QUEER VIEW MIRROR 2

QUEER
VIEW MIRROR 2
Lesbian & Gay Short Short Fiction

Edited by
JAMES C. JOHNSTONE &
KAREN X. TULCHINSKY

ARSENAL PULP PRESS
Vancouver

QUEER VIEW MIRROR 2

ARSENAL PULP PRESS
103-1014 Homer Street
Vancouver, BC
Canada V6B 2W9

The publisher gratefully acknowledges the assistance of the Canada Council, the Book Publishing Industry Development Program and the British Columbia Arts Council.

Typeset by the Vancouver Desktop Publishing Centre
Printed and bound in Canada by Printcrafters

CANADIAN CATALOGUING IN PUBLICATION DATA:
Main entry under title:
Queer view mirror 2

ISBN 1-55152-039-7
1. Gays' writings, Canadian (English)* 2. Lesbians' writings, Canadian (English)* 3. Short stories, Canadian (English)* 4. Canadian fiction (English)—20th century.* 5. Gays—fiction. 6. Lesbians—fiction. I. Johnstone, James C. (James Compton) II. Tulchinsky, Karen X.
PS8235.L47Q84 1997 C813'.01083520664 C96-910820-6
PR9197.33.G39Q44 1997

Contents

Acknowledgements

We would like to thank Brian Lam and Blaine Kyllo at Arsenal Pulp Press for their belief in and ongoing support for *Queer View Mirror* and *Queer View Mirror 2.* We also would like to thank our friends, mentors and supporters in and around the queer writing community: Rob Atkinson, Tommi Avicolli Mecca, Neil Brock, Michael Bronski, Paul Brownsey, Julie Varner Catt, Penny Chalmers, Lawrence Cloake, Gerry Davidson, John Egan, Gregory fitzGeorge-Watts, Crusader Hillis, Roy Johnson, Michele Karlsberg, Kanani Kauka, Richard LaBonte, Barry Lowe, Maizie Mah, Geoff McMurchie, Mike Nightingale, Richard Rooney, Lawrence Schimel, Don Smith, Keith Stuart, Robert Thomson, Rowland Thomson, Charles Q. Williams and Michael Wynne.

We are indebted to Allie Johnstone, and Mike for the use of the beautiful Harley Davidson, and for all the work they did at the photo shoot. Also, thank you Susan Stewart and Val Speidel for the gorgeous cover. A big thank you also goes to our fabulous and very patient models, Terrie (Cookie) Hamazaki, Brent Hrubizna, David Kiesman and Constanza Silva.

We would like to acknowledge the many individuals, magazines, newsletters, organizations, writers' clubs, bookstores, radio and TV shows around the world who posted our call for submissions and helped us get the word out about the book.

We would also like to thank Geoff Chiasson, Harry Grunsky and the staff at Harry's, Trigger and the staff at The Lotus, Charles Dyer and Mary Brookes of the Heritage House Hotel, the management and staff of Little Sister's Bookstore, Woody's, Tallulah's Cabaret and, of course, our trusty postie, Sandra Fellner.

A special thank you as well to the *Queer View Mirror* road trip support team across Canada and the U.S.: David Drinkwalter, Mohamed Khaki, Bob Tivey, Arlene Tully, Paul Yee, James Willett, Faith Jones, Mark Redmond, Richelle Raven, John McCarthy, Steven Simms, Chea Villaneuva, Jess Wells and Alan Workman.

We also remember our friends Lea Dawson, for connecting us, and Shawn Feeney, for bringing us back together.

Dedicated to

the memory of

Alan Alvare

1947–1996

Introduction

Two years ago we had an idea to put together the first international lesbian and gay anthology of short short fiction. *Queer View Mirror* included 101 stories by ninety-nine lesbian and gay writers from Australia, Belgium, Canada, Ireland, Israel, New Zealand, South Africa, the United Kingdom and the U.S. Half of the stories were by lesbians and half were by gay men.

Since the book's release in the fall of 1995, we have travelled all over North America to host book launches and readings. In each city, it was a thrill for us to meet and to hear contributors read their stories in their own voices. We were keen to see who our book had reached and to listen to the responses of the men and women in attendance.

We were encouraged to hear from many that an anthology which included writing by both men and women was both refreshing and important—that for a lot of people, *Queer View Mirror* offered the first peek many had had into the literature of queers of another gender. There were also those who appreciated the opportunity to read stories by lesbian and gay writers from countries other than their own.

Many readers expressed affinity for the short short format. People are reading *Queer View Mirror* at bedtime, while waiting for the bus, on coffee or lunch breaks, and yes, even in the bathroom. *Queer View Mirror*, and gay and lesbian short short fiction in general, seems to have found its own niche.

The 101 stories in this second volume come from lesbian and gay writers living in eight countries. The stories vary in style and mood. Some are lyrical, poetic narratives, others are stark, staccato monologues. They cover a wide scope of topics and themes: lesbian creation myths, humour in the face of AIDS, the childhood trials of the tomboy and the sissy, coming out as a femme, tricking and the horrors of the morning after, the abyss between political correctness and sexual desire. There are happy-go-lucky stories about breakups and piercing, as well as sobering accounts of queers who struggle to survive in rural areas, small towns, or countries where homosexuality is still a crime punishable by imprisonment, or even death.

We are delighted to feature a story from India, and several other stories, which are written in a particular voice, accent, or even dialect: Pidgin English from Hawaii, Scots brogue, New York Italian-American, Caribbean-Canadian, and the delightful New Zealand, Australian and even Chinese-Australian accents.

Many of the stories, through the power of description and the use of language, convey a vivid sense of location and/or season: an army base in Israel, a Muslim school in India, a high-rise construction site looking out over the Hudson River in New York City, a suburban trailer park in Washington State, Xmas-time in a bush town in Australia, the first snowfall of the season in Montréal, a bicycle ride in the country in Northern California, and the rough city streets of downtown Vancouver, home to a young street hustler.

Like its predecessor, the order of the book is alphabetical, all except for one story which called to be placed—well, at the beginning. We gave serious thought to ordering the book by theme, topic, even gender and nationality, but the overwhelming response we received from readers of the first *Queer View Mirror* was that they enjoyed the surprise of discovery—that they liked how the themes, tones, voices and genders of the authors of each story constantly changed. So, rather than impose a subjective, arbitrary arrangement, we made the decision to present the stories alphabetically, and allow the reader to find their own way.

We hope that *Queer View Mirror 2* will continue to build on the work of the first volume, to provide a multiplicity of mirrors in which we can not only see our own reflections, but each other's; a venue for lesbians and gay men around the world to glimpse different worlds which, in the end, aren't so different after all, motivating more forays and browsing through the other side of the bookstore, so to speak.

In that tradition, we proudly present *Queer View Mirror 2*, short short fiction by lesbians and gay men from around the globe. We hope you enjoy reading this parade of queer short shorts and the unique perspectives and images of queer life they mirror.

—James C. Johnstone and
Karen X. Tulchinsky
January 10, 1997
Vancouver, B.C.

Merril Mushroom

In the Beginning

Shemaya didn't remember exactly when it was that she realized she may have made an error in judgment—or perhaps the error was in not paying enough attention to what she was doing or what was happening. But, then again, maybe the error was fated to happen, or it even possibly might not have been an error at all.

It all began in her philosophy class, with a brief discussion of solipsism. Shemaya was fascinated by the idea. *Could it be possible*, she wondered, *that everything in the world actually is a figment of my own mind, a creation of my thoughts?* At first, she gave the notion only passing credibility, but as time went on, the idea began to appeal to her more and more until, at last, it obsessed her.

The first time it happened was because of a petty annoyance, the neighbour's cat, who meowed all night beneath her window. Toward morning, in her rage over sleep deprivation, she thought, *Make believe it isn't here. Just pretend there is no cat. It exists only because I acknowledge that it is.* And she focussed all her energy into believing there was no cat. The meowing stopped.

The next time it was a co-worker who had been harrassing Shemaya for a date. She had told him no repeatedly. He persisted. She complained to the bosses, but they simply told her to ignore him.

So one evening, when she went home, she decided he would no longer be. The next day, not only did he not show up at work; no one even seemed to know who he was or that he'd ever been there at all.

After that, un-making became easier and easier—dirty dishes in the sink, unwanted trash, leftover food, dust balls, mosquitoes. She progressed to drivers who cut her off, rowdy children, people who were rude, ugly buildings, abandoned cars. As the environment disappeared from around her, Shemaya became more and more involved in the practice of solipsism.

She may have gotten a little carried away. Suddenly, one day, she realized that there were no more people at all left in the world and very little of anything else, and she stopped for a moment. Looking around at the bareness, she thought, *Now is the time for the greatest test of all—can I un-make the world itself just through the power of my mind?* Immediately, she found herself alone among the stars. *So, now, what about the universe?* she wondered, and she was suspended in nothingness. She had no idea how long she remained in this state before an even greater idea occurred to her: *Now that I remain, only I am left, truly the greatest un-making of all would be myself!* And she willed herself out of existence.

Nothing happened.

Hmmmm, she thought, *I don't know what's going on here.* And she tried again.

Still nothing happened. She tried and tried, but try as she might, she continued to remain.

No telling how much time passed then, but Shemaya became increasingly bored and increasingly lonely. Finally she decided to do something about it. *I suppose I'll just have to will everything back into existence again*, she thought, *starting from the beginning.*

And she did.

The whole process took Shemaya six days, and on the seventh day she rested.

Donna Allegra

Strapped

Okay, I got the pipe in place, Kenya."

"Great, whatever you do, don't let go. Where's the strap?"

"On the ledge. Reach into my tool pouch for the ratchet."

Kenya stretches from where she stands at the back of the ladder to clutch the ratchet and a spin-tight. Darcella focusses on the four-foot level that hangs magnetically attached to the bottom of a pipe. She balances like a tight-rope walker, tottering ten feet above the floor.

Kenya flicks the ratchet handle, the nut tightening to the bolt with every click. The bolt is just about set to her satisfaction when Darcella says, "Can you hurry it up, partner? I might want to have kids someday."

Kenya smiles at the V of Darcella's torso, which emerges from her waist like a tree rising from the earth. Ooooh, can I be the daddy? she thinks, but says, "It's a done deal, you lazy wench. You can let go now."

Kenya places the ratchet into her tool pouch. She stretches and arches her back like a cat, then leans her elbows atop the platform of the ladder. Darcella stands on the rungs in front, studying the length of pipe they have hung.

Kenya's face is aligned with Darcella's chest as Darcella inspects the level to check the pipe for plumbness. She smiles up at Darcella like a fond mother indulging her child's seriousness.

"C'mon now, girl," she says. "You are probably the only electrician on the job who gives a hoot that a pipe-run hidden in the ceiling be absolutely level and perfect."

"So humour me," Darcella says. "When things aren't balanced, they tilt and fall down." She surveys her work and smiles. "Damn, we're good."

"Yeah. That pipe fits like it grew there. And you know your foreman put us on this job because he didn't think we could do it. Bob would rather have us fuck up so he can complain about women in the trade than set us up to do the job right."

"Oh, so he's my foreman now. When I first came on the job and got teamed with you, he was everybody's fore*skin*," Darcella kids. "Well, he's going to lose his mind when he sees we've got this baby rolling."

"You think he has a mind?" Kenya smiles and plunks the spin-tight and ratchet into the pouch resting on Darcella's hip. Darcella shifts her weight to her left leg, one rung below her right foot and inhales Kenya's scent.

She looks at her watch. "It's way after nine," she says. "Mark's late with the coffee, again. What is it with that boy? When I was an apprentice, I got back with the coffee order on time or I'd hear about it all day long. You ask for anything, Kenya?"

"No. I've got my thermos of tea in my knapsack."

"Yeah, I figured. You only ask him to get you *Radical Women's Chronicle* once a week."

"Coffee!" Mark yells from down the hall. Kenya and Darcella turn toward the door to see the young, scraggly bearded man lumber into the room. He sets a cardboard box down on the floor. Darcella rummages through the brown bags and coffee containers to find a box of Tropicana orange juice. As an after-thought, she takes a plastic coffee stirrer to chew on.

Mark looks around the room and says, "The foreman got you girls working all by yourself without any help? That's not nice of him." Mark tries to engage Kenya, but she keeps her back to him and looks out the window.

"We're a team, Mark. We work together and help each other," Darcella says as if instructing a child.

Mark picks up his box. "The shop superintendent's on the job and word is that the boss is coming by some time before lunch," he says. "Watch your time, girls."

Kenya turns around to roll her eyes at Darcella who frowns, visibly reining herself in from saying anything more to Mark.

"Let's go outside on the scaffold, partner, our usual spot," Kenya says, massaging the nape of Darcella's neck. Darcella doesn't smile but doesn't resist either.

She pauses at the window to let Kenya pass through first. The fiftieth floor overlooks the East River where it joins the Atlantic Ocean. The two women can see Battery Park, the Statue of Liberty, and water unfurling like a bolt of iridescent fabric that seamlessly joins the sky.

"This view is one of the things I love about construction work," Kenya says. "You can't buy a picture like this on a postcard."

Darcella nods eagerly. "You say what my heart thinks sometimes." She speaks so quietly that Kenya has to strain to hear. She leans toward Darcella. "I wish I could make words do that," she says.

The scaffold they sit on feels spongey. Darcella leans sideways on her elbow, then changes her mind and sits upright and cross-legged as she opens her container of orange juice. Kenya readjusts her position too. She stretches the length of her body like a cat and crawls across the plank. Just as she swings her leg across Darcella, the board upends, sending Kenya half over the edge. Instinctively, she grabs the cold metal frame of the scaffold. Her legs flap in the air like a fish struggling to swim on land. The panorama of the Atlantic Ocean and the wide blue sky reshuffles like kaleidoscope particles. Her view now takes in the cement wall of the building, the probability of the hard city streets below.

"Oh Jesus, oh Father," Kenya whispers as Darcella carefully pulls Kenya's torso to her lap like a piece of braced pipe, her container of juice plummeting to the street below.

"I've got you, babe. Just stay loose. I'm not letting go. Now listen, Kenya, pretend we're up on the ladder. I have the weight, you strap it. Turn and reach for my waist. Go slow."

Kenya doesn't breathe. She captures a hand-hold on Darcella's tool pouch, then another on the belt of Darcella's pants. She pulls herself up until she can snuggle her upper body to Darcella's chest, then finally into her lap.

"I'm on something solid. You go into the window. I'll follow," Darcella orders.

Kenya crawls, chanting, "Thank you, Mother." She collapses to the floor, hitting it over and over with her open palm, shaking her head from side to side. Darcella follows immediately behind and cradles Kenya to her.

"I wasn't gonna drop you, partner. You know I don't like working with boys. Can't depend on them to carry their weight. I'd never let you go. I'd never let you go," she whispers over and over, until the words don't sound anymore, but still she can't stop saying them.

A chill runs through her. It's the smell of fresh cut wood.

Alan Alvare

Widow

Here it is, the Blue Room. There's the coffin—the casket, as the funeral director calls it, leading me over to it like a horse to strange water. Will I drink? Will I look? Apparently I'm supposed to form a "memory picture," my last look at Carl. The first seems like only last week. He was lying down then too, face down on a log at Wreck Beach.

Well, I look. His face looks bloated, a relative term, of course. Maybe it's just the constrast to the way he's looked since he got sick. The funeral director looks pleased at his work, having magically restored the weight melted by Carl's illness. I still don't like calling it AIDS. Stupid of me, considering how often the word comes up. Unless I'm mistaken it's coming up less than it did a couple of years ago. Are we getting tired of it? Is this whole production a bit passé? Carl wouldn't have liked that. He always said it's better to be baroque than five years out of date.

The funeral director is saying something. He purrs, pleased about something, but I'm not sure what. Inside me there's this juggling act going on. I'm trying to match the lines of the face in the coffin—sorry, casket—with the face I first saw when he turned over that day at Wreck Beach ten years ago. Ten years exactly on July 25, our anniversary, which he won't be here for.

So it's taking me a few blinks to remember that face and the neck and the sculpted brown body on the beach, the eye that squinted in the sun and the mouth that smiled and said, "Hi." Who would have thought I'd see that mouth painted over by this funeral man and God-knows-what cosmetics?

I watch the funeral director, who is still smiling down at his product. When this funeral director—what's his name? Len—when Len met me at the door tonight he said my name and then I couldn't figure out what he said after that. I guess it showed. He just smiled and took my arm and led me here. Actually, to be fair, he did tell me Carl wouldn't look the same. I remember that now, but at the time all I noticed was that he had taken my arm. Nobody's touched me like that for a while. It felt good. It feels like he actually cares. He must see dozens of dead bodies a month. Does he remember them all?

It's not that I haven't been touched at all. Friends have given lots of hugs, even people I hardly know, who knew Carl. I talked to my parents on the phone today. They won't be coming to Vancouver for the funeral. Dad said he isn't feeling well, and Mum thinks she shouldn't leave him. Annie's coming, but she's just over in Kits. She left Campbell River about the same time as our other sister, Peg. Our paths don't really cross. Peg says she and her husband are very busy this week. That's vintage Peg—being busy. All my life I remember Peg in a rush. Just after I met Carl, Peg got born again, so she was suddenly even busier when I suggested getting together. Peg met a man as busy as herself and she sank out of sight.

"AIDS widow": It makes me think of the First World War and widows rolling bandages for the front and selling war bonds. Or something out of Greek tragedy. I love Greek food. Carl and I did get to Greece five years ago, just before his diagnosis. He got sick while we were away. Holiday sickness has plagued me all my life, so I thought, "Here it is again," only this time it's got my lover instead of me.

"Widow." To me it suggests a permanent state of half-life, the other half swathed in black and purple crepe. The crepe part would be dramatic. Carl was always dramatic—appropriate for an actor, I suppose.

Somewhere I read or heard that you start saying goodbye the first time you say hello. Maybe it's true. Like you start dying the minute they cut the umbilical cord. That first slap on the bum is to wake you up so you'll be able to fall asleep. Staying awake is the hard part. Carl was always very awake. That's really what made him dramatic. The doctor's first slap on his baby bum woke him up, but that was nothing compared to the slap of finding out he was positive.

Actually, he didn't know what hit him. Home from Greece, he got better and we put it behind us until he collapsed at work. So now he lies in a casket with that smug, artificial look on his face. He always wanted to do horror. Maybe he'd love this role. I can imagine him opening his eyes, then curling those painted lips back into an evil grin. "Good evening," he'd say, resting a claw on the coffin to pull himself up. I laugh at the image. So much for memory pictures.

Len puts his hand on my shoulder. He thinks I'm hysterical. Just what he wants on his hands tonight, a wailing widow. At this time on a Saturday night he's probably getting ready to go out to the Shaggy Horse—probably wishing he were there already, away from me. He asks if I'm all right, then says:

"I think you could use a drink."

I know Carl's funeral is tomorrow. But tonight I've had enough of this widow business. I nod, and we're on our way. I think Carl would approve.

Lawrence Aronovitch

Night and Day

"Are you working?"

Max shrugged. "Sure."

"How much?"

"Depends. Let's start with fifty."

"Okay."

"Did you have somewhere in mind?"

"My place is pretty close."

"Okay." The two left.

"My name is Steve."

"Max."

"I work on the Hill," Steve began. Max observed the restaurant windows they passed and the snatches of other stories he glimpsed in them. A short plump woman laughing merrily, a secretary perhaps, probably Revenue Canada; a balding bearded bureaucrat, self-important as he traded gossip at a corner table.

Steve was an assistant to a Liberal MP, a peculiarly naïve species in the political bestiary—especially when they worked for the Opposition. Max felt a familiar mingling of contempt and pity for the guy as they came up to his place. Just another driven member of the political class, dedicated supremely to the task of helping his Leader win the next election. Pretty boring.

And yet, Max observed, Steve was not unhandsome. Dirty blond hair, a well cut suit—where was he coming from in a suit at eleven? Not a bad body, he could see, as Steve took off his jacket. Maybe there was more to this guy after all. Max decided to listen a little more closely. "So how old are you?" he asked as they sat on the bed.

"I'm thirty-two." Max draped his leg on Steve's and let his hand caress Steve's shoulder. It was time to go to work.

"So how long have you been here?" Max asked the question casually, almost as a distraction for Steve, as his fingers began to move down onto Steve's chest. Under the cotton Max found a nipple. He began to play with it, tug at it, arouse it. Steve turned his head and gave Max a shy smile.

When he got to the finance department the next morning Max found a note from Karl reminding him to finish crunching his numbers for the meeting with the industry department. Why bother? he thought. Regardless of what he might have to say, however brilliant his analysis, it wouldn't matter. Even if the outside world did not conspire to track dirt through his finely honed numbers, the system would. During the two years since he had taken his degree, Max had learned all about the system.

At university a prof asked him whether he felt any passion for his careful models of the economy. "Passion?" Max asked, as if nibbling at some exotic fruit from a distant land. When he got home that evening he couldn't get the question out of his head. Max wondered whether he had ever felt passion for anything.

Max excelled at his studies. On his prof's suggestion, he joined the cadre of junior government analysts. They burbled with excitement about being in Ottawa, effecting change, pushing policy, *making a difference*. Max snorted and watched. Someone would write a memo, someone else would rewrite it, and someone upstairs would send it back down. At the end of the day, nothing changed, their influence remained nil. They made no difference at all.

As his tedium grew, Max began to look for excitement outside the office. It wasn't hard, but he found no passion in the streets either. Just frightened civil servants far from home.

His mother came to Ottawa once and took Max to lunch. Hers was an old Tory family and she wanted to see how he was getting on. She asked after his social life—was he making friends, did he like his job, should she talk to some people his father knew? For an instant Max wished he still drank. Then lunch was over, they said goodbye, and he returned to his office.

Max thought about Steve, with his breathless excitement for the dying

Meech Lake Accord. Max had tried to get Steve to focus on the matter at hand instead. "After all," he explained, "it's what you're paying for, isn't it?" But in the end Steve decided he was too tired and just sent him home.

"Max." Karl caught him by surprise. "Time to go. Are your numbers ready?"

Max gathered his papers and followed. How dreary, he thought. At the meeting Max skewered the poor sucker from the industry department. He was good; even the industry suits conceded as much. But their minister came from Québec and had his own ideas about money well spent. The meeting wore interminably on.

Dull, congenial Karl. Steve had found passion in his politics even as he sat in his dingy little apartment. Was Karl passionate? He was certainly devoted to his job. He played the endless game, enduring a tedious commute to enjoy the quality of life his suburban villa afforded. But Karl didn't seem to spend much time there as he scrambled through his nights and weekends trying to appease his superiors. He was indentured to his mortgage, his car payments and his kids' toys.

Steve worked the same hours—that explained his suit last night—but he did it out of devotion to the cause. Karl did it to hang on. Perhaps Steve would look back at all those nights with pride; Karl would not. Steve. Not a bad looking boy. Shy, yet passionate. Then again, thought Max, how passionate could he really be if he sent me home?

The meeting ended. Max returned to his office and stared at his phone. Maybe, he thought, maybe I should call him. Suggest a follow-up session. He bit his lip. Should he call? Would Steve be there? What would he say?

He decided. He called. A woman answered. He asked for Steve.

"He's just left for lunch. Would you care to leave a message?"

Max was stuck. What would he say? To Steve he was just Max, the boy he'd picked up on Mackenzie behind the Château Laurier. "No." He hung up. He felt numb.

The day crawled by.

Max didn't phone again.

A colleague poked her head into his office. "Want to go for a drink?"

"No," Max said. "I'm working tonight."

Tommi Avicolli Mecca

The Last Laugh

for simeon meadows white

A sect of Christian Gnostics believed that the devil created the world when God turned his back. It was Joshua's favourite heresy.

Joshua read a lot about heresies and myths. He could tell you creation stories from scores of cultures throughout the world. When he felt the most hopeless, he'd sit in the wicker chair on his patio or by the living room window overlooking the garden, light a joint and open his book of Larousse Mythology, musing over turtles that bore the world on their backs, or deities that sprang from someone's head.

I met Joshua at an anti-war rally in Philadelphia in the late sixties. This tall, dark-skinned, handsome man with the incredible cheek bones was easy to spot in his trademark multi-coloured dashiki covered with protest buttons. For years, Joshua didn't attend a demonstration without it.

As a teenager, Joshua spent time in jail for organizing a sit-in at a segregated lunch counter in his Georgia hometown. His action aroused the wrath of a then-unknown radio talk show host who is now one of America's most homophobic, and popular, TV evangelists.

When he turned draft age, Joshua became a conscientious objector. He said it was the only way he knew to be Christian. The government didn't agree and threw him in jail. When he got out, he moved to Philadelphia to continue his anti-draft work with the American Friends Service Committee, the left-wing arm of the Quakers that worked throughout the world promoting peace.

Joshua and I argued a lot about religion and politics. We were both progressives, but his activism was inspired by his Southern Baptist roots; mine was fueled by rage against the Catholic Church, which, as far as I was concerned, didn't speak out enough for civil rights. The Church also supported the Vietnam War. "Religion'll never be our friend," I said. Still, for Joshua, throwing out religion was tossing the baby out with the bath water. I thought the baby wasn't worth saving.

For a year we lived in the same communal household. Once, stoned out of our minds, he invited me to spend the night in his bed. I was terrified: Did he see through me? How could anyone know I was gay? I was attracted to him, but sleep with another man? Even someone I admired as much as Joshua was out of the question. "I need my space tonight," I replied.

On several occasions in the next few months, I tried to talk to him about that night. But each time, I couldn't pull the words from my throat, and only after I quit trying did my heart stop quaking.

Joshua moved to San Francisco in the late seventies to join the battle against the Briggs Initiative, aimed at banning queers from teaching in schools. He wrote me at length about the emerging gay culture in his new hometown. He was the first person I came out to, and the first person to tell me about a terrifying new disease that was killing gay men.

I came in contact with AIDS soon enough. Tomas and David died in 1984. Scared of getting sick, I all but stopped having sex. Seven lonely years later, I found myself late one night crossing out twenty-five names in my address book. I threw down the damn thing and smashed my fist into the wall until it numbed. But I couldn't anesthetize my anger and despair. In the summer of 1991, five friends died in one month.

I was reading names on stage at the first Philadelphia showing of the Names Quilt, a few days after the fifth friend died, when the floodgates broke. I couldn't stop crying. Friends helped me offstage. "I'm not gonna make it," I kept whimpering.

I sold most of my possessions and moved to San Francisco. I was walking out of a Castro grocery a few days after arriving in town when I spotted Joshua. My heart sank, I thought I would lose my lunch. I knew instantly that he wasn't well. Maybe that's why he didn't respond when I wrote to tell him I was moving.

We didn't talk about his health. But I thought about it all the time. Late at night sometimes, a heavy feeling settled in my stomach and I sobbed uncontrollably. I didn't tell him, but I resented the fact that in all those letters he wrote, he never prepared me for this.

Joshua decided to run for the San Francisco Board of Supervisors. He asked me to be his campaign manager. We were pulling together his first mailing when he took sick. From his hospital bed, strapped to machines and short of breath from the pneumonia, he dictated notes to me. Rest was out of the question. "This is the last thing I gotta do," he'd say.

He decided to die in his own home. He let few people in to see him. The disease claimed his gym-toned physique, leaving skin and bone; the chemo, his long braided hair; the various infections, his beautiful almond colouring. But it couldn't take away his dignity.

"You gotta do something for me," he told me. "When it gets bad, I want you to hold my hand while I take some stuff I got."

"I can't—" I whispered through a throat that had closed in on me; my vision was so blurred from the tears I could barely see.

Within weeks he could hardly move or talk. One night when the nurse was out of earshot, I whispered, "Where's the stuff?" I didn't know how I was going to do it, but Joshua didn't deserve to die like this. I was trembling like someone had poured ice water on me; inside, I felt like I was on fire.

He shook his head and laughed. "Don't worry about it. You know, the funny thing is—there ain't no fucking god in sight. All those damn stories and not one of them got it right."

I asked again about the pills. "Tomorrow," he said.

When I returned in the morning he was gone. The Larousse lay on the side of the bed next to an empty bottle of morphine and a brown paper bag with my name on it. The note said simply, "Always remember when." It was his dashiki.

I stood at the window for the longest time, too worn to cry. I was angry that he never gave me the chance to say goodbye. But I was also relieved that I didn't have to help him do what he did.

Sometimes in those quiet moments of the night, I can hear the devil laughing.

Damien Barlow

Postscript to the Tuesday Man

You don't notice me watching you. You are preoccupied with other things, like your daughter, who is pushing one of those miniature shopping trolleys. I watch you pack the station wagon; the way your arse stretches, the sweat marks appearing on your starched shirt. The scarlet baby-on-board sticker glows like some ominous full-stop. I watch you secure her seat belt, adjust the rear-view mirror, and drive out of my carpark. I also note the way you turn your head to observe the beat, knowing it is only Monday.

The trolley boy hears his name crackle throughout the supermarket; checkout five wants a price check on Tasmanian smoked salmon and Queensland pawpaw. His eyes shift from the speaker above his head to the brick veneer toilet block, which sits like a centrepiece, a feature, in the trolley boy's carpark. The beat is partly concealed by a chip-bark garden of hardy Australian natives; scrappy gums that drop balls of larvae and spiky grevilleas, occasionally stabbing the arms of wayward children. The summer air is still as the trolley boy does a round of the carpark. His legs feel as if they are burning in his black pants. The red bow-tie seems to strain against his thyroid gland, while the name tag on his white shirt seems like it could melt, or at least become a blur of letters, in this asphalt-enhanced heat. He notices an old man, the one who always smacks his lips at the urinal, leave the beat. A moment later, a man in Army greens emerges, shaking water from his hands and spitting on the cement path. He is followed by a reversing bike, and a boy, who has moist patches of cum on his school uniform. The trolley boy has had them all, at least once, sometime or other.

I used to call you JOZ, after your numberplate, but once I discovered your routines, you became known as the Tuesday man. I first met you about six months ago now, when I got this job, and discovered that a beat existed at the heart of this urbanized country town. I remember you appeared as if from nowhere and never said a word. I didn't even see your cock that day, only felt the stubble on your cheeks and the thickness of your ex-rugby player neck. You sucked me 'til I came, accidentally, all over your padded-executive shoulder. I also remember your wedding ring got tangled in my pubes. Later, I would read this as a sign.

The trolley boy wanders the main streets of Wodonga, which even in the early evening, still exude a strange petrol-based heat. He searches the carpark of a rival supermarket for stray trolleys, stacks a couple, and watches some kids from his school go into the Christian youth group next door. *Had your father, and yours,* he thinks, as they warm up their instruments and voices. As the trolley boy walks back, he hears the echoes of their performance. They sing as if they were in *Jesus Christ Superstar*.

You weren't the first married man I ever had. There are others like you in this town. I've caught many a husband at my carpark. Some still taste of their girlfriends, others smell like wet wife-kisses. I leave my mark too, but occasionally it gets mingled with the hot breath of their sons. You sometimes arrive with the odour of nappies—baby-shit-stained hands guiding my cock up your arse. Other Tuesdays you have smelled like my father, reeking of expensive business lunches, the type that sees you fondle the breasts of topless waitresses.

It is Tuesday. The trolley boy knows that he will appear soon. He absent-mindedly fiddles with a fruit display; fingers linger over half-devoured grapes and disturb the fruit flies that suckle on partly squashed and overpriced mangoes. The speakers announce that someone has dropped a litre of milk in aisle three. With an old mop and bucket, he soaks up the spilt milk and resumes his daydreams about the Tuesday man's arse, the way he will suck and bite the older man's nipples. He recalls the taste of married flesh in his mouth. As the trolley boy puts the "wet floor" signs in place, the Tuesday man's daughter comes crashing against his thigh, her miniature shopping trolley spilling lamingtons and jam rolls everywhere. *Is he here already?!* thinks the trolley boy, as the little girl begins to howl. From around the aisle, the Tuesday man's wife, with baby, appears. He explains, she apologizes, they say goodbye. He notes she still looks pregnant and wonders, as she leaves, if the discreet scratching at her groin could be related to the crabs he discovered after last Tuesday?

The wife opens the door of her car as the Tuesday man drives in. The trolley boy watches as they talk, as he kisses her and comments on her new dress. He hides his bow-tie in a pocket, and while undoing his top shirt buttons, leaves the air-conditioned interior of red spot specials and frantic shoppers. With her back to him, the trolley boy gains the Tuesday man's attention, disrupting him in mid-sentence. His wife looks around, but the boy is nowhere to be seen. The Tuesday man whispers something in her ear and closes her door. He waves goodbye as she drives off.

The trolley boy thrusts from behind. The Tuesday man goes with the boy's rhythm, but sways too freely, grazing his forehead against the graffiti-covered cubicle wall. The trolley boy hears a dull chink against porcelain, withdraws, and comes up the man's spine; some even mingles with his private school haircut. The boy wipes his cock, then the Tuesday man's back with a tissue. As the trolley boy drops the claggy tissue-ball into the toilet, he notices the Tuesday man's wedding ring, ambiguously glistening in the murky water.

Russel Baskin

You Linger On Inside Me

A young girl wakes in the middle of the night to hear sounds from her mother's room. She finds her mother on the bed crying, tears bursting from some empty place deep inside. Climbing up onto the bed the child tries to ease her mother's grief, but she's too young to know how.

A love has ended. Only the pain lingers on. This woman's loss is her parents' relief. Now they won't be ashamed in front of their friends. Now they can tell their daughter it is for the best, how it never would have worked. This man was not one of them. He was not a Jew. He would not be accepted. They do not try to ease their daughter's grief. They are too old to know how.

A woman lies crying on her bed at night. Her love has ended. Only her desire lingers on.

KISS

It all began with a kiss. You ask. I say yes. I have no doubts. This is an unknown place I know I want to enter. I allow my body to take over and lead the way, into your arms, into your bed.

There, I am awkward at first, not sure what to do, the familiar now unfamiliar, the unspoken spoken. I am shy, hesitant, until slowly over time I let myself drown in my pleasure, follow my desire, respond to yours.

JOY

The joys of new love. A flower bursting through the earth in spring. A singer who wants the whole world to hear her song. I am a child playing innocently in the sand.

Your pleasure, your enjoyment of me is balanced with a healthy paranoia integrated into your life long ago. You're constantly alert. You know tension as normal.

I am untouched, having lived as a heterosexual all my life. I take my privilege into your world. I want to flaunt my love for you. I want to claim you, be claimed by you.

LYING IN YOUR ARMS

One morning, lying in your arms, I wonder what we look like together, how I look beside you. Something I never thought about with men. In my other world I could not escape the idea of my body next to a man's. My life tied to his. Now it is hard to find a picture, a movie, a book, anything to validate, to acknowledge my existence with you. My desire for you. My lust for you.

One morning, you lying in my arms, I wonder why something so beautiful, so pleasurable, full of love, care, respect, could cause another person to feel hatred, disgust.

Later that night when you make love to me, at the height of my pleasure, I feel the same disgust. Hear the same voices. I cry out. Push you away. Don't want you to stop.

DESIRE

You identify as male. Now I see male/female roles as constructions. We use them. Play with them. This is not acting out or pretending to be man and woman, yet in some ways it is. Our bodies, the bodies we come back to, are the same in their differences.

I touch you as a woman touches a man because that's what you want, who you are. I fuck you as a woman fucks a woman because that's what you want, who you are. I lie wrapped around your body and you around mine, so neither knows where one begins and the other ends, and when you lick me it is as if we are joined cunt to mouth, mouth to cunt, then mouth to mouth. You tasting of me, tasting of me.

You love everything about me I learned to hate. The shape of my body. The flow of my blood. The sound of my voice. The smell of my sex. With you I push against edges, explore desire, find my hunger, feel my pleasure. We share fantasies, acting some out, listening to each other's fears. With you I both lose and find myself. I reclaim my sexuality independent of men. Independent of you. It resides within me.

WOMAN WHO IS ALSO MAN

I love your power, the way you take charge so I can let go. I love feeling the leather straps of your harness when you fuck me. You moving to my rhythm, looking into my eyes, knowing you are possessing me as I am taking you inside. After I hold you in my arms, when not being in a man's body is hurting you more than you think you can bear, you say making love to me is so sweet. So painful.

I want to heal your wounds, but feel helpless. I want to be by your side while you explore the possibility of becoming the man you know you are. But I also love the parts of you that speak woman to me. The softness of your breasts when you hold me in your arms. The wetness of your cunt when I touch you. I want you, woman who is also man, to lie in my bed, hold my hand, share my life.

INVISIBLE BOUNDARIES

My time with you passes. I notice changes. Not in my love for you. Not in my desire for you. But in the way I am with you in the world. I find myself pulling back instead of reaching out. I think twice before holding your hand while walking on the beach. I long to kiss you but don't. I feel protective and scared. Angry. Afraid.

Our inner world is familiar. I bring the same baggage to you that I brought to my relationships with men. I fight the same fights. The same struggles. My outer world is different. We enter a restaurant. Heads turn to stare. We walk down the street. Two men ask, "What have we got here?" We kiss in the snow. An elderly couple stops to look. They wonder if you're man or woman. With you I cross an invisible boundary, step over an unforgiving line.

WANTING

One morning in bed you say something is missing. You want to leave. I am hurting. You are hurting. I pull back, wanting. Now I have to find out who I am without you.

The young girl, now a grown woman, lies crying on her bed. She hears the sounds of her tears, the same sounds her mother made long ago, rising from some empty place deep inside.

She will not ask her parents to help ease her pain. They never knew her joy.

They would be relieved. Now they won't be ashamed in front of their friends. They would tell their daughter it is for the best, how it never would have worked. It would not be acceptable for her to love another woman. They would not try to ease their daughter's grief. They are too old to know how.

A woman lies crying on her bed at night. Her love has ended. Only her desire lingers on.

Michael Bendzela

Gentle One

There was once an aluminum rectangle full of deep-green chlorinated city water which would scald the throats of children who accidentally inhaled it, and burn the rims of their eyes so that by the end of the day they would all look as though they had been crying.

The children would line up outside the tall chain-link fence early in the morning, all vying to be first in, first up the ladder, first to run across the algae-carpeted deck and jump with a *ker-sploosh* into mirror-still and tepid bleach, in spite of the sign: NO RUNNING NO JUMPING.

Among them, a gentle boy, towel scrolled under one arm, new flip-flops on his feet, the requisite swim trunks on his hips: NO CUT-OFFS. SHOES, TOWEL REQUIRED.

Swimming's free, but there's a head count, only so many allowed in. The lifeguard watches too, from his high chair, one hairy testicle lolling out the leg of his bright orange trunks, a plop of white on his nose.

The gentle boy salivates a little in the sharp air and the dancing light of the pool as he waits for the gate to be unchained.

A grinning older boy, Timmy, has brought a new pencil with him to the gate—a straight pin sticking up out of the eraser. This kid won't be allowed in; he's barefoot and wears cut-offs, and no towel, either. He holds the spiked eraser up to the face of someone in line and says:

"You're standing in my spot, girlie."

The child only curls more tightly around her towel, using one hand to pull a strand of hair out of her eyes.

Timmy smiles and makes a feint with the pencil. The girl brings a hand up to protect her face. The straight pin embeds itself between the first and second knuckles of her hand and detaches from the eraser. She stares a moment at the head of the pin against her skin then quickly plucks it out and holds the back of her hand up to her mouth.

Timmy gapes around at the others. "Did you *see* that?"

The gentle boy with towel, flip-flops and swim trunks knows little of anger and less of rage. But something black and sour now rises in him at the unfairness and cruelty of this Timmy, who always seems to get what he wants, whose muscles have always been more sleek and intimidating, who greets every situation with that predatory smile. Before he can consider the possible consequences of it, the boy blurts out:

"Why don't you just leave her alone?"

Timmy turns away from the girl as if she doesn't exist and glares into the gentle boy's eyes. "What are you gonna do about it if I don't?"

The gentle boy knows he can do nothing and so says nothing.

"You want to fight about it?"

The gentle boy knows nothing about fighting. He has brought along only flip-flops, towel, the requisite trunks.

"Come on, queer," he says, shoving the gentle boy up against the chain-link fence, which goes *clink*. "If you're a man you'll fight." *Clink*. "Or are you a mouse?"

The gentle boy wants to take Timmy into his arms, say, "Why can't you just be nice?"

"Come on"—*clink*— "a man or a mouse?"

The other kids in line glower, fearing what will happen next. The girl weeps a little, the back of her hand still pressed against her mouth. The gentle boy, hugging his tightly-rolled towel, opens his mouth but can say neither "man" nor "mouse."

"Say it. Man"—*clink*— "or mouse?" *Clink*.

A hole opens up in the gentle boy and he falls entirely into it. His eyes are like windows with the glass broken out of them. Shame envelops him like a rash. He only wants this other boy to leave the girl alone, leave him alone, leave everyone alone.

"Mouse."

Timmy blinks. "What? Say it again." *Clink*. "I said say it again, fag."

"Mouse! Mouse!"

"Goddamn right, a mouse."

Suddenly the gate opens, and children flood through, leaving Timmy and the gentle boy alone by the clinking fence. The gentle boy can see disappointment crossing out the disgust in Timmy's eyes.

"Hey, Mouse. Let me see those sandals."

The gentle boy slips off the flip-flops.

"And the towel."

He surrenders the towel. He would peel off his swim trunks if asked to. He doesn't feel much like swimming anymore anyhow.

The man in orange kicks Timmy out because of the cut-offs. (Strings from cut-offs clog the filter.) The gentle boy is permitted in to retrieve his flip-flops from the pool. Lucky, for he would detest the sensation of hot tar squishing between his toes all the way home.

Persimmon Blackbridge

A True Story With Lies

The Job

I got the interview at Sunnybrook because I put on my application that I had worked at an outpatient clinic in Ontario.

Actually, I'd been a patient there, but I knew the jargon and I knew the routines, so what the hell.

I went there dressed for success: new panty hose, borrowed shoes, a dress with nice long sleeves that covered the scars on my arms. I was interviewed by Dr. Carlson, the head psychiatrist. I think he wanted to hire someone quickly and get back to his important work. The interview was short.

"I understand you've worked with teenagers with learning disabilities," he said.

"Yes," I said.

"So you must be used to dealing with some pretty anti-social behaviour."

"Yes," I said.

"But you've never worked with retarded people. That's unfortunate."

The word retarded bit like a playground insult in his proper mouth. But that's not the kind of thing you mention in a job interview.

"But you do know behaviour mod?"

"Oh yes," I said.

I know behaviour mod.

"Good. Very good. Well, then. I feel I must tell you: the girl we hired last month for this position quit. One of the residents bit her. Quite badly."

He looked at me. I didn't flinch, and the job was mine.

Shirley

The first time I met Shirley, she was sitting on a chair in the hallway on Ward D.

"Hi," she said, "who are you?"

"My name's Diane. I work with Mary."

"Oh boy, Mary. Better work with Pat instead." She shook her head. "Mary. Oh boy."

"I just do what they tell me to. And they told me to work with Mary."

I thought maybe I should ask Shirley a few things about Ward D, things I didn't think Nurse Thompson would tell me, but just then an orderly came running up to us yelling, "Don't talk to her!"

"Go away," Shirley told her. "We're busy."

"Ummm, what's wrong?" I asked.

"You're supposed to ignore them when they're on that chair. It's behaviour mod," the orderly said.

"Oh yeah, right," I said.

"Excuse me," Shirley said, "I'm talking to this lady. She's telling me about her job which is not a very good one."

The orderly smiled at me, turning her back to Shirley. "Don't worry about it. You're new here, you'll learn. But you've got to watch out for Shirley. She's a troublemaker. You'll see. She's a real manipulator. And she talks too much. And another thing: she's a lesbian. So be careful."

"How do you know?" I asked.

"It's in her file."

"Oh," I said. "Okay."

I couldn't think of anything else to say.

I looked at Shirley. She rolled her eyes.

The orderly ignored her.

It was behaviour mod.

Lesbian Social Service Professional

My girlfriend said if I was having such a hard time at work, maybe I should join the Lesbian Social Service Professionals' Support Group. I could talk about my job to people who would really understand, and avoid Social Service Burnout.

I went to Sappho's instead and downed five Blues in quick succession. Shirley was there, a hallucination, sitting at a table of loud butches.

That was okay. At this point in my life hallucinations didn't worry me too much.

I shot sneaky glances at her between beers, and considered my life.

I hadn't actually explained to my girlfriend about the outpatient clinic and the lie on my job application. *No one knew about the outpatient clinic except for my friends in Ontario who were mad at me for being too weird.* I hadn't told her about my current official diagnosis, or the one before that. I hadn't really gone into my spotty employment record in any detail. She knew I couldn't type or drive or fill out forms, because she helped me with that type of thing. She knew about my scars because I did occasionally take my long-sleeved shirts off. I wasn't sure what she thought about it all. I guess she thought I should go to a Lesbian Social Service Professionals' Support Group. It didn't really make sense.

I had another Blue. Then I switched to tequila to see if I could find wisdom there. No luck. Then Shirley sat down beside me.

"Are you trying to pick me up or what?" she said.

Rock Me

It wasn't actually Shirley. She was taller, with a butch swagger that the real Shirley could have punctured with one pointed remark. Unfortunately I wasn't that sharp.

"I was just—I wasn't—you look like someone I know," I stuttered.

"Oooh, I've heard that one before," Shirley-Butch replied. "Haven't we met? Somehow, somewhere, across a crowded room? Wanna dance?"

"Sure," I said.

It was the least stupid thing I could think of.

We danced. I was a bit unsteady on my feet but so were half the other babes on the dance floor.

Shirley-Butch had a casual, too-cool-to-dance shuffle. She wore these sort of pressed polyester pants and a bowling shirt instead of jeans and tank tops like everyone else. But she was cute. She had big shoulders and crooked teeth. She had the same out-of-control red hair as Shirley. As "Rock Me Baby" segued to "Love to Love You," she pulled me into a slow dance that made my palms sweat.

"I think I have to go," I yelled, barely audible over Donna Summer's disco orgasm.

"And here I thought you were coming home with me tonight." She pushed her pelvis a little tighter into mine and then stepped back.

"I can't. I, ummm, have a girlfriend and all."

"You looked more like a girl getting very drunk all by herself than a girl with a girlfriend. But I guess I was wrong."

She blew me a kiss and disappeared back to her table. David Bowie was singing "Rebel, Rebel" and I stood stranded on the dance floor, thinking about the Lesbian Social Service Professionals' Support Group.

Allen Borcherding

Bus Ride

I spot these two guys waiting at the bus stop and I'm liking it. Two sweet looking men obviously together, as in, a couple, together. And none too subtle about it, either. They are so enraptured of each other, I'm surprised they even see the bus when it roars up to the corner and smothers us in a fog of diesel exhaust.

Probably new love.

I hang back a little, fumbling to find my pass, and let them get on first. I plan to choose my seat carefully. I want to sit where I can see them.

Luckily, the bus is nearly empty. If it usually is at this time of day, I don't know. Most days I get off work a couple hours earlier and I'd be home by now.

On this particular bus we have a young working stiff reading the personal ads, a dozing matron leaving head grease on a window, and the ubiquitous weird person up front, stuffed into two grimy coats and a bursting nylon vest, muttering and rearranging her plastic bags of God knows what every time the bus takes a bounce.

So I sit across the aisle, one row back, where, if I sit a little sideways, I've got room to cross my legs, recline ever so slightly, and keep tabs on my boys.

They are more than a few years younger than me, but just a couple years younger than I wish I felt. And cute. Especially together. The way couples are even cuter because they're couples. One in particular catches my eye. Maybe it's the wispy blond hair that trips down his forehead. Or the rolled-up shorts, even though the season's long gone, bulky knit socks and ankle-high boots.

Sometimes that clone look annoys me, but in this case, I make an exception. After all, it works with good legs, if good legs are what you've got—and he does. A savoury package, altogether.

The other has black hair, cut in a way a little too pretentious for these parts, in my opinion. He's wearing those great-view-from-the-rear jeans, cinched at the waist, and a button-down shirt with the sleeves turned halfway up. Around his neck this spider web of a gold chain lures your eye down the front of his chest.

Obviously, these two are a lot more out than most. Like just now, when the one closer to me tries to make a point, he puts his hand on the other guy's bare knee and, no fuss, just leaves it there. Easily I can picture them walking out of a late movie holding hands. Maybe not at your average *mall* theatre, but in the right neighbourhood, for sure.

These two hold my attention so completely, I don't know why I bother with my magazine. I'm at the point where I've scrutinized them so much, I think I know them from somewhere. For most of us, I think, seeing other gays out in public, especially in unlikely places, is a real trip. We're here, we're queer, you know the rest.

As the bus lumbers toward downtown, rattling from one stop to the next, I become infused with their confidence, their self-assuredness. For a while we hardly pick up anyone, but as we get closer to downtown, the bus slowly fills.

The two are getting cutesy now, teasing each other. One pins down the other's hands. Then he pokes for a ticklish spot and the guy on the aisle almost squirms off the seat. When that outburst ends he leans over and actually nuzzles his friend's neck.

An old woman in a frayed tweed coat, sitting in one of the side seats, looks back just about then, and sees him sit up. Good, I figure. Now they'll settle down a bit. Then the guy on the aisle leans toward his friend and, my God, from this angle it looks like he's about to kiss him. No—he whispers something. That's almost as bad, I think. Considering where we are.

I see these three cocky teenagers climb on the bus. I feel like clearing my throat or something, to warn the boys. Cool it, fellas, I'm thinking. But the first of the three has a pile of transfers in his pocket and blocks the way while he figures out which might still be valid.

The bus pulls out and the three shove each other toward the back. I see one eye the gay boys, but nothing comes of it. I'm tensing up a little and wish they would, too. Especially in this part of town.

The aisle-guy has slipped down in the seat now, with his knees up on the back of the seat ahead. His shoulder presses against his boyfriend's arm. Any second his head will drop onto his friend's shoulder. The knot in my stomach chafes like a ball of coarse twine. We're almost downtown, where I hope they'll be getting off.

Then he drapes his arm over the other's bare leg and my spine stiffens. Clearly they have no sense. The bus slows for the next stop and I see a large, scowling man in a camel overcoat. The coat might have been fine once, but now it's dirty, a little threadbare. Probably second hand. This guy is big, a couple inches taller than me, with hair shaved short, and a neck as thick as his head. He's carrying a grey, plastic lunch pail, and looks ready to punch more than just a time clock.

I look across the aisle and they haven't moved. Hey, guys, I think. Butch it up a little. Slowly I uncross my legs, prop them apart. My triangle pin disappears under a fold of my jacket. The man in the overcoat clomps down the aisle and stops just short of the gay guys, still acting like faggots. I can feel his stare. I shift in the seat and look away.

Oh boy, I think. This is it.

Jacob Bowers

Jackson Park

I used to say, "I'll write, I promise," but when it came to actually writing letters, well, I never did get around to doing it. I come from a town of six thousand rednecks. Windsor, Ontario is the closest city, its Peace Fountain looking like a napalm bomb, with radioactive-coloured water gushing out of it. To the north and south, the United States looks like a cesspool of slums with phantoms swallowing the horizon, and the only evidence of civilization are speeding ant-like vehicles and the Ambassador Bridge.

I often wonder why it took me so long to realize I was gay, but in a county like Essex, it isn't hard to understand. Most people there are sheltered, isolated and ignorant. I remember sitting by the fountains in Jackson Park, a place where gay men used to go meet, until the cops started busting their faces open for doing what their heterosexual rivals were allowed to call love.

Even cars were targeted: if the people inside were heterosexual, they were allowed to stay. If they were fags, their car was ticketed, towed, and then they were bashed. I remember pulling into a parking space with my best friend for a smoke. A policeman came over, shone his flashlight into the car, cupped his hand to the window, and peered in. He stood by the car until we finished our cigarettes and drove away.

Jackson Park is where I came to grips with my sexual orientation, the place where only a year before I came out, my friend Cory told me that he was gay. He drowned himself a few days later. There are flowers now in Jackson Park, and the fountains don't look the same.

It's sunny today, and there's a warm breeze that caresses me, much like I wanted to caress Cory the night I last saw him, the night he told me his secret. I'm sorry that I left the park that night, but I didn't know what to do. It hurts to know that maybe if I'd have been a better friend, and just stayed with him that night, he might be here today.

There are so many things I want to say to him, but I just don't know how. *I miss you, Cory. I want you back. There are so many things that we could have done, so many things we could have shared.*

I never got the chance to tell him that he wasn't alone, that I was still his friend. I didn't even tell him that I too thought I was gay. Maybe I just didn't want to admit it yet. I only knew of my attraction to him. Knowing both his secret and mine was too much for me that night. His words brought to mind things I didn't want to see in myself, much less admit to. I wasn't ready then, and he's not here to listen to me now.

Where are you, Cory? Do you watch me sleep, or are you off in heaven, chasing boys more honest than I was that night in Jackson Park, better friends than I proved to be, in your white sterile robe? I miss you, Cory.

I wish I had written while I still had the chance.

Maureen Brady

Amour, Amour

I. First Kiss

We walk the river park, gazing out, then back at each other, our eyes sparkling with blue, yours more like the water glinting green. I want to hold your hand but hardly know you. Hardly know how to say why my heart keeps wanting to home in next to yours.

Your hands are busy, possibly nervous. You tell me how you embarked to see the world in youth, your European travels. The couple you stayed with in Germany who made love in front of you. I see your innocence standing side by side with your determination to escape the provinces you grew up in and become worldly. Remember my own rickety shuttle through youth: the man on the train who reached for my crotch behind the screen of his *New York Times,* the photographer who wanted to shoot a toothpaste commercial of my smile but said it would be necessary for me to expose my breasts as part of the audition. *People do things like this*, I thought but did not say, that same determination overriding my dismay.

The mention of sex from your lips makes me study them all the harder, and this only makes me want to hold your hand again. We are sitting on a step by then. I lean into your shoulder, press it for a second. You say you are moving to the other step because you need to smoke a cigarette if I don't mind. I don't. I want to smoke myself again for the first time in over a decade, watching your small ritual—your fingers holding the cigarette, your breath imbibing it, the smoke curling upwards. I wonder if I am going to get myself in trouble if I draw up the courage to kiss you.

You more or less ask how lesbians decide to kiss each other, confessing that you've nearly always been with men. I relate my coming out, the agony of the days I waited for the woman to seduce me, before I realized she was patiently, respectfully, awaiting me, since I'd declared myself straight.

All the way back up beside the river I think about your hand, how nice it would be in mine, how awkward it feels to keep apart like friends, like strangers, like birds flitting from branch to branch but landing beside each other.

Later, after you feed me the delicious pasta sauce you've stirred all day, making it into an aphrodisiac, I bump your shoulder again, this time with my head, as if I am a lowing sheep, and you grab it with your arm and hold it for a moment. Then before thought can come again, I hold your hand and you hold mine and who can say who made that happen. It doesn't matter. It makes me bold enough to lean across and kiss you.

Some days down the line, you say, "You can tell if someone will be a good lover by the way they kiss, don't you think?"

"I could tell about you," I say, remembering your desire, how it captured my upper lip and pulled at me and made me want to go into your tide, utterly.

II. Possession

I think I am too tired to come. Maybe too tired to have sex. But then I think I'll let you do what you want to, anyway. And you go exploring with your fingers. You rub my clit, which seems almost indifferent for a short time, though for all the past days our sex has never been ordinary.

You work at it. You don't give up. And then you go with your mouth licking me, and somewhere in there I feel your energy come into focus. Your power becomes the shape of a cone, as if you are a tornado touching down and I am the earth you want to ruffle.

My head falls back further, my limbs go slack, my cunt goes open. You come back up and hold me, one arm surrounding me as if I were a baby. You lift me onto your leg and fuck me with your other hand and watch me swoon and come to you. And come some more. Circling high into the sky. Leaving this planet for the moment. Yet never leaving you behind. You take me everywhere I go. You take me.

III. Separation

You disappeared. How could you disappear so utterly, when I thought you were right behind me? It's what I fear the worst, the most—complete desertion and disappearance. You told me we were close to danger, that I should back up. I thought you meant retrace our steps to the other subway line. I thought you were right behind me. I went single-mindedly, my head never turning around, trusting you were in my footsteps. When I turned around you were nowhere. There was blank air. There were strangers. There was silence and frigid air.

My heart fell down an elevator shaft into a bottomless hole. There was no landing. I was lonely right away like I'd been before I met you. Before you arrived in my life looking wholesome, possible, eager, lovely. I peered at all the people, called your name, not out loud, which would make me seem crazy since you were not there, but silently I prayed your name. Retraced my steps, searching as one examines the weave of a fabric for a misstitch. How could the weave come apart when it had been coming together so exquisitely? When your head laying upon my shoulder had come to feel placed there by an angel. When your popping an apple slice into my mouth had come to be an anointing.

You have been gone one day and one night and this is what I dream.

IV. Reunion

You fly home in bad weather. I don't want you flying in an ice storm but I don't want you to be late, either. I've borne our days apart with whole segments of me submerged in a holding tank, and I don't know if I can bear another.

We undress each other slowly. Our bare chests touch tenderly, our breasts get kissed and greeted. My eyes search your face, roam your body, learning you all over again, while recruiting memory of the routes which have become familiar.

A pitch of fear mediated by desire into a high, thin note hangs in the air vibrating. We dart from our memories of separation to our memories of union. We are new again and yet your smell has gained a hold on me with ancient remnants to it. I fall headlong into your spell. Your mouth is so soft I am amazed once more at the power it has to flood me.

Length to length, our pants kicked off, our hearts joined, our mounds shimmer a current from one to the other and back again. We create a sensation that both anticipates and quite possibly surpasses the pleasure of orgasm. I say, "Can I die now? Because I think I've gone to heaven."

And you say, "No, I want you right here, on earth," and know you have me.

I lick you until enough light teems out of you to adorn the crown of my head, which makes me wonder how sex ever got associated with badness, when it is good enough to tell us we are home.

Alison Brewin

Daylight

My head. I don't want to wake up yet. The pain.

I squeeze my eyes shut in an effort to blank out into sleep again. But that hurts more. I want to throw up. It smells in here, of stale cigarette smoke and some kind of alcohol she pulled out of a drawer last night. What will I see if I open my eyes? What will she see? Is she even here? I don't feel her body, but maybe this is a big bed. My eyes want to stay shut.

The bar. I was at the bar last night. It was fun, I think. Must have been. Heat, bodies, loud voices. She was there, watching me laughing with my friends. One of them elbowed me, then I saw her. Lights, music, lots of drinks. She kept on watching me, and then she was gone. Where did she go? I looked for her. She was in the bathroom, washing her hands. Beautiful hands. Those hands, later, on my body.

I open my eyes suddenly, remembering our early morning sex play.

Is she here? I'm afraid to breathe. Across the messy room is a large chair with tattered, cat-scratched arms. We sat in it last night. Together. She was touching me. Now it's empty. My shirt hangs over the back of it.

The bed I am in, I remember, is small.

She is not here.

I roll over onto my back. My head. My mouth tastes like shit. We didn't brush our teeth last night. I hate that. My tongue feels thick and coated. The sun shines through the window, onto my face, across my body. My skin. The heat is too much. I roll away from it and back onto my side.

I didn't speak to her in the bathroom. I smiled at her and went into one of the stalls. Later, on the dance floor we flirted. I was high. That was Diane's idea. She said I was trying too hard, that I needed drugs to have fun. Let loose. Let my hair down. It worked. I flirted with her on the dance floor. I know how to dance. Comes from hanging out with gay men. It's what you do with your hips.

Where is she now? Is she coming back soon?

I don't know where I am. My foggy mind struggles with last night's details. We can't be far from the bar because we walked. At least I think we walked. Yes. Stopped at that pizza joint on Abbott, then walked down Hastings. Laughing. That giggly pre-sex laughing. As though we were in love.

Ugh.

Her name. I can't even remember her name. Lynn? Linda? No. It wasn't that simple. It had a "y" ending, like Buffy. Ha. It definitely wasn't Buffy.

I heave myself up to sit at the edge of the bed. I'm naked. The mirror across the room reflects my pale, flabby stomach. Hungover again, ugh. My greasy hair. Is that the drugs, or do I always look like this in the morning? I shake the image away.

There is a piece of paper on the dresser. Is it a note? I get up to look.

No. A Visa slip. From the bar. Did I really spend that much money? Long Island Iced Tea. Buffy liked Long Island Iced Tea. Between that and my scotch. . . .

"I refuse to drink blended scotch." Did I say that to her? I did. What an idiot.

My jeans are in a pile on the rug. I pull them on without looking for my underwear. We sat on this threadbare, dusty rug last night. Smoking drugs and sharing drunken dreams. I was going to be a famous lawyer, as if there is such a thing. She hoped to make assistant manager at the bar she worked at. I was full of advice. Of course she would make it. When I was struggling through school I just told myself, where did I want to be in three years . . . blah, blah, blah.

Why am I such a shit? Why do I think my life matters? Did I offend her? Bore her? She hadn't seemed bored.

I go to the window. I look out. I'm still downtown. She lives here. I'm in an apartment/hotel downtown and it's not one of those fancy ones. Far from it. People live here. I'd always known that, but I could never imagine what it was like. I look around. It's not so bad, I suppose. Small. Just a room. High ceilings. The ceiling is moulded, but cracked, as though it once aspired to greatness, but the chance had passed long ago. Now it's too late. The furniture is old. Stuff that might have been antique, but didn't quite make it. Like the building. The brown, arm-tattered chair. The dresser with the mirror, etched twirls of art deco design in the corners of the glass, but panelling missing from the drawers. The small, narrow iron bed. Old, tired furniture.

Buffy is nostalgic, though. A golden-coloured teddy bear lies on the floor. Knocked off the chair during our quiet wrestling. Photos are jammed around the mirror's edge. Most of the figures are Asian. Her family, I presume. There are photos of a large white woman. She has short brown hair. In one, the woman is alone. She wears only shorts, hiking boots and a necklace with five coloured rings. It hangs between her breasts.

I am struck by how much this woman looks like me. How much *is* she like me? Does she drink scotch? Is she a lawyer? Was Buffy disappointed by my stupid rambling last night? She did cut me off with a kiss. She did shut me up with sex.

I turn to pick up my shirt and see the note on the floor. It must have fallen.

GONE TO GET BREKKIE. WAIT FOR ME.

LINDY.

Lindy. That's it. Is my name not on the note because she can't remember it? Or is she better at drunken details then I am? Should I wait? Suddenly I'm struck with panic. I find a pen, turn the note over and write:

SORRY. LOADS OF WORK TO DO. GREAT NIGHT.

I'LL CALL.

SUSAN.

XOXO

I add the XOXO as an afterthought. The note seems harsh without it. Will I call? I don't know. At the moment, I don't care.

I pull my shirt on, grab my bag, stuff my underwear in a pocket, and flee. My head still hurts. The hallway smells of urine. Why didn't I notice that last night? Where is the elevator? I get my bearings and head left. Is she on her way up? The hallway is long, the elevator at the end. I vaguely remember our giggles as we bumped our way down to her room. Is there a bathroom here? As much as I don't want to run into her, I have to pee.

A door on my right stands open. As I approach, another shabby room comes into view. There is a woman sitting on a chair at the window. She is skinny and old. As I pause, she turns to look at me. She is not old. Her eyes are half closed, her skin an unpleasant shade of yellow, her hair an unnatural blonde.

"Hi. Uh. . . . Is there a bathroom here?"

She laughs. "Whad'ya think, idiot, we pee on the floor?"

"Ha. Yeah . . . I mean . . . course not . . . ha." Jesus. Get me out of here.

She turns back to the window and points with her thumb down the hall.

Quickly. Move quickly. I hurry forward to a door marked Ladies, though someone has scratched that out with a black marker and written "Women" and below that someone has written "Whores." Despite my expectations, the bathroom is passably clean. After a hurried pee, I stand at the door listening for the sound of footsteps. None. I head out. The elevator is there. It's not moving. No one is coming up. But there are stairs. Oh, hurry.

I push the button and hold my breath as it cranks up toward me. Will she be in it?

The doors open. It's empty. I exhale with a hiss.

Will she be in the lobby? This stupid machine is way too slow. Please let her not be there. The elevator stops with a bang. The door slowly slides open. The lobby is empty. She isn't there.

I walk out onto the street and duck a little. I wave at a cab. As I lean back in the seat, tears of relief and frustration come to my eyes.

David Lyndon Brown

Why I Never Learned to Swim

The sea was a seething scribble far away on the top of the horizon, and the air boiled above the white hot sand. I was building a battlement of turrets around the blanket where my mother lay, but the sand was dry and the turrets kept collapsing, invading the blanket, infiltrating the paper bag full of warm tomato sandwiches and the coloured plastic tumblers sticky with orange cordial. It was impossible to restrict the sand to the beach. I lay down on my back staring straight at the sun until it turned black and then I got up and staggered around with my arms outstretched, like a blind boy. Then I looked at my mother for a while, waiting for her to come back into focus.

"I'm going for a walk," I announced. "I'm going exploring."

"Well, don't go too far, and don't go in," my mother said, turning herself over, slick with a home-made marinade of oil and vinegar.

The heat from the sand entered the soles of my old-fashioned sandals and rose up my legs as I walked toward the distant ocean. I walked with crossed legs, then hopped a bit, then galloped on one hand and one foot. Everyone would be astonished by these weird tracks and wonder what strange creature was at large on the beach.

Suddenly the sand dipped and the waves came crashing in. They were tall and loud and kept hurling themselves down and getting up and rushing out again. I dipped the toe of my sandal into the frizz of foam that was spat up along the tide-line. It looked like the stuff that emptied out of my mother's washing machine, or what you sick up after drinking too much lemonade. Further up the beach, I could see some children dashing in and out of the surf, and I walked slowly toward them, popping the beads of a seaweed necklace the sea had chucked out. The boys were brown and glossy in their little togs and sparks shot off them as they raced from the water. There was a man with them. A great big glistening god of a man. He grabbed the boys, swung them high into the air and launched them into the waves. Then he sat them astride his massive shoulders and cantered along the beach like a centaur. I stopped not far from them to watch. I was bewitched by that colossus and my eyes ranged over his immense limbs like hands, always coming to rest on the blue satin bulge between those mighty thighs. I sat down on the hot sand to unbuckle my shoes. Part of me wanted the man to rush over and sweep *me* off my feet, but I felt dry and opaque next to those luminous kids and self-conscious in the matching shirt and shorts my mother had made out of a stupid old curtain. I took off the shirt and stuck it under my sandals. My skin was as pale as milk.

I was shuffling, up to my ankles in the water, sifting the sand through my toes, when the ball the boys were playing with plopped into the water in front of me.

"Get it," they shouted. "Get it before it goes out." The red ball was bobbing in the trough between the big waves. I waded toward it. Up to my knees. Up to my waist. And then suddenly the sand dropped away beneath me and I was under the water. I could see the red ball above me and beyond it, the yellow ball of the sun. It was so quiet under there. I thought I was breathing underwater like a fish. I can swim, I thought as the ocean sucked and dragged me. I'm swimming. I found my feet and staggered up into the air but another wave bashed me and another one tumbled me, rolling me along the bottom.

The hot sand was burning my back. I was lying in a circle of upside-down boys. The big brown man was kissing me on the lips. His big hands were rubbing my chest. There was a halo of sunlight around his head. I looked up at him through my eyelashes and then turned my head and deposited a little pile of red and white vomit onto the sand. Tomato sandwiches.

"Where's your Mum?" the man enquired. I sat up to disguise what was going on in my shorts.

"Did you find the ball?" I asked.

T.J. Bryan

Good Gyal Gets *Hers*

Khadija's under my skin like a disease. Six voluptuous feet of Afro-lesbian goddess with a real African name (used to be Sarah-Jane). Got a head fulla locks too! You know, it's only conscious sisters who have the dedication to grow locks like hers. And that voice! When she speaks I can feel her commitment to the struggle deep down . . . uh . . . inside.

Last week she came to my Black Wimmin's Sing Along & Drumming Group. Afterwards, when I got home, I went for a pee and found my underwear and my genitals moist with . . . uh . . . desire. It wasn't surprising considering the times our eyes locked as we measured out syncopated beats on our drums.

Tonight's rehearsal went smoothly and later the whole group was talking about a revolution at Sister Nzingha's place. I nearly fainted when Khadija came and asked me to twist her locks. There we were: her between my legs and me in heaven. I went extra slow to make it last. But eventually it came to an end. She thanked me for a job well done. I just stood there, wanting to do much more than twist her hair, not knowing how to ask. Feeling uncomfortable as her eyes crawled over my body like I was a piece of veal in a butcher shop.

"This thing work for you?" Her velvet-toned voice broke the silence as she reached out to finger the African fertility goddess pendant I always wear around my neck.

I stifled a giggle. She was so calm and composed. Really had her act together. I didn't want to seem a fool in front of her so I came back at her with: "What do you think?" When she didn't answer, I lost what cool I had and blurted out: "I was wondering if we could go somewhere for some tea and talk about tonight's meeting?"

She walked away, pausing only long enough to ask, "You comin'?"

I didn't say goodbye to my sistren with a hug, as is customarily my practice. I just snatched up my drum and followed.

Her place is on a street lined with huge, imposing maples. I enter a dark hallway and begin taking off my coat. Then she's on me. Strong arms pin me to the wall. Long tongue invades my ears, my throat. Rude hands claim my breasts, slide down my zipper and into my pants. Not what I expect from a feminist sister at all. Her aggressive pawing makes me uncomfortable. My heart isn't beating right. Should never have come. I push her off me.

"Get out," she says. The look in her eyes tells me she's not joking.

"I don't understand."

Sandalwood and sweat invade my nostrils as she moves closer. Although she's smiling, her eyes are dead serious. "It's real simple." One of her hands closes around my throat, cutting off my air. "If you stay, you're gonna have to do what I say. Got it?" I nod. Her other hand slowly twists one of my nipples hard enough to make me cry out.

"That's not good enough. I need to hear the words."

My damned pre-menstrual clitoris responds to the pain she's inflicting. My brain valiantly tries to counter its influence but the signal is fuzzy. All I receive is a steady throb, throb, throb from below. The gist of this clitoris code is something like: *Now girl, I don't have arms or legs. but you know I'm in control. Do not, I repeat, do not fuck this up with your happy clappy, anti-sex, penetration and lust equals abuse and misogyny shit, okay?*

I struggle to free myself. Meanwhile inside me a war's ragin'. Good Black Gyal, the upstanding activist, member of one anti-porn task force and two anti-prostitution patrols is arguing with Slut/Whore, who demands control of my clitoris at times like this. If Mommy and Daddy ever found out about *her*. . . well, Good Black Gyal can't even think about that.

The struggle in my head keeps my tongue tied. And my clit doesn't help matters any. It's pumping like mad inside my panties. Slut/Whore is daring me to break through my fears. *Tell the truth. Expose that proper, political Black lesbian warrior image hanging like a boulder around your neck. Deep six it, girl. Cast it off.*

But I can't. Not when Good Black Gyal *has* to wear psychic chain mail just to walk down the street everyday. *Take it off!* Not when someone needs to take care of business. *Why does it always have'ta be you?* Mommy and Daddy raised me right. *I wanna see you whimper, scream and grovel. If you can't let go I can't come. Let somebody else run things. Let* HER *do it!* Slut/Whore wrestles control from Good Black Gyal long enough to force one of Khadija's hands down to the wetness between my thighs. "Can you feel how much I want this? Let me prove it to you."

Khadija glares at me. "Don't say things like that, little girl."

"I'll do anything to sleep with you, *anything!*"

"I'll do *anything* to sleep with you," she taunts. "That what you think's goin' on here, babe? *Sex*? Makin' *love*?" I hang my head in confusion. "Novice." She grabs me by my hair and drags me into the room across the hall. My eyes adjust enough to the darkness for me to make out a beat-up black leather bag positioned nearby. She picks it up and throws herself down into a big over-stuffed couch, resting the bag on her lap. The grip she's got on my braids compels me to kneel before her. She shoves her feet toward me. "Tha boots."

Slut/Whore sets to work obediently trying to remove them. The sound of Khadija rooting around in the depths of that bag pricks up my ears. She leans over to get a better look at my rear end, or so I think. And faster than you can say *Kwanzaa* my behind is on fire, stinging from the lash of whatever she's pulled out of the bag. "Ouch! That really *hurt*. What is that?" Good Black Gyal nearly stops breathing when she catches sight of Khadija holding a small, leather flogger.

But Khadija doesn't care. "Don't take 'em off," she orders, pushing me back down between her spread legs. "Clean 'em good . . . with your *tongue*."

Now, I like the smell of leather. What's not to like? Though some of my feminist sisters may not be able to stomach that combination of what they call "murdered-animal skin" and shoe polish, there's nothing like a dyke in black leather steel toes to excite Slut/Whore. But nobody said anything about licking somebody's *stink*, dirty boots.

She sees my hesitation and *whap!* Another lash connects with my skin, bringing tears to my eyes.

"Shit for brains, ain't this what you *want*?"

"Khadija—"

The bony back of her hand connects with the side of my face and I taste my own blood. "That's *sir* to you. Can't even admit that you wanna be freed from yourself. Ain't got the guts to say you wanna be my slave, *do* you?" She's slapping my face with increasing force. Driving my head back and forth. Beating Good Black Gyal into a hasty retreat. "What do you want from me? Answer *now* or get out!"

Slut/Whore's need is stronger than Good Black Gyal's fear of defeat. So I speak, tongue dripping with lust. "Sir, please do what you want with me."

"Then be a good little feminist and get to work." For emphasis she crams the tip of one mud-caked boot into my mouth.

I don't know what's worse for Good Black Gyal: being treated like a slave by a sista or the fact that Slut/Whore loves it. Stuck in the middle with no possible compromise in sight, I crack. My pussy opens shamelessly as tears roll down my cheeks, pooling on Khadija's cold, hard boot. Slut/Whore eagerly laps them up.

"That's it, bitch. Suck it. Lick it. Keep that up and maybe I'll let you come." Slut/Whore, caught up in the grip of her want, squirms with delight. All Good Black Gyal can do is blubber and moan as her tongue is used to lather up the now shiny surface of Khadija's boots.

After eight years of living, loving and playing with Deej, I can relax and trust her to set up the scene I envisioned. My woman knows exactly what I need to tame the Good Black Gyal in me and open the closet where my Slut/Whore sleeps imprisoned, in bondage.

Together we mine the perversity in our free, Black souls and unleash the defiant power of our pleasure. Relishing the ways my demonic sista lover can bend my iron will, I willingly submit to her not-so-tender mercies.

Giovanna (Janet) Capone

Her Kiss

I'm leaving because of it. I'm eighteen and in love with a woman for the first time. Right after graduating high school, I'm leaving my family, New York, and everything I've ever known. I've shelled out ninety-five bucks for a one-way bus ticket from Manhattan Port Authority to Texas.

I'm leaving because of her kiss. Believe me, it was delicious, and I'm obsessed. With Dee going back home, it feels like someone has pulled the plug on me, sucking everything down to the Southwest. My destiny is in Texas with her, and nobody is gonna fuck with that.

I met her in high school English. A native Texan, born and bred. So different from me, an Italian from the Bronx. I wanted to know all about her and that lilting, chicken-fried accent. I looked up Texas in the library and checked out five books on the Lone Star State. But soon printed matter wasn't enough. I wanted more.

I still flash on that night in Dee's room, the night we first kissed. She started it, but I reciprocated. Her lips were soft and warm. She kissed my neck and my earlobes. I pressed my whole face into her breasts and thought I'd reached nirvana. Goddamn! It's what I'd always wanted.

I saved money from part-time jobs, bought myself a few pairs of shorts and the bus ticket. Hell, I was young, ripe and ready for a change. I got Mario, my father, to drive me to Port Authority Greyhound Station. That was no small feat.

The two of us are speeding down the highway in the family station wagon. He's talking my ear off, telling me I'm making a big mistake.

"What the hell ya gonna do in goddamn Texas, *stroonz?*" (It means turd.) "You got rocks in your head?" I stare out the window at the cars and cabs speeding by, everyone racing on to the next important thing in their life. I'm racing too, but I'm also scared.

My father looks over his shoulder, about to change lanes. He doesn't know why I'm leaving. Or does he? Poor Mario. All his kids are turning out wrong. Now this one's a dyke. I kind of feel sorry for him.

"I'm over here breaking my ass to give you kids a few things, and teach you what's right," he says. On the word "right," he steps on the gas and the car lurches forward.

I knew I wouldn't get outta town without a lecture. I may not get out alive.

Yesterday I got a lecture from my mother. She's positive Dee's been brainwashing me. She even thought she might be giving me drugs. I caught her snooping through my stuff one afternoon.

"Ma, what the hell are ya doing?"

"I'm looking," she says defensively. "I'm your mother and I'm looking."

"I know you're my mother. What are you looking for? You run out of underwear?"

"Don't get smart with me, young lady. Are you on something?"

"I'm on my period."

"You keep giving me answers," she says, shaking her finger in my face. "But you ain't giving me the right answers." The sweat is beading up on her lip. "Ever since you've been hanging around that girl you got all these crazy ideas in your head. Now you wanna go down there with her. Whatsa matter? Everything she does, you gotta do?"

"I'm eighteen years old and it's my life," I yell. "And stop snooping in my stuff!"

"I have a right to know what the hell you're doing," she yells. "You're not telling me the truth!" She grabs my arm like she's gonna hit me. "And you're getting too free and easy with that girl, hanging around, talking a lotta crap."

"Get off me!" I say, pushing her away. She hauls off and slaps me right across the face.

"Ow! Stop it! Get the fuck off me." I push her away. She's screaming and hollering. Says I'm selfish to move so far from the family.

"You only care about yourself. You think you're better than the rest of us."

"Leave me the hell alone!" I shout, and run out of the house in tears.

I didn't come back 'til past midnight. Who does she think she is? She'd run my life if I let her.

Now, I sit back and brace myself, expecting more from Mario, with less fanfare and more guilt.

"I'm breaking my ass," he says, "and for what?" He flicks the fingertips of one hand under his chin. "*Va fan' culo!* They'll piss on my grave when I go!"

He keeps driving. "*Gesu Crist!*" he says under his breath. I don't utter a word back or it'll extend the lecture.

It figures he'd try guilt. Them and their martyr complex. I'm sick of it. They work and work and never feel appreciated. Who told him to go and have so many kids?

We approach the exit and he looks at me, shaking his finger in my face. "You got thick skulls!" he says, and I know immediately he means all of us, all his wayward kids. Vinny's been getting drunk at the bars every night. Rosemarie's off to college. She moved out early, after that big fight about boyfriends. Screaming and hollering in front of the neighbours. Thank God I never had to have boyfriend fights with Mario, like my sisters. But we've got other fun issues to fight about.

"Gotta do things your own way," he says, gassing the pedal. We pass a Wonderbread truck in silence. I stare at the red, white and blue dots. I never knew what Wonderbread was 'til I went to school and saw kids eating baloney and cheese sandwiches on sliced white bread. I never envied them, nor felt like I was missing anything special. Mario always bought Italian bread or whole wheat or dark rye, and that's what I prefer today. Red peppers fried in olive oil is a lot more appetizing than baloney. Actually, I love the traditions of my culture. I'm proud to be Italian. But they'd never guess it, especially lately. When I'm angry and feel suffocated, the last thing I wanna do is appreciate them.

Mario tries a new angle. "If that girl wantsa go down there, let her go. That's where she's from. Isn't she?" I don't answer. "Well, isn't she?"

"Yeah, she's from there. Her family lives in Texas. Some of 'em."

"Well you ain't from there. You're from here," he says, pointing at the floorboards. "Your family's here. What the hell ya gonna do in goddamn Texas?"

The more he talks, the more I feel like a liar, a gutless liar. He doesn't know the real reason I'm leaving and neither does Ma. I can't tell them I fell in love with a woman.

"You gotta make your own decisions," he says, pointing at me. "Don't let nobody influence you."

"Influence me?" I yell. He looks surprised, prepared for a fight. "You piss me off! Both a you. Would you just let me do one thing for myself? Would you?"

"Yourself, yourself! All you think about is yourself," he says, getting louder. "All you kids are alike. The whole buncha you. What about your family? What about us?" he goes on, but I'm blocking him out. My mind is gone. I'm tripping so hard on the assumption that I can't make my own decisions. If he only knew the half of it! I've got cousins my age getting married and multiplying like rabbits. Mario, I'm making my own decisions.

"*Tu sei pazz'*, Fran. You're outta your mind." He taps the side of his head and continues driving. But the whole time we're arguing, he never once refuses to drive me.

When we get there, he helps me with my suitcase and a huge cardboard box of stuff including my dismantled ten-speed with socks, t-shirts and shorts packed around it, still protesting the plan he's helping me carry out.

We say goodbye and he stuffs some money in my hand. "You got a head like concrete," he says. "I don't know why you gotta do this."

I hug him goodbye and get on the bus. I throw my backpack on the floor and find a seat, grinding my teeth. Mario's final question rings in my ears. "I don't know why you gotta do this." Damn him for making me doubt myself!

The bus pulls out of the station. I wave to Mario as he gets back into the car. He has a way of holding his shoulders that always looks like he's burdened by so many responsibilities. He is, I guess, with five kids and my mother. They work their asses off. Work for their kids, work for the family.

But now I need to grow in a way they don't understand and can't help me with. I watch him drive away. Tears flood my eyes as he leaves.

Justin Chin

The Cooking

When I fall in love, I always seem to end up cooking for the person I'm smitten with. It's not an easy process and sometimes, I find myself calling my mother long distance at ten forty-five at night, saying things like: "Mom! What's flan and how do you cook it? Where can I buy one?" Only to have poor Mom on the verge of tears saying over and over, "Are you taking drugs again? What's wrong with you?"

Once, there was a person I was so taken with, I spent two days making a pasta sauce. The whole process involved grilling peppers of all different shapes, colours and tastes on the oven racks for hours, then slowly stripping them of their skins. The denuded peppers, in all their squishy aromatic splendour, were then put, along with whole cloves of garlic and some tumeric, in a large earthenware pot overnight to undergo some kind of miraculous change rivaling the Miracle of Lourdes. Next, it was rescued and diced into a nice soft mush which was added to the frying mixture of minced garlic and onions, fresh basil leaves, a small sliver of ginger, a sprinkling of coarse black pepper, and random dashes of ground spices from the spice rack. The whole frying mixture was then introduced to a huge heap of finely chopped and diced fresh tomatoes and a small pot of tomato sauce. The sloppy mess was cooked, simmered, and cooked again.

When we finally sat down to dinner, I lied and said the sauce was really no problem at all, less than an hour I said. If I had told the truth, would he have loved me more? Would he have stayed and not left me for that tile salesman from Colma?

Kent Chuang

Lento Con Expressione

Lento con expressione: Slowly with feeling, that's what it said on the top of the page. So I put the cello between my legs, placed the hair of the bow on the strings and pulled. Slowly, and with feeling. The vibrations began penetrating, deeper and deeper inside me. Suddenly it hit me.

The same thing happened last night while I was driving home through a back lane. I pressed my foot on the accelerator and gradually the car sped up. As if in a timewarp, ghostly moonwashed terrace houses began to fly past me on both sides, faster and faster. There was a rush of adrenalin, excitement, and that's when it first struck me.

Life's like that. Before you know it. . . .

The melody plunged into a long and uneasy note before spiralling upward again.

Just like our family dinner last evening, in one of those Chinese restaurants where people talk faster than chopsticks and Peking Ducks land like UFOs. I was suffocating from the noise around me, generations of simple-minded bliss.

In the middle of watching the king prawns sizzling, my two sisters began to bicker over the best future for their children. Their husbands were comparing the fuel consumption of their new BMWs. Even my Calvin Klein Eternity faded as Mum manoeuvred another chicken foot toward me, so I took it like a man, welcomed it onto my bowl of rice and played my part in this, our "normal and happy" little family.

"How was your weekend?" asked my "favourite" brother-in-law.

"Nothing special, sodomy on Saturday and Ecstasy on Sunday. More tea?"

How does my sister put up with him, and for over twenty years! Can't she see that the next twenty will be just as predictable? If that is love, I'll take masturbation.

Mum added, "Why no stick to same man? Why play Russian Roulette?"

What could I say?

"More rice?"

I looked around the restaurant. Everywhere there were fish tanks filled with happy little crustaceans nonchalantly bubbling away. I felt as if I was Esther Williams, trapped by a chilli crab.

Well, I should be thankful. Two years ago when I told Mum and Dad, in Cantonese of course, "Me no want Susie. I want man. No grandson. Extra daughter. Better!" They broke down in tears and shouted, "Shame to family. Shame to ancestors. Shame to neighbours!" Dad tried to straighten me out with a psychiatrist. Mum rang her acupuncturist, but in a fit of desperation decided to defy God. She sent me to a brothel.

After that failed there was just silence. I guess that's when they started to blame themselves. Two months ago Dad stopped asking why. He died.

I took a sip of green tea and momentarily the whole restaurant reeked of what our family could have been and how happy we once were, stir-fried into what we were then, in that noisy, oily hole.

The final note of the solemn melody lingered in the air before disappearing. The empty room waited in anticipation.

I paused.

Allegro con fucco.

Fast with fury. That's what it said on the top of the next page. The music exploded at rapid speed, there was no time to think, my fingers were on automatic. The bow jumped back and forth between strings splattering notes like hot oil in a fry pan.

I'll never forget Lava. It was Buddies Night at the baths, and that night I crouched on tiptoes peering through the glory hole, only to be hit between the eyes from her explosion. I lost my balance and landed on something cold and wet. Lava just continued exploding, and simultaneously belted out bursts of excruciatingly painful squeals and fabulously exaggerated aaahs, sending shock waves through cubicles, dislodging condoms from their dispensers.

Rapidly tissued, we bolted out the door. Bang! It was fate. Love at first sight. What would life be like without Lava?

What was life like with Lava?

Together we almost re-invented domestic bliss. If we had children we'd send them to Sunday school. Instead we stayed home on Buddies Night to watch re-runs of *Melrose Place* and on weekends we planted tulips in the garden. I even perfected Mum's special shark fin soup.

This mindless bliss lasted just short of our local gym membership. Then slowly I began to feel as if I was acting out the predictable life of my brother-in-law. I even dreamt about polishing his BMW, and that was the beginning of the end.

Poor Lava, he saw no reason not to wash our car.

Gradually we started returning to Buddies Night. The tulips in our garden turned into dandelions, we ate home-delivered pizzas. I picked out the anchovies and left them on the plate, then waited to see who would say it first.

With a big crescendo the fiery music climaxed. Exhausted I let out the final breath. The tension between my legs slackened, the grip on the instrument limp. Breathing softly again I raised my head, opened my eyes and saw.

Out through the sunlit window, our lonesome conifer stood proud against the deep blue sky. Even with swarms of insects buzzing around, it refused to budge. It was smiling with a certain phallic charm.

I hope Lava is having a great time with Bruno.

Yes, why no stick to same man?

Why no play same music?

I turned the page.

Lento ma non troppo.
Slowly but not too.

A. J. Crestwood

The Colonel and Me

Ingrid and I sit on the couch, hip to hip under the pink and blue Afghan Ingrid's mother made for us. We are waiting for The Kiss.

Not one of our kisses. God, no. After ten years, two kids and a mortgage the size of Miller's Cave, our kisses, though frequent, are not heralded by such . . . *anticipation.*

In fact, Ingrid has a cold, and being the conscientious medical person that she is (Ingrid's an orthopedic surgeon), we are not allowed to kiss tonight. Germ theory.

No. The kiss we are waiting for is on prime time television. The Monday night made-for-TV movie. Some time before 11 p.m., famous mainstream actress Glenn Close will kiss famous mainstream actress Judy Davis. At some point in the narrative, the actress portaying Colonel Margarethe Cammermeyer—the highest ranking officer in the U.S. military to be discharged because of sexual orientation—will kiss the actress portraying her artist girlfriend, Diane, the woman who made her aware of said orientation. At some point, the TV people will have to show, somehow, that these two women are, in fact, *lesbians*—without offending my mother (who may be watching this on the other side of the country).

Ingrid is making her way through a bowl of apple crisp and milk and staring at the TV screen. The lights are out (except for the one in the hall), and the tube casts a bluish light on her face. She looks a bit like Glenn Close: same purposeful nose, same no-nonsense cheekbones. Bigger though, a strapping blonde, with shoulders muscled from sawing and hammering bone.

We have waded through the introductory part: the soldier's work, the divorced mother of nearly-grown boys, the shiny four-wheel-drive vehicles rolling through shade-dappled suburbs. Then the love interest: the first look, the twig of attention, the Colonel helping the artist to her feet during football on the beach. More looks. The first date: *I don't know what I'm doing,* says the Colonel. The artist smiling.

"Are we taping this?" Ingrid asks. She is brilliant in the O.R., but the VCR is beyond her.

"Yes."

"Good. Can we go to bed now?" Scraping her bowl.

"Wait 'til the next commercial." Another twenty minutes by my reckoning.

"Okay." A hint of resignation as she lays her bowl on the coffee table and puts a weary arm around me.

I burrow my face into her neck. "Which one would you choose, if you *had* to?"

"What?"

"Which of the two women would you have a relationship with, if you had to?"

"Oh. Neither, really. Well, let's see, if I had to . . . Judy Davis. The Colonel's a bit *military* for me."

"You know, you remind me a bit of the Colonel," I say fondly. "I could see you doing that, being honest in spite of the stakes. Plus you have great posture."

She laughs. "Well, you know my feeling about the military. Anyway, what about you? Who would you choose to be involved with . . . if you *had to?*"

"Judy Davis."

What does that mean: both of us attracted to the *femme?*

"You remind me of *her*," she says. "Of course, you're younger."

"Not much." Possibly not at all. But I will always be younger than Ingrid.

The movie's on again, so I shush Ingrid, though she is not making a sound. Then, naturally, there is a noise upstairs. One of the kids?

"I'll go," I say, leaving the cozy darkness of the living room. Up the stairs. Zack first, then Katey. Both warm and flushed and peaceful, smelling like clean pyjamas. Quiet for now.

"Well, Colonel, what did I miss?"

"Please." She arranges the Afghan over me. She has tolerated being called Vanessa, Emma, or Meryl—depending on the movie—but "Colonel" she will nip in the bud. "She's meeting her lesbian-lawyer, and the lesbian-lawyer's friends."

"Oh. They don't look like dykes." Too feminine. *Feminized.* For my mother. Ingrid hates it when I say stuff like that.

"And what does a lesbian look like?"

"Like you."

Another batch of commercials.

"Can we go to bed now?" asks Ingrid, toes fumbling around the carpet for her slippers.

"Next commercial."

"That's what you said last time."

"Yes, but I missed most of it checking on the kids."

"Oh, all *right*."

And so I eke out the evening, the commercials coming faster and faster, the story deepening. The coming out stuff: boys, father, hostile ex-husband, hostile woman in the street. The lovers: a ring, a conflict, the second ring, the Colonel crying, the artist hesitantly unbuttoning the Colonel's jacket, stiff with medals, not actually touching her—because my mother may be watching.

Then the porch scene (I knew it, it's five to eleven), the cover of darkness, the look (affection, respect, loyalty, love, not quite lust), the tentative brush on the shoulder. It's coming. . . .

There is a noise upstairs.

"For God's sake!"

"That's okay, I'll go," says Ingrid, stretching.

And then I finally see it. The Kiss. Both women facing the camera, the artist slightly behind. The Colonel turns her head *significantly* to get on target, and even then—as Ingrid says later—it looks like she's hitting the cheek (corner of the mouth, max). Not a surgical strike. The hands come up. Matching rings. Hold that pose. Music. Titles.

Must have taken quite a few takes.

Ingrid's back. "Did I miss it?"

"Yeah, but we've got it on tape."

And so I replay it for her. Once. Twice. In fact we practice it ourselves. It's as tricky as it looks. But we get it. Hands come up. Matching rings.

No titles though.

Daniel Cunningham

A Few Minutes at the Fringe

Glen should have seen it coming. When he looked up and saw the young man standing across the street—the young man wearing black paratrooper boots, the loose-fitting field jacket, dark glasses, the Marine Corps cap—an alarm should have gone off in his head. But it didn't. Instead, he just laughed and said, "Military drag." Anyone else would have done the same, but then Glen wasn't like anyone else, and he should have responded differently. No one else here had served four years in the military. No one else had special training in guerrilla warfare and antiterrorist tactics. Glen should have realized what was about to happen, but he didn't.

He was too busy thinking of other things. He had left the service six months earlier and was contemplating something he considered more important—freedom. And what a freedom it was. No more rules or regimentation. No more kissing ass in the line of duty—just in the pursuit of happiness, and Glen had been following his heart's desire.

Nocturnal performances that drained both him and his partner David dry—that's what Glen was thinking about. Of cock and ass, together and apart. Of two bodies in rhythmic motion and then at rest. Was it any wonder that he didn't give the young man who stood across the street a second thought?

Glen turned and directed his attention to his immediate surroundings—the AIDS Network information booth at the Fringe Festival. Two other people were in the booth with him. David was in the back sorting boxes, while Maria, another volunteer, was rearranging pamphlets. She was talking to Rebecca, her daughter, who stood on the other side of the counter. Rebecca was playing devil's advocate. She wanted to know why anyone would affiliate themselves with an overtly gay organization, in Alberta, after the re-election of the Tories.

"You worry too much, dear."

"Mom!" Rebecca hated it when her mother talked to her as if she were still a child. "This isn't the Age of Aquarius anymore." She turned to Glen. "I suppose I have you to thank for this reblooming flower child?"

Glen laughed, "Me?"

Rebecca laughed too and continued. "How long do you think it will take the provincial government to pull the plug on an organization that provides condoms and promotes safer sex?"

Glen considered her question.

"The provincial government," she repeated. "Or someone else."

Suddenly, it all became clear to Glen. His head shot up just in time to see the young man pull something out from under his field jacket. It was metallic and reflected the sunlight. Glen recognized it immediately. It was an MP5 submachine gun.

The man strafed the booth, killing Rebecca. Her blood and pieces of her flesh splattered its canvas walls.

Switching the gun to semi-automatic, he pointed the barrel at Maria and fired once. Glen saw the bullet enter her forehead, blowing away the back of her skull as it exited. Only a 9 mm hollowpoint could do that.

Glen should have hit the ground—that's what he had been trained to do—but instead he leaped toward David and knocked him down.

A lot of good this is going to do, he thought. Only a piece of canvas, which hung from the bottom edge of the counter, separated them from the killer. It offered no protection, but at least they were out of sight, and perhaps out of mind.

Through the gap between the counter and the canvas, Glen saw the young man turn toward the crowd. He emptied what was left of his first magazine in less than a second. Quickly changing mags, he emptied a second, a third, and then a fourth. No one remained standing.

Glen surveyed the area. There was better cover over to the right, behind the brick buildings. But how would he get there? More importantly, how would he disarm this lunatic before anyone else fell victim?

Changing tactics, the young man dropped his submachine gun—a makeshift harness kept it from hitting the ground—and from underneath his field jacket, he whipped out an M65 hand grenade. Its smooth steel casing fit snugly in his right hand. Pulling the pin, he shouted, "Die, you AIDS faggots!" and hurled the grenade into the booth.

Glen could still hear Master Corporal Hadley's voice droning in his ears: "The M65 has an effective radius of eleven metres. It destroys any structure within that range and kills any man who does not take cover. . . . Upon explosion, the steel casing breaks up into shrapnel and travels at fifty metres per second. . . . Once the pin has been pulled and the spoon released, the M65 will explode in three seconds."

As the grenade sped through the air, Glen started counting backwards. When it hit the ground inside the booth he was at two. He tried to grab it in the hope of throwing it out of the booth, but its momentum carried it to the back and out of his reach. One.

Suddenly, David cried out. Had he been hit? Glen spun around. No, David was not injured, but fear had contorted his face, giving the impression that he was.

At that moment, Glen wanted to see David smile again, like he had that morning and every morning for the past six months. And he wanted those six months to become six years, and then sixty. He wanted them to grow old together. He wanted to be able to recall the memories of a lifetime. Most of all, he wanted to hold David in his arms. Looking at him as he did in that split second, Glen knew exactly what he had to do.

Without hesitation, Glen turned and threw himself on the grenade. He could feel it jabbing into his abdomen, at the base of his rib cage. He was yelling so loudly, he didn't hear it go off.

Harlon Davey

Unlikely Fuckbuddies

Today, I listened to my saved messages and savoured an old one again. His voice was kind of mocking, or was he nervous? Maybe he was just incredibly horny. He wanted to know if I had forgotten about him. He said he just came across a military uniform that he wanted to dress me up and rape me in. Then he asked me to call him, in that same voice, which I now recognize as loneliness.

We met about three months ago. He slid his hand along the crack of my ass while I ordered a beer. Then he grabbed me and kissed me and asked me where I had been hiding. He told me he had been watching me, that he thought I was handsome. He had beautiful eyes, big hands and a nice basket. All the things I like in a man. He was a great kisser. A pig. A performer.

He said that he wanted to tie me up and fuck me. I told him I had a boyfriend, and later, as I was leaving, he said he'd like to sleep with me and hold me all night. I smiled and said good night. Neither of us were too good at saying goodbye. His lover had died about a year and a half earlier. He wasn't over him, if that's the right expression. He had stopped working, stopped going to the gym. He had withdrawn. He was lonely. I was afraid that I wasn't loved anymore. I was afraid of getting sick. I was afraid of being alone.

He stayed at home getting stoned, drinking beer and looking at old photo albums. He'd call ex-tricks and leave them dirty messages but wouldn't pick up the phone when they called him back. He'd go to leather bars and charm strangers. I'd go to bars and find the darkest corner, where I would lean against the wall and stand alone. That's where we would find each other.

Later, he left messages saying he understood my situation. That he'd been there. I talked to friends and they'd tell me how they had fallen for him once too. They said he was all talk and no action. I figured that's what I probably wanted.

I went to his apartment one night. He showed me pictures of him and his boyfriend nude. He held them out for me to stare at like I wasn't supposed to say anything. Like I was supposed to memorize them. I just looked and didn't say anything, admiring his former glory. He waited, looked sad but didn't cry. I admired the photographs of his chiselled body and beautiful cock. Once he was truly beautiful. Now he had faded and folded inside his apartment.

He touched my nipples and reached under my leather vest to pinch them. I leaned to kiss him and then nibbled on his tits through his khaki t-shirt, slipping my fingers underneath the worn fabric to feel the stubble on his shaved chest. He slid his hands firmly down the back of my pants to cup my ass. I was nervous, awkward, almost intimidated by him. It was like trying to have anonymous sex with someone I knew. I kissed his lips, his neck and the back of his skull. He smelled good.

I wanted him to strip me and take me to his bed. I wanted him to put his weight on top of me and fuck me. I wanted to feel the skin of that handsome man I saw in the pictures he showed me earlier. I wanted his fingers inside my mouth and his cum inside my butt. Instead, he just stared off into space. Then he narrowed his eyes and looked at me, but didn't smile, like he was wondering why I was still hanging around.

He sat down and told me a few things: that he had a lot of baggage right now, that he's not a good person to be with, that he'd only bring me down. He's broke. He's sad. He's not over his lover's death yet.

I told him I'm in a stage of my life where I need to discover my courage again and get my shit together. I didn't tell him that I just needed some attention.

We agreed the only thing we could be right now was fuckbuddies.

He said he didn't want to damage my relationship.

I told him that's my problem not his.

"I'm not good for you," he said.

"I'm probably not good for myself," I replied.

He said we should get together every now and then, "and I'll give you an incredible fuck. Call me when you're really horny, we can be fuckbuddies," he added with tenderness.

He pulled his dick out of his pants again. I was so hungry for him. His cock. His pain. His cum. His baggage. So I knelt down and sucked his dick. But he just sat back looking vacant.

He continued to leave dirty messages on my answering machine, telling me that he wanted to suck my toes and eat my ass.

He never picked up the phone when I called back.

Lisa E. Davis

God's Law

for Melanie in Florida

Working for the county, they move you around a lot. They put me in her office, the first of the month.

"Lenore," she said right off, "we've got to do something about your typing."

I couldn't help but feel bad.

"It's okay," she said, and leaned across my desk. "I'm gonna bring you in a typing book, and you can practice."

She was pretty as could be. Like a teenager in her little skirt and blouse.

But Preacher helped me to see what she was after. They're trying to take over the world, he told me, voice shrill as a high wind.

"I'm a married woman," I said.

"Don't matter," he said. "They don't respect God's law."

My girlfriend brought it up at lunch. Bent down low over the table, she whispered to me. "So, Lenore, how you like working for a *les-bi-an?*"

The word went through me like a knife.

"Naw," I said. I figured she had a boyfriend, pretty as she was.

"That picture on her desk ain't no man," my girlfriend said. "You take a good look, and don't you go getting friendly with her."

She was right. Up close, that picture looked more like a handsome boy than a man. Big, soft eyes.

That's what I told Preacher. "The body is the temple of the Holy Spirit," he hollered out, eyes like lightning striking in a pine thicket.

Next day, seemed like she couldn't stay on her side of the desk. "Lenore," she said, leaning over me, "you have *got* to learn to use the dictionary."

That skirt she was wearing about reached up to her crotch. I didn't want to turn around.

"Are you all right, Lenore?" she asked me, like butter wouldn't melt in her mouth.

"Spawn of the Devil!" Preacher said.

The one in the picture on her desk came to pick her up, grinning like a Cheshire cat. Looked just like a man, and had that same low voice I heard a hundred times on the phone. "How are you today, Lenore?" Made my skin crawl.

Preacher said they mock God's law, pretending to be like married couples, and that they oughta make her take that picture off her desk. Decent people shouldn't have to see it.

The two of 'em live together, out on the highway. I drove out by there to see, late at night. Just one light on. It must be the bedroom.

The Preacher said they'd pay dearly for their sins.

I woke up covered in sweat, hollering in my sleep. Joe came running. I couldn't tell him I was dreaming her and me was sitting out on the front porch. She put an arm around me, and tried to kiss me on the mouth. Joe tucked me back in. "Ain't nobody gonna hurt you," he says, and goes back to the couch. Joe's always understanding.

I heard the two of 'em talking on the phone. They're going on vacation to New York City. "Sodom and Gomorrah," Preacher said. There they can parade their filth and abominations, where they'd never dare do that around here. He said they touch the bodies of women and little children in orgies.

Lord, show me the way!

When she came back, she looked at me the way she does, eyelids all aflutter. "Did you manage all right without me?" she asked. I felt like I had no clothes on.

Then she put her hand on me. Preacher said to get her for that.

She said to me, "Lenore, you've been coughing all day. You feel like you've got a temperature."

Where her hand touched, I felt like she'd put a spell on me. I couldn't stop coughing, and I couldn't sleep. I was feeling sharp pains all up my legs, and in my private parts. Preacher said they have laser beams now, can shoot from a long way off. Joe took me to the emergency room in the middle of the night. I told 'em I thought a laser beam was burning into me. They didn't know nothing about that, but they gave me something to help me sleep.

She sat down next to me at lunch, right where everybody could see. "Here's that typing book I promised you," she said, and patted my hand. My face was like a coal on fire.

Preacher said it was time to press charges.

"I'll ask for a transfer," I said.

"What if she won't let you go?" he said, his voice low like he was talking through a hollow log. Like to scare me to death.

They wouldn't have me in the supervisor's office when they called her in. But I saw her when she came out, eyes all red and streaked, hair falling down over her face. She saw me and looked away. I guess I didn't expect her to speak.

They asked me to be in person at the next hearing. Could Joe come with me? I asked. She'll be bringing a lawyer with her, they said.

It dragged on. Preacher told me to take sick time. When I came back, she looked like she'd lost ten pounds. She was doing all her own calling and typing.

I got me my transfer. She's not working for the county anymore. When they asked her, she admitted to what she was. No shame, and she didn't want to change. Her lawyer was some smart Jew. He said to me, "Mrs. Pitts, when you talk about 'sexual harassment,' do you know what you're accusing Ms. Marks of?"

"Against God's law," I said.

I kept the typing book she gave me, and I do try to practice some.

Nolan Dennett

Tallman

Sometimes I approach men living on the streets. Sometimes we just talk. Sometimes we'll end up fooling around. It's a way of getting next to a straight guy. Larry was one. I saw him off and on for three years.

One time I asked him why he did it and he said, "You're the only one who wants anything from me."

When he couldn't find a place to stay, he'd sleep under a bridge.

We met when my landlord hired him to do some odds and ends on the mobile home I was renting. Larry would show up on Saturdays and putter around. I had a washer and dryer on my back porch. Through the window I'd see him leaning, smoking a rolled cigarette.

One day he walked up to the screen door and asked me if he could wash his clothes.

"I don't see why not," I said. "Just throw them there and I'll put them in with the next load."

He stripped—didn't even turn his back—and then stood there grinning.

"Do you want to take a shower?"

"Sure, man. Thanks."

His smell followed him into the house.

Eventually we worked out a routine. When he'd finished for the day, he'd strip down on the porch, throw his clothes in the washer, and then he'd come inside and take a shower. We'd sit at the kitchen table, get high, and wait for his clothes to dry. He would wear just a towel. I could see his dick hanging out from between his skinny legs.

He would always make me ask. Indifference gave him control. I think he liked showing off his cock, though. I'm not sure how much he enjoyed the rest of it.

"I like it when you put your hand on my shoulder when I'm doing you."

He wore a red and white baseball cap to cover electrocuted hair. He had missing teeth and looked like he could be a relative of Ichabod Crane or Lurch. He was skinny, cadaverous really. But he had an incredibly deep voice that seemed to echo up from his big balls.

He would bring me things—an Indian head penny, a blown-glass swizzle stick with a parrot perched on the end, a pencil with no eraser that was covered with strawberries, an unopened bar of soap. He would pull them out of his pocket when he would first come in the door, like a little boy showing off a treasure.

"I wish you would ask *me* sometimes."

But he never did. Unless I asked him to ask me first.

He told me that when he was a kid an older neighbour boy shoved dog shit up his ass.

"Ya, with a stick. If I saw him now I'd kill him."

"How old were you?

"Five."

"Did you tell anyone?"

"My dad, but he just laughed and told me I was imagining it."

"How old was the other kid?"

"Eighteen. My dad did talk to him, eventually."

"Well at least he did that."

He said that it changed his whole life.

I would tell him how proud I was of him whenever he got a big hard-on. He told me that's why his name was Tallman—tall man, tall dick. . . . He invited me to go to the welfare mission and have dinner. Once, he even told me a poem. He said he made it up. Maybe he did.

Spring Birth
by
Larry Tallman

I like the wind to sweep a snowless path.
I like the rain to soothe the winter's wrath.

I like the spring to have an early birth.
Now all the flowers are in blossom.
And the trees are swaying, bending, and tossing.
And now I see spring has had an early birth.

It was really cold a couple of nights ago and he came knocking on my door. Late. He had never stayed over before.

"This bed reminds me of the ground."

"Why, because it is so hard?"

"Ya. Where my camp is? My bedroll is over a root. It killed my back at first. But you know, I got used to that root."

With the instincts of a beast he curls around the living thing most close at hand, not unlike a leaf turning to find the sun.

I said to him, "I wish you would ask *me* sometimes. If you always act like you don't really want it and make me ask I don't enjoy it after a while."

A little later he pulled down his shorts and asked me if I wanted to suck his dick.

In the middle of the night I woke to find his hand resting lightly across my back.

Nisa Donnelly

Glass Splinters

Night falls too slowly in summer and I wait, without shame. I am always waiting. Now. When I was a child, I would wait to wake up, wait for the darkness to break. The night was that long, that terrifying. Now I embrace it like a lover, calling it to me, cool and dark and forgiving. I wait for the dark to block out the memories and the lines.

I draw lines in my life and do not cross them. I simply rearrange the lines. Integrity is a personal habit, but one not to be taken too seriously. I am a creature of compromise. Capitulation, according to my last lover. She imagined the lines in her life were more firm than those in mine; imagined she was kinder and more gentle and more certain than either of us ever could be, at least with each other. We drew lines—all lovers do—and when we crossed them, we had gone too far. It was over.

Lately, I have been drawing lines with drinking. Now, bourbon and vodka and tequila, and even Southern Comfort, are on the other side of the line. They all made me sick or humiliated. Wine is on this side of the line. It makes me warm, makes me smile, colours the bad memories the way pastels wash a landscape. After a few glasses of wine, I can be the woman I'd like to be, the woman I believe I should be.

I go for days, sometimes weeks, without drinking. And then, almost without thinking, I reach for a bottle. No, that's not true. I do think about it when I reach for one of the bottles of whites—all from small wineries up the coast—which line the bottom of the refrigerator. (The idea slips in, almost unnoticed, like a glass splinter in soft flesh. And nothing can be done, except wait for it to work itself back out again. Painful. Bloody.)

Drinking is easy. Easier than drugs. Easier to get. Easier to keep. Easier to digest. There were lines with drugs, too. Now almost all of those are on the far side of the line, beyond even the vodka and the tequila and the bourbon. I don't think about drugs. No glass splinter there. (The year I turned twenty, my brother, Duff—the one everybody loved—was first home from Vietnam. We lost six months to the opium he smuggled back in the heel of his boot. Then we lost Duff. Too many glass splinters for him.)

Now, I drink wine alone, most often in the kitchen, sitting on the window seat, under the cup rack where a dozen faces that are supposed to look like dead movie stars, but mostly don't, stare out through dust and neglect. The eyes are too blue, the smiles too shockingly bright and pink. The hair is right, though: dark and wild with curls, or blonde and sleek. A lover I don't like to remember left them behind, a long time ago. She always wanted to fuck a movie star, one of the great and tragic beauties. All I did was tell jokes. I kept her laughing. For a while. She probably got tired of the same show night after night. No new material is the curse of failed entertainers and lovers. I've used up too many lovers and jokes. Careless, I suppose.

The people I have loved best were careless with me, and I am careless with life, the way warriors are careless with death. I don't use the term "death" lightly. It's something I think about, sort through, examine like some poor trapped spider under a microscope. Neither enemy nor friend, it simply is. That's what I see when I look across the expanse of day, waiting for night, waiting to slip into a void of tightly woven lies and selfish evil. What evil is not selfish?

Some nights I dress the woman I've become and go into the night, a snake dressing for summer. I take myself into rooms of strangers. And I take them into a world that is as false and as real as they want it to be. Women whose names don't matter tell me I am beautiful. Talented. Lucky. They do not know me at all.

I light candles. There is a certain comfort in the way the flame shoots blue and gold, hot and clear against the darkness when the match catches. Life is easier at night. The sun is an alien and angry god. I once loved a woman who came from a land where the sun shone all the time—or so she said—a land where pilgrim believers bled themselves on Good Friday morning, droplets splattered in the dust like rubies. They were seeking absolution. There is no absolution. The pope is an old man in a white dress encrusted with fine lace made by virgin nuns, who live in a convent high on a hill, whose prayers wash a sanctuary draped in purple velvet and red. (Does a sad-eyed Jesus in a blue robe kneel in a garden, red tears of stained glass splinters streaming down his luminous face?)

I drape my bed in purple satin and red. Tie my lovers to me with tears and blue velvet ropes. I grow my nails long, paint them the colour of red tears, plunge them into the women I've loved and love, and the women whose names don't matter, rocking them close—closer, to the only heaven any of us will ever know. Baptize them with my tongue, while they wash me in tears. No lines, there.

"Too good," I tell them, "too good." They don't understand, but give what they think I need, what they want me to have. In that moment between pain and passion, sleep and wakefulness, they dream of dancing and of lightness and sometimes of death. And when sun washes across the bed on Sunday morning, we don't think of the devil or of God, only of glass splinters working free.

Annette DuBois

Red Ribbons

for S. W.

I am walking home from a funeral. Another one. I'm on Sanchez Street and it's cold and rainy and the wind is blowing, that San Francisco wind that never stops on days like today. I'm walking and I'm thinking about the pictures and the flowers and the people breaking down and crying as they tried to talk about my friend—my friend who didn't live long enough to really become a friend. I'm thinking about how each one of those photographs and letters and clippings on the altar is all that's left now of a story he could have told me over a cup of coffee someday, only now he never will. I'm remembering how I moved a box while I was setting up the altar. A brown cardboard box, not even very big or important-looking, only that box had an urn in it and all that was left of a man I was talking to only a few weeks ago. I never thought I'd be able to pick him up. He was so much larger than me.

And I'm remembering that room full of shocked faces. How was this memorial different? He knew so many people, so many very different people. Old people and teenagers, black people and white people, gay and straight. There was a couple with a new baby they'd named after him. So many people, and so many who'd never lost anyone to AIDS before, which was incredible to me. I heard someone say, "He was so young," perhaps seeing her own mortality for the first time, like when my uncle died and Mom called me to say that she wasn't used to people so near her age dying, and I realized that I was. Mom's sixty. I'm thirty. Young? In another world he would have been young, but the face smiling from the altar is framed with greying hair. I find myself thinking he was lucky.

The best picture of him was the one on the programme, with the Marin Headlands in the background. I see that face smiling, that warmth, and the red ribbon pinned to the programme. So many people took those ribbons and wore them, but I couldn't.

Red ribbons make me too angry. "AIDS awareness"? What in hell is that supposed to mean? Are there still people anywhere in the world who aren't "aware," and how could a piece of cloth make them aware if all the headlines and face after face on the wrong page of the newspaper haven't?

"AIDS awareness." It's not that I go to any special effort to be aware. It's just that people I know keep kicking off before they've had a chance to live. It's just that every time I turn around someone else has tested positive. It's just that I watch the people I see in the café every morning getting thinner and thinner. Life just keeps reminding me. Do I wear a ribbon to show I'm aware of the air I breathe? And now everyone wants in: pink for breast cancer, blue for child abuse, green for political prisoners in whatever country it is this week. Maybe in another life I'd wear them too, if I thought there was a chance that someone who really didn't know about AIDS or incest or Bosnian Muslims might see and ask and learn something. I've been known to use those stamps on letters to the Midwest, but here? In San Francisco, in the nineties? It's become so trendy I'm not even sure that the people who wear red ribbons know what they mean. If they do, they probably think wearing a ribbon is enough.

The ribbons they gave out today had nothing to do with this man's life. After the ceremony, they won't even stand out as a sign of mourning. "Someone I love died of AIDS, and all I got was this lousy red ribbon." Maybe if we'd all wear one ribbon for each person we know with HIV—only some of us wouldn't be able to see our clothes. They can't show the whole quilt at once anymore. I remember stumbling across the Vietnam wall in D.C. late at night, amazed by how small the names were, all of them.

I miss the man whose life we honoured today, but the sadness comes from a great distance. My sadness is tired. Face after face in the obituaries and always, always someone I love knows someone who's sick. Maybe that's why no one in this city takes the time to get close, when they don't know if you'll be here tomorrow. My sadness is tired, and my anger at strips of bright fabric tries to burn through a numbness as heavy and grey as April rain clouds.

Gary Dunne

A Bush Xmas

For the past few years, our town's pre-Xmas decorations have hit the front page of the local paper and the local television news. Over on the cemetery side of the park each household makes a display in their front yard. Whole streets are brilliantly lit—houses, trees, shrubbery and fences all stitched up with lines of party lights. Front lawns are transformed, each family trying to outdo their neighbours in conspicuous festivity.

It's generally home-made rather than hi-tech: there are hand-painted plywood cut-outs of Santa and his reindeer on roofs. Old truck tires are cut and painted into swans. There are pop-up witches, mechanical elves and waterfalls constructed out of old bathtubs and garden hoses.

Late in December, just after sunset, a crowd of locals and tourists turns up every night to wander the streets, take in the scenery and chat. A couple of years back, when I started senior school, we considered giving it a miss, then decided that as it was the only real Xmas tradition we had, we should keep it up. So every year Mum and I stroll over at least once for a look.

This year it's bigger than ever. There are tourist buses parked along Mullens Street and the crowd has spilled out from the footpaths to the street. Flashing lights, tinsel bells, cut-out Santas going down the chimney and Willie Nelson's latest CD blaring out—it's like we're walking down into a technicolour movie set.

The little kids are in their pyjamas. Home-owners sit proudly on their porches, Vic Bitter or Diet Coke in hand, and exchange pleasantries with the passers-by. Uncle Arnold, our local Mr. Whippy, is doing a roaring trade. So is Mr. Johnson with his open boot and esky full of ice cold beer. The air is thick with excitement, mosquitoes, ghetto-blasters playing carols and the pungent smell of insect repellent.

The gang of guys from my year are huddled in the bus shelter at the top of Henry Street, trying to smoke inconspicuously.

"If your father catches you, David O'Malley, you'll cop it," calls Mum.

"He's up the club, and you're not going to dob us in, are you, Mrs. B?"

"I should. It's bad for your health."

O'Malley stares at me and I stare back. He's big and hunky, destined to be a thickset oaf like his old man. I never understood why Brett fancied him so much. But Brett was convinced that under the muscles and attitude, the class football rep was one of us, and was interested.

I outstare O'Malley. He looks down, spits and examines his cigarette. Early this year he worked Brett out and started giving him a hard time. Just kept on hassling him. Lots of little things, nothing he'd get in real trouble for; stealing his books, mimicking his voice, calling him Brenda. Brett was getting it at home too. His dad was on at him relentlessly. Anyway, one night Brett got the old man's rifle, stuck it in his mouth and pulled the trigger. The school had counsellors in. I said nothing. No one was going to get me. O'Malley's still guilty enough to not start, but it's only a matter of time 'til he calls my bluff.

Mum and I keep walking.

"He's a mongrel, like his father," says Mum. "You watch yourself next year at school."

"Don't worry, Mum. I'm a survivor."

We stop in front of my favourite house. The Hanlons always have a wonderful spot-lit tableau featuring the manger, the crib, Jesus and his mum plus an assortment of guests: two shepherds, three ninja turtles, a wise-person, Blinky Bill and two bananas in pyjamas. The visitors have all brought gifts: frankincense, pizza, myrrh and a box of Cadbury Roses chocolates. Every year the number of visitors increases. Mum and I agree that this year's addition, a cut-out talking pig, is perfect.

Not everybody in Kanangra is filled with such festive fervour, however. The fundamentalist Christian homes are conspicuous by their darkness. As Mum used to say, "Their Christmas is as drab as the rest of their year." Two doors down is Brett's place, sandwiched between two gaudy, over-lit extravaganzas. Planted in the middle of their empty lawn and concrete is their small sign which says the same thing it says every year: JESUS IS THE REASON FOR THE SEASON.

Mum puts her arm around my shoulder and we keep walking.

At home I've got a Gay & Lesbian Mardi Gras video. Actually it's Brett's. We used to watch it when Mum was on a late shift. He had this crazy scheme. We'd hide costumes in our backpacks, catch the train to Sydney, change clothes at Central, go in the parade, sleep in a park and catch the early morning train back.

Late last summer, when the Mardi Gras was shown nationwide on the ABC, Mum and I watched it together. I said very casually that I wouldn't mind going to see the parade live next year. Mum said, equally casually, that I didn't have enough muscles to be a marching boy and anyway, I wasn't old enough yet.

In the distance we can hear the sound of a siren approaching. It gets louder, then suddenly the local fire truck comes around the corner, all decked out with red and green Xmas bunting, lights flashing, bells ringing and Santa perched precariously on the ladder at the back. As it passes us, Santa opens his sack and starts hurling out handfuls of sweets, like confetti. In his wake, there's a swarm of eager kids, all scrambling for lollies in the dust.

Next year I turn fifteen, and my plans are more practical; leave home, move to Sydney, get a part-time job and go to tech. I haven't told Mum yet, but I think she knows anyway.

John Egan

Ethiope's Ear

It seems (he) hangs upon the cheek of night
Like a rich jewel in an Ethiope's ear;
Beauty too rich for use, for earth too dear.
—*Romeo and Juliet,* Act I, Scene 4

I get really bored in the house, but I hate playing outside. Patrick and Joseph are always outside. When they come in, they smell like the outside, and it makes me gag. They like to dig in the woods and plug up the swamp and play football. I read and watch a lot of TV, in the TV room. I like to sit real close. Sometimes I push my nose against the screen to see the mark. I got in a lot of trouble yesterday, so I'm not even supposed to be in here. But Mom said it was okay, if I stayed out of the drawers.

If it's nice out, I get the TV as soon as I get home, 'cause my brothers go out and play, and my sisters play in their room. I like to play with Maureen and Mary more than the boys, but they make me leave if any of their friends come over. They say I embarrass them. My brothers and the other guys on the block won't even let me come near them. They throw things at me, or chase me away. I'm no good at sports, 'cause I'm afraid of the ball. And they call me crybaby.

Sometimes my Mom hugs me when I cry, and sometimes she don't. Daddy calls me a crybaby too. He will give me something to cry about if I don't stop. So I try to stop, and that's really hard to do when you're crying. Once when my brother Joseph didn't stop crying, Dad hit him in the face so hard his nose got crooked and bled a lot. So I always stop, 'cause I don't want to get hit. But it's hard.

Another good thing about lying on the floor right next to the TV is you can switch it easy. I already broke the handle once, so it has a popsicle stick in it so you can turn the channel. If the stuff on is boring, I turn the thing on the knob that makes the picture go kinda fuzzy, and stare at that with the sound off. If I close my eyes real fast and hard, the picture goes inside my head, and spins around and around. I sometimes forget to breathe when I'm watching it like that, and I kinda get buzzy. And if you look close at the speaker, you'll see a bunch of holes I made with my pencil. I like the feel it makes when you push through the speaker, it kinda pops. And if you stick things in it when it's on, the people sound like they are talking through wax paper. My brother Joseph says I'm an idiot and I broke it. But it still works, so it isn't broken. He's the idiot.

A lot of time I just have the TV on, but don't watch it. A lot of the time the noise covers up me fooling around with stuff in the TV room. We aren't allowed to close the door, so I have to be quiet and careful, especially if I go into Daddy's closet. There isn't a lot in there anyway, except his bank. I take quarters out of there sometimes so I can get ice cream. So far he hasn't noticed. Most of the time I play with the stuff in the drawers. The big drawer has magazines and a whole mess of stuff that don't fit in the small drawer. The small drawer has cards and pens and pencils and pins and tees and all the little stuff. Junk. It's a lot more fun than the other one.

I've been in it lots, so I never expect to find anything new, but I always do. Yesterday, I found this funny earring. Once my sister put some on me and they hurt my ears and I started crying, so she took them off and made me swear not to tell Mom and Dad. Those ones were like ladybugs, but this one was shiny, like a car's bumper. It didn't hurt like the other ones, and it looked neat when I turned off the TV and looked at myself. I forgot I had it on.

Daddy saw it as soon as he came in. When I saw his face, I pulled it off my ear and threw it behind me. He grabbed my arms and started squeezing and saying what the fuck is that in your ear, an earring. And I told him no, because he would've killed me if I had told the truth. And he kept saying is that an earring, is it, you little sissy? And he shaked and picked me up and I thought I was dead. And I was crying, and Mom and my sisters was crying, and I kept waiting for him to hit me and it would stop, but he wouldn't stop. He kept shaking me and laughing and I was bawling and Mom was yelling stop it Gerry, stop it. And the girls hid behind Mom and the boys just stared at the TV and then he put me down. *Fucking fairy.*

My foot kicked the earring when he put me down, so I stood on it barefoot, and it hurt. But he was gonna kill me if he saw it. Then he pushed me down and left and I pooped myself and sat and cried and everyone else left. Mom was crying and then she left. I picked up the earring and threw it out the window, in case he came looking for it later.

Mom took me in her bedroom after Dad had gone to work, and asked me why I lied to Dad, because I was never supposed to lie to them. And I told her that he would've killed me if I didn't. And she didn't say nothing.

Siobhan Fallon

Work of Art

She hit me again.

Yes, Natalie hit me again and then she started crying, asking why didn't I just hit her back? She says that I'm stronger and quicker and my fists would teach her a lesson. She says that I get so silent and cold that she feels like she's with her sister. She says that the only way to get my attention is to scream and swing and contact her hard knuckle against my cheekbone. . . .

Natalie says that sisters always fight like that.

I was silent at first, silent as I had been each and every unforgotten time before, packing the duffel bag she had given me when we first moved in together. Silent while she wept and begged, screamed and yelled, wept and begged again. But I broke as I always break, went to her, held her shuddering body with its scent of smoke and spiced rum, let her hot tears burn my neck, and I whispered that it didn't hurt very much, that it was only a bruise, that I loved her, that I'd never leave her alone. I didn't say that I dream of slipping away in the night while she sleeps heavily beside me. I didn't say that I try so hard not to flinch when she reaches for me in the dark.

So I've run to my dim studio to escape our apartment. I had to sneak away from the happy pictures of us on the wall, from the kitchen of dirty dishes and streaked cabinets.

And I'm scribbling away in this pencil-smudged notebook as if writing all this down will make it go away, make it someone else's fiction, make Natalie just another melodramatic character in some cheap, best-selling book. I try to tell myself this is my life, this is my throbbing cheek, this is the woman I love who pushes me into the wall. It's me who walks down the street with my eyes on the sidewalk while people stare and think I'm just another battered wife, wondering why I don't stand up to the bastard, stick his ass in jail, get a divorce and a new life.

I don't want them to know that a woman did this to me, that I forgive her each and every time.

Tonight's fight was about my work, the work I shape with my hands. Funny, I just couldn't figure out what to sculpt until now, until the moment my right eye went red with broken blood vessels. Natalie's boss wants to see a sketch next week. That slimy gallery owner in his imitation Armani suits. Somehow Natalie convinced him to commission me to sculpt the "epitome of woman's repressed frustration." Natalie wined and dined him, hoping to get a raise out of pimping my art, pimping my anger, beating it out of me. Now Natalie's so scared that I won't get it done, asking every day if I've started, finally screaming, "I work my ass off trying to make you a success, how can you do this to me? I need you to impress him, you lazy bitch." And the lights went out, then went red, in my right eye.

Now I know what it's all about. I can see the clay, feel its red mass wet and thick between my fingers, even as I write this. The womb. The enormity of its cavern, its power to give life. Torn. Red like fire, like anger, like rape. The womb, woman's source of creation, melted in the blast of fear, of stunted hatred, deflated and empty. All resting upon a phallic white marble stand, the cool paleness of marble a contrast to the livid red of the organs skewed above. And, the final touch, the umbilical cord trailing out of the uterus, down the exposed birth canal, dangling from the white marble stand. But there is no life on the other end. The life is lost. Lost.

I'll get it done, Natalie, in this drafty little studio with its crooked sink and dirty mattress on the floor. This is the one place you won't disturb me with your shouts, salt tears and blind fists. I'll have peace with my pack of cigarettes and warm pitcher of whiskey sours, the clay so cold and lonely in my hands. And while I work with the dead, red clay with my living hands, I'll think about the spiced scent of you, the strength of your arms pulling me down, your mouth swallowing my words and eating the beat of my heart.

Laurie Fitzpatrick

Mine Field

There's an addictive little game on my computer at work, called Mine Field, that consists of a grid of buttons that have a certain number of mines hidden beneath. When my boss goes to lunch, I play the game obsessively. Using the mouse, I click open free spaces and mark hidden mines with red flags. If I hit an unmarked mine, the screen flashes red, accompanied by a synthetic blast, and I lose. Should I open all the free spaces and flag all the mines, I win. Love is a lot like this game. Only much harder.

Through many years of dating, I'm a seasoned veteran when it comes to discovering and avoiding the explosive psychic mines hidden in women I've chosen to become involved with. Case in point, to say "I have chosen" is to take responsibility for my actions, and to place a big red flag over a mine of my own. Believe me, I have plenty. So when I'm on a first date with Ms. New, I imagine each of us surrounded by a field of hidden mines, seeding the space between us. Skillfully, we navigate through the evening's conversation. If there are few explosions, there will be a second date. After more dates and further manoeuvering, I might begin to feel that things will work out.

Tonight, I'm going on a date, the first in what feels like a lifetime. My last relationship blew up so badly that I stumbled through eleven bleak months—numb—seemingly without sight, hearing, or feeling.

Leah and I meet for coffee at a little café a couple of blocks from my house. She looks wonderful, wearing a colourful silk scarf draped over her shoulders, and silver rings on her fingers. Her short hair balances her feminine outfit, letting her dark eyes dominate her face. I look good too, more androgynous than feminine, not quite as exotic. Our conversation flows. She smiles a lot, flirting with me across the table, more so than before I asked her out. I met Leah three months ago when I began volunteering at the women's reproductive health clinic where she works full time. She has this way of looking at me, zeroing in, with a smile full of pleasant secrets. I've wanted to kiss her since the first moment she pinned me with her eyes.

She had accepted my invitation to go out almost too eagerly. I sit back and assess our situation. To an outsider, we might look mismatched: the hippie with the yuppie. I wonder, if she could see the real me—missing most of my heart and my psyche webbed with scars—would she still find me attractive?

Then we start hitting mines.

She says, "I don't get out to eat very often. Have you ever been to Rose of Sharon?"

"Oh yeah, many times." I exaggerate the truth.

"Don't they have a vegetarian menu?"

Boom.

"Oh. I never noticed." She's a vegetarian. Obviously, I'm not.

She digs in her purse and pulls out a pack of cigarettes. "Mind if I smoke?"

I fake a casual shrug, then pluck an ashtray from the empty table beside us. Setting it before her, I say, "Go right ahead."

Boom.

She lights up and grey smoke drifts all over me, clogging my sinuses as the stale odour seeps into my clothes and hair.

As the coffee kicks in, we tumble into our second half hour of conversation. She says, "In past relationships, I acted as if I had one foot out the door. That way, I could leave them before they left me. But I'm in therapy now. I'm not as bad as I used to be."

I make a mental note of three existing mines: "foot out door," "in therapy" and "not as bad." I wonder if she's being honest, or is the caffeine propelling her out of control? Planting a big red flag in a mine sitting between us, I say, "When I start seeing someone new, I ask myself, what's this person going to do to me?"

She considers this for about a second, then skips on to another topic, something about an interesting schizophrenic she recently met.

Boom.

Such eerie allusions scare me.

I figure the game is lost, then she starts talking about her job and her computer at work. She says, "You know that little mine game they include with the word processing program? I can't stop playing it. Sometimes, I'll close my office door and play for an hour."

Interested, I ask, "What are your best times?"

"Nineteen seconds Beginner, 130 seconds Intermediate. But I'm not sure for Expert. It's enough to just get through that level."

She had me beat at the beginner level, but not at the intermediate. I sit back and re-evaluate her, then say, "Sometimes I think that game is like love."

"I've thought it too," she chuckles, "and whenever I win a game, I think it means that I'll win at love someday."

Around midnight, we're exhausted from talking and drinking caffeine. We walk to her car, then she drives me to my small row house in a not-so-nice neighbourhood. Before getting out, I manage to say, "I had a nice time."

"So did I," she admits shyly.

"Maybe we could go out for dinner soon? We could see if Rose of Sharon has a vegetarian menu."

"Yeah, that sounds good." She smiles, her eyes glittering. Her lips part, inviting me.

I lean over and brush my lips across hers, then pull back a little, staying there. She quickly bridges the gap with a hungry kiss.

For a moment, the field of mines—those blown, those flagged, the many waiting to be discovered—becomes transparent and we slip beneath the grid, connecting in the vast grey space, safe and warm for now.

The crowd quiets as the women take focus and seem to gather their thoughts into one. The silence is broken only by the turning of a single leaf of music and with a synchronized breath, the four women begin. A woman near me places a hand on the collection of beads at her breast. A silver-haired, saggy-faced man turns to a woman at his side for her reaction and all around people are checking for the response of the audience at large. My awareness of them gradually fades as I become transfixed.

No, the sound is not the sophisticated, well-oiled sound one would expect on a twenty-dollar ticket for such an event. In fact, it is chaos, and the notes seem sour, punctuated with the high-pitched squeal of a bow losing hold of the string. This has to be an elaborate hoax—these four women sitting here, rocking and rowing their instruments like large children for their parents' approval, with no care or concept of the quality of their performance. Two violins: the first in her chair like a great scoop of cinnamon ice cream with a short afro and spectacles; the second a big-boned gal, perched and high yellow, cornbread coloured with a mess of silver curls, shaking loosely on the top, like a pile of dirty grey pantyhose. The bass player is a dark-skinned woman, with a shape that brings to mind the Venus of Willendorf, with its great round torso and limbs that, here, are wrapped around the body of her instrument. The cellist is the most formal of the group—stiff-backed and utterly in control—daring the music to take her. Her honey face is expressionless, heavy and mysterious as the Sphinx, tight and impenetrable as the abundance of nappy braids collected at the back of her head. Four black women, each as unique as the instrument she holds, creating a noise that is all of music and none of it. Their sound is that greasy-faced Ornette Coleman free jazz sound—not music but conversation. Theirs is the sound that was heard in my mother's or aunt's or late grandmother's kitchen when I was a child and would sit amongst those heavy ankles and listen to them argue and cuss and pray. A music stand becomes, here, a bag of green beans for snapping and, there, the pot for boiling out chitlins or colla'd greens. I am a spy again in that kitchen, where I could overhear the brash explosions of laughter, the mythic cackle with heads thrown way back and mouths with big swollen tongues shaking inside like big pink slices of fat. I can smell the salt pork thrown in to flavour the black-eyed or crowder peas. I anticipate the swing of the wooden spoon and the dull thud of it on my hind parts and scampering to safety under the table and the joy of having been for a moment the centre of attention.

If you had asked that child that was me what he wanted to be when he grew up, he would have said a writer or performer, but that was only because he did not—could not have found the language to express his true desire—at least, not in a way that any sensible adult could understand. In these days of political correctness, that largely accepted verbal tyranny, and after television with its broad-faced and pop-eyed representations of loud, smiling, frowning, sassy, affable, dutiful, matriarchal, self-sacrificing negresses, the idea was not only too scandalous, but somewhat self-effacing. I picture little white children crying "Mammy!" running to me in tears for comfort at my bosom. I feel the movement of my character in the sway of those heavy torsos. My sexuality is the steam from the smoking pot and the crushing weight of thick ankles. My nipples grow erect and I'm laughing out loud and my lover has taken hold of my jeans. I feel myself pulled back into the seat next to him from the waking dream. I'm in love with myself and the space around me. I feel like I'm on Ecstasy.

The man with the sagging face turns to see me smiling and giggling like a wicked child, and I am shrouded in the music of these goddesses—the four black women rocking and plucking and weaving—casting their tiny spell on me alone. The cellist looks in my direction and I'm sure I catch her winking at me. I feel my lover's gaze and I blush with the thrill of my secret. I feel a twinge of guilt in the deceiving of one so dear to my heart. He will sense the difference, but will think it only a trick of wine. He will not know tonight, when I am writhing above him in the throes of my orgasm, that he is part of an orgy. His hands will fall on my flesh, but tonight he will make love to four black women.

Rhomylly B. Forbes

Forsaking All Others

M*arried?*" I screeched, causing the other patrons of the White Raven Bookstore and Coffeehouse to give me startled looks that turned soft as I continued to announce our business. "Oh, Celia, that's *wonderful!* Barbara must be *so* happy!" I had actually scooted out of the booth to give my best friend a congratulatory hug when the look on her face stopped me.

"I'm not marrying Barbara," she whispered softly. "I'm marrying David. In April." I slowly slumped back down on my side of the table.

"What? *Why?*"

Celia could not look at me. She fidgeted with her spoon as she groped for words. "I . . . it's my parents, Joanna. Well, David's parents too, I guess. They've been pressuring each of us to get married, so we thought, you know, if we *did,* then they'd leave us alone."

"But Celia, this is the nineties! 'Gay marriage' means same-sex unions! Hell, being gay is *in!*"

"Not at my house," she said softly.

"So tell them," I challenged, confident and secure in my "out" status.

"I can't." Celia swallowed hard. "I . . . really can't."

"How do you know unless you tell them? C'mon, I bet your mom and dad would get over it. Most do, you know. They love you. It wouldn't be that bad."

"Yes, it would." Celia's voice was a tortured whisper. "Joanna, listen to me, please. I have . . . I have a sister four years older than me. She was my best friend in the world and told me she was a lesbian the summer I turned twelve. A couple of years later, she came out to my parents during a fight about her curfew or something. My father was so angry. I'd never seen him like that. He . . . he hit her. I think he broke her jaw. She left that night and I never saw her again. My parents never mention her name and my mom took her pictures out of the family albums. Do you know what it feels like to see carefully cut holes in your childhood memories?"

I was in shock, as much by the story as the fact that Celia, the toughest butch in town, was sitting across from me in tears. I was crying too, but that's not unusual. I took her hand in mine and held on as tight as I could.

"God, Cel, I'm sorry." I felt so guilty for my earlier superior attitude. "What can I do?"

"Would you . . . would you be one of my bridesmaids?" she sniffled, a little ironic smile playing about the edges of her face. "Barbara is going to be my maid of honour and David's lover, Steve, is going to be the best man. This . . . hasn't been easy for Barbara. Steve either, for that matter. I thought maybe you could, you know, be there for her, keep an eye on her for me that day. Please? I need you." I took her hand again and nodded my consent to what she'd asked. Celia was too good a friend for me to let her down.

By the time the actual wedding rolled around, I was heartily sick of the entire thing and sorry as hell that I'd agreed to be part of it. Celia's mother was a royal pain, flaring her nostrils in disgust every time she caught a glimpse of my short hair or the labyris necklace I refused to remove for the ceremony. Celia's father was even worse. I had met him before, a small mild-mannered scholar—the last person in the world you'd suspect of punching his child in the face. Now, at his youngest daughter's wedding, he was loud, jovial and over-friendly to all of Celia and David's friends; all, that is, but Barbara. In his eyes, she simply did not exist. I felt sorry for Celia, and wondered briefly how she'd managed to grow up and be such a terrific person, with these flaming homophobes for parents.

But the person I felt sorriest for was Barbara. In spite of the unimaginable pain she must have been feeling, she handled herself beautifully, arranging and hosting an exquisite wedding shower, making sure we bridesmaids made all our dress-fitting appointments, even managing to look completely radiant as she walked down the aisle, looking for all the world as if she were absolutely thrilled by her "best friend's" nuptials.

I gritted my teeth when the minister asked, "If anyone knows of a reason why these two should not be joined in matrimony," and the vows were even worse. But Barbara didn't flinch, didn't even blink, as she watched her lover of seven years "forsake all others until death do us part" to a man she would never, ever sleep with. I hoped God knew they were lying. I prayed He understood why.

Finally, the travesty was over. On the way to the reception, Barbara grabbed my arm and dragged me into the small Sunday School bathroom in the basement. I instinctively locked the door behind us as Barbara grabbed a handful of those awful coarse brown towels, spread them carefully on the shoulder of my dress, and burst into tears. I held her as tightly as I could. I was afraid she would never stop.

Later, as we were repairing the damage to her face, she said, "Ever since I met Celia, I've wanted to marry her. I love her and I want to be with her forever. That should have been me up there. That should have been *me!*"

"I know."

"When, Joanna? Dammit, is it ever going to be *my* turn? *Our* wedding?" Her eyes were begging for answers.

I didn't have any.

Michael Thomas Ford

The Crown of Heaven

Picking through the glittering remnants of my eighth summer, the clearest memory I have is of kneeling behind a station wagon in Mickey Whitlow's driveway and saving the soul of a girl named Susan. I have forgotten Susan's last name—or likely never knew it at all—but I do remember that she had a pinched face, startling green eyes, and frizzy red hair. We were frequent playmates, usually racing our Big Wheels up and down the street in mad delight, and on the day in question I had taken it upon myself to show her the road to heaven.

"You have to pray to Jesus," I told her as we knelt on the scratchy asphalt, the tar warm under my bare knees. She looked at me and blinked. "Like this," I said. I folded my hands and tried to appear as earnest as possible. "Dear Jesus," I intoned solemnly, "Please forgive me for all of my sins and come into my heart."

Susan repeated my plea in a quiet voice. When she was done, she frowned. "I don't feel any different," she said. "If he's in my heart, shouldn't I feel it or something?"

I nodded. "You won't for a while," I reassured her. "But he's there. Now, no matter what you do, you won't go to hell."

We had spent a long time on hell before getting to the actual moment of salvation. I had described it for Susan in the fullest and grimmest of terms—all fire and burning and endless centuries of torment. I assured her that without Jesus she was headed there immediately, should she suddenly be struck down by a car while riding her bike or choke to death while downing the contents of a Jumbo Pixi Stik from the 7-11. That's what finally sold her on the Son of God and all he had to offer. That, and the fact that I told her that her dog would be waiting for her in heaven when she got there.

"Is that it?" she asked, picking absentmindedly at a scab on her elbow. She seemed to be expecting some big finale, like a musical number or something.

I thought for a minute, staring at our distorted reflections in the slightly rusted chrome of the station wagon's bumper. I didn't want her to go away thinking she'd been cheated. "Now we sing," I offered.

Her face brightened. "What do we sing?"

I chose at random a song I had heard my sisters playing on the stereo. "Don't stop, thinking about tomorrow," I warbled. Susan joined in, her thin voice mingling with mine as we chanted the familiar chorus together. "Don't stop, it will soon be here." Thus sanctifying our act with the words of Christine McVie and Lindsey Buckingham, I declared her Born Again.

That night at dinner, I told my mother what I'd done. She beamed at me over her meatloaf. "You'll get a jewel in your crown for that," she said, as she spooned peas onto my plate.

This was the first I'd heard about jewels, or crowns. "What kind of jewel?" I asked. I had visions of something vaguely tiara-like, similar to what Miss America wore on her runway walk, or perhaps something more reminiscent of the crown the Burger King wore in the television commercials for his restaurant.

"Was Susan Catholic?" my mother asked.

I looked at her blankly. I really had no idea.

"Was she Jewish, then?" my mother suggested hopefully.

"I don't know," I said finally.

My mother sighed. "You really must find out," she said. "It's important."

"Why?" I asked. Quite honestly, I didn't really know there was a difference. I'd just assumed there were Baptists, like us, and then a general multitude of sinners. Until her salvation by my forceful message of grace, Susan, I had believed, was simply one of the latter. Now, if I was hearing correctly, there were actually categories of the unsaved. Secretly, the thought delighted me no end.

"It's important," my mother explained, "because when you get to heaven, you will get a crown covered with jewels, one for each soul you've saved while you're here as God's messenger. You get different kinds of jewels for different kinds of souls. For Catholics, you get sapphires. For Lutherans, you get emeralds. For all of those eastern types you get rubies. And for Jews," she said triumphantly, "you get diamonds, which are the best of all."

"I think she was Catholic before," I said doubtfully. Although Jews were clearly the bigger prize, to my mind sapphires seemed somehow much more festive than diamonds.

My mother smiled. "That's fine, dear," she said, seemingly satisfied with my achievement. "There are so many of them; it's good when we can show one of them the right way."

I sat through the remainder of dinner contemplating this new information. If my mother was right—and I had no reason to believe that she was not—the choice of which souls to lead to salvation held far greater importance than merely swelling the ranks of Christ's army. Where once I had thought it enough simply to snatch my peers away from Satan's fiery grasp, now I understood more clearly what was really at stake in the cosmic battle between good and evil.

As I thoughtfully consumed my meatloaf, I envisioned the crown I would one day wear in glory, the construction of which would be my life's work from that moment on. Now that I knew the rules, I feverishly designed in my mind the exact pattern of jewels I would work toward. Not to be satisfied with any old hodgepodge of gems, I was determined to meet my Lord dressed in a smartly-encrusted crown of diamonds and sapphires, with perhaps a hint or two of emerald, if I could scare up a few Lutherans.

Later that night, alone in my room, I dug out the school annual and found the picture of my class. I ran my finger down the list of names, counting the numbers of souls waiting for the deliverance I, with the helping hand of Christ, could offer them. With a red felt tip pen, I carefully wrote in Cs next to those students I felt must surely be Catholic, and Js next to the ones who seemed, by whatever vague criteria I was using, to be Jewish. Those I was unsure of, such as Annie Chang, received question marks. When I was finished, I had a list of nine Catholics, five Jews, and four question marks. Folding it neatly, I stuck it into my notebook, where I could easily find it when the appropriate time came.

I dreamt that night of Jesus. He came to me in a long white robe, His face rosy with celestial delight. I approached, and He beamed, His mouth curling into a beatific smile. In His hands He held a crown—my crown—glittering with blue and white, the accumulated reward of a life spent in faithful service. As I stood before Him, holding my breath, He placed it on my head. I felt its weight settle around me, and looked up into my Lord's adoring eyes. As the heavenly host broke forth in song around us, He leaned down, bathing me in all His glory.

"Fabulous," He whispered in my ear. "Absolutely fabulous."

Debbie Fraker

Baby Butch

She's standing in the corner of the fenced playground sulking. Instead of the plaid girl's jumper, somehow she's gotten a pair of the blue boy's pants. They're a little too big, hanging long over her feet, with a web belt just below her waist holding them up. Her white shirt is also the type the boys wear, with a button-down collar instead of a Peter Pan. Her shoes used to be white sneakers. Now they are dingy brown and hopelessly scuffed. One toe digs a hole in the dirt where she stands. A corner of her shirttail is hanging over the top of her trousers. Her hair is short like a boy's. In fact, in places, it looks like she might have cut it herself, and then her mother had smoothed it out as well as possible. She really looks like a boy, down to the dirty band-aid on her elbow. But I have always known she was a girl.

I'm sitting on a swing watching her, wanting to go talk to her, but unsure how to approach. Only minutes ago she was running through the playground with a girl's shoe clutched to her flat twelve-year-old chest. Three girls had chased her until they caught her. Dragging her to the ground, they pulled at her arms, trying to wrestle the shoe loose. She never squealed or giggled like most girls would. She just held tight to the shoe, throwing her shoulders back and forth to keep possession of her prize. Her face was wide and bright with a grin. I wished it was my shoe.

Then Sister Mary Paul marched toward the four of them, her skirts swishing across the ground, raising dust. She grabbed the two girls on top by the backs of their jumpers, pulling them out of the cluster. When the third girl didn't notice what was happening, Sister yanked her back by the hair. Only the boy/girl was left on the ground, still holding the shoe, looking up at Sister with a stubborn challenge on her face. Sister

Mary Paul yanked the shoe out of her grasp and found the foot it belonged to. The other three girls skulked back to the hopscotch squares. When Sister grabbed the boy/girl by the ear to pull her up off the ground, I winced. That hurt. It hurt her pride more than her ear. But she looked Sister Mary Paul in the face defiantly with her jaw clenched and her eyes narrowed until Sister slapped her across the cheek and shoved her away. With her back to me and her hands jammed into her pockets, she dragged her sneakers across the dirt to where she now stands.

Her name is Sarah, but she'd rather be called Scott. I know that much about her. I think she's been crying, even though I'm sure she won't admit it. When I talk to her, I'll call her Scott, to let her know I understand. I'll give her my hanky to wipe the dirt off her face.

david michael gillis

Killing Arthur

So anyway, it was ugly. He's never taken things well when he's not in charge. Arthur is the great initiator, the great planner and executor. When I told him, his face dropped, and I thought he was going to have a tantrum. But then he got that cold look he gets when he's forced into talking about things he'd rather not. He went to the fridge, grabbed a beer, sat down heavily on the sofa and stared at me. Those fantastic, stupid, beautiful crystal eyes looking up at me, putting me in my place simply, efficiently. "So," he said, "could you just repeat what you said a moment ago? I may not have heard you correctly, old troll that I am."

"Please, Arthur."

"No, really. Say it again. I need to hear it one more time out loud, and I think you do too, Roger."

I started for the closet to get my coat. "I think I'd better go out for a while. You need to cool down." As I reached inside the closet I heard him get up. Then there was a paralyzing pain in my neck and shoulder where he grabbed me. I shrunk as my knees began to give out under the pain. He put his mouth next to my ear and said in a quiet, steady, menacing hiss, "You're not going anywhere until we have this out, bitch. So get your sorry little butt back in the den."

Arthur is violent; he's hurt me before. When he gets like this it's best to comply. I sat in the over stuffed recliner facing him on the sofa. With the same menace in his voice as before he said, "So. To recap, could you repeat what you said during dinner?"

I sighed deeply. "I said that I was seeing someone else and it looks like it's getting pretty serious." I looked down at my hands. They seemed to be doing their own little dance, wringing around one another.

"No, no, no," Arthur said. "That's not exactly what you said. Come on, repeat it."

"This is too fucked up, Arthur. Don't pull mind game shit with me. You heard me the first time."

"That's right. I heard it, but I don't believe it. You said you were seeing a woman. A woman, Roger? Does she know you're a fucking queer? Does she know you dress up like a bitch every chance you get? Does she know you've got a closet full of dresses?"

"She knows that I've explored certain areas of my sexuality. . . ."

"Explored?" he laughed. It was an ugly laugh. I cringed when I heard it. "Honey, you've been a faggot all your fucking life. I mean, in all the time we've been together, how many times have you taken the top? Huh? Tell me. I mean it's always been the same with you. 'Oh Artie, please, please. I love your cock. Stick it in me, Artie.' We've been together ten years, Roger. All that time you've been my bottom. Now you're telling me that you've been fucking some woman? If you wanted to fuck somebody, why didn't you fuck me? Maybe I'd like to be on the receiving end for once."

My hands continued to work at each other. Arthur had stopped his rant. He was seething.

"I can't live as a gay man anymore," I said. "It's been all wrong from the start. I'm not saying I understand what's happened. The whole thing has been tearing me apart."

"So that's it. It's over. Ten years down the toilet."

"If that's how you want to see it."

"Roger's coming out of his closet. He's a closet hetero no more. Let's all watch him blossom. Tell me, Roger. Did she fix you? Are you cured of your horrid malady? Gonna move to the fucking 'burbs and have kiddies?"

"Arthur, don't. . . ."

"Fuck you, Roger. You've been a fuck-up from the start. You know why I went for you at first? Because I felt sorry for you. I've wasted all this time on someone I have no respect for, only pity."

That was it. We'd gotten over the hump. We'd gone way past the point of no return. Short of a phenomenal act of will on both of our parts, we would never get over this. We were finished.

In a bar on the east side of town, Julia was waiting for me. I'd told her that tonight was the night I'd tell Arthur about us. We'd arranged to meet afterwards. I got up and made for the door, not bothering to stop at the closet for my coat.

"I'm getting a hotel room tonight. At some point we're going to have to get together and work out who gets what, but I'm too exhausted right now. Maybe in a week or so."

Arthur sat deflated on the couch, hands at his side, limp in surrender. "What's her name?" he asked. "Just a first name. I don't want to stalk her down or anything."

"Julia."

"Ah, Julia. Is she sexy and wonderful and voluptuous and mysterious and . . ."

"Stop it, Arthur. You can't compete with her. It's a different league."

"A different league? Fuck, you little slut. It's a whole fucking different species. What could she possibly see in you?"

"She likes me because I'm gentle. Men have hurt her before, same as me. Why do you hate women so much?"

"I don't hate women in general. Only the ones that steal what's mine."

He was up off the couch now, rage starting over again. In four long strides he was across the den and at the door, in my face. His fists clenched, his lips drawn tight, grinding teeth exposed. I'd always had a feeling that he was capable of violence above and beyond the normal domestic variety, and now it was about to come out. Instinctively, I reached for the door knob, but his hand gripped my wrist and he threw me back into the apartment. I stumbled over the coffee table.

"Before you leave," Arthur said, loosening his belt, "how about one last go around, for old time's sake?"

"Fuck you."

"That's right, bitch. Fight it. I love seeing you fight and lose." He was taking off his pants, and I was just starting to get my footing after my fall. He laid a well directed fist into my stomach. The force from the blow winded me. For a moment, breathing again was all I cared about. As I gasped and choked, Arthur pulled the phone out of the wall and then the cord from the phone. I knew this drill. We'd gone through a lot of phones this way. This was where I got tied up with telephone cord and fucked. Not this time, though. With a burst of energy I grabbed the heavy brass cast lamp from the desk and held it like a fool, thinking its presence alone would ward him off. He laughed and just kept coming, holding the cord in his hands, implicitly inviting me to submit.

At last I let my hands fall to my side. I nodded. "Fine," I said. "One last time. But you better use lube. None of this dry fucking stuff."

"No promises, bitch. Turn around."

I began to turn and then swung back around with all my strength, hitting him on the temple with the base of the lamp. His head caved in at the point of impact, his eyes rolled back into his head, and dark red, almost black, blood splattered the room.

Three days ago Arthur died having never come out of his coma. The cops are looking for me. I don't phone Julia anymore because I don't want to cause her any trouble.

The air down here in New Mexico is wonderful. I've been sleeping in ancient native ruins high up on a piece of table land that looks over the highway miles away. The other day a couple of tourists came across my camp, and they were interested in who I was and how I'd come to be living here. I told them that I was a manic-depressive and a drop-out. I was trying to find God here in the desert. None of this was a lie. They gave me some of their food and a couple of dollars, and for a couple of nights they shared my camp with me. They had very good, expensive equipment, and slept in a Westfalia van. I'm pretty sure that when they slept, they locked their doors against what I might have been.

Of the two nights they stayed in camp with me, the second was the best. There was a meteor shower that provided a spectacle that kept us up until nearly dawn. We talked about our families, work—little things. It was then, in the middle of it all, that the enormity of what I had done struck me. I was a murderer. I could never go home. I cried, and then fell silent. My two guests said nothing as the blackened skies above sparked and flashed, and the shapeless night with all its animals, monsters and ghosts flowed by like a river.

In the morning they left. I could hear their van's motor for twenty minutes after as they made their way down off my mesa. I watched them turn onto the main highway five miles away, a metallic speck shining before a rooster tail of desert dust hugging the curve of the planet.

Gabrielle Glancy

The First Time I Saw Vera

We agreed to meet at La Boheme.

We made the date for four o'clock on a Thursday. It was a chilly spring day.

When I walked in, I looked around. I saw a handsome young man with blondish, wispy curls sitting at the table by the window. He looked like a lanky, foreign angel. He was reading intently. Otherwise, the place was empty.

I crossed to the left side of this boy, who couldn't have been more than seventeen, and went to the counter to order. I surveyed the room. I was looking for my five-nine, brown/brown, unsociable, unpredictable, complicated, perverted, disbalanced, artistic, narcissistic Russian/Jewish pessimist—that's how she had described herself in her ad. I ordered a tea. While the woman behind the counter was steaming out water, I tried to see what the boy was reading. The cover of his book was yellow. That was all I could see. He saw me looking at him, for an instant looked up at me, then looked down.

"Place is empty," I said to the café worker. She was a cute, dark-haired girl, slim, straight short hair. I liked her smile.

"Is it always like this?" I was nervous.

"Yeah," she said, handing me the pot of tea over the counter. She smiled sweetly. "Gets busy around six."

I thanked her and went toward a table by the door. On my way, the young boy lifted his eyes. I had the very conscious thought then, that he looked like Tadeuz from *Death in Venice*—he had a most lovely face—square jaw, soft eyes, blond curls.

"Are you Vera?" I asked.

She nodded.

"Would you like to move to this table here?" The table she was at seemed crowded into the most exposed corner of the room.

She conceded and walked toward me with her book.

"What are you reading?" I asked.

"Nabokov."

I tried to read the title, but it was in Russian.

"*Glory*," she said.

"I don't know that one."

She lowered her eyes, large sad eyes that were more yellow than brown. She was very tall and I could see that, under her sweater, she had high, firm, lovely breasts. They were exquisite, in fact. I took note of this and referred to it later. It was not until I dropped her back off at the café, however, after I took her to my house to show her my photographs of Natasha, my first Russian girlfriend, that, as she walked away from me, I realized I was in trouble. I could fall for that girl, I thought. And I was right.

So I tried to read the first line of the book. I had learned the Cyrillic alphabet just that week and attempted to sound out the words. She laughed. We talked for a brief few minutes. Then I asked her if she wanted to go to my house.

At my house, that very first day, she sat in the chair by the fireplace. I sat on the couch.

She was quiet, timid. We sat for a long time in silence. I looked at her every once in a while, but mostly we both looked at the plant, a *false arelia*, on the other side of the room. She had a darkness to her, and a femininity which wound through her boyish curls. I thought to speak but it didn't seem appropriate. I was thinking. And listening, actually. I was listening to the silence between us.

Finally, she asked, and it sounded like she was making a joke, "So what would you say you write about?"

"What do you mean?" I said.

She laughed.

Then I laughed.

Again we were quiet for a long time.

"You want to know what I write about?" I asked, shyly.

She nodded.

"Hmm," I said, "that's a hard question."

I can't remember now exactly what I answered, but it was something kind of pompous, something like, "I write about the relationship between the visible and the invisible."

"The invisible . . . ," she repeated.

I thought for a moment she didn't understand what the word meant, but then she piped up: "The relationship or the intersection?"

For someone with so heavy an accent, who had only been in this country for about two months, this seemed like a pretty sophisticated question.

"Both," I answered.

"On the plane of the vertical or the horizontal?" she said, sort of laughing.

"Both," I said again, coyly.

Now we both laughed. Then, for the briefest moment, we looked at each other. I mean really looked.

We sat for a long time that day. She told me she had to get back to that same café, that she was meeting friends at seven. It wasn't until later I found out she had another date.

I knew, as one often does, everything I needed to know about Vera at the moment of our first meeting—it was all there, all of it, raw signs which time and interpretation would only obscure. Everything was right there out in the open, the end woven into the beginning, just like that, except, I suppose, the answer to the question I'm asking now: "Where was Vera?"

I returned her to the café. In the car, I blasted the heat and played the Russian music Natasha had sent me from Moscow.

At the corner of Mission and something, I dropped her off.

"I'm going to want to see you again," I said.

She didn't answer. Then, after a long pause:

"I think it's my grandmother you remind me of."

I was a little startled, but I continued. "Do you think you'll want to see me?"

"But you look like my mother. Yes," she said, "my mother's family."

I realized I was not going to get a straight answer from her. In any case, this was more than she had said all afternoon. At the time, I found the *non sequiturs* charming.

When I looked at her, I could see she was looking at the floor of the car.

"Well, take good care," I said.

She nodded.

"Can I call you?"

She nodded.

Then I nodded, as if to say, "Okay, now you may go."

Vera got out of the car and walked back to the café.

I knew how it would end and I didn't.

How could I have known, for example, that just two months later, I would be sitting across a table from her mother in St. Petersburg, Russia, waiting to be introduced to the man, a boy, really, Slava, to whom Vera was promised at the age of six, and that upon my return, she would be gone?

That, of course, is what happened.

When I got back from Russia, Vera was nowhere to be found. I had spoken to her from New York just two days previously. "You will call me when you come home?" she had said. But when I got there, I found her phone disconnected, her apartment vacant. Kind, but completely disinterested, her landlord, a ruddy carpenter-type, held the door open for me as I ran my eyes over every inch of empty space where once the aura, the spirit, the scent of Vera had presided. He was no help at all in answering my questions.

How could I have known?

I knew and I didn't.

In any case, on this particular day, the day I met Vera for the first time, I very consciously watched her walk away from me. I watched her deliberate sway, her slim, full buttocks. I thought to myself looking at her—*I could do that*—meaning I could fuck her, she could be my girl.

What can I say? She was beautiful.

I wanted to see her again. That much was clear.

Robert Oliver Goldstein

Loleeta Takes Her Place in the Scheme of Things

Loleeta Morales reclines to read her fave alternative magazine—*The Utne Reader*, a sort of *Reader's Digest* for middle-class girls who pump adrenalin from thinking themselves liberal. She would like to offer the following quote from an article entitled "The Place of the Poor in our Cities": "Poor people have taught us so much about being fully alive in the world."

How they must bore each other, Loleeta thinks. She thinks she should hop on down to Fisherman's Wharf, she could be a member of the underclass who truly leaves them invigorated.

Loleeta writes:

"I can teach them how to walk. It says so right here: 'Poor people have taught us so much about how to move rhythmically and melodically down the street, about how to use colour and ornamentation to say new things about ourselves, about how to bring out the rhetorical and theatrical powers of the English language in our every day talk.' I can teach them how to walk, talk and dress."

She decides to prepare herself for the task. First, she must fully wake up. She pops a couple of No Doze. Next, she will place herself in some especially well-swept section of The City. Is the Castro genuinely colourful or is it in need of flotsam? Where will her gift of trashiness be most appreciated? And what shall she wear? Her wardrobe expands with possibilities. She decides on the educator's look of faded, shit-stained chinos and tie.

Loleeta writes:

"I never thought I would see this day. When I would be given a place in the design of a city. For this I am grateful."

She crosses herself and prepares to enter traffic. Lights change when their colours displease her. She looms over San Francisco like a Godzilla in search of King Kong. Her jaw flops open and she roars: "How many girls wanna be Loleeta Morales!" Dozens, she decides. As if the hills were alive with the joy of Loleeta. She storms 18th Street like a mob with convictions. There was *money* in her mailbox today. Her stipend for going crazy.

Loleeta writes:

"What wonderful times we live in. No one paid my mother. She had to go crazy and *work for a living. That was no kind of thing to do to a girl like my mother."*

With that thought in mind she storms into the Bank of America.

"Cash my cheque!" she demands.

"Gladly!" the teller answers.

And Loleeta takes her place in the scheme of things.

Candis Graham

A Second Time

I went dancing, after weeks of thinking about it. I wanted to get out and meet new women, but I'm never comfortable in crowds—even crowds of dykes. Still, it's better than being alone every night.

I found myself sitting at a table with some women I knew by sight. That's when I spotted her. The woman beside me noticed her too.

"She has quite the reputation," she said.

I turned. "She does?"

"Yes. She's here every week. She's always alone. She was involved with a woman for years, three or four for sure. They split last spring."

I watched her walk across the room, winding her way around tables and clusters of women. I said nothing to the woman beside me. The band had taken a break and the silence was wonderful. It wasn't silence, not really, but the heavenly sounds of women talking and laughing, rather than loud, pounding music.

She stopped to talk to someone. After a brief conversation, she resumed her trip across the huge room. She walked with a lazy stride, as if she had all the time in the world.

I couldn't resist asking the woman beside me, "Do you know her?"

She lifted her mug of beer. "Kind of. I know about her." She drank from the mug, deliberately taking her time. "I know her name." She took another drink. "Her name's Erin."

Erin. It suited her. The perfect name for this woman with short short hair and over-sized purple glasses. Erin of the lazy stride.

"She sleeps with everyone."

My mouth fell open. "How do you know?"

She gave me a pitying look. "Everyone knows."

Everyone knows she sleeps with everyone. Everyone! Rumours. Innuendo. Don't we relish the distorted details, speculating about the lives of others? It entertains us, as long as it isn't about us.

"Yes, she has quite the reputation." There were sounds of satisfaction in her voice.

My fury astonished me. I wanted to yell at her. Erin sleeps with everyone, does she? Well, I'd bet money that she's celibate. That's how much faith I put in idle rumours. I tried to ignore my inner voice and asked, "Do you want another beer?"

She smiled. "Sure."

I walked away quickly. I had no intention of getting her a beer. She could faint from thirst before I'd get her one. But I wanted a beer myself, so I headed toward the bar.

I joined the line-up. Erin was right in front of me. I hadn't planned it. I'd watched her walk in the direction of the bar, true. But I was only here because I was thirsty.

I wasn't angry anymore. I felt excited standing so close to her. I looked down at the floor, trying to calm my racing heart. She was wearing bright yellow running shoes. I have a friend who says you can tell a lot about a person by her shoes. Do women who wear yellow running shoes sleep with everyone? I almost laughed out loud.

"Why are you smiling?"

I looked up. Erin was grinning at me, waiting for my answer.

"I had a funny thought, that's all."

"What were you thinking?"

Her eyes were looking into mine, hazel eyes behind the glass, inviting me to look back. Usually I am tongue-tied, especially around women I admire, but words came easily. "You wouldn't be amused. Trust me."

She laughed. "Try me."

It was her turn at the bar. She ordered mineral water with a slice of lemon. As she took her drink and started to walk away, I ordered my beer and called after her.

"Wait!"

She turned, still grinning.

"I'll tell you."

"I can't wait," she laughed.

I took my beer from the counter. "Come out here, in the hall, where it's quiet."

She followed me. She was following me! What could I say to her? She would not be pleased if I said I'd been told that she has a reputation for sleeping with everyone. The band started playing loud, energetic dance music as we left the room. Maybe I'd ask her to dance, after I'd figured out how to explain why I was smiling at the bar.

The hall was deserted. We stopped in an alcove beside a water fountain. I turned to look at her, to see if those hazel eyes were still warm and inviting.

She bent forward and kissed the end of my nose. "I couldn't resist. Do you mind?"

I shook my head, speechless.

"Why were you smiling back there? You said you'd tell me."

I nodded. What if it was true, her reputation? What could I say to those hazel eyes?

She leaned toward me and put her lips on mine, warm lips. My heart started to pound. I wanted to shout for joy. I wanted to hold her close.

"I've missed you," she whispered.

I put my arms around her, trying not to spill my beer, wishing the mug would vanish. "I've missed you too, Erin."

"So, why were you smiling?"

I moved back a little to look at her. "I was thinking your yellow runners should be scarlet, to match your reputation. Did you know that you sleep with everyone? That's what I've been told." I hadn't meant to blurt it out like that.

Tears welled in her eyes. Wet, hazel eyes. She was always able to express her emotions as she felt them. I'm more inclined to control my feelings. I pulled her close to me again.

"I sleep with myself!" She cried the angry words against my shoulder.

"I thought so." Her smell was just as I remembered. A hint of lavender soap, mixed with freshly-ironed clothes. "Let me put this beer down so I can hug you properly."

"You never do anything properly."

I grinned. "Wanna dance?"

She took off her glasses and wiped the tears from her eyes and cheeks with a forefinger. "You want to dance with a scarlet woman?"

"I'd be honoured."

She laughed, put her glasses back on, and reached for my hand.

Mikaya Heart

A Nice Scottish Story

A've always liked car mechanics. A like the shiny steel, the way it's cold tae the touch, but heats up sae fast. A like its resistance, A like the way it glows red when yi pi' a torch tae it. A like bein' able tae make a broken down vehicle run agi'n. Of course, sometimes it's hard tae make them run ag'in, sometimes yi jus' cannae work ou' wha's wrong wi' them. Dinna ever le' anyone tell yi that a car is just a piece o' me'al. Cars are enti'ies, they have minds o' their ane. Yi hevta ge' in tune wi' 'em if yi wan' tae work on them. And sometimes they dinnae wan' tae be fixed.

The worst thing abou' car mechanics is the bullshit.

A like takin' cars tae bits. Pi'ing them back taegither isna always sae easy. But A like the challenge of a nu' and bolt that are hard tae undae—there's nothin' mare pleasurable than that *crrrack* when it finally goes. A like takin' the pieces off bi' by bi' until A've gor it a' stripped naked, laid out in fron' o' me. And then yi piece it back taegither, until everythin's neatly back in place, each nu' and bolt tightened down just righ'.

Of course, A prefer auld cars. New cars are made so yi cannae work on them wi'out thousands of pounds worth o' equipment. A like auld cars, that were made simple and solid, made tae last, made so yi can ge' a' them.

The bullshit. Aye, there's a lot o' bullshit around car mechanics. Women fall intae it, but men are incorrigible. Especially Sco'ish men. It's verra rare to meet a man who doesna bullshit abou' mechanics. Yi cannae trust a word they say. Chances are A'll ken ten times mare than any man who starts tellin' me wha' tae dae. A've learned tae tell them to leave me alane. They often dinna pay any attention until I'm rude tae them. I dinna like bein' rude tae people. But when someone isna treatin' me respectfully . . . well, yi havtae stand up for yersel'.

Sometimes it's mare than lack o' respect.

A do a lo' o' repairs fer *mot* testing. A only work oot o' a backstreet garage masel', of course, so A have tae take ma cars somewhere else tae be cer'ified. A've been through a lo' o' places. It's the same thing every time—at first the blokes are all intrigued tae see a woman in overalls, covered in oil. They act really condescendin', but they're helpful—a woman's presence brings ou' the chivalrous male, yi ken. They look o'er the car, full o' 'helpful' advice. Sometimes they'll be especially magnanimous—because, efter a', A'm only a woman, who cannae be expected to ken wha' she's daeing.

Gradually, their attitude gets belligerent, as A bring in mare and mare cars, and they begin to realise A do ken wha' A'm daein'. They no longer offer assistance (that part's a relief). They make snide remarks wi' sexual overtones. They're short wi' me. They keep me wai'in'. They find one excuse efter anither tae fail ma cars. So A move on tae anither *mot* place, and go through the whole cycle ag'in, wi' a whole new bunch o' assholes.

It's lonely work.

One place A took ma cars tae for a while. They started gettin' nasty wi' me and A prepared to move on. The last car A took there was ma ane car—A knew i' inside out. They said they couldnae fi' me in right away so A left it there, and went back la'er in the aftenoon, as they were closin'. The bloke handed me the failure note wi' a sly grin. I was surprised it failed— A ken ma ane car verra well, and A knew it shoulda passed. A looked over the note, and A was even mare surprised. Bad windscreen wipers, handbrake adjustmen' incorrect, headligh' aim high, seatbel' torn. This was awfi strange—A knew there wasnae anythin' wrong wi' any o' those. A wen' tae the car, i' was parked outside. A looked i' over, and A got really angry, A mean, *rrreally* angry. Those motherfuckers, they'd cu' the wipers and the seatbel', and they'd rese' the adjustmen' on the headlights and the handbrake. A *knew* A'd set them correctly before A ever took the car tae them. So there was nothin' else tae think. They sure as hell were grinnin' a' somethin' when they gave me the note. Those assholes. Bad enough they make fun o' me and keep me wai'in', bu' when they start tae fuck wi' ma car. . . .

Well, A dinnae like tae be treated bad. So A drove away, as though

A'd niver noticed anythin'. But A went back la'er that night, verra la'e, when the streets were empty. A poured half a can o' petrol over the front doors tae their garage. A threw a match and it went *whoosh!* A mass o' flame sucked a' the doors. A ran off, up a back alley ontae the nex' street where A'd parked ma car. A love that car, she's an auld Morris Minor. A walked up tae her jauntily, and ran ma hand o'er the wing. The metal was cold and smooth. A go' in and drove away. A glanced behind once when A reached the corner. A vivid orange glow filled the sky.

A'll no tolerate bein' treated disrespectfully.

Thea Hillman

Having Holly

It was so hot. Can I just say it was the hottest sex I've ever had with a woman practically fully clothed the entire time? As good as the best boy sex I've ever had. Except it was Holly.

Maybe it started when I could crack sexual innuendos, and she fired them right back; she was nasty too. Or showing up at her birthday. We were the only women wearing flowing skirts in a room full of argyle and crew necks. Or her room. The pillows on her bed—flushed peach and blue, red—pastel, but not shallow; light. Embracing. A flash of me holding Holly on that bed was how I realized I was attracted to women. And more specifically, Holly.

So is she going to call or what?

Years of moving around ensue, but somehow we stay close. I come out to her via airmail. She writes back she is, too. She flirts with me over the phone. Goes to a wedding nearby and is too busy to call. She's scared, I think.

I mean, it wouldn't be so weird if we hadn't gotten together.

Another year goes by. Then we see each other. I've changed a lot. She's intimidated. I think, good, I'm not attracted to her anymore. I go to dinner to meet her mom, her aunt, her grandparents. And it's all so innocent that we drink wine, and I make her family laugh, and they like me, and I'm sleeping over.

If only she didn't stroke me afterward, caressing me with so much tenderness.

After dinner, lying in her high-school-pink-ruffled bed, teenage girls at a sleep-over, I wonder why we keep returning to the subject of sex. And why when her lover calls and she breaks their date, she lets him wonder what's going to happen that night.

I tell her I'd rather have my hair played with than be fucked.

Cuddling, friends, "non-sexual" of course. She holds me. It's nicer than I ever could have imagined to be held by Holly. She jokes about how beautiful our children would be. My head against her breast. Her fingers in my hair.

Neither of us is taking responsibility.

Excruciatingly, strokes lengthen. Fingers stray close to sensitive ears. Fingers splay open over faces. Hands slip under t-shirts. Hair is tugged. Strokes are held—hesitating—then deepening. Strong hands are complimented. Little moans escape. Bigger moans. Bodies shift. And it's not so suddenly that I realize sex is happening with Holly. And the girls who usually have so much to say to each other are silent.

I don't want to be sexual with Holly unless I can knock her socks off.

Years of wanting, denying wanting, unconscious jealousy, and fear fill my fingers as they love Holly. The same love that's always been there, open, that's no longer being mentioned, that's completely different now, or might be.

We scratch, using nails through scalps, down necks.

I can't seem to do anything wrong. Holly moves with every touch, and all I want to do is keep her moaning with my "non-sexual" strokes. Her head is tilted back, mouth open. I'm too scared to make a sound; she might stop running her fingers through my hair, might stop getting closer and closer to my breasts as she rubs my back. The only thing I'm thinking is, come on, bitch, stick your fingers in my cunt, bitch, touch my breast. Over and over, until she finally does make a move. I tighten my legs around hers and let my fingers dig in.

We don't kiss. That would make it real.

We grind. Rubbing through underwear, boxers. Rip t-shirts off. Don't talk. Grab asscheeks. Bite, hard. Scratch. Sweat so hard we slide against each other as we clutch and push our bodies as close as they can get. I want her so badly; I enjoy sliding fingers along her asshole. All I want is to make her come. For her to see how hot we are.

She's told me she loves me, but she's never called me amazing before.

And she's close to coming. And we stop. Holding each other, stray hairs clinging to our sweat, we laugh. She speaks first, whether you like it or not, you're soft and sweet.

I call first. She says she's happy it happened. She'll call me later on in the week.

Phrases fill my head like you know I'm not expecting anything. I know

Holly's track record with women, and it scares me. But she's glowing, and stroking me with so much care, that I decide to expect the best from her. I'm just not sure what that is, and I worry because it's clear to me that I could fall in love with Holly.

She still hasn't called.

And I call her. She isn't stressed or upset. I take this as a bad sign. I cook dinner. She makes sure I know she put on lipstick after she got off BART on her way to my apartment. She brings me flowers and asks me when I grew breasts.

Holly, what is it about you that makes me write?

I think of calling her in New York sometimes. Urgent. Because she might get married at any time. Because I need to tell her how much I love her. Because I am in love with her.

Writing Holly is having Holly.

But I don't. And I can't seem to write to her. So I use her name. Write her. Because in writing Holly I am loving Holly.

Again and again.

Welby Ings

The Fairy

I'm not a man who likes to believe in fairies, so my first encounter with one came as a bit of a rude awakening. I was travelling on a bus heading into the central city when he stumbled up the steps to the driver's seat, thinly disguised in a business suit and a polyester raincoat.

"Oh God!"' he gasped. "I thought that you were going to leave me. How much is it into the city? "

He poised himself beside the collection stand and touched a flick of hair back into position.

The driver looked at him.

"Eighty cents."

"I beg your pardon?" he asked.

"Eighty cents."

The fairy raised his hand and touched his chest lightly with the tips of his fingers. "Oh, is it that much? I thought it was only forty. . . . "

The driver raised a weary eyebrow and glanced back through the rear view mirror. "It's cheaper if you use your broomstick," he said.

The fairy looked outside at the drizzle.

"I just hate days like this," he sighed. "I haven't used public transport for ages. All this confusion, but what's a girl to do when she can't find a taxi?"

The women on the bus glanced up from their magazines and watched him as he balanced his umbrella against the ticket stand and rummaged furiously through the compartments of his wrist wallet.

"Just a moment," he said, "and I'll see what I've got in here. . . . "

The driver flicked off an orange ticket and eyed the man impatiently. "Eighty cents," he repeated.

"Eighty cents? Here we are." The fairy smiled and tossed the coins like a shower of blessings down into the collection bowl.

"I try to avoid carrying loose change on me, you know," he said. "It really is such a business trying to find the right—"

He didn't finish. Sighing impatiently, the driver swung out from the curve with a strategic jolt, sending the fairy stumbling down the aisle in a flurry of polyester. He lunged blindly between the support bars and finally fumbled his way into the seat beside me.

"My God!" he gasped. "James Dean on the A.R.A. bus run! Do they all drive like this?"

I looked up from my paperback and smiled at him.

"Really! I've heard of showing a girl to her seat, but this is ridiculous!" He laughed, gasping a falsetto and folding the flaps of his wet raincoat onto his lap. "I'm sorry," he said. "Did I drip any water on you?"

I shook my head and flicked a page of my book with embarrassment. People were looking at him.

He sighed.

Richmond Road frittered past the windows. The houses with their leafy verandahs and ruptured footpaths, the wind-torn banana palms straggling over fences; a never-ending line of tropical suburbia. I gazed at my reflection in the window, watching the street corners as they rippled through my forehead. I could see him mirrored there, over my shoulder. He was sitting with his legs crossed, licking the tip of his finger and stroking the corner of his hairline into place.

I moved an inch closer to the window.

There was a shuffle in the seat in front of us and two girls, suspended in puberty, flicked their wrists and giggled at each other. I wondered why the hell he had to stumble into the seat beside me. I picked out a middle-aged woman who was watching us and rolled my eyes with embarrassment. She smiled.

The fairy lowered his head and examined the tips of his fingernails.

God, I thought, it always happens like this! Every time that you climb onto a bus. You find a seat somewhere tucked discreetly up against the window and just when you think that you're looking your most unobtrusive, every freak or vagrant takes it as a sign to move in on you.

When the bus stopped at the corner of Ponsonby Road, an elderly couple got up and ambled down toward the driver. The old man muttered something at the door and the driver, glancing back across his shoulder, swept us both with a wry smile. When they had gone, he flicked the lever and the door closed behind them. He looked down at the ticket stand. The umbrella was still sitting there, dripping indolently into a puddle on the floor. He glanced up at the rear view mirror and smiled to himself.

"Hey, fairy," he said. "You've forgotten your wand!"

There was a ripple of laughter throughout the bus and the girls in front of us turned around and grinned at the other passengers. I buried myself in my book. But the fairy sat poised, his eyes fixed on the rear view mirror and his lips pursed into a pout of humiliation. He rearranged his raincoat as the driver, laughing, threw the vehicle into gear and lurched out from the bus stop.

He was silent for the rest of the journey.

At the top of Queen Street, there was a graceful shuffle beside me and the fairy raised his arm and pushed the emergency button. The bus veered over to the footpath and stopped.

The fairy stood up. He flicked his hair back in a swish of contempt and minced like a leading lady in a Broadway production, down the aisle to the front of the bus. The driver caught him in the rear view mirror and reached out for the umbrella.

But he missed. When he looked up, the fairy was standing there like he was in some Bette Davis movie, poised with the umbrella above his shoulder and looking like he was set to kill. The bus fell silent.

He turned, paused and surveyed his audience with razor-sharp eyes. Then he touched the driver lightly with the metal spike of the wand and screamed:

"Turn to shit!"

Alexandra Keir

Cows

Come o-o-on, cows. Hey, come o-o-on, cows." God, do they have to be way down there this morning? My back aches. How long will it take them to walk up here if I don't go and get them? Waiting until the cows come home is a helluva long wait.

Kelly starts off across the paddock, rubber boots slapping jeans. She stretches and steps carefully over the electric fence wire into the pasture. There's a heavy dew and though the sun is up the morning is cool, autumn is coming.

"Come on, cows." A few look up. If she can interest Sarah Bell maybe they'll come on their own. Doesn't seem likely this morning. "Heeey, cows." Here they come. "Come o-o-o-on, cows."

Kelly thinks, *I'm sure he's abusing her. She reminds me of me when I was fourteen. I wish someone had done something for me. Didn't anyone see? Well, I see her and I know. I have to do something.*

The milking machine's steady rhythm fills the barn. Between washing an udder and putting the milking machine on the next cow, she joins the row of cows and pees in the gutter behind them.

It seems like I hardly know Erin and yet I feel so sure. She's quiet. She cowers when he's around. She sticks so closely to her mom, she's practically in her lap. It's that "take care of me I'm your little girl" stuff. I wish I could talk to her or her mom. Of course, I don't think Joan would hear me.

Kelly pours the fresh, warm milk from five-gallon buckets into the cream separator. It whines as it gains speed. The first stream of skim milk plunks hollow into an empty plastic bucket. Chicken feed.

Joan would have a shit fit. Imagine. It would be the end of our friendship, that's for sure. But what about Erin? I wonder if she'd tell me if I asked.

The fine rivulet of cream pours slowly into a stainless steel bucket. There is a lot more milk. She needs to keep the cows pregnant to keep the milk flowing. Like women and other mammals, cows only milk after they've birthed. A steady cycle of calving and milking, calving and milking.

What to do? I suppose I ought to call Children's Aid. If only someone had done that for me. Although, what will they do? As if they have any place to put her. Erin, Erin, what can I do?

She scrapes dried manure from a sleek, tawny summer coat. She loves her cows. Loves their warm softness. She lives with the contradiction of loving them and yet tying them up and keeping them pregnant. She does let them calve in the field in the warmer months, unlike her neighbours who tie up the cows for calving—pulling calves out with chains lest something go wrong. Not so different from doctors. The baby could die. We must pull it out. The woman could die.

She understands this. She watched a calf half born, hind feet first, take its first breath and fill its lungs with fluid. She moves on down the row scraping, patting, expert eye assessing each cow's well-being.

How can I stop this? Here it is, women protecting children from men again. Imagine asking him. Or her. Imagine what they'd say. What Joan would say.

One more cow to milk. She nudges it over with her shoulder so she can kneel to remove the machine. She remembers she had leapt into the pen and pulled the calf out. Slapped its sides. Reached a finger in to clear mucous from its mouth. Blown gently into its warm, slippery, wet body. Too late. She pulls the milker away from the last cow.

Joan would yell. "You fucking bitch. How could you do this? What were you thinking? What have I ever done to you? Why didn't you talk to me first? Why didn't you talk to me? What are you trying to do to us?"

Silence is immediate when she turns off the milkers, the space filled with shifting animals, burping, chewing their cud and slurping from automatic waterers.

"I was abused. I know what it's like. I know what she's going through. I had to do it. I am not doing this to you. He is. He is doing it to her. I'm sure of it. Ask her. Ask him. They are lying. They have to lie."

Neighbours are not that close, a few kilometres between each of them. They like the privacy. There is a certain tolerance or respect for differences as long as you're a good neighbour.

Unclipping their collars, she urges the cows back out into the morning. "That's it cows, out you go. Get on cows, get on there." Kelly pauses in the doorway, feels the breeze lift damp hair from her forehead and looks out over her herd as they settle into the pasture. Her gaze continues past them across to the mountains, Erin's mountains. She sighs, hooks the fence wire, closing her cows into the pasture and turns to the milkhouse to wash up.

K. Linda Kivi

Cherries Are Her Angels

The day Sue choked her, Karen ate three pounds of cherries up in Gyro Park. The Food Co-op in town had just received their first shipment of local, organic cherries. They were fat and firm and summer perfect.

Out in the blank daylight, Karen avoided the town's main drag and slipped into a back alley instead, heading toward the park at the other end of downtown. She was afraid she'd cry if she ran into anyone. That they'd notice the blueing, banana-shaped bruises on her throat she'd tried to disguise beneath a turquoise bandanna. No matter how she folded it, the bandanna never covered her entire neck. The long neon marks of Sue's hands glowed against her pale skin and seemed to expand right before her eyes. It was as if it was written on her face, a tattoo that she was stuck with.

Karen peered both ways then scurried across the last street before the park. As she approached the top of the lane, she noticed a young East Indian man negotiating footholds in the stone wall that banked the hillside. He was dressed in climbing gear, a silky yellow jacket and pants with cinched wrists, waist and ankles, shoes with grip. He hoisted himself up off the asphalt. Karen skirted the wall and started up the road, passing the man just as one of his hands, in black fingerless gloves, reached up onto the sidewalk at her feet.

She clutched her bag of cherries closer, absentmindedly rubbing the globes of fruit through the plastic. They were good cherries, these cherries, she told herself. Firm and dark, almost black, the way good Bings are supposed to be. Taut. The word did not swallow well. Taut. She tried it again.

Taut.

Tight.

Tighter.

No!

Let go! The words she had not uttered. Swallowed, every last one of them.

The road curved to the right around the bulkhead of rock upon which the park perched. The rock climber had crossed the road and was beginning to scale the sheer rock face in front of him. It didn't have the obvious footholds of the stone wall.

Karen couldn't bear to watch. She hastened her step. She sucked the juice from the cherry in her cheek and separated the pit out with her tongue. Turning to spit the stone over the railing, she caught sight of the man again.

He was partway up the rockface, a yellow flower bonded to the cliff by sheer will. Crazy man. There were easier ways to get to the top. Didn't he know that? What was he doing there? Stupid, stupid man. It would be his own fault if he fell. His own fault. Fuckin' idiot! she wanted to yell, but hunted for another cherry instead.

The fruit was smooth in her hand, small. She squeezed, slowly. Juice exploded in her palm, cool and wet. Cherry flesh pressed out between her fingers. She opened her hand. Red. She quickened her step.

At the lookout, Kootenay Lake stretched out to the East and snaked silvery between the rising Selkirk Mountains. Closer to town, Elephant Mountain slept. Karen leaned over the railing. But where was the guy in yellow?

She scanned the cliff, moving along the curve of the railing until she spotted him. From the top, he was all arms and head, a yearning to rise in his face, his hands grasping for solidity on the face of the steep pitch.

She watched as he pulled himself up, shifting carefully, methodically, from foothold to foothold, finding always and only a reliable crevice.

Karen couldn't bear to watch. What if he fell? She wished he wasn't wearing yellow. It made her think of eggs, eggs smashing onto hard pavement. Broken, burning.

Adjusting her bandanna, Karen lowered herself onto the slatted bench behind her. She stroked her throat, and swallowing hard, opened the bag of cherries. Methodically, she began to eat. Pop, burst, chew, spit the pit, swallow. Her magenta-stained fingers turned to purple as the juice dried on her skin. The bruise would turn too. From blue, to green, to olive black and finally, sullen yellow. She couldn't imagine it completely gone.

Pop, burst, chew, spit the pit, swallow.

Swallow, remember to swallow.

She tried to propel the pits over the edge. Many fell short. She couldn't gather the necessary air to force them out. Were there obstructions in her throat? Had Sue's hands ruptured something inside? Could she still speak? She hadn't tried. Not since.

What was there to say?

She closed her eyes and saw her lover's face over hers, her dark hair electric, her eyes squinted in anger. "I'm going to kill you, I'm going to kill you, I'm going to . . ." How many times did she say it before she let go? What if she hadn't let go?

She thrust two linked cherries into her mouth.

Chew, just chew. Swallowed everything. Pits, skin, flesh, hands. Just swallow, girl.

A terrible screech resounded in her head. But no, the sound had not come from inside, but from a car. Where? Below? The guy in yellow! Oh shit!

She raced to the cliff's edge. She scanned the black below. No yellow.

No.

Tears puckered the corners of her eyes for the first time in weeks. No. It was only two cars. Two cars, bumpers nosed close in defiance. The man was still on the cliff. Still on the cliff, cautiously nearing the top.

There were three cherries left when a yellow leg breached the air. Through the blur of tears, she had not noticed his hand, the moment of arrival. He pulled himself up and over the railing, dusting off his yellow suit as he turned in her direction.

"Cherry?" she asked, her voice cracking silence.

Swan K.

Calling Me Home

The year is 1977 and I am hurrying through early fall sleet on Michigan Avenue in Lansing, the capital of Michigan. I am pulling my long out-of-style raincoat tightly around me for warmth—and because I'm wishing I could hide. Every time I turn a trick and I'm not high enough I have this sense of grey gunk filling me up inside, so much so I get nauseous. My eyes can't focus. I get panicky and I gag too easily when I'm giving head. Tonight, I wasn't high enough.

I stop at a corner store where I buy a pint of tequila—I don't mind there's no lemon or salt. People stare as I wait in line. I ignore the wet warmth on my cheeks. My mascara's probably running. The clerk takes my money and I leave, walking behind the building so no cops bust me. I down the pint of tequila, ignoring the burn in my gut, and pitch the bottle still in the bag at the corner of the building, smiling when I hear the bottle shatter.

I turn and hurry, anxious to get to Pine Street, hoping you're home, hoping you're not too drunk to fuck me. I need you to erase the smell of the trick, the feel of the man's rough skin. I start to weave a little as I cross Capital Avenue. I don't mind, I'm almost home. At least we have a home, I think, suddenly grateful for the thought of lying in our bed, staring at chipped paint, glow of street lights on the ceiling, the sound of a bus rumbling by.

I try to wipe the mascara from under my eyes with my index finger; I try to adjust my pantyhose so you don't see the runs. When I open the door, you are lying on our bed, only a little buzzed. I see you've barely begun to drink, most of a fifth of Jack Daniels sits on the floor. My mind is filled with images of your shirt off, arms around me, lean breasts against me.

I'm all desperation now. . . . You look up, rise, pull me to you, kiss me deep. You say, "Hey, gorgeous. You are mine now, hear?" I nod. I am giving myself up to you as I shiver, tears rolling down my face. You pull me to you again, bruising my mouth with yours. I want to give up totally to you, but I am not ready yet. I force myself to think of every ounce of my skin which has been touched by the john tonight, how it is now being touched, sucked, bitten, held, licked by you. His smell burned away by your scent.

"Fuck me," I say. "Please, just fuck me." You groan, I hear your breathing get shallow. "Take me rough," I plead, needing more than caresses, needing to feel you, know it is truly you. I feel I am dying as you slip on your harness. You slip my dress up and my panties off. I know you by your skin, the taste of your sweat. You call my name over and over as you slam into me, bringing me back to our world.

Soon I am feverish, my sweat runs with yours and I am murmuring back to you, moaning out the passion I finally feel as, in a rush, I return to my body, return to the butch I love.

Robert Labelle

War Story

There's a crack that runs all along the outside wall of St. Paul's Cathedral. It's about shoulder height, or at least it was just after the war. It's getting higher and higher as I get older. I have to reach up now to touch it, but it's still there. They say it was caused by the bombardment, the Blitz. Somewhere I have that photo of St. Paul's dome rising out of the smoke. "The crack doesn't represent any real damage," the newspapers had said, which sounded to me at the time like a rather miserly condolence for someone with a broken heart.

His name was Coogie. He said he was named for Jackie Coogan, the Hollywood child star. I guess Coogie got slapped with it because of his boyish looks—a babyface, quite defenceless-looking despite the coarse woolen uniform—but it was also musical-sounding, jazzy. He played the trumpet.

It was because of jazz that we met. The Americans brought it over, just like they would that awful rock 'n' roll a generation later. St. Michael's Hall in Manor Park, way in the East End, started having jazz nights around the time Coogie arrived in London. They were put on by the American servicemen because a lot of them could play. Every second Saturday, this staid, rather impoverished Church of England community hall was transformed into a smoky American jazz club—or what we imagined one would be like. Different shades of khaki would show up—Brits, Canadians and Americans. The British looked the most affected by the war, whereas even the most depressed-looking American seemed to glow all pink and healthy. Of course, they hadn't been in it for very long; they'd only arrived toward the end—to tidy things up.

So there I was in St. Michael's Hall, standing off to the side. I didn't mix well. I was intimidated by the soldiers, and I was generally ignored by the other civilians. These were mostly young women in sad print dresses. They would hover in small clusters like shivering flower patches hoping to be approached by an American.

They say we Brits are natural-born actors. Being a male of age without any apparent physical handicap meant you had to evoke a kind of stoic frown to show you were dealing with some incurable ailment that kept you out of the war. I put up a good show. Of course, beneath it all, everyone knew you were just a queer.

I stayed at the hall until the end, until the lights came up bright. Then I quietly edged my way near to the stage as they were putting things away, and stood there for a while, quite paralyzed. I had been watching him play his trumpet all evening, indiscernable amongst the other brass, until he pulled out one of those caps that they hold over the end of the instrument to make that comical, baby wah-wah sound. It seemed to suit this child so well, like it was his voice.

Our eyes met. I couldn't say anything. He smiled. "Looks like you could use a drink," he said finally, saving me, sounding like an American film.

We went and sat in the little room behind the stage while other men bustled around, paying us no attention at all. The fact that we were so ignored was significant to me later on, but at the time I was glad of it. "Coogie," he said, shaking my hand. I never told him my name. I think I was too fascinated with the sound of his to respond. He poured some darkish liquid, which I, at first, had to force down. I think it was cheap brandy, like something meant to be burnt on top of an elderly aunt's Christmas pudding. He kept feeding me more of the stuff, the two of us hardly speaking. Finally after the third or fourth drink, I was feeling bold and quite drunk. I might have done something else, but I was still aware of the other men hanging around, so I picked up a yellow pencil stub I found lying by my foot, and wrote these words on a scrap of paper: "Do you fancy me?"

He took the paper and looked at it. I watched his lips form the word "fancy"—unfamiliar to him, in *that* sense. Then he took the pencil out of my hand, and started to draw on the word, illuminating it, adding vines and leaves to the "f," turning the "a" into an upside down heart.

I took him back to my miserable Chelsea bedsitter. The both of us, so thin, took the place of one person in my single bed. The next day, and the day after, we hardly left that room. I made him a good English breakfast, or tried to. My meager wartime cupboard produced two pallid eggs cooked in that awful Betford's lard (greatly redeemed by its other uses which Coogie and I discovered), toast with gummy old marmalade, and tea without sugar.

I didn't want him to leave, but was fearful for him. He must have had to report somewhere. "Are you going AWOL?" I asked, experimenting with the words I'd seen written in the papers. He laughed at me and said no, that he was on "extended leave."

I called in sick on the Monday, but by Tuesday, I had to go to my stinking clerk's job at McClaren and Stern Solicitors. Coogie was supposed to be there when I got back. We'd even planned to go out together that evening. The note I found lying on the bed (made up so tightly you could bounce a coin on it), was addressed to Fancy.

"Got my walking papers. Heading back to the USA today!"

Later, in the middle of the night, I sat up suddenly in bed. I'd been awake anyway, but now I had this new, astounding idea: I had been an incident, a crime, used to get Coogie out of the war. Those other men who seemed to be ignoring us in that church hall were really paying attention. In fact, Coogie had let it be known that they should pay attention. Perhaps they'd even followed us.

It was a strange betrayal, one without much consequence for me. No one ever questioned or even approached me about it, though I never returned to St. Michael's. I thought of what Coogie would face back home—certainly not a hero's welcome, but I guessed he thought that anything would be better than Germans shooting at him. For me, the incident turned into a quiet little scar, my own battle wound that, if it were visible, I would have shown off to my grandchildren—if I'd had any. Instead, whenever I want to remember, I just go for my walk 'round St. Paul's, and reach up to touch that wartime crack.

Larissa Lai

Traitors

Karla should burn Trinity's letters. That's what she tells herself, but she can't quite bring herself to do it. She's not so pathetic as to read them over and over, but she fingers the soft brown paper, deepening the creases of the tripartite folds between two ragged fingernails.

She doesn't read the words, but she knows they are there. At night, though she longs for the acceptance of the cool dark, the words set her on fire, become hot fingers tracing her bum. The words burn like breath at her neck. She turns her face into her pillow, but tears won't put out the fire.

Sarah is trying to be her friend. In the safety of daylight, Sarah brings groceries so Karla will eat. Nabisco Shredded Wheat and lactose reduced milk—"for your digestion," says Sarah. Ramen and beansprouts and canned sardines, because Sarah knows that Karla is a lazy cook. A bag of miniature chocolate bars—"to cheer you up," says Sarah.

But at night, Sarah goes to Trinity's house and sits in front of the fireplace where the logs blaze and crackle loudly. Karla doesn't know what they do there, but she can imagine. Despite Sarah's boyfriend, whom Karla thinks of as boring and bad-tempered anyway, Karla imagines the worst. She thinks Trinity is conniving. She thinks Sarah is a traitor.

Fortunately there's Jane and her pack of cards. Jane and Karla play Crazy Eights on Jane's futon all afternoon until the sky begins to fade. Two of Spades, pick up two, Two of Clubs, pick up four, Two of Diamonds, pick up six, Two of Hearts, pick up eight. Karla slaps down an Eight. Change the suit. Anything but Hearts. She wishes for stars. She wishes for the quiet dark.

Jane heats up a tin of cream of mushroom soup and suggests a game of Memory, but Karla asks her to take out her guitar. They sing old college radio tunes until their eyelids begin to droop. Karla crawls under the covers with Jane, but when Jane tries to touch her she rolls away and curls against the cool white wall.

Jane and Karla go to Illuminares, the lantern festival at Trout Lake. The lake is alive with half-remembered histories, horses and fish and planets made of light and paper. A knife juggler. A fire swallower. But spectators and magicians alike all dress in fleece and gortex. Jane and Karla giggle.

Karla's mirth vanishes when she spots Trinity under the light of a paper moon. Sarah is beside her laughing, but Trinity is holding hands with another girl. *A white girl.* Karla's heart sizzles like a steak on a hot grill. Jane is white too, she thinks, for the first time. But somehow it's not the same.

Sarah smiles and waves. Trinity seems embarrassed, but looks Karla in the eye and nods politely. Karla grabs Jane's hand and pulls her behind a copiously skirted woman on stilts.

Back at Jane's apartment, Karla can't stop crying. Jane hugs her, but Karla shrinks from her embrace. Jane heats another can of mushroom soup and feels helpless.

At three in the morning there's a phone call. It's Trinity.

"You better come over," she says.

"How did you get this number?" demands Karla, indignant.

"Just come. It's an emergency. You can bring your friend if you want."

Sarah is almost unrecognizable. She won't let anyone touch her. Blood is growing crusty on her face.

"Boyfriend lost it," says Trinity. "I think it had something to do with me."

"Sarah," says Karla.

Sarah turns her head ever so slightly to acknowledge that Karla is there.

Michael Lassell

Three Drops of Blood

There were three drops of blood on Hollywood Boulevard, across the street from the Chinese Theater, in front of the Hamburger Hamlet, on a pink star no celebrity had yet laid claim to. They formed a triangle pointing south, and slightly west.

There were three more drops in exactly the same configuration on the white marble steps that led from the back of the building into the parking lot, and three more on the next corner, where a dozen pudgy brownish girls were trying to become cheerleaders on the Hollywood High track.

I studied the drops while the teeners tried to decide if I was cruising them. That's when I realized that, if a line were drawn from the first set of drops to the third, it would pass directly through the second—which is to say, the drops of blood formed an imaginary bee-line. Obviously, I had to follow it.

The next set was on Sunset, in front of that Mexican restaurant where Anglo singles go to drink margaritas after snorting movie-biz cocaine all day in faux-Elizabethan studios where Charlie Chaplin used to make silent films. The next was on the west side of LaBrea near the discount Korean luggage bungalow, the next just west of Arturo's Florist on Fountain, and the next on Detroit, just behind the remodeled McDonald's.

The last was on the south side of Santa Monica, near Formosa, where they keep trying to tear down the old Chinese cocktail lounge, and the bus stop in front of the Goldwyn Studios (where *Dynasty* was shot after they got kicked off the Fox lot). It's one of the corners where hustlers hang waiting for tricks. Tricks in trucks. Long johns with silver.

The sheriff deps know they're selling, of course, but there's no law against sitting on a bus bench, not even in West Hollywood—where it's a lot harder to be a street kid now than it was before West Hollywood became its own city and the Homosexual Majority on the city council had to prove to the *L.A. Times* that they were good upper-class Bruce Bawer-type Republican queers, not some no-account disenfranchised fag prostitutes.

What was interesting was that there were three sets of three drops each, all of which formed an even bigger triangle.

And there was this kid sitting on the bench blocking the Star of David Mortuary ad. He looked like he was sixteen. He was thin, dark. He wore a ponytail that glistened in the sunlight and an earring that didn't.

"Is this your blood?" I asked.

"No," he said, as if he didn't know what I was talking about, and he said it like a question.

I sat down next to him, waiting for the bus that never comes.

"You know anything about it?" I asked, casually putting my arm up on the split plywood bench so my hand brushed up against his denim shoulder.

He shifted his weight and uncrossed his legs so the frayed crotch of his jeans pointed in my direction.

I took him home anyway.

He was Shoshone and said he was from Idaho. He was adopted, so he wasn't really eligible for tribal politics or anything. He was raised in Seattle, or so he said, and had no accent of any kind, so he could have been from the San Fernando Valley. Or Ohio. He said he was twenty, which was close enough. He had a soft flat stomach with coarse dark hair that reminded me of the scalps I had seen at the Indian museum in Harlem. But maybe if I didn't know he was an Indian, I would have thought of something else.

I told him my grandfather said we were part Cree.

"It's not the part that shows," he said.

In bed he let me do anything I wanted—so I did it all. Except kiss him, of course. Many a hustler will not kiss, no matter how much you pay them, which is a thing worth knowing in advance. I can spend all night kissing a man and never come and think I've had the greatest sex in the world. Which is probably why they don't do it. Always leave them wanting more.

That night it began to rain. It rained for six days. Hunks of the coast slid into the ocean. Cats drowned when underground parking lots filled with murky water. Cars were washed down Laurel Canyon by walls of rain. January in Paradise. When the sun came out, the blood was gone.

A few weeks later, I was walking down the boulevard and ran into a couple dozen people in wheelchairs carrying sledge hammers at the corner of Hollywood near the Roosevelt Hotel. It seems the Hollywood Chamber of Commerce said it wouldn't make curb cuts in the Walk of Fame, which pretty much meant that people in wheelchairs could just stay off Hollywood Boulevard, which meant out of Hollywood. Could tarnish the tinsel, you know?

So these wheelchair people just called the papers and showed up with sledge hammers and said that if the City of Hollywood wouldn't make the curb cuts, then they would. There were curb cuts going in by the very next day, and people on wheels were taking Instamatic shots of the Michael Jackson star just like everybody else.

The thing to remember is, if it's raining, the Hollywood Walk of Fame is slippery as ice.

So a few weeks later Mahalia Jackson's name went down on the blood star. Or maybe it wasn't that one. Of course, Mahalia herself had been dead for years. There was the usual ceremony. Somebody sang. A woman. It was supposed to be a spiritual. And maybe it was.

I never saw Tim again, either. That's what he said his name was.

His nose could have been on nickels.

If he had killed me, I would have forgiven him.

Joe Lavelle

Ten Budweisers

You notice him at the Lisbon as you knock back your first Budweiser. Light brown hair, green eyes. Five-ten. Weight? Who knows. Slim, though. Through the tautness of his t-shirt you see the definition of his upper abdomen and chest. Great arms too. "Definitely DWB"—definition without bulk. The ideal. Despite his smile you go to the Curzon. It is only nine-thirty. The Lisbon is dead. The Curzon might be busier. Might offer other alternatives.

The Curzon *is* busier, but the selection is poor. Midway through your second Budweiser you notice DWB enter as you stand by the entrance. He smiles at you again. You smile back. Then Andrew approaches you, launches into a conversation—a monologue, really. Something about Phoenix. As Andrew talks you watch as DWB orders a drink and wanders to the back of the bar. After the conversation you wander to the back. No sign of him. You order another Bud and return to talk to Andrew. You are more attentive this time. He'd split with Phoenix. What did he want—sympathy? Andrew bought you your fourth Bud. You go for a cruise.

You know lots of guys in the Curzon tonight. Some nod at you, acknowledge your existence, but only just. Nothing changes. No one meets your eye. Andrew returns. Babbles about fuck-all, except Phoenix and your being drunk all the time. What about him? When was the last time you saw Andrew sober—truly sober? That's possibly why you're friends.

At midnight you go to the Palace. You wait patiently in the queue. When you get to the front the doorman gives you the once over. Maybe the Palace isn't such a good idea after all? Though the doorman hesitates he nods you in. Maybe your previous visit hadn't been as you remembered. You pay the entrance fee—the equivalent of three Budweisers. You wait for what seems like ages to get served at the bar counter. The Palace doesn't serve Budweiser on tap so you settle for a bottle. A voice in the crowd behind you says, "That fucking drunk's in again." You think, Does he mean me? Then forget about it. The Palace has "entertainment" tonight. During your sixth Bud you finally realize that the drag act is drivel. During your seventh Bud you realize you are bored with male strippers too. So much for entertainment. You notice DWB talking to an older guy. The older guy buys him a drink. A coke. You smile at him. DWB smiles back. Andrew arrives and you dance. The Palace loses its allure. As you exit DWB winks. You wink back at him and stumble.

At the Escape you order another Bud and feel paranoid from the joint you smoked as you walked up from the Palace. The Escape is bouncing. You aren't. You think of the past—all thirty-four years of it. You think of the bills you haven't paid. You think of work in the morning. You think of your family, lovers and almost-lovers. You think of sex and that brings you out of it. That and the fact that you realize that DWB is standing next to you. You ask if he wants a drink—no introduction, no hello, no "Hi, I saw you earlier." Just, "D'ya wanna drink?" He wants a coke. You buy him a coke. You have your ninth Bud.

DWB's name is David. Lives in Bootle. He's twenty-five. Said he was from London, but has a Manchester accent. You pick up on that. "Well, I lived in Manchester for six years," he says. You accept it. He asks if you want to dance. "Nah," you say. Too drunk. He asks if he can go back to your place. He can't—you're living back with your parents, temporarily. He lives with his sister. He's seen you around. Doesn't say anything about you being drunk. He's either lying or being polite, you think. His next statement makes you forget that. "I really wanna fuck yer!"

You share a joint as you walk toward an alley. In a doorway, just inside from the street, he kisses you. A great kiss. He wants you. Fondles your cock—hand down the front of your Levi's. Doesn't let you reciprocate. Undoes your belt. Undoes the buttons on the crotch of your Levi's. Your Levi's drop. Smooth hands. Warm hands. Caring hands. You pass him a condom. The weight and warmth of him against your back then. . . .

At AA, three weeks later, you sit and listen. Your mother has forced you there. Losing your job was the last straw. It is your second meeting.

Karen Leduc

Chocolate Chip Cookies

As I dialed the familiar number, I could feel the lump in my throat build. It had been a few months since I last spoke to my mom. I hoped she was home; I wasn't ready for the usual difficult conversation with my dad.

It took her a few rings to reach the phone. "Hello," said the voice.

I twisted the telephone cord around my hand. "Hi Mom, it's me," I replied, trying to sound relaxed.

"Well, hello, Diana. What prompted this call? You're not in trouble are you?"

Mom, I'm in love with a woman.

"No, Mom, I'm fine, really." I took a deep breath, trying to calm my stomach. "Actually . . . what I wanted was to . . . get your chocolate chip cookie recipe. It's for a potluck." I felt my voice changing, accommodating. Why did every conversation with her make me feel like I was eight years old again?

"Oh, well then, hold on a moment while I get my recipe cards."

Mom, your daughter is a lesbian.

I could hear her walking across the pale blue linoleum, saw her steps around the cluttered room in my mind. She'd been sitting at the little pine table Dad made years ago, no doubt reading some women's magazine, as usual. Muffled voices filtered through the phone, probably a daytime talk show. How many times had we sat in that smoky kitchen together? Throughout my entire childhood the only stable thing in our lives had been that kitchen. There, over cups of hot chocolate in Grandma's china, we connected at least on some level. She would never understand my life, and often wouldn't try, but together in that room we could forget about our differences for a while.

Mom, she's so beautiful and strong, I know you'll like her.

"Okay then, dear, do you have something to write this down with?"

"Uh, yes, I do. . . ." I could feel myself shrinking into childhood behaviour. My fingers were entangled in the phone cord, and I was hugging my knees to my chest. Why is it so hard to tell her? I'd already come out to almost everyone for several years, including most people at work. In person we would find this conversation impossible—she would not be able to look me in the eyes once it was said.

Mom, please be happy for me.

I could hear her voice and watched myself automatically write down the words, but I felt detached from myself. Why should she have this influence over me? Does it matter at all if I tell her? It really doesn't make any difference in her life whatsoever—why was I finding this so hard?

"Did you get all that, Diana?" her voice cut into my thoughts.

"Yes, Mom, I think so. Thanks."

"Your father will be so upset that he missed you. He's out with some friends this evening. You remember the Rosens? You dated their son for a while? Well, you'll never believe it, but he's getting married this year. I certainly never thought that boy would settle down. Are you sure you're doing well? You don't need anything? You sound upset."

"I'm fine, Mom, honest. I don't need anything, really. I guess I'll talk to you again soon."

"Oh, well, all right then, dear. It's been good to hear your voice again. Remember you can call anytime, don't be a stranger."

"Okay, well, bye. . . . "

"Bye, dear." She hung up the phone.

I sat for a while staring blankly at the telephone. It was the sound of Kathryn's keys unlocking the front door that finally broke my reverie. I had missed the chance to free myself.

Mom, this is your daughter who loves you.

I grabbed a sheet of paper and rolled it into the typewriter.

Denise Nico Leto

The Bicycle Riders

She comes in the door and a wind seems to pick up around her, a whole weather system follows the blush in her cheeks and settles comfortably in the small of her back. I see her moving this way, then that, changing course, colliding gracefully with unseen elemental forces, holding them close, breathing in and out so that all the molecules are at once touched and transformed. And I am the only one who sees this. To the naked eye of everyone else, a woman walks in a door. But to my eyes an inescapable violet sea rushes in and I am carried by its beauty; made to break and open and fall again. And this is the shore. The place I arrive at with her. All this within seconds, with no words spoken, without her knowing, without my really knowing.

We ride together. *This is what we do*. I have rarely seen her sitting or walking. I have no idea what she looks like standing in a line, say, or reading a book. I have sometimes seen her eat, and again, I am made to see all the underneath things. A geological view upwards from warmth to sea level. She picks up an olive. A kalamata with an oily sheen, skin the colour of flushed wheat; she picks up this tiny oval and carries it to her mouth. Her mouth opens; oval meets oval. The olive is gone. She chews. Swallows. I watch. A gesture as ordinary as it is old and yet what I see is not ordinary at all: as in typical. This is ordinary as in two women breaking bread. Ordinary as in *I am born, a tree grows, lightning strikes, the wind comes up*. Ordinary as in a bond, certain as breathing. It is just that love is a conduit of infinite direction and her eating is one direction, my eyes watching another. And on and on and on. How else can I explain it? Spin us all out on a wheel and somewhere our spokes touch the centre.

Our riding is an invocation. It is a little otherworldly and childlike.

Remember long ago in childhood time: playing until late, missing dinner, night falls, you are in trouble and nothing could be more beautiful. "We are wonderfully and fearfully made." O yes. Heaven. Our riding is an invocation, to what, I don't know. Others speed by with neon toe clips and nylon outfits and tight-fitting black lycra shorts and helmets that look like they deflect a little too much. And we are in our own world. We are in a certain time in a certain place and no matter where we are, we are in our own world.

For one thing, we know that on our rides we must eat. Not because our stomachs are empty; not because we need it to fill up all the missing places; but because it *tastes* good. Because it is fun. Because it is what we must do. We pedal to a stopping place, pull over and eat. Ravioli from the deli dripping with sauce. Blood oranges that we peel and look at for a long time before we bite into them, wine-coloured juice running down our fingers. Almonds and dried pineapple and banana chips. Popcorn buttered and speckled with parmesan cheese. Popcorn that makes our hands greasy and leaves tiny husks from the kernels clinging to our teeth. Bright orange cheese crackers that we wouldn't normally eat become delicious, become somehow necessary. All this spread out on a red and white checkered tablecloth in the reeds, in a marsh, in a park, in a city somewhere on a map no doubt.

Though we never read a map. I believe we travel wholly without them. It is hard to think clearly or along a sensible line when seas are being formed and whole memories invented. And when I am seeing things come bursting to life, I must pay close attention and wave unnecessary details by. It is still and always important, however, to wear our helmets which we seem to do when we are the lone riders on a safe and soft downy country road and which we seem to completely forget when we are riding somewhere in The City. Fighting traffic, and wind, and exhaust, and terrific buses which clog and sputter and take up all the space in the road leaving us only a thin line on top of which we must balance everything that could ever come to pass. Beleaguered, we laugh at our bare heads, bobbing fiercely, exposed and free and vulnerable as peeled eggs.

We laugh, she and I. On our rides we laugh because things have depth and dimension and therefore mirth. Even if in the depth there is sadness, we can see a suggestion of the joy which ambles softly just out of reach. And we laugh. Something charmed suspends between us. Something out of time and place. We laugh because our love engulfs us. Spreads out before us in tablecloths and sea shores and thin white lines in the roadway. Sitting on a bike in San Francisco in 1996 with a strong headwind; two lesbians must either race frantically or giggle. We giggle.

Once, in the middle of our picnic, a dampness hit the air. A gauzy mist and then suddenly a storm. Rain pounded around us, surly golf balls of water bouncing frenetically. I ask you, has the rain ever been so fast, so ferocious? Our bikes were sluggish and protesting. Water and wind and leaves and gusts of everything temporal and unknown swirling, exacting visibility to nearly zero—scratchy twigs and bubbling puddles and slimy rocks. Mud the colour of eggplant splashing up onto our legs, our bellies, our mouths. And I fall. I glide helplessly from my bike. I sprawl out into the muddy path. My knee stings. Rain falls mightily. Mistakes are forgotten. I am in a slippery, delicious world. I suspect snails and underwater currents press against me. Forests soar above. Clouds dash over trees, giant green branches hang heavily down. The water is a thick syrup I drink. The rain is fast, unpredictable, stunning. Everything else is slow and falls out of focus. Since when has my body pressed firmly into mud and *when* will I lay like this again? This sinking lulls me and I slowly rise. Although my body moves, my limbs are disconnected from skeletal imperative. I ride with pine needles and twigs in my hair, my mouth is full of mud, my feet move like a lazy windmill round and round and though I can see very little, I do not fall again.

The rain enveloped us, hurled us into water as never before. And we rode carefully with the weather and the only thing left that mattered was the warmth we finally found in the car. The damp, steamy warmth. The way the windows fogged up and the way the mud hardened on our skin. We laughed because things unplanned are most believable.

Consider the iced coffee she places in her water bottle. Consider the condensation that settles around the bottle as the air whips around it warming the mixture, settling it. She must have her coffee and places it happily—dripping and brimming and frothing—into her plastic water bottle. No other bicyclist in the world has done this, or ever will. Propriety or embarrassment would get in the way. But this one cares less for that than the way coffee sweat glistens in the sunlight. "This is perfectly delicious," she says, "this is heaven. You must taste it." But my heaven tastes and looks nothing like coffee, iced or hot, and so we ride. She

Shaun Levin

Luscious Fruit

Hey! Wanna suck my dick?"

I open the gate and the cooks make their way into the base.

"Hey, Amos," Ziv says. "Let the poor guy give you a blow job."

My eyes are in my book. On the page. I read. There are words here. And I concentrate on each one. On each letter. As if I didn't know this would happen. It always comes to this in the end. It's just a matter of time before they start. And standing here on guard duty in the early hours of the morning, like a sitting duck, is just asking for it. So I wait, and listen. My eyes are still on the page. I know they'll have more to say before their boots stop pounding the tar and they disappear into the kitchen.

"What's the matter with you?" Amos' voice is further away now. Almost at the kitchen door. "You think I let any old arsehole touch my pipe?"

Amos grabs his crotch, makes a whistling sound, and thrusts his pelvis out at me. They roar with laughter.

"Come and get it."

And they laugh. They love it. Just like yesterday, that boisterous giggle, as if they had some secret to share. But everybody knows they're the ones. Who else would have done it. Not that it bothers me, really. After all, not everyone gets to star on the toilet door. Just me and Shosh the switchboard operator. Shosh gives good head. Call . . .

Then, at lunch today in the mess, aluminium trays of deep-fried schnitzel and mashed potatoes on the tables. Facing me, a young corporal is eating. He eats only with his fork. He's new at the base. Someone asks him, and he says he was a paratrooper before he was wounded up north. And there's something about that red beret and those maroon boots of his. I try not to stare. I try not to. So I concentrate, and slice my schnitzel into thin strips, stick my fork into each one, and crown it with mash.

"Could you pass the bread, please?" the paratrooper says.

I slide the faded green bread basket across the table.

"Thank you," he says.

"Where were you wounded?" I ask, looking him in the eyes.

"Near Tyre." The paratrooper takes the bread and says: "Thank you." Again.

But I want to know where the scar is. Where it lies on that oh-so-beautiful body of yours. I want to lick your skin, you see. I want to search for that healing wound. Across your chest and stomach and groin. With my tongue. Oh, lucky surgeon singled out to draw the bullet from your flesh.

The paratrooper eats in silence and then leaves.

Sari comes over to the table after he's gone. We pick at the cold potato mash with our forks.

"Mm, isn't this delicious?" she says.

"Oh. Yes."

"I could go on eating forever," she says.

"Insatiable. Aren't we?" I say.

Dana and Sigal join us. Three girls at one table—Sari, Dana, and Sigal—and it's just all too much for Amos. An opportunity not to be missed. He struts out of the kitchen like a fly to. . . . Chest out like a peacock.

"Hey, baby, baby, baby."

Ziv is left in the kitchen to do the dishes. Amos settles in now. Folds his legs, folds his arms, rests his elbow on his knee. He takes a puff from his cigarette and grins at Sari.

"Feel like a little dessert?" he says.

"How little?" she says.

And they all laugh. The girls laugh.

"There's enough to go round," he says.

Sari raises her eyebrows, turns up the corner of her mouth.

Amos puts his cigarette out in left-over mashed potato, and brings his chair closer to the table. He rests his elbow on the table, his palm open to arm-wrestle. He looks Sari in the eyes.

"Give me your hand," he says.

"Pick on someone your own size," Sari laughs. "Let's see you and Danny."

"Nah," Amos says. "Let's go outside. Like men."

Quick calculation: better to arm-wrestle. I could never win a fist-fight. Never been good at one-on-one combat. Although I'd love to watch my knuckles sail through your pink face and collide like a hammer with your pug nose. I'd love to see those brains of yours splattered on the kitchen wall.

The girls crowd around and Amos pulls up his sleeve. His skin is so smooth and tight. The veins run up his thick arm. Such beautiful green veins. If only. Smooth tummy, as well, I suppose. Protruding belly-button. And nice sweet-smelling sparse wiry pubes. He clears the table. Dirty plates, cutlery, bread basket all swept aside. If only you were here to see. We face each other across the table.

"Go for it, Amos!"

"Show him, Danny!"

This is going to be mine. Watch me. By the strength of my arm. By my mighty hand.

"Let's go outside," Amos says. "Like men."

We clap palms together. His skin is soft. Amos' fingers are around my hand.

"Let's get this over with," he says. "One, two and *hop*."

Now. Puuuuuush. Down. Yes. Down you buttfucker. This is for DANNY THE FAGGOT on the bathroom door. Went in for a shit yesterday, crouched down on my haunches over the hole and right there. Bright red on grey. On the back of the door. Still there today. You did it. Who else would have? Down down, this is mine. It's mine. Come watch this. Look. Come look. Ben Rosen, dark face with stubble and black eyes, jumping out of his sleeping bag. At me. Thick hairy forearms. Coming for me. Hands flying. Oh my big boy. Come watch. And that night, the car swerving in to cut us off. Onto the side of the road. That young boy, fucking teenager. Maybe he's got a knife. Just drive away already. He runs up to the window. Open up. Open up, fucker. Just drive, drive already. The car won't start. Just go. The engine's dead. Open the fucking window, he says. In my face. His hand. Shit. Didn't feel a thing. All numb. Can't get away. Drive, just drive. My boy. Down down, fucker, down you go. Oh my big strong boy. Come watch. My big big big strong boy. Joel

Cohen, come on, mommy's boy. Big strong boy. By the bike-shed near the *sukkah* and laughing. Everyone laughing wildly. Cry baby tit. Suck your mommy's tit. Yes. Down. And if it's nice. Take a slice. If it's sticky. This is it. I'm going to do it. Down. Watch. My big big big strong boy. Lick my pippy, cocksucker.

"Agh," Amos says, getting up, shaking his hand, moving back to the kitchen. "We should have gone outside, like men."

Later that evening I'm at the gate again. On guard duty. Ziv and Amos are coming down the path. My book's in my pocket. I slide the gate open.

"Amos, Amos, let's give it to him the way he likes it!"

Their boots march down the tar road. I watch their backs.

"Amos, man. What's the matter with you?"

R. Zamora Linmark

Kalihi in Farrah

Everybody in Kalihi wants to be Farrah. The name itself sounds sultry and expensive. Who doesn't want to be the reigning queen of pin-up posters thumb-tacked on every wall of every house? A swimsuit goddess with long and graceful legs, pearly-white teeth, glossy lips, roller-derby hips, and a million dollar smile on a King-size waterbed next to none other than the six-million dollar man himself. Who doesn't want that full-volumed, sunshine-gold mane: side-combed, then feathered at the top, and curled along the sides? Who in Kalihi doesn't want to be Farrah?

One:
Ernesto Cabatbangan, a Freshman at Sanford B. Dole Intermediate, doesn't want to be Farrah; he wants to be inside her. He bought on discount all her posters from DJ's Record Store because his calabash cousin manages the Pearlridge branch.

He says he can't get it up unless she's there watching over him, smiling. At times, it gets so bad he sprays the room, bull's-eyeing Farrah's mouth.

Two:
The two-hour season premiere of the hit series *Charlie's Angels,* starring ex-*Rookie* Kate Jackson (Sabrina Duncan), commercial model Jaclyn Smith (Kelly Garrett) and newcomer Farrah Fawcett-Majors (Jill Munro) attracted 5,483,097.99 households, according to the Nielsen Ratings. A week later, Edgar Ramirez formed the Triple-FC, the Farrah Fawcett Fan Club, with him acting as the President, Katherine Katrina-Trina Cruz (1st Vice President), Caroline Macadangdang (2nd Vice-President),

Jeremy Batongbacal (Secretary), Judy Ann Katsura (Treasurer), and Loata Faalele (Sergeant-at-Arms).

The Triple-FC's primary goal was to keep the TV show on the air and the blonde bombshell's career alive. This meant watching the weekly detective show, including re-runs, wearing t-shirts with Farrah Fawcett iron-on stickers, buying the Jill Munro doll, playing the *Charlie's Angels* board game, trading *Charlie's Angels* cards, and praying the *novena* every Wednesday with Father Pacheco at Our Lady of the Mount Church.

Once a week, the club met at Edgar's house to: 1) write letters to Farrah Fawcett c/o ABC Network; 2) show off their collections of Farrah memorabilia—cut-outs from glamour magazines, Farrah's latest swimsuit poster; 3) roleplay scenes from the show; and 4) discuss socio-politically-charged issues the show tackled, such as prostitution, lesbian undertones and Orientalism.

Though they were a bit bitter after Farrah left the top-rated show, they continued their Farrah piety, anxiously waiting to see if she would burn up the screen with her movie *Sunburn.* Unfortunately, it received no tans on the big screen and the Triple-FC fizzled and died.

Three:

Orlando Domingo's favourite letter is F, not F for Filipino, but F for Farrah, and he won't answer to his friends and classmates who call him Orlando, his teachers who address him as Mr. Domingo, and his mother who nicknamed him Orling.

Just call me Farrah, he says, as in Far-Out Farrah, or Faraway Farrah.

It all started with *Charlie's Angels* and his addiction to Farrah's hair. One night he borrowed his mother's box of curlers and curled his hair before going to bed. When he woke up, he propped himself in front of the vanity, and blow-dried, at an extra-high speed, the rows of hair caged in pink. Then he removed the curlers and began the arduous task of styling his hair until he achieved the million-dollar mane coveted by Farrah wanna-be's and Flip queens.

Farrah, Farrah, what's the secret to your hair? they ask him. And all he says is, Once a Farrah Flip, always a Farrah Flip. Or, A Flip is a Flip is a Flip. Or, Secret.

He's flipped out, his classmates at Farrington High told each other the moment he entered the classroom sporting Farrah's hairdo. The next thing you know, he goin' be packin' on make-up and dressin' up like her, too.

Sure enough, on the day after the *Charlie's Angels* episode titled "Consenting Adults" was aired, the one where Farrah as Detective Jill Munro goes undercover as a call girl and delivers her immortal line "I-never-give-anything-I-can-sell," Orlando strutted into class wearing a fire-engine red polyester long-sleeved shirt tied around his twenty-four-inch waist, yellow bell-bottoms and Famolare platforms. His face was painted courtesy of Helena Rubinstein's "The Paris Boutique Kit," which includes lipstick and nail lacquer, and Aziza's "Shadow Boutique." Twelve shimmering eye colours for every occasion.

What next? the teachers asked during their lunch break. Principal Shim must do something about this. *Ahora mismo!* The following week, after Orlando viewed the episode called "The Death of a Roller-Derby Queen," he wheeled onto campus on black leather Cobra skates, wearing see-through Dove shorts, red Danceskins and red-and-white knee and elbow pads. And, as always, fully made-up with Farrah's hairdo that withstood the Kalihi breeze with the aid of an entire can of unscented Aqua Net hair spray.

We gotta do something before our boys catch this madness and start huddling in skirts and pompoms, the football coaches Mr. Akana and Mr. Ching told Principal Shim. You gotta do something. *Pronto*. Suspend him, expel him, we don't care, but you gotta keep him away from our boys if you want the team to bring home the OIA title.

Principal Shim leaned back in his vinyl chair and stared at Orlando Domingo's file. He thought of the possibility of expelling or suspending him on the grounds of disturbing and endangering the mental health of the other students, especially the athletes. But he couldn't. Not after he examined Orlando's records:

Born in Cebu in 1962; Immigrated to Hawai'i at the age of ten; Lives with mother in Lower Kalihi; Father: Deceased; Speaks and writes in English, Spanish, Cebuano, and Tagalog; Top of the Dean's List; Current GPA: 4.0; This year's Valedictorian; SAT scores totaling 1500 out of 1600; Voted Most Industrious and Most Likely To Succeed four years in a row; Competed and won accolades in Speech and Math Leagues, High School

Select Band, Science Fairs and Mock Trials; Current President of Keywanettes, National Honour Society and the Student Body Government; Plans to attend Brown University in the fall—to take up law.

I can't expel him. Maybe suspension. Then he squirmed at the thought that Orlando could easily turn the tables and charge him, Mr. Akana, Mr. Ching and the Department of Education for discriminating against a Filipino faggot whose only desire was to be Farrah from Farrington, as in Farrah, the Kalihi Angel.

Principal Shim closed the file and threw it on his desk.

L.D. Little

Graham and Colin

When Graham was twenty-one he knew no one would ever love him. Several men had tried him, then disappeared. His own father's gaze focussed beyond him, as if seeing another son, the one who should have been.

Colin Redpath chose him out of the crowd. He spotted him at the bar where Graham was waiting tables, asked about him, cajoled him, courted him for weeks, took him on his knee. Graham, dazzled and laughing in relief, hugged his neck and kissed his thinning temples. Colin drew him close and told him all the things people never tell; pulled back his skin and showed him the wounds on his soul. "You're the only one I can trust. The only one who understands." And Graham knew it was true.

Graham gave up his job downtown and moved into Colin's house in Etobicoke.

Graham polished the candlesticks. He shopped for the crispest head of Romaine, brightest starfruit, ripest avocado; prize offerings to their love. After dinner they lay on the rug in front of the fireplace, finishing a bottle of wine. Graham served a dessert cheese. Colin traced Graham's face with his finger.

"You'd look better with short hair," he said. "It's too red."

The next day Graham made an appointment with a hair salon.

Graham read novels, cleaned the spare rooms, watched *All My Children,* then *Another World.* He called a young man he used to work with and listened to him chat breezily about restaurant politics. He felt a stab of envy. And fear. He made the Scallops Mornay that Colin loved.

"I was, uhm, thinking of going back to work. . . ."

Colin's eyes froze. He stopped chewing, pushed his plate away. Graham felt a huge arctic silence engulf him, freezing his lungs until it hurt to breathe. He stammered over bits of explanation, reason, as Colin stood, crossed the room and spit a half-chewed mouthful into the sink. The colour drained from Graham's face. Colin retreated upstairs and locked their bedroom door. Next morning Colin stalked silently off to work and returned home, late, all sadness and gin. Graham felt he would drown in regret. He didn't want a job. He followed Colin through the living room, reached out to touch his back, "Colin, please. I love you."

The silence exploded, cracked suddenly by a flying lamp, a torrent of shouts and a slap that sent Graham sprawling across the hearth. A flash of pain sprayed, like buckshot, up his arm. The door slam rattled the windows, shook the house. Terrified, trembling, stunned, Graham lay where he had fallen, curled in on himself.

When Colin finally returned, he brought roses and wine and promises. He cried into Graham's lap. Kissed the bruise on his arm. He was sorry a hundred times. All Graham had to do was forgive. Just this once. It was the easiest thing Graham had ever done.

The next time didn't count because Colin had drunk too much wine and Graham had made him angry and the bruises were very small. And Colin made up with a honeymoon vacation to France. They made love all through the long mornings, strolled the cafés in the afternoons, and found a beach where they could kiss and lie naked. Graham was the happiest he had ever been.

On Graham's twenty-third birthday Colin gave him a beautiful, long-haired kitten with swirls of white and butterscotch and rich, smoky grey fur. Graham melted in joy. He named her Margaret, for his mother. For the kind of love that goes on forever.

Graham felt badly about the time he ended up tumbling down the stairs and spraining his wrist. It hadn't really been Colin's fault. But Colin took him out to dinner for two weeks so he wouldn't have to cook. Graham wished Colin wasn't so jealous. He did everything he could to prove he loved him.

Colin's job gave him a lot of stress. Colin needed him. Graham tried to keep things nice at home. He grew flowers on the window sill. When Colin drank, Graham shrank into silence, but never far enough. In the empty mornings Graham played the radio and danced waltz after waltz with Margaret, burying his face in her luxurious coat.

Graham wanted so badly to go back to university; just a course or two in English literature. Someone to talk with. But Colin didn't like him going out alone. Colin and Graham were invited to a party. Graham sparkled, laughed at stories, held out his glass to be refilled. Someone touched his leg. Someone squeezed his shoulder. Colin drove home, blood roaring over Graham's protestations. Punched to the floor, a flashing kick left him groping like a fish. For air.

The fist-sized bruise brought cherry chocolates and a rose. Colin offered the world; Graham asked for an English course. He felt like a whore.

On the day of registration Colin changed his mind. "It was only a little slap, for chrissake."

When Graham first began shaving dollars off the grocery money, hiding them away in a secret envelope, he told himself it was to buy something nice for Colin. On their fourth anniversary Colin took him out to dinner and Graham, lingering a heart-beat behind, stealthily pocketed their waiter's tip. He felt deeply ashamed.

Margaret made a nest in Colin's black woollen overcoat; cozy, deep, lined with her own long silky hairs. In the morning Graham heard the curse, felt the whiz of the body past his ear, the thud, felt the crack like it was his own spine. He sat forever, stroking her limp body.

The next day Graham read the want ads, then cried for hours before rushing to have dinner ready on time; bathing his face in cold water to shrink his puffy eyes. He made arrangements. On the first of the month he packed what he could carry: summer clothes, clock radio, three novels, his childhood collection of Christopher Robin. He had one month's rent and thirty-eight dollars left for bus fare and food. He wore his good suit and shoes; too bulky to pack.

At twenty-five years of age Graham sat on a bare mattress, in an attic room all his own, and trembled with freedom.

Jannathan Falling Long

Ketchup

Ronnie cornered me, knocked my breath out," Garland said.

"I'm goin' to wire your jaw shut, boy, if you don't shut up," his dad yelled. They were speeding in the pick-up truck, the right tires spinning in the gravel.

Ronnie had also grabbed Garland's ass and had said *Next time, this*, but Garland didn't dare tell his dad about that. What was it Ronnie knew about him?

That was yesterday. Now Garland sits at the kitchen table, wearing his sister Debbie's underwear.

He has emptied the kitchen cabinets and broken all the plates—some were difficult to crack. Everything is off the pantry shelves. But the oatmeal his mom made for them this morning is still on the stove. . . . He's saving it for her.

The fridge is empty too. Its door is wedged open by its former contents. Shards of glass stick up from the pile of food on the floor—ketchup, old salad, beans and milk, all mixed together, smelling sweet and ridiculous.

If he throws himself on the glass, then everyone will finally know how very different blood and ketchup look.

Garland wipes tears off the note. He has a gun. He dares himself—not to kill himself; he's gathered strength enough for that—but to write the words, *I am gay*.

Just two words, he thinks. Three, he corrects himself, and laughs. They will look funny beside what he already has written—*I love you, Mom.*

Garland starts. There's someone at the door! He scrawls out the words, *I'm gay*.

There, he thinks, now it's two words. And he laughs again. He lays down the pen, picks up the gun, and points it to his temple.

This is like a dream, he thinks. He can't understand why everything is so funny.

The door opens.

What if it's Prince Charming, he wonders, smiles, and pulls.

Michael MacLennan

The Adjudication

I bought new sheets, $125 percale, and I don't even know if he'll sleep in the bed with me. I washed them in hot water to get rid of the creases and then gave them a light iron, which I never do, but you can always tell when a sheet's been ironed, like in hotels.

He's on the ferry over here now, his legs stretched up on the seat opposite him. I bet he's slouching so that his jeans ride up his thighs, wrinkle at his crotch which he might brush absently—maybe reading a book, maybe looking out the window and wondering about me.

I've mopped the floors in case he's allergic to cats and scrubbed the stains in the kitchen's ochre arborite. I even planted some pansies in the barren, slug-infested bed in front of the house. I bought foods I've never cooked with before: mangoes, couscous, fresh mint. I don't know what to do with them, but I wanted different things around.

He phoned me two days ago and just the sound of his voice, the smile of it coming through, made my heart leap. I've written him four letters in the last four months, sending measured volleys with careful determination. It hasn't bothered me that he doesn't write back. I figured my last letter went too far. Anyone could tell by the handwriting how much my heart swelled just writing his name at the top of a page. A week later he phoned. To ask if I could put him up for the night before he catches a flight to Amsterdam the following morning.

We met when I was in Victoria for a youth theatre festival. I was the technical adjudicator; my job was to judge design and stage management. He judged acting and directing. He lived in Victoria. They put me up at the Empress Hotel. I invited him to my room for our final deliberations where we picked the top three plays and figured out which one would go to the national competition. He tromped in, going on about how wide the hallways were. I cracked open the lock on the mini-bar.

"Look at this bathroom!" he said, running his hand over the black marble counter.

"They upgraded me," I said, like an apology.

"Listen, I'm wrecked—could I have a shower in there?"

He was already kicking off his Birkenstocks and sliding down his pants so I just squeezed a towel out of the steel rack and handed it to him. He gave me a wink that was either an invitation or just saying isn't this rented opulence fun, and turned on the taps.

I stood at the bathroom door and watched his darkened form humming behind the translucent shower door. The steam flowing past me expired on the cool glass, the sky darkening outside. I thought about stripping, sliding the glass door open and stepping in. But chances were he'd laugh and tell me just wait a minute until he got out, or he'd punch me and call me faggot, or maybe I'd catch him jerking off. I looked down at the tiles, the jockey shorts in a pool of pale softened denim. I could have picked them up, held them a moment, but I was afraid he'd notice.

The fitted sheet shrank in the wash, so I keep pulling off one corner when I attach another. I must look like a fool, a clown in a bad gag. When it's finally done the cotton floats splendidly on the mattress, tight as a drum. Even with new sheets, the bed still smells of me. But I think he might like that. At the end of the night I'll just say, "Why don't you crash with me? I can set the alarm for you." The top sheet's off-centre, so there's more on his side in case I'm a sheet hog.

Mark came out of the hotel bathroom steaming, his skin flushed by the heat, by so white a towel resting on his narrow hips. He had a second towel as a turban because he had all that hair, and it didn't look weird.

I've never had a fling before. It's not that I'm ugly. I'm not. I just don't know how to make moves, to make something I feel into something I do. I'm not really sure about Mark, but he must be getting the idea if he knows anything about courtship. How else could he sit there in a towel and talk about the best play we saw, his knees wide open and slouching off the couch toward me like I was a magnet. I could see what was underneath and just tried to keep thinking about the plays but he saw my hard-on and was smiling at me sitting there asking him what he thought, getting a wet spot on my khakis and trying to cover it with my notes. And when he changed back into his shirt and jeans, he did it right in the doorway to the bathroom so I could see him. He kept talking and didn't even put his underwear back on, just shoved them in his front pocket. Gave me his address. Said he had to go and then he did.

So tonight I'll either be tearing back the bedsheets as he throws me down on the squeaky mattress, and neither of us will care about the cotton's softness or if candle wax or lube or cum soaks into the new cloth. Or it will be him in a sleeping bag and me sliding into the cool sheets alone, whishing my legs between the sheets back and forth like blades, so smooth nothing catches. I look at the bed now, the careful folds betraying the eagerness of the maker. They'll be kicked off, those sheets. No matter what, they'll be kicked to the bottom by morning.

Tom McDonald

Paying the Rent

My twentieth birthday and I'm squatting down on the largest dildo I've ever seen much less taken. Suddenly there's a loud pop and Gordon, the director, says "Fuck!" and we're taking an early lunch. Artie, the sound man, argues with Richie, the lighting guy, about how to make white clam sauce. Next they talk about auto insurance and then Artie's passing around snapshots of his grandkids, getting pissed 'cause I get lube on his grandson's little league photo. Eventually the camera's fixed and I've got a butt plug bigger than my fist up my ass and Gordon's telling me to lick my lips and twist my nipples and then I come.

"You're a fucking natural, Nicky," Gordon says. He asks me to do another shoot, the next day. Rimming. My tongue up some guy's butt for an hour. I say no. I'm tired, want a few days off, maybe look for a real job, go to a few legitimate auditions. Then Gordon quotes a price and it's next month's rent and the rest of a down payment on a new car.

So the next afternoon I'm smoking a cigarette and reading a script, which has me pissed, because I'm stoned and not into memorizing shit, plus it's stupid. I'm in prison and I'm working in the laundry room and I get caught sleeping on the job and the guard's going to tell the warden unless I become his sex pig and Gordon's got me wearing this blue uniform that doesn't fit, but I keep thinking *new car*, *new car* and I go to the bathroom and pop some more valium.

Then I come out and the guy I have to rim is there and he's absolutely beautiful. Tall, dark, hunky. "Mike," he says extending a large hand, a smug little smile on his face. At first I think it's because he knows he's got it easy for the next hour or so. A few lines like, "Yeah, shove that faggot tongue up my ass," and "You like that hot ass, don't you, boy?" and a lot of genuine moaning and groaning. But it turns out he's really nice. Sweet even. He talks about working out, the weather, good places to get Chinese food, shit like that. I sit back, listen, smoke a cigarette, watch as Gordon covers up Mike's ass pimples with foundation.

Then the scene takes forever and Gordon's pissed because I keep fucking up. It's not even like rimming's that hard or anything. Open mouth, extend tongue, lick. But Mike's got to be the only porn actor in L.A. who doesn't shave his butt and even though I'm into it, I keep choking on his ass hairs. Then there's a light problem and then the sound screws up, but eventually we both come—on me, of course. Gordon gets Mike a bathrobe, pats him on the back, tells him what a great job he did, offers him a beer, a cigarette, tries to talk him into doing more videos. I don't even get a fucking towel.

And outside my car won't start and I'm about to lose it when Mike comes out with a hearty "Yo, buddy!" He checks under the hood, plays around with some wires, mutters some shit about electrical connections. He gets some tools out of his jeep, plays around for awhile, looking hotter in his faded jeans and work boots than he did naked. He tells me to give her a crank and when I do the car starts!

"Thanks," I say, smiling widely. He smiles back and I think how I could get into a guy like Mike, someone sweet and hunky and handy, someone to put a little reality back into my life, remind me there's more to it than videos and late rent payments and drinking and drugs and waiting for a break to finally come my way. I'm about to offer to buy him lunch when he leans toward me. "Wow!" I think and close my eyes, prepare for the kiss. But he doesn't kiss me. No. Instead, he plucks one of his ass hairs from between my teeth, holds it in front of me, winks, lets it fall to the ground.

"Keep up the good work," he says, sticking out his tongue with a laugh. And then he drives away.

I get in my car and cry.

Jim McDonough

Ring Cycle

My friend Suzy called me in tears late one night. I hesitated before I picked up the phone. You see, I hate telephones. Working six years at the phone company will do that to you. As far as I'm concerned, telephones bring only two things: bad news and phone bills. I can live without either.

I had other reasons for not wanting to answer. Suzy had warned me that she might be calling after her date with Lester. If I didn't hear from her, she was enjoying her first man in five years. Leave it to a lesbian, getting laid before me. If she did call, the date was a disaster. I could have told her—first clue, girlfriend—any date with a man named Lester is going to be a disaster. As usual, Suzy wouldn't listen.

"Suzy, it's okay. He's just a man." I couldn't remember how many times I had been on the receiving end of that comment. Although, I secretly hoped to myself that I had inspired the same in other late night phone conversations.

"But I spent so much time preparing dinner. I even went to the farmer's market to get fresh arugula."

"Suzy, straight guys don't even know what arugula is. We've been having dinner together much too often."

"Eli . . ."

"Are you sure he's even straight? I mean, this *is* San Francisco."

"Yes, I'm sure."

"Are you ready to listen to me now?"

"Huh?"

"Remember Eli's enlightened rules for entertaining men? Rule number one: never cook a man dinner before he's taken you out to a restaurant at least once; preferably one that has a week-long wait list for reservations. Rule number two . . ."

"Eli, you're such a fag."

"And you're supposed to be a dyke."

"Well, I'm a lousy dyke."

I met Suzy the next morning at eleven at Café Flore in the Castro. I didn't have to go to work that day. In fact, I was in the middle of what turned out to be a ten-week nervous breakdown after I convinced my shrink that I couldn't cope one more day at my job or I was going to do something drastic. I'm such a drama queen—a woman on the verge. Until I had to go back to work Suzy and I were having the time of our lives, spending my disability check and her unemployment.

I didn't say anything to Suzy about her puffy eyes. She must have been up all night crying.

I ordered my usual lime Italian soda and grabbed an empty table in the crowded café. Suzy had her usual latté.

"You feeling any better?" I asked as I stirred my drink, which was the colour of my mother's kitchen in 1977.

"You were right, Eli. But I don't know why I even listen to you. How many weeks have you been pretending to be crazy?"

I grinned and tried not to laugh. "I'm not pretending. It's been six weeks now."

"Aren't you afraid that you might not be able to convince them you're sane again?"

"Well, if I don't, who cares? I mean, it would be like a major miracle if I turned out to be the only sane one in my family."

While Suzy sipped her latté, I scanned the café for cute guys. I still held out hope that I'd get laid before the turn of the century. We didn't say much. We didn't have to.

Suzy sighed. "I'm going to stick to women from now on."

"Good girl. Now that you're okay, what do you want to do today? It's too early for lunch."

"I don't know. You want to go get something pierced?"

Suzy and I stopped at the ATM on Market Street to get some cash. While she was depleting her bank account, I cruised this hunk who was on the stairmaster in the gym window next door. I briefly thought about ditching her and trying to meet him, but Suzy dragged me by the arm and we walked further up Market.

"What do you want to get done?" I asked.

"Something nobody can see."

"With my love life, if it's not my nose or ear, nobody's ever going to see it."

"Come on, Eli. You just need to go out there and find somebody."

I ignored the comment, stooping down to gaze at the lower shelves covered in metal rings of various sizes and colours. I should never have even mentioned my love life.

"I was thinking about getting my nipple pierced," I said. "I wonder if I have enough to do both."

"Are you two together?" asked a man in black. His name was René—René the piercer. He looked the part of the consummate professional with a shaved head and a large bone through his nose.

Suzy started giggling. I didn't know whether I should be offended or not. Suzy was the one considering going over to the other side, not me. In all my years, I had never once considered playing for the other team. I will admit that for the last several years I had been pretty much fed up with gay men and was mostly enjoying the company of my dyke friends. It was typical. All my life I had been an anomaly. I mean, there isn't even a catchy little phrase like "fag hag" to describe a gay man who hangs out with dykes.

Suzy and I came to a decision—matching twelve-gauge stainless steel hoops would be inserted through our navels.

"Who's first?"

"You go first," I said. "Ladies before gentlemen."

"Eli, you're a bigger lady than I am."

"Yeah, but you're the one having the crisis, not me. Promise me one thing, though. If I call you some night after midnight crying about some guy, you'll come with me the next day and get something tattooed."

Suzy just smiled and followed René into the back.

Rondo Mieczkowski

Trial by Tofu

The solitary health food store employee kept staring while Adam shopped for tofu and a few other items. Young, skinny and cute, the clerk sported his very first, very soft beard. He reminded Adam of his first beard in college and his rampant vegetarianism back then. Adam remembered making his mother cry at Thanksgiving by refusing to eat turkey.

Eventually, he stopped coming home at Thanksgiving, Christmas, Easter or any time at all. California was about as far away as he could get from his family and he stayed there. This trip back to his hometown of Toledo, Ohio was an unusual duty. Something, like so many things, that Adam wanted to do before he might get too sick.

As he approached the check-out counter with his tofu and Evian, Adam realized that the clerk was staring not at him, but at his black leather motorcycle jacket.

Adam gave his jacket the once-over. There wasn't a new rip or fresh stain on it. It was pretty ordinary, just another ninety-nine-dollar motorcycle jacket from Pakistan. Surely by now they must have heard of James Dean in Toledo?

Adam smiled and attempted conversation, but the man with the downy beard kept a sullen silence. After ringing up Adam's tofu the clerk leaned across the counter and snarled, "You know, killing animals for clothes is as inhumane as eating them."

So that was it. "Oh, don't worry," Adam answered. "This is my childhood pet, Daisy. She died peacefully in a meadow of natural causes. I skinned her myself. Do you want to see the pictures?" The clerk glared as Adam tried to slam the electric door on his way out.

Adam sat in his rent-a-car, angry, shaking. He hated fascists of all kinds, but especially vegetarian fascists. When he disavowed meat in college, he never presumed to tell other people how to live their lives. Now, all sorts of people voiced their concern about what entered Adam's orifices—vegetarians, his doctor, his family, Bible thumpers and safe sex police.

He wondered if the clerk would have stared the same way if Adam wore a short-sleeved shirt, the Kaposi's dancing on his arms. Actually, there were only two lesions on his arms and the one on his ankle, hardly enough to trip any light fantastic. Closing his eyes he focused his still simmering anger onto his lesions.

This had been a point of contention within his AIDS support group back in Los Angeles. The majority of members believed in a lovey-dovey approach to HIV infection. By loving one's virus you created an aura of understanding and peace, as opposed to fear and guilt. The lack of negativity would deprive the virus of its power source and it would disappear.

Adam belonged to a distinct but vocal minority that believed that AIDS, and society's murderous apathy toward those afflicted, was one of the greatest evils ever to be perpetrated on a people. To unleash all your hate and frustration on the virus was to harness the energy of the mind and destroy the foreign invader in your body.

Neither group acquiesced to the opposing view, and it was impossible to judge who was right. So far, an equal percentage of people from both camps had died.

Adam, decidedly of the "hate is great" school, sat in his car and brought the brunt of his frustration with the health food store clerk to his three lesions.

Shortly after the lesions appeared—three at once, a troika of impending doom—Adam decided to name them. He wanted something that could immediately conjure up his fury and unleash his full rage on the festering inside him. So he named his lesions Reagan, Nixon and the ugliest, most misshapen one—Miss Helms.

Adam imagined each of these vermin hidden just below each diseased mark. He visualized a stream of light entering his crown chakra. A warmth spread past his head, down his neck, over his shoulders and into his torso. The warm pleasant glow, really more of a silver liquid, flowed into his legs and arms. He felt bigger than himself, filled. Quickly, he fired laser bursts at the loathsome creatures that were the source of his lesions. Speared by the light, each of them writhed and twisted. Reagan and Nixon began to smoulder but Miss Helms exploded into a bright flame. Adam figured that must have been because of the higher fat content.

Adam screamed his mantra. "Die, you sons of bitches! Die! Die! Get out of my body! Die! Die!"

The offending creatures gradually withered into crispy cinders and vanished. Adam relaxed, enjoying the calmness that usually followed his lesion meditation.

He imagined himself floating on a raft in a quiet stream. The sweet scent of lily-of-the-valley wafted over from the banks. Ducks honked overhead. The sun warmed his face. The ducks honked again, and again, louder and louder until Adam snapped his eyes open.

He was back behind the wheel of his rent-a-car. Some idiot was honking at him to pull out, so he could take Adam's parking space. Adam returned the interruption with a blast on his own horn. He gunned the engine, slammed into reverse, and squealed out of the lot.

Dalyn A. Miller

Filling Station

I used to fuck Pedro Medrano Garcia, the guy from the filling station, on Tuesdays and Saturdays when his wife and kids would leave for Our Lady of Grace to try and become millionaires at bingo. We would make love for hours in his rented four-room apartment, above La Discoteca Grande, to the sounds of the crazy salsa crowd on Saturdays, and the lessons for the would-be dancers on Tuesday afternoons at the rate of five dollars an hour. I would wait across the street at the pay phone jabbering nonsense at the steady dial-tone drone until Pedro's family rushed out, flagging the bus as it almost passed them by. I would tap lightly on the door with the worn green paint and the tarnished aluminum number five and wait for Pedro to let me in. I thought of spies meeting in a dark alley when he would ask if anyone had seen me, and then, assured that no one had, he would secure the four locks creeping down the edge of the door and bury his sharp whiskers in the flesh on my throat as he began his twice weekly seduction.

He was a strong man with powerful arms and thick sinewy legs, both covered with a fine coating of coarse, black hair.

On his right arm he had a tattoo, four small faces, and the words *Mi Familia* arced over them.

"My wife at sixteen when we met," he once explained, pointing at the first of the tiny faces. "My oldest daughter at seven, my middle daughter at five, and my son at four." Then he pointed to a spot with nothing on it. "My next son," he said, and tapped it a few times for emphasis. "When he arrives."

"Is your wife pregnant?" I asked, surprised and alarmed.

"No," he said, "but someday."

I wasn't supposed to believe that Pedro would ever leave his wife for me. During our first meeting he clumsily blurted out, "Men have sex, not love," and he shook his head. "It's wrong." A warning, I guess, that if I wanted anything more I needed to look elsewhere.

He always wore the same thing when we would meet: a muscle t-shirt and a pair of cut-off shorts. It was a change from the sharp pressed uniform he wore to work; the same uniform he'd been wearing the first time I'd seen him and fallen so hopelessly in love. He was a clean man, yet the intoxicating smell of gasoline clung relentlessly to him.

"It's in my blood," he once said, as I breathed his scent from where my head rested on his chest. "Too many years at the filling station."

When we made love, his hands would work busily undressing me as his mouth made its way from my neck down to one nipple and then across to the other. He would pull my jeans off from the cuffs and the change in my pocket would rain down onto the crisp white sheets of the bed. The shiny coins stuck to our sweat-slick skins and I imagined exotic belly dances as the copper and silver clinked together over and over again.

On Saturday afternoons the fights from Mexico City were on Univision TV 6 via satellite. We would make love while in the background crowds jeered, announcers screamed in Spanish and men beat each other down to the stretched canvas floor. When sex was done we would lay in bed watching the end of the fights together. If I persisted, Pedro would sometimes translate the announcer's outbursts for me.

"What is he saying?" I asked one afternoon while the announcer screamed the same thing over and over again.

"He's down for the count," Pedro mumbled, not taking his eyes from the screen.

I lay next to him staring down at our legs entwined, dark skin and light, the smell of gasoline and sweat hanging in the air. I thought about Pedro and our two very different lives. I watched as he clicked off the television and rushed around the apartment picking up clothing and cleaning away traces of me—preparing for the return of his family. I thought of his wife at sixteen, immortalized in a tattoo, and wondered if his whiskers digging into her flesh hurt her as much as it did me.

At night, in my own bed, on the other side of town I dreamt about me on Pedro's arm: one blonde head amidst three dark ones. *Mi Familia*, like an umbrella protecting us from the rest of the world raining down.

Tia Mitchell

A Gay Day at Harrison

We had no money so it was time to go on a holiday. Away from the stress, away from the fears, away from the future.

Christine had gone a day earlier. She went by bus and the experience greatly amused her. It was only the second bus ride of her adult life. Before the ride was over, she had met nearly all of her fellow passengers. Most of them were going to visit family or friends at the prison in Agassiz. Christine always encounters like-minded people on her journey.

We spoke that night. I was tired; she was playful; we were both lonely. Telephones can be such instruments of torture—but not to connect would have been worse. We finished talking and I resisted the urge to call her again and again and again.

I left work at noon and headed east to Harrison, wondering what it would be like to travel across Canada by car, understanding why people in Ontario have air-conditioned cars, as the little Tercel started toasting me from inside.

I stopped at a place called Echo Chocolates and bought six for my love.

I knocked at the room, 6613. I heard her voice, and my heart stopped. She fumbled for the lock and I held her in my arms, warm, soft, naked, sleep-tousled. "I knew you'd bring chocolate," she laughed.

Later, in bathrobes and bare feet, we headed for the pool. Flash bulbs greeted us at lobby level. We were crashing a high school prom. Noble young women in velvet gowns and pimply young men in black and white tuxedos backed away from us, as we strode through their surging hormones. We did a little dance in the middle of the foyer and flashed our ankles as we laughed ourselves toward the water.

We mused as to how many young women would lose their virginity that night. We wondered how many would some day marvel at learning to love. We wondered who would be happy.

After the chocolates were gone, we made love. We rocked ourselves into tenderness. I told her I wanted to play with her and I did. Nipples, stroked softly, rose to pointed little peaks. Soft strokes and caresses guided by the power of words caused her velvety softness to moisten and move. We surrendered to sleep and, in the early morning, we touched again. Christine rose to look at the dawn breaking over the lake. "We missed it," she said as I laughed and held her again.

We went paddle boating that day, in a turquoise boat to match her clothes. We were the only ones on the lake. I was mesmerized by the swallows skimming the surface of the water. Christine was fascinated by the dance of shadows and light on the mountains.

We had dinner with straight friends with kind hearts. Did I call Christine "Darling" during dessert? I no longer remember, no one really cares, and our friends are too polite to speculate. Christine says it is difficult to be gay in a straight world. She fears that I am naïve and will be hurt. She may be right.

We had a drink in the hotel lobby later that night. I leaned forward and kissed her. She looked around nervously and asked: how could I do that? I smiled and said, If anyone says anything, I work for the Human Rights Commission and will take their comments in writing. We laughed together hysterically and danced again in the lobby; we were so full of joy.

On our last day, we bought two paintings we could not afford. We had coffee at the Black Orpheus and had our tarot read: no change before the fall, money problems for Christine, the chance of travel. It felt good to honour the intuitive side of our nature. My heart felt torn apart to be returning to Vancouver. We took the windy road and the trees were our friends. The silence and the pain were part of our journey. We knew, when we started, the road would be long.

Letizia Mondello

Hurt

I made the phone call. She agreed to meet me. I had decided I would spit on her in public, outside the florist where I used to buy her the large tropical stems which she loved. Spitting on someone in public, I knew, was supposed to be a particularly Sicilian thing to do. Whatever I did, it had to be public, but more importantly, it had to be swift. I then realized that I would find it impossible to turn my back on her, because no matter how difficult things had been between us, I had never once walked out. So I practiced on the white tiles in my kitchen. An about-face and departure of military precision.

Just as I had anticipated, it was a dreary afternoon. We talked in a café about movies and books. I soon felt so indifferent toward her I didn't want to discuss our relationship. I had never seen her so unanimated. Her irises, which had been a sharp blue, had faded into an unappealing nondescript grey. I decided that I didn't really want to spit on her after all. My life, I realized, had moved on, and the indignation and sense of betrayal I had harboured somehow drifted away without me willing it to go.

So I decided to leave it. The *che me ne frega piu* attitude which was my natural disposition was a bonus in this situation.

So we stood outside the florist, next to the café, saying goodbye. I just wanted to shake her hand, which would have been a true reflection of what I had been thinking in the café, but she started to hug me. It was then that I saw her new girlfriend, the one she had ditched me for, sitting in the window of the café on the other side of the road. My face flushed with intense embarrassment and I felt something clench in the pit of my stomach. I was catapulted back into the weeks after the breakup when I dry-retched over the bathroom sink daily because I couldn't stop myself imagining her fucking the woman I simply referred to as "that thing."

Before I could control myself the insults I had rehearsed came out of me completely jumbled. "Do you know what I've been doing while you've been screwing your ass off . . . the agony you put me through," I said, to the woman I had once loved and who had once loved me. "Look I don't believe you need to stay with someone forever, but your weakness kills me." "That," I said, pointing to the woman across the road, "is so dishonest it makes me sick." I was trying to say four words that would not translate. Words I hated to use because they sounded so melodramatic. *Hai spezzato mio cuore.*

I felt the saliva gather in my mouth, but instead of spitting I raised my arm and hit her across the face. My open flat palm whacked her. Flesh. It makes an awful sound.

I had hit her so hard it unbalanced her. She fell across the buckets of daffodils stacked outside along the roadside and tumbled into the gutter. Meanwhile I saw her new girlfriend run across the road. Some jerk was trying to park his car in the exact spot where the girl who had said she wanted to be with me forever was now lying. The store owner and the customers in the flower shop came rushing out.

I felt dreadful. I couldn't move. This isn't me, I wanted to say, but no sound came from my mouth. Jealous, violent, lesbian, scum was what I expected to hear. But no one said anything.

I just stood there while the store owner hurriedly restacked his flowers and the customers surrounded this woman I had once shared a bed with. Her mouth and nose were bleeding. As I stood there, I remembered that when I was practicing the spit, I had thought that perhaps she'd love me again if I got angry, just once. Just once if I did something spontaneously unsettling.

I watched her new girlfriend help her across the road away from me. Then it started to rain and the droplets of water landed on my glasses so I couldn't see too clearly.

Somehow I managed to move. When I found my car, I sat behind the steering wheel, shivering. I tried to start the car but the engine refused to turn over, so I sat there. I pulled myself up so I could see my reflection in the rear view mirror. I wanted to look at myself to see if I had become someone else, to see if I could recognize myself. It was then that I noticed that some of her blood had splashed on my face.

Lesléa Newman

Final Exit

for Sarah Shulman

The stupidest thing I ever did was kiss Barry goodbye, peel myself away from his hospital bed, dash down the stairs, rush uptown to Penn Station, jump on the Long Island Railroad, leap off the train, grab a cab, and tell the driver to let me off in front of my mother's house. I usually visit my mother once a year. On her birthday sometimes. Or for Passover. Never on a Tuesday. Never unannounced. Never with tears and mascara streaming from my eyes.

I rang the bell and peered through the bevelled glass beside the door, until a small, watery image of my mother appeared. She floated toward me like a dream in her green polyester slippers and robe, growing larger and larger until her entire image consumed the glass, then disappeared as she stepped aside to disengage the burglar alarm before opening the door.

"What is it?" she asked, filling the doorway.

"Barry's dying," I whispered, because to say those two words any louder would make them more real than I could possibly bear.

My mother remained motionless in the doorway. She did not say, *I'm so sorry*, or *You poor thing*, or *Is there anything I can do?* She did not open her arms and draw me into a warm, bosomy embrace. She did not reach across the endless distance between us to wipe my wet cheek with the back of her hand.

She just stood there. At first I thought maybe she hadn't heard me. But then I saw the news wash over her face: the crease between her eyebrows smoothed; the corners of her mouth rose to resume their neutral position. I thought of that old TV commercial, how do you spell R-E-L-I-E-F? My mother was relieved that there was no real emergency here.

Her crazy daughter hadn't been in an accident or gotten herself arrested or decided to move back home again, God forbid. No, it was nothing really. Just another one of those friends of hers, Barry—or was it Larry?—was dying of AIDS.

As I watched my mother's face, her eyes met mine and then leapt to the sky. "What happened to the sun?" she asked.

"It's gone," I said, though I wasn't talking about the weather. I was talking about my want, my desire, my gut-wrenching need for this woman's love. It was gone, as suddenly and completely as Barry was gone, though I did not know that yet. All I knew was I felt much lighter and much heavier as I turned from my mother's door and walked away without looking back. Which is the smartest thing I have ever done.

Laura Panter

I want to fuck you with words

I want to talk so dirty that you come before I touch you. Cup your breast in my hand like a comma—slide a run-on sentence up your thigh until you quiver. I want to fashion a dildo out of exclamations and take you by surprise. I desire a life with no periods. I want there to be no conclusion. I long to invent a word that describes the way your cunt feels when you wake up. Create a new language that narrates the way your hip meets your ass, the way you push your body into me while you turn your head away. In this language there is no fear; there is no word for walls.

I want you to give me so much that you don't know what you are saying. I crave a garbled stack of sounds that never utter "love." Sounds that come from somewhere deeper inside you. The way a moan escapes through clenched teeth as if it was beyond you to suppress it. I don't believe in "love." It is a word spoken by people who fear more. It is a construct; tiresome and indeterminate and never meant to describe us. It is the scripted utterance of people who covet safety. I want you to describe what lies beneath the words—what sea rushes with fervent colour under the concrete boredom of language. I demand more than what we know. I yearn for parts of you I have never touched. The parts we cannot speak of. The essence of you beyond words.

I have not found you in any language. I searched with such a desperate ache, trying to create you. Aching to possess you—slamming words on paper for vicious months as if I could direct our paths with sentences of lust and denial. Who else could ever know this urgency? I wrote as if I could make you tangible; as if I could create your swell on my tongue. Late nights I was scribbling you into my life while you slept miles away. With such panic, writing fantasies as if I could make them real. Never accepting that words are only constructs: mere creations. Until you came to me. And when you finally surrendered in such beauty, all language was deserted. You could not be revealed in words. What expression could ever describe your body that night, the streetlight slanting across your glistening stomach, your eyes drawing me to frenzy?

I want passion to choke me. I wish to stumble the way I did that night, when no utterance could describe you. No longer hiding behind linear paths. I need to imagine language as curved as the lines of your body; that reads as smooth as the small of your back; that rushes like your cunt with my fingers inside you. I want our bodies to spiral away from everything safe, and created. I want to resist everything redundant, and predictable, and known. I want to fuck you with words, spin tales off my tongue until we are naked, and whole, and can see ourselves completely.

Gerry Gomez Pearlberg

Lying in the Lap of Chronos

The bus was due at seven. It was past nine. Already it was phenomenally hot, which was why I was lying in the dust. The road was so long and flat and straight that you could see almost to the edge of the world in either direction, where heat and light bend everything into an eyeball cocktail, a liquid mirage.

There was no bus in sight, but no one was even bothering to look for it anymore. Anticipation and irritation had given way to a kind of suspension, a restful stillness like the pause between lyrics. Some napped beneath the holy pipal tree behind the bazaar. Others sat in the unlit bar no bigger than a hen house, swamped in shade, drinking in the dark. And I was lying in dust the colour of wild rice. Stretched out in the middle of the road, which not a single motor vehicle had traveled all morning. The ox carts and dogs, which moved in slow motion because of the heat, simply veered around me.

Way down the road, heading in our direction, came a woman. She was driving a small group of chickens, herding them with a stick. At first, she was a small speck on the horizon, but even from a great distance, one could tell that she was very old. The chickens were like a whirlpool of dust at her feet. There they were, woman and chickens, dot and whirlpool, silent as an old movie flickering away in black and white.

As she drew nearer, the chickens became audible. They made a racket clucking and arguing, flapping and fluttering, but the woman was absolutely silent, barefoot in the dust. I wondered how many eggs those chickens had laid in their lifetimes, how many children that woman had borne. I tried to imagine eggs, with their shells and yolks and fluid whites, hovering inside those chickens before being laid. It was very hard to envision this, like a double-exposure X-ray taken by a surrealist: the see-through chicken with white balls messily floating inside, a hubbub. How much more soothing to imagine a chicken calmly sitting on her nest with the eggs formulating themselves beneath her warm feathers, independent of her body. A spontaneous generation, the way scientists once believed flies came into being, emerging fully formed from rotten meat.

The old woman's face was deeply wrinkled, the colours of tobacco, yellow and brown. She was smoking a flat stub of cigarette, the norm for a woman of her age and tribe. She made me think of Georgia O'Keefe in her later years, mythic and stern. I'd once hung a picture of her on my bedroom wall, a talisman toward the possibility of aging with power. I wondered if there could be such a thing as aging with power in the world that America was becoming. I wondered how long it would be before there was even such a thing as "growing old." Maybe the elimination of old age would be a kind of mercy. I feared growing old and vulnerable in America. I feared it so much that it ate up my youth.

And I wondered how there could be such a thing as aging at all in a place like this, a place of oxen and terrace farming, where whole mountains are carved by generations of hands over centuries to resemble the ripples in a placid pond. I wondered if one could sift time like flour by lying absolutely still in the dust of a road leading nowhere. Resting in the lap of Chronos, that old, old man whose beard splits in two, a forking path, future and past. Lying in the dust on a road hidden behind that beard, sheltered by it, like a three-legged toad beneath an emerald leaf that time skips over entirely.

I told myself that when the woman passed me and disappeared from view, I would go into the bar and get something to drink. I was dying of thirst, but also drugged by heat. Who wanted to move? There were flies everywhere, the kind that come out on the dot of sunrise, and feed on you continuously until dusk, whereupon the nocturnal insects take over. Nature's synchronicity is astonishing: like those swallows that return to Capistrano on the 19th of March every year. Or the seventeen-year cicada, whose nymphs sleep underground for exactly that long. The whole world runs on the invisible clocks of animals.

The woman did finally pass me, and in greeting I moved my arms up and to my sides, the way kids make snow angels. An effigy of dust spreading bread crumbs leading back to this moment. All around me, crickets sprung up, disturbed by my motions, like tiny black clock springs. This excited the chickens, who began zig-zagging around me, attacking the crickets, muttering as they swallowed the shiny violinists down. Amidst this cacophony of insects and chickens, America seemed impossibly far away, more like a place existing in another time than in another location. There could be no America, no laptop computers, no modems, no Baby Doll Lounge at the corner of Leonard Street and Avenue of the Americas, where my ex-lover dances for gold. That other world as unlikely as fully formed eggs suspended inside the body of a bird.

At dusk, when crickets sing, the sound is always a short distance away, a bit out of reach, so that when you approach the source of the song—a bush, perhaps, or a glade near a river—you are suddenly met with a wall of silence, as if a door has closed, and moments later that very sound begins to emanate from somewhere else, also a short distance away, also just out of reach.

That's how America seems when one is in a place like this: an entity incapable of existing simultaneously with the rising song. Or with the intense, palpable stillness of moments such as these. Time throws its voice like a ventriloquist against Space, a disinterested stage.

The woman and her chickens did, of course, finally disappear from sight, and my arms did, of course, stop moving like the hands of a clock, but I did not keep my promise to get up to go to the bar. I remained where I was: in the dust, on the road. It was the day Chronos tied the ends of his split beard tightly around his neck and hanged himself to death.

Jane Perkins

God's Gift

One Friday after school I was in Nancy's kitchen waiting for her to come out of the bathroom so we could go down to Liggett's for a hot fudge sundae. We do this just about every day, although sometimes I get hot butterscotch instead. It's our dinner. My dad isn't home until nine or so, and my mom doesn't live with us, so I'm lucky. I get to have whatever I want for supper. Nancy's mom is just as glad to get us out of her hair so she can be alone. So Nancy's lucky too.

Her mom was playing a Patsy Cline record in the next room. I peeked through the space between the curtains that separate the kitchen from the parlor and spied on her. She doesn't like it when people look right at her, so you have to sneak. She had her teeth in that day, and purple eyeshadow on her lids which matched her lilac pedal pushers and flipflops. There's so much hair in the curly black wig she had on that you could hardly see her blouse, but I think it had purple check marks on it. I like the red silky wig better, the hair is straighter and shinier, but I guess red clashes too much with purple.

She was waltzing with herself, with one arm across her belly and the other on her chest, holding her shoulder. Her eyes were closed and she was crying and singing along with the record, "I fall to pieces. . . ."

She sat down and lit up a Pall Mall, then took a puff, staining the cigarette with lipstick. Shaking her head and mumbling, she picked a piece of tobacco off her tongue with her thumb and middle finger, then took a sip of her drink.

I imagine walking through the curtains into the dark, smoky parlour, and bringing beams of light in with me, like angels do.

"Let me help you," I tell her.

She looks at me for a second, then holds her arms out to me and I go to her, my halo light shining on her face and making it look plated in gold.

I have a beautiful embroidered handkerchief given to me by God, and I take it out and wipe the little blobby tears left in the corners of her eyes.

"I wish I was dead," she says.

"Nonsense," I say, like Mary Poppins would say it. "Here, let me kiss you." A kiss from me is like medicine that can free her to be happy. I am the Prince and she is Sleeping Beauty. I will kiss her right on the mouth and probably get lipstick on me, but that's part of my job. I can wipe it off with my handkerchief.

She looks at me and smiles. "Come closer to me, little girl."

She takes off her blouse down to her gleaming white bra. It's the lift-and-separate kind, like my mother's. The one which I keep under my pillow. Only Nancy's mom doesn't fill it out like my mom does—there are pointy wrinkled spaces where the rest of her boobs are supposed to be.

"Kiss me here," she whispers, then she cups my face in her hands and brings me to the little flower that sits between the two bra cups. "This is what I need from you."

"Then that is what I must do," I say. I kiss her on the flower and then she holds my face in her hands and says, "You have made me happier than you could ever imagine. Thank you, thank you."

The toilet flushed and Nancy came running down the stairs. I took my red face out of the curtain just in time.

"I'm going to ask for a cherry on my sundae," she said.

"Me too," I said. "And walnuts, not peanuts."

"Absolutely," she said.

Edward Power

Love, Frankie

They looked at the same spot halfway between them, but their eyes didn't meet there. Something smouldered now where love must once have been. Shy sorrow. They said little. Their kids had grown and gone, and taken something with them. Sometimes it felt like they'd taken everything. Except the silence. It was time to begin to shape new memories, but they didn't know how.

Sciatic, he sat humming and hurrumphing to himself, keeping time with his walking-stick. One of his old war-songs. Something he imagined he still marched to. She sighed in his wake. The sighing annoyed him, she knew, but she couldn't help it, and that was reason to sigh all the more. She punctuated everything with sighs. The song he hummed, he hummed before he met her. She felt some vague significance in that.

She looked at him, thinking to catch a glimpse of the old courtship in his eyes before the war-song burdened him again, but his gaze fell helplessly onto the hearthstones. Above his head, halfway between the crown of his hat and the smoke-coloured ceiling, she saw herself standing beside him in their wedding photograph: he's seated, because he's taller; she's solemn, but he almost smiles. She looked from the picture and felt they'd both fallen from that sepia moment onto the chairs they aged in now.

A week ago, he'd been ill in bed. He still looked pale to her and not quite recovered. But it wasn't just the illness. It was the photograph—the old one he kept in his prayer book. Not an *in memoriam* card. Someone he'd known, someone who'd died, perhaps.

The boy in the photo was about sixteen. His eyes were soft and amazingly open. She came upon it accidentally when he'd asked her to bring him the prayer book from the shelf where he kept all his books and papers. The shelf was almost beyond her, though she stood on a chair. She fumbled and fought for balance, while some inserts fell from the book: *in memoriam* cards, the boy's picture.

At first she thought it was of a girl, and her heart leaped jealously. Unreasonable, she knew, but real just the same. But it was of a soft-eyed, fragile, very handsome boy. A trench-mate, she guessed. Sadness that such a face was fossilized in time. Two words in copperplate on the back: *Love, Frankie*. And the date. 1915.

A keepsake he'd been asked to pass on to a relative or girlfriend, she supposed. But something about the boy, something in his eyes, in the brittleness of his features, pleaded against this. The boy looked out with a kind of helpless hunger. "Love, Frankie," he seemed to say, still said, silently invading her curiosity until it grew into something else.

She had watched him hold the prayer book often—intently, sadly gazing at prayers, she thought, his lips moving over chapter and verse. Now she knew, somehow she knew that it was on the boy's face that his eyes had lingered and his mimed words fell.

She remembered how, in their early years, he'd made love to her with a frenzy she didn't understand. Sometimes, afterward, not asleep, she heard him crying quietly beside her. Filled with seed, and an unknown sorrow, she'd slept. She remembered, and the words "Love, Frankie" echoed in her mind as if she'd always known them.

She gathered the cards and replaced them, aware that she'd put them in random places. She hoped he wouldn't notice. He lay on his side in the bed, waiting. Her hand shook a little as she handed him the book. He looked up at her in shocked surprise.

"Some of the pictures fell out," she said.

He started to speak but something caught his voice.

She sighed. "I put them back as best I could."

He nodded and looked toward the window, avoiding her eyes and her explanation. She saw his eyes well with tears.

"I'll make a cup of tea," she said, and left the room. She heard him rustle the pages. "Looking for his son," she thought. "He'd have been too young to have had a son that age."

The kettle was on the boil, but she didn't go in immediately with the tea. She felt a fear and a weakness in her legs, but also wanted to leave him to himself for awhile. She didn't want to expose him to her painful need for explication.

His eyes were still red and puffy when she went to him with the tea. The prayer book lay on top of the locker and she placed the tea next to it.

"I'm sorry," she said, tearful now. He looked at her, but said nothing. She looked at the book, picturing the boy inside it, and feeling a strange maternal love in her reach out toward him.

The old man's face told her that Frankie was dead or irretrievably lost. "I'll say a prayer for him," she said.

He lowered his head slowly. The silence between them then was the most potent, mutual thing they'd ever known.

"I'm . . . sorry," he said, his voice suddenly breaking the space between them.

"Drink your tea," she said gently. "It's getting cold." She felt his wet eyes follow her as she left the room.

Later, when she collected the empty cup, he lay asleep with the picture on the pillow next to him. Where her head usually lay. She opened a bottle of stout and was grateful for its dark comfort. It went to her head and warmed her.

Next day, it was as though nothing had happened—as though the boy in the photograph had never existed. He was up and about, humming and hurrumphing, his eyes averting her gaze. The silence was more tangible than ever, but she heard it whisper, "Love, Frankie." It whispered to both of them. The name on the photograph now lay indelibly between them and, when their eyes did meet, the boy's image filled the wordless space, reawakening the mystery of love.

Someday, she thought, he might tell her about the boy, but deep down she knew she needed no telling. It made her sad and understanding. She dreamed of the boy in the photograph—beautiful, sensuous, pleading. He was the last offspring of their marriage. One who wouldn't grow old or fade away.

Cynthia J. Price

Canada

"How was Canada?"

"Cold!"

"I could've told you that, and saved you an airline ticket!"

It's been fifteen years since I saw you last, and already I'm trying to make you laugh, remembering how the corners of your mouth turn up and the small lines creep out from the edges of your eyes. Remembering how that makes me feel.

Pam and I had been bumping slowly through the crowds in the streets of Margate, looking at the stalls on the pavement displaying goods under gas lamps and weak, naked bulbs plugged into long, trailing wires from the closed shops. It was an evening of slowly turning over bits of home-made jewellery and pottery and flipping through other people's cast-off records and books. Music from at least three live bands filled the background and the whiff of *boerewors* cooking somewhere in the crowd told us that we were hungry.

You were standing in front of the fire, the smoke from the coals making a halo of light around you as you spread tomato sauce on your bread roll. I didn't know whether I would be able to find my voice to say hello to you.

You laugh at my little joke about the airline ticket and introduce your husband, who cannot shake hands because he has a *boerewors* roll in each hand and is trying not to drip sauce on his shirt.

"Lynda and I used to work together in Durban," you tell him.

I am standing here talking to you with my hands jammed in my pockets, like a sullen schoolboy, and Pam probably thinks I'm trying to look butch to impress you, but I know that if I don't keep my fingers occupied, playing with the loose change and crumpled till slip in the deep recesses of my denims, they are going to reach out and touch you. They will trace the grey strands of hair that have appeared on your temples since last I saw you. They will gently wipe away the spot of sauce that sits in the crease at the corner of your mouth. They will trace the outline of those lips that once kissed mine and then pulled away hurriedly.

"Did you ever go to Italy?" you ask.

"Yes, Pam and I went last year. Really great!" I answer.

I think back to the lunch hours we spent together on Addington Beach, watching the ships leave the harbour and wiping away the tears when the big boats honked their farewells to Durban. We'd both felt that we had somehow been left behind. You had always dreamed of going to Canada and I had dreamed of Italy, but we both knew that these were just dreams.

That was why I couldn't believe it when I heard you had actually gone. Why didn't you tell me?

We had seen a movie together on Wednesday night and had gone back to my flat for coffee. When it was time for you to leave, I had joked about a goodnight kiss. I think that kiss frightened both of us, because you ran down the stairs to your car without looking back to wave goodnight, and for once I didn't have something funny to say to bring you back and make you feel better.

You were very quiet at work for the rest of the week and when I went into the office on Monday morning you weren't there. "Oh, she's gone to Canada!" they said. "Didn't you know?"

Why didn't you tell me you were going? You told me all the dreams you had about going and what you would do if you ever got to go, but you forgot to tell me when you eventually went. All I could think was, "I didn't tell her how much I loved her."

Now you are telling me about Canada and Pam is hanging onto my arm, something she doesn't usually do in public. She is sensing the feelings I have for you and feeling vulnerable. Your husband hasn't noticed anything. He is too busy trying to look down Pam's blouse. And I still don't know how you feel.

Why didn't you tell me about Canada then? And why didn't you tell me how you felt? Maybe it was all my imagination and you never felt anything at all.

The band at the far end of the street is playing a familiar thump, thump,

thump, and I try to force my ears into recognizing the tune, but the song is muffled by the voices and laughter swirling off the crowded pavement.

A young girl comes out of the crowd and links her arm in yours. She has the same creases around her mouth as you and the same little smile lines around her mouth and I realize that she must be your daughter.

"This is Lynda," you tell me.

The girl gives me a hesitant smile. "Lynda with a Y," she says, and her shyness is broken by her feeling of pride in the special name you have given her.

Why didn't you tell me about Canada?

Gary Probe

Pink Shag Triangle

My mother pretends she doesn't know I'm gay. Serious. I probably told her the first time when I was sixteen just to piss her off. I walked down the hall to the back room where the light from the window doesn't put a glare on the TV screen. I watched her from the door for a few seconds until she looked at me and then I said it with a bit of a snarl: "I'm probably gay, you know." Nothing. All she says is she's got to get off the night shift at the hospital. I mean, I know it's a shock for parents and everything and that you've got to absorb it, but she said the same thing when I told her the next three times.

"I gotta get off the fuckin' night shift."

We have this big section of carpet in our living room that's a couple of shades lighter than the rest of the rug because my mother had a fight with the carpet cleaning people and they walked out half-way through the job. See, she'd had too much to drink that day and decided to pour a little vodka in with their cleaning soap to give it some extra oomph. She always says that vodka's this miracle stuff, so she pours it everywhere when she's drinking it—in her plants, in the cat dish, washing machine, you know. It makes it seem like everybody's having a snort.

Well, the carpet guys didn't like it and told her to leave their equipment alone. My mother told them that while they were in her house that she was the boss and if they didn't like it they could go fuck themselves. So they did. It was embarrassing for a kid to have his mother swearing at the carpet guys. I remember them packing up their stuff and this long, unattached hose flipping around, dripping carpet cleaner and vodka out the front door, my mother kicking at it and yelling at them to go to hell. And that was it for finishing the carpet. I grew up in a small city where there are only two carpet cleaning outfits and they're owned by two brothers, so my mother couldn't get the other company to come and finish the job either.

"Those people were ruining the carpet. What the hell made me call those people in the first place I'll never know. I've gotta get off the fuckin' night shift!"

Just to piss her off, subtle-like, my brother and I would hum the song from their radio commercial, "Dream Steam your Carpet Clean, it's Service With a Smile," and then act all innocent when she told us to shut up.

She wouldn't let anyone rent a carpet cleaner from the store, either, because to her that would have meant that she'd lost—like, that bright blue plastic bottle of leftover Easy Off cleaner would laugh at her from underneath the kitchen sink.

So the carpet stayed that way—three-quarters red and one-quarter vodka-bleached pink. If you sat on the floor in the opposite corner and looked straight ahead, the pink part was in the shape of a triangle. We weren't allowed to talk about that pink rug triangle in the same way I couldn't talk about being gay. Just one of those things that sits in front of your face and makes you think about how shitty being white trash is when you know in your heart that you're not.

Only I wasn't really sure what I was. For a long time I was a lot like a vampire: I didn't have a reflection when I looked in a mirror.

Everything about my life was pretty fuckin' nuts. Firstly, from as early as I can remember I needed to bang my head on my pillow in order to go to sleep. If I didn't do it, I couldn't breathe. Serious. And I had to sort of sing a song while I was doing it too, so my parents would know I was still alive and hadn't suffocated. It was just the way it was. My little brother did it too but I don't think he ever *had* to on account of how he always copied me. My songs were better than his but his were louder.

Secondly, we both peed the bed 'til we were teenagers. For that one I don't think he was just copying me. I remember when I was little my mother took me to the doctor about it and he prescribed speed for me.

"He's wetting the bed because he sleeps so deeply he's near a coma, Cheryl," he told her. "I want you to try giving him these."

She did let me try them for a few days until she figured they'd do her more good.

My bedroom back then was in the corner of the basement and from there the world radiated outward. That was where sexual awakenings started piling up. It's not like I ever got overwhelmed by sex or anything. From the first time I figured out how to do it, I set up a regular schedule: jerk off twice a day, as soon as you wake up and just before you go to bed. I remember the morning that my Dad walked in on me to tell me it was time for school. He didn't blink more than twice and then he said, "As soon as you finish get your butt upstairs. It's time to go." I wasn't even really traumatized much.

In the beginning, anything about sex made me horny. My pals and I found a box full of straight porno magazines by the train tracks and we split 'em up except for one with some hot pictures from a movie called Boxcar Bertha. We'd pass that one around this circle jerk that we'd get together for every now and then. It wasn't too long before me and this other guy Mike started forgetting to call over the other guys to participate. It'd be me and him making it in our own circle. He was my first boyfriend, the one whose name my mother could never remember after I told her that he was my boyfriend.

Things started to get a lot clearer during those times. I started to find people who actually knew a few answers for some of my million questions. I could even make out a reflection in the mirror after a while.

Now after all these years, my father is ripping out the carpet in the living room so he can expose the hardwood underneath. My mother says she doesn't want anything to do with it.

"I'll stay in a motel until you're finished ruining my living room," she says. "Call me when it's safe to come back."

Mansoor Punjani

Shakil and the Mullah

See how ruthlessly my Arabic and Koran teacher Mullah Dawood Khan is beating me, for my most simple of mistakes?" Shakil, my young lover, showed me the marks on his palms, back and buttocks.

That day I saw the welts from the beatings this cruel mullah meted out to him, and to the other young children for the slightest mistakes in their lessons. I kissed him very lovingly all over his body and his tear-filled eyes. I vowed to him that I would teach that self-righteous bastard Mullah a lesson he would never forget.

I thought it over all that day. I knew Mullah Dawood Khan was a widower, in his early fifties. He had a beautifully trimmed beard and always wore pure white robes—the sign of purity. He must be sex-starved, I thought. Why not take him in our clutches by seducing him into homosexual acts? That night, I gave careful instructions to Shakil. He had to be very tactful and slow.

The next day, Shakil was studying alone with the mullah. Just as I had instructed him, Shakil, as if by accident, gently brushed against the mullah's cock through his unstitched white cotton *lungi*. (The lower garments many Indians wear.) At once, the mullah's unused cock sprang an erection. Shakil said, "My apologies, sir. This was just an accident." The mullah did not say anything and did not beat him very hard that day.

That night, Shakil reported what had happened. I told him, "See? Sex is the weakest point in a man, be he an ordinary person, high priest, or anybody else. Now be bold and act according to our plan."

The next day at studies, Shakil reached out and put his hand on the mullah's cock. At once, the mullah's pious, yet sex-starved *lingam*, grew erect. Shakil did not remove his hand but started to play with, and lovingly fondle, the mullah's member.

"Just a minute," the mullah said, and he got up to close the door and window. He sat back down beside Shakil and slowly lifted his *lungi*. The cruel mullah had fallen into our trap. That day, instead of learning any lessons, Shakil played with the mullah's cock, for a long while, until at last the mullah groaned and came in Shakil's hand. That day the mullah did not beat Shakil at all.

Shakil found the mullah waiting eagerly for him the next day. As soon as the mullah had closed the doors and window, Shakil shyly removed his shirt. The mullah drew near Shakil and kissed him on his lips, and on his pink nipples. Shakil removed his pants. The mullah started to fondle Shakil's hairless buttocks. Shakil took off the mullah's *lungi* and started playing with his cock, then slowly like I had taught him, he started licking the mullah's big circumcized penis very slowly. The mullah went mad—totally mad at this wonderful sensation he had never experienced before. That day there was no lesson at all.

Next day, I instructed Shakil to close the door and window himself, but not to use the stopper, only close it. I took my camera loaded with film and went to the mullah's house. I peeked through the window. They were already naked on the mullah's bed making wild, uninhibited love.

My camera ready, I slowly opened the window and silently entered the house. They did not see me. The mullah's back was turned toward the window. I smiled, raised my camera, and took a photograph: the mullah's huge cock in Shakil's mouth, his finger in Shakil's arse. The mullah jumped away from Shakil, a look of shock and terror in his eyes. He started pleading. I told him to keep quiet or I would shout and all the neighbours would come running. Mullah Dawood Khan started to shake in fear. I sneered, "Just do what I tell you and no harm will come to you and your precious pious reputation." He obeyed, like a lamb caught hold in a butcher's hand.

I took a few more photos as the mullah continued to shake and beg for mercy. Poor mullah. He was so scared. I assured him that I wouldn't do anything but that we would be back to play the last act tomorrow. We left in a hurry. Another student was due anytime.

That night I developed the film in my own darkroom and made a few black and white prints. They came out perfectly, each clearly showing the mullah caught in the act of seducing an immature child, caught in homosexual acts strictly prohibited by Islam, the religion he professed to teach.

The next day we took our pictures to show the mullah. The poor man was shaking like a leaf in high wind when we arrived. Right away, I asked him where he kept his cruel notorious cane by which he ruthlessly beat his poor students black and blue. He brought the cane from the corner and I told the mullah to hand it to Shakil, which he did. Then I asked him how many strokes he gave to the students for the mistakes they made in lessons. He confessed that each day the students received at least seventy to eighty strokes on outstretched palms, on back and buttocks.

I ordered the cowering mullah to first stretch out his palms, and told Shakil to give the mullah twenty strokes on each palm, very hard, just like the ones he used to give his poor students. Shakil was a bit hesitant, so I took the cane from his hand and caned the mullah until both his palms were red like Shakil's had been. Then I caned him on his naked back, then his bare buttocks, leaving red welts like those he gave to Shakil and the other students. Mullah Dawood Khan wailed like a small child.

"See how it hurts?" I said. "Imagine how your poor students feel each day. I won't use these pictures I have taken but you must promise me that from henceforth you will not use this cane on anybody."

The mullah took the cane into his still throbbing hands and broke it into pieces.

That night my family was out of town. The house was ours. Shakil and I made wild lusty love, happy in our success. My Shakil was safe at last from the mullah's cane. Since that day, Mullah Dawood Khan has never caned any of his students. In return, I let Shakil give the sex-starved, lonely old man sexual pleasure once in a while—to keep him happy.

Wendy Putman

There Are No Lesbians in This Picture

The air is stuffy. It's four-thirty in the afternoon, and we're standing in the corridor outside a courtroom of the Supreme Court of British Columbia. The air is thick with arguments: of opposing parties, of lawyers to judges, of words used as weapons of justice.

The court has just awarded custody of a one-year-old child to his grandmother. The corridor is empty but for the two of us: lesbians of middle-age spread facing one another, eyes darting back and forth with the speed of code, speaking volumes too complex to articulate. I am the grandmother. The other woman is my lawyer.

"Despite the complication," she says, her statement deceptively simple. She turns on her sensibly-shod heel, and strides down the corridor toward the elevators.

I nod at her back, with perfect understanding, the sharp edge on which my emotions have been perched, dulled to a tolerable thickness.

She had been my first choice of lawyer. I had begun the client-solicitor relationship bluntly. "There's something you should know. I'm a lesbian."

"Ah, yes. Well, so am I."

"I know. I'm counting on you to handle that complication when it arises."

The judge, a middle-aged man with thinning white hair, seemed not to notice me in his courtroom. I look neither stereotypically grandmotherly nor lesbian. My dark hair is cut stylishly, and the Chanel number I am wearing, the one I call my corporate drag, is prim and black, smudging the distinction between me and the lawyers filling the courtroom. Perhaps the judge did notice me and ignored what he could not prove, deciding that my home *is* the best place for my grandson, despite any reservations he might have. I'm certain the judge would have mentioned it, though, had he known. I understand that awarding custody to a lesbian is not something the court does lightly.

What the judge did notice was the report of the family court counsellor, which graciously ignored the fact that my apartment has only one bedroom, that the dining area now houses my bed, and that the dining room chairs now rub arms with the sofa. Instead, he said he found my home full of the stuff an infant requires: warmth. Love. The types of stimulation and challenges a child needs to develop. I read the report thoroughly, searching the subtext for the single obvious fact that's carefully been ignored.

When the court counsellor visited my home, I began the interview with the blunt admission, "There's something you should know. I'm a lesbian."

"Ah, yes." His tone was guardedly neutral. "Are you involved with anyone right now?"

I decided to reveal the truth. "No. As a matter of fact, I've been celibate for a while now." Oddly, *this* I am embarrassed to admit.

I find a pay phone, tease coins into the slot. Listen to them jangle in time with my wearied nerves, call the social worker. She will be relieved that the case has concluded; otherwise, she'd have to prepare for the more complex hearing against the child's parents. There, we'd all squirm through the sordid telling of a tale of neglect and abuse, of a child removed to a foster home; a child placed with his grandmother and thriving under her experienced eye, being given free rein to develop his uniqueness in a way denied him until now.

The social worker wants to know details. What less-than-savoury anecdotes had been told, whose reputations sullied? She wants to know what I did that allowed a staid court to pass over the issue of sexual orientation. What magic weave of facts held the strongest argument?

"What did you say about the kids?"

"The truth. That they mean well but can't cope. That they can't control their tempers, that they squander their money and don't feed the baby properly, that they're too lazy to take him to the doctor when he needs medical care."

"And what did the kids say about you?"

"That I wouldn't be able to cope with a baby because of my lifestyle." I hasten to add, "It seems I'm too active."

"Active," she repeats, her tone flat in disbelief.

"Yes, as in 'too many causes'," I say, in a laugh that gains an edge of hysteric relief. I search my pockets for a tissue to wipe my eyes, oblivious to the passers-by who give this curious woman a queer look, as if they know.

The parents have shuffled out of the stuffy courthouse into the fresh air beyond, where the smokers congregate outside the front doors. As I walk by, they turn to each other, their backs shutting me out. But I know even *they* are relieved it's over, though they would never admit it. They went through the motions of contesting, knowing they would lose. They would never admit that, either, but I know it all too well. They had called me a few days earlier, to arrange their next weekly visit with their son; it's hard not to read the defeat of the gesture.

I walk to my car—I drive a mini-van now parked in the next block. I slide back the rear passenger door and kick my shoes onto the floor, replacing each high heel with a heavy oxford. Driving shoes. My coat, wearily tossed in the back, catches on the baby's car seat. I breathe deeply, pulling fresh air into my lungs. The rainbow sticker on the back window is oddly comforting. There is a definitely a lesbian in *this* picture.

Carol Queen

Hot 'n' Hunky

Tonight we had the wildest storm of the winter and the lightning had the air crackling with ozone. I'm just on the cusp of my period and I need some red meat to call it down. There's always meat on Polk Street. I duck into a burger joint just as the rain stops pelting the pavement.

The bartender ignores me—I don't belong; the counterman is friendly, but he doesn't look too good. Pictures of Marilyn Monroe everywhere, and at the next table a couple of conventioneers—no, they're old gay guys from Dubuque. I'm dipping cold fries into a pool of catsup, red as the blood welling up in my womb. The burger is starting to get cold too. Bad dissonance between the jukebox and the bar stereo—on one a doubtless-by-now-dead-herself jazz chanteuse, no, *belt*euse, repeats, "Mose kicked the bucket, Old Man Mose is dead" in every rhythmic pattern she can devise. On the other, the Pet Shop Boys are doing their bit for morale and this is playing in gay bars all around the world: "Yes it's worth it, yes it's worth living for."

I can't tell if the group of kids outside is old enough to be out this late. Street kids, making a clubhouse out of a recessed doorway. One of my first gay acquaintances—at seventeen—was a boy who'd left home at twelve and by the time I'd met him, had made his way up and down the west coast, hustling. I know what to look for. The boys are talking, energized by the storm. The doorway belongs to a travel agent, closed now. The boys make a ring. They could be any gang of boys, but even from here where I can't hear the cadences of their voices, their gestures are different.

So I am shocked to see one of them start to push another, his mouth forming a shout I can't hear. I had just been fantasizing about a john coming along and buying them all burgers at Hot 'n' Hunky so I could eavesdrop on their street kid dish—maybe the trolls from Dubuque have a trick's largesse. The white boy who moved to push the black one is pumped up, dancing like a dog, suddenly all macho gestures. My prejudice shows: I wonder if he's straight. The black kid pushes back and feints. He hops backward into the street, like a boxer. My fries lay greasy and tangled in their plastic basket, the kind fries came in in the cafés at home where boys really acted like this, really fought. I am shocked—I can't believe this.

One has his arm cocked back and ready to slug. The other one meets him and they dance around like straight men who need this insane polka for an excuse to rub off on each other's legs. Their friends aren't paying any attention to them.

As suddenly as it started, they have their hands in each other's hair and they're kissing.

The song about dead Mose fights for my attention, but my body is following the Pet Shop Boys and all the years of gay bar salvation. I leave the burger half finished. Warm carmine blood stains my lips.

Keith Rainger

Spokane

She would not believe how much warmer it was in Spokane, he said. It had been minus twenty-seven when he left Calgary that morning, but there it was just minus five. It felt so warm he had had to open his coat as he walked to the airport bus. Yes, he was fine, the hotel was fine. He expected to be back in four days or so. *Love you.*

Louise looked forward to Rick's occasional business trips—five or six times a year—Vancouver sometimes, Winnipeg and Toronto, Seattle too, but quite often Spokane. She enjoyed the space and time to be by herself, to catch up on some of the more ambitious and disruptive household chores which she would prefer not to be doing when Rick got home from work. She brunched with one or two of her neighbourhood friends, took in a movie, wrote at length to her mother.

She supposed they were happily married. It had never been the greatest romance of the century. The sexual side of it had not lasted long—long enough for Jamie to be born, of course—but over coffee her girlfriends gave her to understand that bedtime ardour was usually short-lived in a man, and she had never thought of herself as highly-sexed. Rick was attentive and dutiful, shared the work about the house, loved and encouraged their teenage son. Louise had reason to think she was lucky when she heard horror stories about other marriages just a block or two away, not least her own sister Karen.

On Rick's second night away, she ate a light meal with Jamie who was hurrying to join the other guys for a session at the gym. She drove him there, promising to be back in two and a half hours. Then she went on to visit Karen. She guessed her sister needed all the support and company she could get. Three young children, none of them easy, though now all safely and quietly in bed, Louise prayed. A moody and neglectful husband whose only hobbies seemed to be beer and television. Karen was glad to see her, but Louise was not sorry when it was time to call for Jamie.

He was not waiting for her at the door of the gym. She sat in the car for ten minutes or so, then went in. One of the coaches met her at reception. Jamie had had an accident, she was not to worry too much, a back injury, but nothing serious. He had been using weights in just the way he had been told not to, but a few days' rest should put him right. They had taken him to hospital as a precaution. They had tried to call her at home. Louise explained her visit to her sister. They called the hospital for her. Yes, he could come home. No school for three or four days. Complete rest.

An hour later, Jamie was in his own bed, liberally dosed with a hot fruit drink, a lengthy scolding from his mother, and a pile of sports magazines. Louise thought to let Rick know about Jamie, but realized she did not have his number in Spokane. Prudent with expenses, they had always agreed that he should make calls so that they could be charged to the engineering company for which he worked. Well, it did not matter. Jamie was not in danger. She would call the company in the morning.

There was some delay before Rick's colleague returned to the phone. He had to check out the computer record which showed which of their employees was away on business. Now he sounded puzzled. He had checked Vancouver, Seattle, their other offices. According to the computer, Rick was not working, he had taken a few days' leave. That was not possible, Louise insisted, she knew her husband was working in Spokane. A brief silence. Spokane? Was she sure? Did she not mean Seattle? No, no, her husband had worked in Spokane three or four times a year for as long as she could remember. Rick's colleague was kindly but definite. He knew Rick. He knew where he worked. The company never took work in Spokane, they had no contacts there. In any case, Rick was on leave. Surely he was at home?

Louise could not remember how she had brought this conversation to an end. She did not have to ask herself what this meant. At least she understood now why Rick insisted he would always call her. She had kept to that rule for such a long time—why shouldn't she?—that he had felt confident she would never find out. But what was she to do about it?

Jamie was sleeping most of the time, and when he was awake, she made sure he did not notice her distress. She thought to call her friends, her sister, but she had never had personal problems to share, and it hurt her pride to do so now. What could she do? Rick would be back tomorrow or the next day. What would she say to him?

Rick drove home from the airport the following day. Louise surprised herself at the normality of her greeting. She told him about Jamie, and then brought him coffee as he sat on the boy's bed, talking him through the accident and the rest he would need in the next day or so.

Louise saw that he had left his suitcase and coat in the kitchen. She did now what she had never done before. She unzipped the bag and searched among the shirts and other clothing for anything that might explain Spokane. Nothing. She tried the coat pockets and opened his wallet. Credit cards, twenty or thirty dollars and a small photograph of a good-looking man about Rick's age, with trim moustache, cropped hair and a winning smile. He had written across the back: "For Rick, with all my love, Ian."

She replaced the photograph and made some fresh coffee.

Lev Raphael

My Brother Says

First flight. Sixteen. I drink too much. Arizona cousins. The dipping dropping plane. The banal rage of light.

Lori, sixteen too, says rest, now rest. I dream of her, or try. Late, we drive deserted streets. She says to me you're beautiful you know. We stop. I kiss a lie. I know her from my brother's words, can picture what a woman is. I find her strange and warm.

My finger slips inside. The biting lips. She directs my hand. Her clench and groan are ugly, watched.

We do things, tour. Cactus, hills, the city spreading from itself, a trailer park run wild.

Her parents do not know. Her father tells me dirty jokes. Her mother cooks and cooks to juice me up. She says.

I wonder why I didn't ask for more. My brother meets me in New York. I write to Lori once a week. She calls. There was a party that was hot, she lost it on a couch. She says. I wonder why I didn't ask for more.

My father never touches me.

My brother, wild, is always high, in debt. I love to fuck, my brother says. My brother has a real man's sheen and strut. My brother is a man, my brother loves to fuck.

Now *I* do well at school, my papers kissed with praise. I write, they say, maturely and with style. They do not know.

I rearrange things when I can. Books and clothes, great nervous piles my brother mocks. I want to get it right.

My brother has a girl for me, he always has a girl. I cannot share. I fear my brother's tracks.

My brother, Jeff, is big and dark where men are big and dark. Unh-hunh. Thin lips, beard, taut muscled man.

My hand has been my brother's, some times at night. A real man's hand on *me*.

I do not feel the way my brother feels and is.

My brother says get laid get drunk you think too much. My brother does not know.

Claire, my brother's girl, in hippie beads and rags, gets stoned with me. Come on. We are not missed, the night's too wild, the party up too high. We talk. My brother's girl. Her scarf has butterflies.

I remember one with broken wings somewhere, looking drunken on a car. Come on. She rides and it is quick, and quick. Half-dressed, I go blind.

My brother asked how was it can she fuck or can she fuck?

I read too much. D.H. Lawrence says that man's great journey in his life is into woman.

I want my brother's name, and everything.

I read that artists like to kill themselves. I do not understand a chosen death. Being sure enough to care.

My brother says that Claire's the perfect girl. My brother settles down and straightens out. I see my brother straightened out.

Hey I can't sleep. We talk in bed, my brother's bed. He is high and hot.

My brother says, Since you had Claire, and holds me down. It hurts.

My brother says.

Jeff Richardson

Smoking in the Rain

I was depressed—no, *suicidal*—so I bought a pack of cigarettes even though I'd quit, finally, after promising Adele for years that I would. I went into a corner store and said, "Du Maurier Extra Mild, large," as if I'd been saying it every day for the last six months, which I hadn't; well, okay, in my mind maybe, but not in reality. It's like Jimmy Carter lusting in his heart: is craving a cigarette sinful if you don't actually have it? Can people on the subway smell smoke on your clothes if you're only *picturing* lighting up? Could Adele taste smoke on my breath when I kissed her just because, for one mere moment, I was mentally sucking on a butt instead of her tongue?

Anyway, like I said, I was depressed going on suicidal, so I went into this corner store, bought the Du Mauriers, took them into a park around the corner and sat down on a bench. My hands were shaking as I peeled the thin cellophane tape off the package, releasing the wrapper. My God, I might as well have been undressing a lover, that's how nervous and excited I was. I slid open the pack: the two foil covers were as neatly tucked about the cigarettes they concealed as blankets on a hotel bed. There they are again—adulterous thoughts—but instead of sneaking off on a weekday afternoon, I was having my quicky with Mme. Du Maurier in a very public park.

Have I told you it was raining? Not heavily, but a light drizzle. Have I told you I wasn't in my own city but, even so, kept furtively looking around as if someone who knew me and Adele and her threat to leave me if I ever smoked another cigarette again was suddenly going to show up in this park I didn't even know the name of, in a city I'd never been to before, and catch me lighting up.

I slipped that first delicious babe out of the pack, touched her to my lips, fumbled with my quivering lighter, inhaled—oh God almighty I *inhaled!*—and there he was, out of nowhere: "How you doin', Bill?"

Harry Banister. Travelling salesman—restaurant equipment—and Adele's first cousin. She has no siblings, so Harry's really, well, more like her *brother.*

I threw the cigarette at him. I don't know how it happened exactly—in my hurry to get it out of my mouth my fingers overreacted. I flung it at his nice trim overcoat. (He was dressed for the rain.) A cigarette hitting a salesman's overcoat should bounce off and fall to the ground, but it didn't. This one—it must have been my saliva on the filter—this one *stuck* to his overcoat, just a little to the side of his left lapel. *It stuck there and burned.*

We both just looked at it. I don't know which of us was more surprised, but we watched as it slipped, in the slowest slow motion, down, down, until it tripped on his belt, did a little somersault, *graciously*, then continued on downward to land on his shoe. Italian leather loafers.

"What brings you here, Harry?" I asked. Maybe I could've pulled it off, distracted him with my false tone of normalcy, if only I wasn't looking at—instead of his eyes—the brown-rimmed hole my cigarette had etched so completely into his overcoat.

"Convention," he replied vacantly. He watched the cigarette continue to glow red on the top of his elegant loafer, then, coming to himself slowly, he flicked his foot, sending the cigarette from his shoe neatly onto mine.

I had to look like it didn't matter, like I kept burning cigarettes on my feet all the time. I still had the pack in my hand.

"Cigarette?" I asked, holding them out for him.

"If you don't tell Adele," he said. "She thinks I gave up a long time ago." He paused a second. "*Hey. . . .*"

We both laughed. Then he took one, and I took another, and I lit them both with a flourish—some overblown, chivalrous gesture befitting Walter Raleigh himself, God bless him/curse him for starting it all—and we sat there, Adele's cousin and I, smoking the whole afternoon. It kept raining. A fine, faint mist coated my glasses and Harry's black, bushy mustache, but we didn't care. We smoked the whole pack and when it was finished, Harry went over to the corner store and bought us more. I would've gone myself, but I was feeling too nauseous to get up, but not so nauseous as to turn down Harry's offer of another, and then another.

I told him I was suicidal and he said, "Yeah, me too," and we laughed. I said I had to leave Adele and he said, "No kidding," which made us crack up even more. And then we started telling each other things, important things, so that you'd think we were guzzling cheap wine, not sucking in smoke, what with all the truths bursting out of us.

I don't know what came over me: I stuck my finger into the burn-hole in his coat. He grabbed my hand to pull my finger out, only then he didn't let go, he held onto my hand, and we started kissing. He kissed me or I kissed him—I don't know which—and part of me wanted to pull away, but part of me couldn't. Part of me couldn't because the taste of cigarettes I found on his tongue reminded me so completely of myself.

"There's a cigarette machine at the end of the hall, right by my hotel room," he said, and I knew then that no offer of infidelity would ever sound sweeter.

Susan Fox Rogers

Exes

"You can be cruel," I say.

"Cool?" you ask.

"No, cruel." I smile because you have never really been cruel. But you have been rough and part of you, I sense, wishes you could be cruel.

"I now know what you like," you say.

I think: *Don't always give me what I like because I'm not so sure what I like.* I say: "You can be cruel."

When we first met you kissed me, then put your hand down my throat. I was thrilled and I thought I would gag. I thought: I cannot do this, I cannot sleep with her. I was very scared.

We are lying on a bed that is not ours in a small studio apartment that is also not ours. It is twilight, my favourite time to lie in bed, to talk lying in bed, me on top of you. I have just gotten off the phone with an ex, really *the* ex: my first woman lover. I talk to her like family, even though I do not talk to her often.

Did I tell you that with her I discovered orgasms, the kind that make me black out? I do not have those orgasms very often now because I learned I cannot trust all women. I did trust her, was so happy I could not imagine we would not live together to the end of time. But then she disappeared into a bottle and I disappeared into an affair and it ended and the orgasms became more cautious.

I called her because we spent part of the day on the Upper West Side, the territory she and I lived and travelled together. We were grad school comrades. She tells me she just finished her dissertation and I think this is wonderful. I have already moved through several jobs and lives and loves. She thinks big, I think many. We still love each other.

When I met her I was a skinny girl. After our first night together I bled for the first time in four years. I was so scared and happy because I was doing exactly what I wanted to do. When I left her I started to miss being scared. So I went rock climbing.

When we first slept together it was in the huge bed that is now ours, but then was yours and hers, even though she was an ex. You were strong and knew what you wanted. You wanted to fuck me. I was still scared. Because that's what I wanted too.

On the Upper West Side, you were not thinking of my ex, you were thinking of your family that is no longer your family. How can a family, so immutable, be ex? And now exes are family.

On the way downtown on the subway you spotted a woman you knew. She is the lover of an ex-friend. You say hello cautiously and introduce me. She looks me up and down. She has known all of your exes.

And then we slept together again. And we had dinner. And we talked on the phone. You knew what you wanted. You pushed my thoughts around and I thought: I cannot do this, have a relationship with you. Who would do the laundry?

This city is haunted with exes: families, memories, friends, lovers. How did there get to be so many? I know that this is what usually happens to a sex life as well: it becomes an ex, and then the person is an ex. That is not happening here, between us, in this bed where your body meets mine and it is warm. No, we are in this apartment talking about exes, but really thinking about the future.

Patrick Roscoe

Sweet Jesus

They searched for mother and they searched for father, then Sister Mary said I belonged to sweet Jesus for eternity. She gave me a picture of a man with a long face and yellow hair floating in blue robes amid the clouds. Now they called me Matthew, but the name felt like my cracked shoes, too tight or too loose, always reminding me of another boy who'd once worn them. The doctors peered down my throat for something hiding there, took pictures that showed what floated inside my head. "If only you would speak," they sighed. "If only you would tell." They wondered again about the red coat that had been wrapped around me in a doorway down on Union Avenue, among the roaming cats and cars. A woman wore the coat, they said, a woman went away. "I was lost," quavered Sister Mary. "But now I'm found." At night the other children cried in rows of beds beneath the crosses and the smell of onions in the dark. I kept the picture of sweet Jesus under my pillow; he whispered when I moved my head. Sometimes, when the thin nuns cleaned the corners and the bigger children played the bad game, I heard a voice from before St. Cecilia's and rainy Portland afternoons. During mass, the sweet smoke curled behind my eyes, a bright red mouth was laughing through the cloud. Veils fluttered inside my skin, something shook me, Sister Mary placed the stick upon my tongue. After, they stopped trying to teach me and the disappointed doctors went away. My broom swept the mute years. I scratched the floor and raised a cloud of dust and the priest with spicy breath showed me inside his lavender robes. In a circle the nuns clapped their hands at Christmas and asked me for one more dance until I was too big, until I had to go away. They gave me to the sour man near the docks. I filled boxes in the back, waited for him to come through the dark. His hot face moaned while big boats moved slowly down the muddy river. The wafer melted on my tongue. Disappeared. One day I lost sweet Jesus, my secret box was empty, another boy belonged to him for eternity. My feet followed red coats in the street, wondered where my prayers would take me. I'll never tell, sweet Jesus, I'll never ask why.

Meredith Rose

Run, Ruck and Maul

On the field you have to want it. Fifteen women on the other side want that rugby ball just as much as you. But you have to want it more. That's how the game works. You have to wear a plastic mouth guard. It gets dirty and sweaty, but you have to wear it and you have to taste it. Victory. Sweet and sharp—like the blood that seeps from your split lip when you peel your face from the field. You have to want it bad.

In the scrum you have to push; in the ruck you have to kick; in the maul you have to pull. Mostly, you have to run. When the ball is in your hands and when the ball is in some other woman's hands, you have to run. Fast. All the time. You have to want to win. You have to tackle and fall down and get up quick for the line out. You have to know the signals and you have to want it bad. If you don't, then you get hurt. Not a broken nose or fractured clavicle. A different kind of hurt—inside—like a part of you is on the field running for the ball, but there's another part safe at home, under the covers with a cup of hot cocoa on the bedstand, the warm milk insinuating that maybe you don't want it bad enough to take her down, to risk the violence. You have to take her down. You have to throw her to the ground, wrench the ball from her hands. The ball is in her hands, cradled in her arms like a warm leather baby, pressed tightly against her body.

Big women are the most beautiful women. You want them on your team: two enormous Props supporting a slim Hooker; two gigantic Second Rows holding up two enormous Props; one solid Number Eight pushing from the rear. Small is a wiry Scrum-Half feeding in the ball; four thin-bellied Forwards on the wing, ready to run. But big is best. Women swear and belch. They fart, then talk about it. They draw blood: it is red.

All lesbians play rugby, but only the fiercest of straight women play. Off the field they are nice. They exchange recipes, compare sewing patterns, but on the field they play like razor blades.

After the game you drink beer. You have to suck it down. You have to sing bawdy songs about sexual intercourse in every possible configuration. The songs are made up by men and sung by women who are tough enough to play rugby. You have to be tough. On the drive home you cram your aching body into the backseat with three other sweaty smelly teammates. Your head buzzes with beer; your shoulder throbs; red crusty patches replace the skin on your knee caps. You wonder if you want it bad enough. Sometimes you simply like the idea of the game: brightly coloured uniforms, drinking and singing, outrageous women. You know you could never walk away from the wanting. You have to charge after it, all the time, though sometimes you are afraid of getting hurt—not running fast enough, not tackling rough enough. You think of bed, instead.

When the game is over you store your mouth guard in the pocket of your rugby shorts. It marks the set of your teeth. On the ride home you slip it in and remind yourself of the way you bite down when you've got the ball in your hands and you're running, galloping, flying across the field, and every other woman wants that rugby ball just a little bit more than you.

Lawrence Schimel

Fear of Falling (Apart)

I*'m leaving, on a jet plane . . .*

Unbidden, the tune kept running through my head. There was a song for every occasion it seemed, even this: running away because I had come home early from work to find Rick in bed with another man. No doubt, there was also a greeting card friends could buy me for the occasion; maybe not from Hallmark, but one of those newer companies called things like Fag Hag Greetings. (Well, it would make sense; statistically, women do comprise the bulk of all card purchasers, and they must therefore need appropriate cards to give to that special gay man in their life.)

I didn't listen to his excuses. They were fucking in my bed. The bed that Rick and I slept in each night, where we made love. How could I trust him after that, no matter what he said?

I stayed with my friend Dave that night, and the next day came by the apartment when Rick was at the restaurant he managed and got my stuff. I wanted to put as much distance as possible between us. I booked a flight to Portland, Oregon, where my best friend from college had moved. Greg had been begging me to come visit for almost two years now, and I was finally on my way.

Airports are very cruisy. I had to keep reminding myself each time someone tried to make contact with me that I was single now. Alone. But I wasn't interested in a quick bathroom suck or anything like that. I wasn't even interested in flirting, at least not until I saw one of the flight attendants on my plane. He was unbearably handsome—not especially tall (maybe five-eight) with dark hair, wide shoulders, and dreamy blue eyes. The complete opposite of Rick, who was blond, tall, and thin; insubstantial.

This time it was me who kept trying to make eye contact. When I finally did, he smiled at me, before walking past on his way down the aisle toward the rear of the plane. I pressed the buzzer on my arm rest to call him back, and desperately tried to think of some excuse before he showed up, other than to stammer: "You have a beautiful smile, and such bright blue eyes." Or, "My boyfriend just left me, wanna fuck?" But I couldn't think of anything to say, and suddenly those blue eyes were staring intently at me, asking, "What can I do for you?"

"Cards," I begged, the word bursting forth from my lips of its own accord. An odd request, perhaps, but inwardly I thanked whatever inspiration had saved me from the embarrassment of silence.

He smiled at me, a flash of those beautiful white teeth, and disappeared once more to the back of the aircraft. I let my breath go, only then realizing I'd been holding it in. He must think I'm a dork. What could I do to change his mind?

He was suddenly back, handing me the cards. He lingered for a moment after I had said, "Thanks," while I tore the plastic from the pack, unable to look up at him though I wanted desperately to drink in the sight of him for a very long time. Looking down at my tray table, I could see from the corner of my eye that he was still standing next to me. Was he waiting for me to ask him to play cards? I looked up at him at last, but just then one of the stewardesses came up to him and stole his attention. He disappeared in her wake, as she continued up the aisle.

Had he been waiting to see what I would play? What choice had I but solitaire? As in life, now so in cards. . . . Would it have been some sort of clue to him that I was single if I had dealt myself a hand of solitaire in front of him? Or was it perhaps like the voyeurism of watching your neighbour across the alley masturbating?

I looked across the aisle and past the two women (mother and daughter?) reading magazines, to look through the tiny window, but all I saw were clouds. I remembered lying on the beach with Rick on our third or fourth date, staring up at the clouds and trying to decide what objects they looked like.

I returned to my cards and, as I shuffled, continued to wax philosophical. I had to play the hand which Fate had dealt me. I was alone now, because my lover had been unfaithful and, overwhelmed by this betrayal, I had chosen to run rather than try and work things out. I had no idea where I was going; figuratively, at least. When I got to Oregon, Greg would be waiting for me, but then what? I would try and rebuild myself a life. I guess.

I began to build a house of cards, stacking them level by level until it had risen four stories. Rick and I had lived in a four story walk-up on Fourth Street. I stared at the top level of cards, imagining it was our apartment. I wondered if Rick were in it right now, and if he were alone.

The FASTEN YOUR SEAT BELT lights flashed on. A stewardess' voice crackled over the intercom, amid lots of static: "We are experiencing a bit of emotional turbulence. The Captain has requested that you return to your seat and fasten your seat belt."

The cute flight attendant hurried up the aisle, but did not smile at me as he passed. The house of cards suddenly crumbled, as if from the wind of his wake, and I watched my apartment, the life Rick and I had shared, fall apart before my eyes.

D. Travers Scott

Alphonse

Oh, hon, it's not that bad. I know. You think we're this tired old married couple that never gets out, but we do, actually. It's just that this is about the only place we go. Really. Look, I'll spell it out:

Obviously, we do not love it here because of that lime and tangerine mannequin in the rubber gloves and feather boa suspended above our heads. Credit us with some taste, please. You've seen our place.

There's lots to like about this bar, and if you'd sit there quietly and nurse your Greyhound like a good boy, we will enlighten you as to why.

Obviously, it's not that scrawny underage stripper over there with the bullet scar on his gut. And it's not these lovely videos of Palm Beach, Provincetown, RSVP cruises and wherever else the owners spend our money.

It's not the dear owners, either: Tessie over there in the gold lamé jogset, with Richard Simmons' personality and Andrea Dworkin's body. Or Dex in the full-length mink, who stared you down when you walked in. They loathe this town, but are not welcome back East.

It's definitely not these Wal-Mart drag queens and trannies that seem to have chosen astigmatic bank secretaries as their feminine ideals.

Here's why we love this place: It's never boring. You know how hard it is to keep a couple of ex-city queens interested in anything more than five minutes. Janet Jackson undulations, steroid strippers, this week's Erasure dub—one expects those things. One does not expect Stevie Nicks, *The Muppets Take Manhattan*, and a beer-gut stripper flipping ashtrays with his jock!

Which is why, one Saturday afternoon, when we had the time and the inclination for a daytime buzz, we knew there was nowhere else to go.

And dead it was. Rockie was working the bar. The videos were off. The tunes were pre-recorded. A half-dozen geriatrics and leftovers from the Bloody Mary crowd lingered around the bar. And there was that smiling Korean girl selling roses.

We got our pitchers and perched near the strippers' arena. We only sit there if they're not dancing, because we don't tip. Some other desperate fool might want to make a down payment on a late-night rental, stuffing bills into those glow-in-the-dark floral skivvies that probably irradiate the hell out of their little hustler nuts. Like those watch factory girls we saw on Discovery. Remember, Babe? These young girls were hired to paint radium on watch faces so they'd glow in the dark. Radium—by hand! But it was the twenties and they didn't know any better. So these girls would cavort around painting their teeth, gums, eyelids and such. Twenty years later: cancers galore. These poor boys here, all they get paid is tips and they have to clean up themselves, even after Jell-O wrestling.

Back to Saturday: This man came in. Sixty-plus. Grey fedora. Long shock of snow-white hair. Apricot ascot. Blinding Hawaiian shirt. Butt-huggin' polyester dress slacks. White bucks. And shopping bags. But he's clean and spit-polished, hon, and everyone says, "Hi, Alphonse," so he's not dangerously insane. He takes a stool catty-corner to us. Before long he's got a pitcher, a pint and a bottle in front of him and he's downed two pills.

That "Boom! Boom! Boom! Don't Run Screaming From My Room" song comes on. Alphonse is digging the song. Rummages around in a Nordstrom bag, pulls out two spoons and starts playing them, all clickety-clackety like castanets.

He's standing up, smacking that flatware against the counter, his stool, his ass. The song collides, in their usual subtle-as-a-thrown-brick mixing style, into "I'm Too Trendy" by Right Bald Fred and his matching brother.

Alphonse sweeps into the spotlight and takes over the stripper's arena, front and centre! He parades on in, whacking those spoons all over. Total tambourine dervish. Got to have percussion. Starts working the crowd. Clacking off his elbow, peoples' heads, pitchers. Clacks all around us, swooning and acting all flirty with Babe here. Gets right in our faces and pops his dentures out with his tongue, then sucks them back in. Charming. This entertainment continues for some time.

Later he comes over and chats us up. Buys us a pitcher. Says how cute this one here is—how he only gets guys this cute when he pays for them, and half the time they insist he also rent out their friend. He gives me an envelope and tells me next time Stud Pup and I bump uglies, I'm to put Babe's load in the envelope and mail it to him.

Yes, it had an address on it, and no, I'm not giving it to you. Hon, if you need money, just ask, okay?

Any-way. He's back out there doing his spoon-dance and this other guy starts cheering him on. Early fifties, dark toupee, bushy moustache. Powder blue dress shirt of that thin acrylic Babe's mother always sends at Christmas. Unbuttoned halfway down, big hairy chest hanging out and, of course, gold medallions.

The tape crash-lands into "Night Fever" and Alphonse and his pal just light up. Alphonse extends his hand, his fan joins him in the spotlight and they start doing this tango all over the place to the Bee Gees. This is how the afternoon continued, 'til we had to get ourselves to Vinnie's for some High-Aggression Meat Combo Pizza.

Here's the final image as we leave: Mr. Donna Pescow-in-Need-of-Electrolysis has sat back down. Alphonse pops his dental work out at us and waves good-bye, still whacking those spoons. And you know who he's dancing with? That tall, skinny guy over there, by the darts machine. Yes, that one, the guy with cerebral palsy.

The man can barely walk straight, but he was up there with Alphonse, just working his disco twitch thang to the living end, grinning like Heaven really is a place on Earth.

And the music, the music, my dear Philistine friend, is Miss No-One-Ever-Knew-My-Name-But-I-Had-That-Big-Cumulonimbus-Hair, with her 1987 fierce disco-rama mix of "I Am What I Am" from *La Cage Aux Folles*.

That, hon, is what we like about this bar.

Ken Smith

First Love

Paul jumped from his hammock wearing floral Hong Kong boxers, not navy issue, but permitted. His erection proudly popped through the open fly, allowing his tight black curls above to peep through. He smiled, his rich, brown eyes sparkling when he caught me staring. I smiled back, shyly, my dimpled cheeks flushing as he read my thoughts.

He was teasing for sure, leaving his cock dangling and decreasing as he yawned and rubbed his eyes, a sliver globule sparkling on the head, remnants of his early-morning entertainment.

With some difficulty, I averted my eyes from this eighteen-year-old seaman, whom I adored.

"Morning, Smudge," he greeted, rubbing the smallest of hands over my head.

"Morning, Paul," I returned, then more bravely, "Nice dream!"

He laughed, boyish for a young man. "Wouldn't you like to know?" I would liked to have known, liked to have known he was dreaming of me, this boy-sailor. This boy who would love him.

"Tea?" I offered, willing to be his slave.

"Bacon and egg, and fries, whilst you're there."

Yes, he was taking advantage, but I would have cooked it, even laid the eggs myself if he'd asked.

His boxers fell to his ankles as I began to ascend to the deck above. His pert brown bottom stared back at me, acorn-brown, not from tanning but from his mix of race. Catching me staring a second time, he winked. I turned crimson, hopping up the metal ladder two rungs at a time, which loudly clanged when I stumbled.

We sat apart whilst we ate, not that there was any distance in this miniature mess-deck which somehow billeted thirty grown men and boys. All the while, my eyes searching, searching for a hint of love, for another smile, for any expression which would give me more importance than the other boys. But Paul was aware of the dangers of appearing too interested, or simply was not, and was locked in "sailor-talk" with older, more rugged men—men, of whom it was clear, saw Paul as a mere boy, not as I did, an Adonis.

He refused my offer to return his dirty tray, and that hurt—a rejection. But I wanted him to want me to do everything for him. More importantly, I wanted him to want me to do *that* for him.

We had different professions and the completion of breakfast separated us. I wouldn't see him again until lunch, maybe—hopefully. I would miss him. His smile, laughter, company. His body—beautiful and brown, firm and fit, flexible. Honed to perfection, pulling hawsers. Freshened by upper-deck air and salt spray splashes. Perhaps, I too would reach that masculine elegance one day, but hoisting flags, I doubted it.

On the flag-deck, I scrubbed the woodwork with salt water, bringing it to the whiteness of my frail chest, the morning Far East sunshine attempting to reverse that colour to the nut-brown of my beloved young seaman.

My tight white shorts flexed around my buttocks as I bent scrubbing the duck-boards upon which the twenty-inch signal lamps stood, sweat and salt water dampening around the crotch.

A stiff slap across my backside jolted my body upright, bringing me eye to eye with Paul, my eyes reaping every inch of him; sowing the vision into my subconscious—his delicate chest—every muscle defined—sporting rich-brown nipples; the concave chocolate-button navel; his hairless arms, youthful biceps formed and solid. The whole beautiful vision was complemented with a sprinkling of pale, pinkish blotches, the result of a skin pigmentation complaint. On his right cheek was a solitary beauty spot.

Yes, I had seen every centimetre of him during the month I had been on board, but I would never tire of that which I desired so badly.

"Bending over like that, Smudge, you're asking to get knobbed," Paul laughed, grasping the bulge in his shorts.

It was sailor banter, common on board ship. Meaningless fun, something to break up the drudgery of the day, but warranting a reply. In Paul's case, one that needed to be daring. That needed to say, without saying, that I was his.

"That's what I was hoping," I bravely confessed.

Paul laughed again, eyes widening and sparkling, but simply replied, "Catch you later."

Why did I want him to do that? No one ever had. A wank with school-friends was the limit of my sexual experiences. But I knew I did. And at which point in one's life was it safe to offer up your soul—offer yourself up for possible crucifixion?

Lunch brought us together, he pulling me into the canteen queue, my body slotted comfortably between his body and a mammoth sailor's, my buttocks brushing into his crotch.

I was not a brave kid, quite shy really, but turned, thanked him, then bravely said, "I meant it. You can if you want to. I'll be down the flag-locker after lunch."

Paul didn't reply.

Suddenly I was afraid. My heart raced and I sucked in calming air. There were no innuendoes in my statement. It was the truth. My desperate desire had pushed me beyond the limits of sailor banter. I'd armed Paul with enough ammunition to blow me apart.

The wait was unbearable. My chest was tight from lack of air, sweat trickling from my armpits. He would not come, or would, but with someone in authority. What had I done?

The metal door swung inward. Paul entered alone, closing it with a clang, causing me to jump.

"Paul," I whispered, unsure of what to do next. "Can I kiss you?"

He didn't speak, his arms gathering our chests together, my lips falling onto another boy's for the first time, passionately feasting.

In youthful frenzy, my mouth was free to savour any flesh it wished, searching the silken frame of my first love. All the while, Paul remained still, allowing me to seduce him. To love him.

My only wish was to please him—give him whatever he desired, demanded. Swallowing that very private part of him sent my head spinning, sent me into sexual oblivion; savouring his seed. Seed I'd never savoured before.

Paul loved me. My heart soared.

Too soon, it came crashing to the ground. That evening I met Paul ascending the ladder to the mess deck. He was dressed in a uniform and shouldering a heavy kit-bag.

"Paul. Where are you going?" My eyes brimmed with tears.

"Flying home," he replied, almost ignoring me.

"Why?" A solitary tear spilled down my cheek.

"My wife's having a baby."

"Your *wife?*" I whispered.

Linda Smukler

Marry

The morning I asked you to marry me we were staying at Bob's and I could not say it out loud so I wrote it first your roses had opened blush pink and were beginning to wilt in the heat you came out of the shower with cramps and I rubbed your belly and wanted you and thought I'm writing a marriage proposal on a simple yellow pad not even mine how strange I've never asked anyone before a marriage proposal in Bob's unlived-in apartment while he's in Massachusetts with Peter who has just come down with CMV in both of his eyes I held you in a brown leather Mies van der Rohe chair and I could have been in my parents' home and thought I am my parents both of them the way I ask you to marry me cling to me be with me the walls were white but I do not speak to my parents and they do not speak to me so I could not even tell them and I had one new pimple and so did you twins I'd say made from our long nights our endless days the stress of our delight I lay you back over my lap on the van der Rohe chair and entered you took you twice you said yes yes like that and yes and you told me you had never said yes before then we got dressed and walked out on the streets and am I different I took your hand so easily but shouldn't it feel different and we walked and I thought how to explain I do not have a ring but I did not say anything I wanted no yellow bands to fade over time if at all a circle of straw or perhaps a stem of mint to be changed every day to renew our vows we accidentally stepped into St. Patrick's because I thought it was St. Thomas' the air heavy with incense and sanctity not a place for us so we walked out and started toward the museum our destination but at the last minute I turned around to fix our mistake we opened the heavy doors to St. Thomas' and found

plexiglass blocking our way into the chapel but the air was clean and clear
and look up those windows with stars eye-hurting blue fall down on us
as I kissed you standing there inside the church

Sam Sommer

Last Sunday in June

Max was seven. A grown-up name for a little boy. His father and mother had been separated for a couple of years and were going through a prolonged divorce. It was a difficult time for all of them, but especially for Max. He loved both his parents very much. There had been so much change already. Max was constantly worried about what was going to happen next. He wanted things to be the way they used to be, but he understood that was impossible now.

Every Friday at seven his father would pick him up at the subway station to take him into the city for the weekend. Max would patiently wait in the car with his mother for his dad to arrive. He disliked the subway, and the city. They were both noisy and smelly and moved too fast. But he loved his dad, and looked forward to their weekends together. He'd camp out on the floor in a sleeping bag, at the foot of his father's bed. They'd eat fried chicken from the Colonel, or pizza, or burgers, and go to the movies and the park, or just stay inside watching TV and talking. Max loved to talk with his dad. They were pals. He really missed seeing him during the week, but it did make the weekends special.

"You up for a parade, kiddo?" his father asked him early Sunday morning.

"Sure. Where's it at?"

"Right here in the city. On Fifth Avenue. I thought we'd meet one of my friends for breakfast, and then head on over to the parade. Is that okay with you?"

"Yeah. Absolutely. Will we be eating in a restaurant?"

"Uh-huh."

"Can I have waffles?"

"You can have whatever you'd like."

"Great!"

After breakfast his father's friend excused himself. He was going to meet some other people downtown. "I'll see you later tonight at the Center," he told Max's dad, and then gave him a hug. "Nice meeting you, Max. Have fun today at the parade."

Max and his dad walked the five or six blocks to Fifth Avenue. The parade hadn't gotten under way yet, and they were able to find a good spot where Max would be able to see—Max sat atop a mailbox while his father stood at his side.

"If the crowd gets in the way, Max," his father said, "just tell me and I'll put you up on my shoulders."

"Okay, Dad."

The parade started right on time. Max watched as the first group on motorcycles passed by.

"Those are women," he whispered to his father. "And you can see their boobies."

His dad just smiled, but said nothing.

Max watched the marchers with their colourful banners, none of which he understood. He cheered along with the rest of the crowd at the occasional float, and clapped loudly in rhythm to the marching band, but he quickly got bored, and finally asked if they could go home. It wasn't the kind of parade Max had been expecting. Nothing at all like the Macy's Thanksgiving Day Parade.

"Can we go, Dad?" he asked. "I'm getting tired."

"Just a few more minutes, Max. Okay? There's still one more group I want to see."

"Okay," he said, to be polite, but really he wanted to go.

"Here they come, Max!"

What was so special about this group? Max wondered. They looked just like everyone else, although it was the first time all morning he'd seen any kids marching. He watched as his dad cheered them on, waving his arms as they passed. They were a small group, and it didn't take long before they were out of sight.

"Now, Dad? Can we go now?" Max implored.

"Sure, kiddo," he said, picking Max up. "Now we can go." He gave him a big hug.

Max placed a finger on his father's face where a small tear ran over his cheek. "Why are you crying, Dad? Is something wrong?"

"No Max. Nothing's wrong. Everything's fine. I'm just happy, that's all. I love you, kiddo."

"I love you too, Dad," he said, and kissed his father where the tear was already beginning to dry.

"I said it first!" his dad teased. It was a game they played.

They both laughed.

horehound stillpoint

In Between Beats

The shifting parade of gogo flesh can be glimpsed only through rifts in the techno fog. The airwaves are full of radio fuck, nailing each moment to the next. Shirtless black man spins his dreads, adding his rain of sweat to the weather in the room. Tall mod insect queen keeps busy whipping up a mini-hurricane of attitude. Latino funkpunk shoots gangster jism out of his nipples like bullets. Wiry young dyke in leather whatever performs calligraphy with her body and the message is lowdown. The many-layered lesbian with multi-coloured hair is calling forth all the immaterial powers of the southeast corner. Thick white misterdick sucks off his own reflection in the mirror. Music chugs out the rhythm of a train on track to infinite nowhere. Macrochaotic strobelights sterilize the room.

The only virus left is memory.

Scarred unit number one is not remembering the first time he fell in love, when he was eight and there were no names for what he wanted. This hardbeat dance-floor shares not one particle with that old neighbourhood, which turned en masse against the child, chiding, scolding, mocking, spitting, and finally pushing him so forcefully that he fell down a staircase. He is not remembering the entire string of events which taught him not to love or desire anyone that he loves or desires. He will fuck somebody's brains out tonight.

It is 1:15 in Metropolis, anywhere, in the end-of-reason dancescape called Paradigm. Upstairs, the third floor beckons with the seamless lust of a one-room sex club. The throbbing purple perfume makes the concrete walls seem thin and transparent by comparison. At no time does the sucking titplay, the fingering buttgrind, the tonguelashing cockstroking, the nudge nudge grope sneer knee-banging action cease. No one is remembering a father whose smoky alcoholic braying laughter accompanies an endless stream of fag jokes.

(This place operates on the same principle as an ancient Eastern zendo: people are encouraged to leave history outside. Yet history is what brings them in.)

Strippers get people in the door, thirsty for a union with oblivion. Downstairs, in the cellar, two pros vie for attention, not from the crowd, but from each other. The male is an olive-skinned hunk in dog tags, military boots and army-issue khaki boxers. The shorts are crawling with little toy soldiers, most especially on the hills of his ass and clinging to his crotch, which houses the mother of all bulges. Grown men imagine themselves as one-inch plastic figurines. Boys gaze at that voluptuous basket and wonder: is it real or is it full of wishes, dreams and a sock full of sand? On the other side of the room, on another rectangular rise, a lily white woman with no hair drifts and sways as slowly as if she were on a cloud. She is naked except for chrome-plated claws wrapped around her thighs, between her legs, around her rib cage and breasts. An orange-haired girl with a huge grin seems unable to take her eyes off this vision. The twinges she feels, deep down inside, are not connected with the chemical hardbrush scrubbings her mother gave her not that many years ago. As a little girl, she liked putting her fingers in her pie— and other objects as well. Her mother's vigorous efforts changed everything and nothing.

Scarred units pack the floor, screaming for the sound of sirens, factories, scare-mongering futurism, and war . . . all the sounds of oppression. If it were not ugly hard fast relentless, it would not be useful to this crowd. The night flutters as if it had wings, and the group mind slips into an overheated bath of no-pain, no-loss. (That skinny guy in the baggy white shirt is not remembering his lover's last drawn-out breath. He is not remembering that he still can't quite forgive himself for their last argument.)

The deejay has ingested a mix of drugs carefully balanced to enhance confidence in his godlike powers. An extra gram or two convinces him to reach for his secret stash of vinyl. Now he is mixing in not-quite-subliminal overlays of the Mahavishnu Orchestra, Johnny Cash, and Diamanda Gala onto a deathray rhythm track. When he phases in Nancy Sinatra, the mob swoons.

A red rubber dildo gets pulled out of a backpack. One colour skin rubs up against another. Winks get passed, intercepted, and used as deceptions for sidelong possibilities. Everybody flashes some piece of hardware: tools, hooks, vices, rings, screws, zippers and grommets catch the light and stir the imagination. Condoms spill out of a pail, a new version of the horn-of-plenty from yesterday. The fires of the day have turned into the lunar tides of those small dangerous hours of pre-dawn. Before this night is through, dried boycum will cloud the mirror and mix the image of gloriously seedy youth with triumphantly haggard veterans. Girlcum will soak old flowery towels handed down by grandmas. And the floor will be pounded to dust, making way for whatever comes next.

The deejay pulls a giant fairydust mirror ball out of his sleeve and hangs it overhead. People look up and see—a miracle—in one frozen moment, a thousand reflections of Beauty.

Everyone remembers everything. Then, between one beat and the next, it all kicks apart.

Ah, disco.

Matt Bernstein Sycamore

Shitpokers

We don't get out of the house until six p.m., rush to the clinic for our seven o'clock appointment. They tell me I have crabs even though a week ago they said I didn't. Gabby's all nerves and a few bumps of coke, waiting for her HIV test results. She turns out negative, we go to Buddha's Delight to celebrate because I'm vegan so we can't go anywhere else.

While we're eating, Gabby sees some van that says Boston Streetworkers, what could that be? I say must be for *streetsweeping*. Gabby says they don't sweep the streets in Chinatown. We leave and the van comes around again, men or boys leaning out, driver screams You gay *son of* a *shit*. Gabby says I am a son of a shit. I say me too, we go to Playland and Gabby gets an Absolut Cape Cod that's almost colourless, I get water in a *Pocahantas* cup. Gabby talks to the owner about buying a wig, this queen comes behind the bar to tell me about her forty-fifth birthday, went out with her friend done up and *no one even blinked.*

We walk to Copley Square where Jeff Barrows can barely say hello because now he's straight. Gabby calls Lincoln and Randy for her make-up so she can do the eyebrow thing, I call a trick who paged me two hours ago. Over to the Westin Hotel to use the bathroom which is packed because everyone's moved there to cruise after the Back Bay Station arrests. I get severe back pain in the Westin lobby and Gabby's strung out or bored.

We go to White Hen Pantry after sitting on the steps of the library where I can't paint my nails because it's too dark. And White Hen is definitely the highlight. This boy, seventeen or eighteen, ghetto style, says why'd you do that shit to your hair, what's up with that shit, that looks fucked up. I say maybe you should put some in your hair. He says what, you look fucked up, he's looking me up and down, are you gay? I say of course I am. He says that's fucking disgusting, he's making a big scene all loud, that's fucking disgusting you're fucking disgusting. I say a few things that end in honey and he's not too happy, yelling out at me and Gabby as we leave the store, you two are fucking disgusting God will strike you down, fucking faggots faggot fuckers shitpokers, why you living in *my* world . . . . And of course the butch muscleboy fag behind us in line who looks all scared, doesn't say a word.

On our way to the T and we run into our friend from White Hen again. He's with five or six other boys who look tough and don't speak, look a little uncomfortable but mostly just laugh. Our friend starts making this scene about how he won't get on the train with us, talking to the T worker, saying they let these faggots on the T? I'm not getting on the train with these faggots. Gabby's scared, I'm filled with anger and adrenaline and scared too but mostly just disgusted. We get on the train, our friend makes a big deal about not using the same door as us but then he stands a few rows away. Gabby says why'd you get on the same car as him, I'm thinking there's only one car but maybe she meant the train, I didn't even think of not getting on the train.

Gabby says you're pushing him on, looks like Gabby's about to cry so I decide not to say anything, which is probably the right choice because this guy just goes crazy, screaming and yelling, all glassy-eyed and sweaty—You fuckin' faggot you look like a dog you think that looks good? You look like a fuckin' dog, you dog woof woof both of you—which one's the man and which one's the woman, you both women or you with the purse is the woman? Pink and blue hair—who the fuck gave you that idea?

I'm staring through him for a little while then reading and trying to look like I don't care. He's imitating RuPaul, saying *Girlfriend you better work, chantez chantez, what's his name? What's his name?* Your fucking dirty assholes, better wipe them off better fucking clean out those assholes. And everyone on the bus is silent of course or laughing but I'm not looking up really, we get to Park Street where the train ends and he screams *faggots,* then goes down to the Red Line.

This woman about our age comes up to us, says I'm really sorry about that, I'm really sorry, I wanted to say something but I couldn't. I think why not but Gabby says well it was too scary. Then another woman comes over, says the same thing, thanks, and they both say I like your hair. And then off of the Lechmere train comes this cute boy who Cookie claims I made out with at the Loft, he gives each of us a soft hard kiss, no idea of what just happened, you girls going out tonight?

We get on the train and everyone's sort of staring. Go to Government Center, I'm painting my nails on the platform and this woman who we've seen here before sits down next to Gabby and starts blabbing about her small paycheque and waitressing and her boyfriend. And she lives on Webster Street where we live, her neighbour complains about the noise they don't make.

The train comes, she says you can't tell how old anyone is these days, how old are you? Gabby says eighteen, she says I'm twenty-four, well there is that six years I guess but no one knows, we look young and everyone buys their clothes at Macy's now, I moved from New York to Seattle to Wyoming to Seattle to New Haven, thought I'll get a job in Boston, went to school for film but I need a job before I get a *job*. I fight with my boyfriend and we're loud, called the cops on him once and they took him away for the night so the landlord holds that against us. But we're not loud, just look like we should be loud, don't know anyone so we don't have parties, don't even play loud music, walk around in the apartment at three a.m. and the neighbour calls the landlord. Before when I was single I had all these plans, now we like to do nothing and have fun.

Robert Thomson

Mantasy

Somehow fantasy came up in my conversation with my friend Marty a few nights ago.

"Sexual or otherwise?" I asked.

"One of each."

"Let's see. I think I'd like to learn how to relax. Have a relationship. Maybe even kill someone if I knew I could get away with it."

"Who would you kill?"

"I don't know. Too many potential victims."

"Come on!"

"Oh, how about Raymond's new lover? No, wait, that's too limited. How about all of my ex-lovers' new lovers?"

"Bitter Betty. And sexually?"

"Oh, that's not too hard. A fit middle-aged man with a hairless body, just hovering over me, holding me down. That turns me on. Oh yeah, he's got to be bald."

"Bald, eh?"

I nodded.

"That's your fantasy?" Marty asked, incredulous. "A bald, middle-aged man holding you down." He snorted and stabbed his cigarette into the ashtray. "That's my nightmare."

"Just a thought," I said. Just a thought. "I think I need to get married."

"I think you need to get laid."

After Marty left I paced around my apartment for a bit and then took a walk. To the park. I got lost a little bit and wound up in this wooded area, unfastening a fat man named Drew's belt and pants and pulling his cock out and jerking him off while he stood there with his hands clenched by his sides. Thought about where I could buy good coffee beans that time of night as I jerked him. He coughed a couple of times and then came. He pushed my hands away and did up his pants, said he had to get home. To his wife? I didn't ask.

Came home last night after work, cleaned the apartment, worked out, jerked off, showered, walked down to Woody's where small clusters of men chatted to each other and all the single men glared at the edited porn videos that glared from television monitors scattered throughout the room.

A bald guy came up to me. He had shorts on—nice calves, thick and round. I thought *platypus*. I'd seen him around before and wondered if he was my fantasy. He smoked a cigarette and looked, what? Intelligent?

We talked about stuff. He told me his name was Carl. He said he'd like to go for coffee, maybe. I said maybe? He smiled. I wanted to ask him what he wasn't saying that he wanted to. I'm hardly shy. So on our way to the coffee shop I said I had tea at home, and a joint. "Why don't we go back to my place? I'd love to take your clothes off slowly and see you in my bed."

He stopped with his hand on the door to the café and looked at me for a moment.

"Where do you live?"

"Five minutes in a cab," I offered. Then I moved to him and whispered in his ear, "We don't really need to have coffee first if we're going to have sex. What's the point?"

"Let's go," he said, moving away from the door.

In the taxi I put my hand on his leg, just below the seam of his shorts and rubbed him lightly. He placed a hand on top of mine and looked up at the driver who just smoked and drove.

"Wait," he whispered to me, turning his head to the side.

"Okay, Carl," I said, trying not to sound impatient. "So tell me, why do you shave your head?" He looked at me as if I'd said something obscene. "You don't have to answer me if you don't want. I was just wondering."

"Well, let's see. I shave it because it was thinning and I liked the look better this way."

"Oh."

"Is that the right answer?"

"No," I said. "There is no right answer. I was just wondering, that's all. I think you look really sexy."

"So you, uh, have a thing for bald guys?"

"Older bald guys."

"You're obviously not trying to flatter me. . . ."

"I didn't know I was supposed to. You're older than me, so I said older. I didn't say old. Relax."

I slid my hand up to his crotch and gave a light squeeze. He responded by pulling my hand away and looking up into the driver's mirror to see if the cabbie was watching us.

"Did you know they have a gay cab service in England?" he said abruptly.

"No, I didn't. I wonder if you can fuck in the back seats."

He smiled awkwardly, obviously wondering if he was making a mistake.

"Sorry. I get a little obnoxious when I'm nervous. I say things I shouldn't."

"You're nervous?" he asked.

I shrugged.

"Is this a mistake?"

I shook my head.

The cab pulled up in front of my building. I pulled a ten out of my wallet and passed it to the driver. He blew a cloud of smoke up toward the roof of the car and asked how much I wanted back.

Carl reached forward, grabbed the ten from the driver and let it fall into my lap. "Keep it, man," he said. "I'm going home."

"Really?" I was genuinely shocked.

"Yeah." He shifted forward and told the driver he wanted to go to Mount Pleasant and Eglinton. Then he turned to me and said goodbye.

"You serious?" I asked, almost laughing.

"Yeah. Good night."

I moved to get out of the cab and stopped before I lifted my legs up. "Come on. I'm sorry if I upset you. Forget it, okay? I'm sorry."

"No. This isn't a good idea anymore."

"Okay," I said and got out of the cab, thinking now I have another man to add to the ever-growing list of people who think I'm psycho. I shut the door and the cab drove off, a yellow blur in the night.

Sarah Van Arsdale

Teeth

My dentist's office reminds me of my childhood dentist. He's got a tastefully retro fifties couch, covered in black vinyl with chrome armrests, and end tables with attractively displayed National Geographics. He's even got a gigantic aquarium, just like Dr. Stanislaus did back in New Jersey.

However, because this is California, he also has a very modern print on the waiting room wall. It looks, to me, in its pinks and reds, like a close-up of a few cells from someone's mouth. Dr. Viera comes in, smiling. He's got good teeth. He's very handsome, dark-eyed, dark-skinned, graceful, and has just a whisper of an accent, and tells me to follow him into the examination room.

Once I'm in the chair, Dr. Viera leaves, then returns with his paper mask and blue rubber gloves snapped on, clips a bib around my neck and says, "Open." He pokes at my teeth; the rubber glove tastes like chemicals, reminding me of the formaldehyde and alcohol of dissections in college biology. When he touches my back molar, I wince, and make a noise in my throat.

"Because that tooth is so sore, I'm going to give you a little Novocaine there; then I can clean it and get a better look at it." Then he says, "Open," and pads my inner lip with cotton that's been soaked in sweet-tasting anesthetic.

I nod, but as he turns and pulls back on the upper part of a long-needled syringe, I start wondering. He's never given me Novocaine for a cleaning before. How do I even know it's him, with that costume on? What if the real Dr. Viera got busy with an emergency, and some crazy person snuck in, slipped on the appropriate accoutrements and settled in to have at me?

Maybe some crazy person with an ax to grind? I try to think of what enemies I have, but Dr. Viera, or his impostor, is removing the cotton pads from my gums, pulling my lower lip, then sticking me. "Now, that'll take just a minute to start numbing," he says. He sounds a lot like Dr. Viera.

He leaves the room, giving me time to adjust to the erasure of sensation. When he comes back, and says "Open," again, I try to look him in the eye, to see if he really is Dr. Viera, but he's pretty well focused on the inner reaches of my mouth. I take that to be a good sign, but even with the Novocaine, which I've always thought serves to soothe the nerves as well as numb the mouth, I can feel the sweat eke down my skin beneath my shirt.

If only I could ask him something, I would calm down. What happened to the chairside chitchat to relax the nervous patient? But of course I can't say anything, because now my tongue and lips are inflating into useless cottony masses, and he's chipping away at my teeth, breaking only to switch his instrument to its even sharper flipside. When he flips it again I see the end that he's been using is coated with blood. My blood.

Periodically he scours out my mouth with the plastic vacuum tube. Chip, chip, chip. Chip, chip, chip. I can see the wall behind his head is just a sheet of bright white light.

Chip, chip, scrape. I can hear the sound of a drill in another room.

Chip, chip. He doesn't seem to be making any progress at all. I shut my eyes, and when I tune back in, he is talking, saying something about children, how children do things they don't mean to and then don't understand the punishment later. Something about children not understanding their punishment.

Chip, chip, scrape. Flip. Wipe. Scrape.

Damn, why wasn't I paying attention? How did he get on this subject, anyway? I frantically wonder if Dr. Viera even has children. All this time I thought he was gay.

"I know children especially hate dentists," he says. I can't see his mouth behind his mask, and he keeps his eyes averted, focused on my molars which apparently have developed a layer of tartar more tenacious than the lime deposits on the Statue of Liberty.

Chip, chip, scrape. Chip, chip.

"My brother was going to be a dentist also," he says, wiping my blood from the pick onto the paper bib clasped around my neck. "But he didn't want a job in which his patients hated him."

I want to protest that I don't hate him, that I think he's probably a very nice dentist who never wanted to hurt anyone. But by now not only is my mouth stuffed with metal instruments and tartar chips and blood-streaked saliva, but also the Novocain he injected has bloated my tongue into a puffy, useless pad.

Chip, scrape. Flip.

"I guess it's particularly bad for pediatric dentists," he says. "My own patients have more understanding." At this, he looks me in the eye. I can't tell whether he's smiling behind the blue paper mask. "But I've heard horror stories from my colleagues: kids biting them, of course, but worse, even. One very good friend told me a gruesome story about how years ago—he's retired now—his house was actually broken into and vandalized after he'd done some particularly extensive work on a young patient."

Chip, chip, chip.

"He always suspected it was this one child, but of course he could prove nothing. He says that to this day he just tries to believe in some kind of divine retribution."

I try to scan the room, but it seems dark, and the building feels empty, and has gone very quiet. What is this? Since when do dental offices shut down at four p.m.? Dr. Viera notices this too, because as he keeps chipping and scraping he says, "Everyone except the receptionist leaves whenever they're done. I guess I'm the only one with a late patient today."

I try to remember the receptionist. Is she by any chance large and brutish, able to tear Dr. Viera's instrument from his hand, lift me from the chair, and carry me off to safety? Or is she in on it too? His accomplice? Come to think of it, she did bear a remarkable resemblance to little Daisy Stanislaus, Dr. Stanislaus' fat daughter that Jo and Tori and I had teased relentlessly. It was through Daisy that we'd learned the Stanislaus family was going out of town that weekend, the weekend after I'd gotten my braces.

Chip, chip, chip.

Innocent, Daisy had talked to us on the promise of our friendship—-we didn't have to stoop to offering her the rootbeer suckers and red licorice whips and sticky Maryjanes we kept stuffed in our jeans' pockets.

No, Daisy had talked to us quite freely, just thinking we'd take her into our circle, not quite quick enough to realize that her frilly pink frock and her white eyelet socks did nothing whatsoever to offset her terrible social impediment of being the dentist's daughter.

Chip, scrape.

She'd even told us where they hid the spare house key. The pet rabbit we'd found for ourselves, caged in a corner of the living room.

I glance down at the bib covering my chest, soaked with my blood and spit.

I look up at Dr. Viera. We were just kids, I want to say.

"Rinse," he commands, and I try to comply.

Mary Grace Vazquez

In or Out?

Jesus, Sister," Sister Mary Catherine whispered softly.

"Stop saying Jesus will you, Sister? I don't think we're in any position to be saying the Lord's name right now," Sister Anne said, also in a whisper. "Look at us. No clothes on, rolling around like two horny high school children. We should be ashamed of ourselves."

"Well," Sister Mary Catherine giggled, "I do feel ashamed but this is such fun and I do love you dearly. What am I supposed to do with these feelings?"

In response to the question Sister Anne gave Sister Catherine a deep long kiss that sent shivers of both shame and excitement through her entire body. Finally breaking away from the kiss, Sister Anne said, "Listen, in the morning we can't receive holy communion. It wouldn't be right. I'll tell Mother Superior that I'm ill and I'm afraid if I swallow the Body of Christ I might throw up."

"What am I supposed to tell her?" Sister Mary Catherine asked, running her fingers around Sister Anne's nipples. "If I don't go to communion, Mother Superior will notice. She keeps her eye on us all the time. It's like she doesn't trust us or something," said Sister Mary Catherine, kissing Sister Anne all over her stomach. "What's not to trust?" she said, running her fingers through Sister Anne's short, cropped, nun's idea of a good haircut.

Sister Anne gently pushed Sister Mary Catherine away. "Listen to you, Sister," she said. "What's not to trust? She must suspect that we're much too close for *her* comfort. Do the words *particular friendship* mean anything to you?" Sister Anne got off the bed and began to put her nightgown on.

"Listen, I've got to get some sleep. This fooling around half the night and getting up at five in the morning is killing me. We'll talk again tomorrow during the recreation hour, agreed?"

Sister Mary Catherine was sitting on the edge of the bed, seriously pouting. "Can't you stay a little longer, Sister? We can sleep," she said with a devilish grin.

"Oh right, I can see it now," Sister Anne laughed. "We fall asleep, the morning bell rings and we both answer, 'Praise the Lord.' Then the two of us trot out of the same room at the same time, half dazed and half asleep? I don't think so!"

"Okay," Sister Mary Catherine said in a resigned voice. "You're right. You win. I'll see you tomorrow." She blew Sister Anne a kiss as she quietly slipped out the door like a cat in the night.

"Jesus, what a woman," Sister Mary Catherine whispered to the darkness as she lay back in bed, wondering if she would ever sleep the sleep of holy innocence again.

"Sit down, Sisters." Mother Superior did not look happy. "Sister Mary Catherine, uncross your legs and sit up straight." She waved a hand toward Sister Catherine. "I have reason to believe that you two spent most of the night together." She glared at the two nuns sitting in front of her. "Am I correct, Sister Mary Catherine?"

I wonder who the snitch is, Sister Mary Catherine thought, none too charitably. Aloud she said, "Yes, Mother Superior, you're right."

"Sister Anne, is that right?" Mother Superior now addressed the other culprit who was staring at the floor avoiding Mother Superior's glare.

"Yes, Mother Superior, you're right," she said in a soft voice.

"Sisters, you both know that you are here to serve God and to love only God. We are not here to serve or love each other. We should of course love each other as a family of God. I do not think that God intended for you to serve Him and yourselves as you have been doing. You both need to make a serious decision," Mother Superior continued, her face a bright shade of crimson.

"Jesus, Mother." Sister Mary Catherine rolled her big blue eyes at Sister Anne.

"Don't say Jesus in vain, Sister." Mother Superior now looked even more upset. She glared at the two sisters. "You both need to decide today if you're in or out. If you're in, then you will conduct yourselves like true brides of Christ, not brides of each other."

Sister Anne wanted to laugh. Whenever she was in a bad situation, she laughed. *Please God, not now,* she thought to herself.

"I want your decision by tomorrow morning after mass. I will be in my office waiting for you. Under the circumstances I don't think it would be proper for either of you to receive communion. That fainting spell this morning did not fool me one bit, Sister Mary Catherine. It only got the Senior Sisters anxious and worried. They were all coming to my office this morning wondering about *your condition.* You may go now to think about your decision and may Jesus be with you both."

Sister Mary Catherine and Sister Anne walked back to their rooms, which were side by side. Sister Mary Catherine had pointed out more than once how convenient that was.

"Now what?" Sister Anne asked.

"It's quite clear to me, Sister Anne. We're leaving."

"Leaving?" Sister Anne gasped.

"Why not? I sure don't belong here. Why wait 'til they throw us out? We'll leave with honour."

"Just where do you think we are, Sister?" Sister Anne asked, holding onto Sister Mary Catherine's arm. "This isn't the army, you know. We're not going to get an honourable discharge. In case you didn't notice, Mother Superior was spitting mad at us."

"No honourable discharge, no farewell party, no nothing? Then hell, let's go right now. Let's just walk out the front door, not look back and live happily ever after. Can you do it, Sister Anne?"

"You're crazy. You know that, don't you?" Sister Anne hugged Sister Mary Catherine. "I can't stay here without you."

"That's it, then. We're out!" Mary Catherine grabbed Anne by the hand and they ran out the front door toward whatever Jesus had in store for them.

Chea Villanueva

In This Prison Flick

In this prison flick you are given one blanket, one pillow, and forced to live in a small metal box with no heat, no toilet, your only company the drain pipe—to catch your urine/shit/vomit/despair. . . . Despair is useless here. Time is senseless and sleeping is no longer a luxury in a place that knows no days, nights, hours, or months. You forget your name, the time you were born, and even your mother—in a place where memory creates pain, pain creates tears, and tears create the breaking point between a wall-less illusion and isolation. You meet and converse with the people inside your mind. Be a gangster, lawyer, doctor, Indian chief, vampire—as you draw drop by drop the blood from your finger, tongue, lips, and write your story on a concrete floor. Twenty-four years later you can finally tell it to the world how little Jackie got locked up in the women's penitentiary for selling drugs to an undercover police man.

"Didn't wanna do no time. Didn't wanna do no time." Only wanted to make a living in a world where rich was better and poor was a dead end street. *"Didn't wanna do no time . . ."*

"Oh baby, don't you weep and don't you moan," she told her girlfriend. *"Don't you weep and don't you moan."* They locked up Jackie for her own protection—from the bulldaggers, switches, snitches, and the outside world where number A-17 was a person; had a name.

In this prison flick you are stripped, fingers probe inside you, alien fingers burning your ass, your cunt. Your body burns with shame. Shame that comes from standing naked while you lift your breasts offering them to the guards who grab them roughly while they look for contraband after each and every visit from your mother, father, sister, brother, your lover—*How many times did your lover offer herself up to you in the same way?*

Your lover who you now speak to behind glass, her voice muffled between telephone lines. Her tears and caresses flow like rivulets of blood obstructing the view from the glass. You think of her kisses. Deep red luscious lipstick kisses forever staining your mind. Your mind—the one part you refuse to give up to them when number A-17 was a person, had a name, had a family, had a lover, lived, breathed, fucked, loved, with a name, with a name, was a person. . . .

David Watmough

Surprise Party

My lover was out of town so I squired Arethusa. It was a party surrounding a new movie about a friend of ours. The film was a National Film Board documentary about Henry Wishart Osborne, a fairly well known novelist who had recently died of AIDS.

And that's important because it determined that a large proportion of the audience was gay. It included a substantial number of dykes who were friends of Henry as he had spent a goodly portion of the past twenty years in striving to keep the two homosexual constituents working together. He was a bit of a crusader where gay unity was concerned. Some regarded him as a gay saint.

Arethusa seemed to know next to nothing about Henry Osborne except she may well have assumed he was gay in that I'd told her he'd had dinner with us from time to time.

I guess I should explain a little about Arethusa herself. She is a tall, fashionably dressed widow in her sixties with aggressively blonde hair in a huge beehive hairstyle, and a dowdy daughter in her late thirties who recently redeemed herself in maternal eyes by making her a grandmother. Arethusa, with her cartload of jewellry and tight silvery laugh, was a frequent visitor to our Vancouver home where she had met a fair number of our gay friends.

That might have been enough to earn her the title of fag-hag but somehow no one said it to her heavily powdered face. Although utterly at ease with a bunch of unmarried men who chatted about the exorbitant cost of new drapes, Arethusa, with true Canadian mien, never heard or saw anything she didn't want to. Brass monkeys were no competition for her *Canuck* discretion.

Not for a moment did I think I was taking a risk in inviting her to the invitation-only première of *The Healing Pen,* but I must admit to twenty-twenty hindsight.

The chatter was shrill in the crowded foyer. There was also the steady clink of drinks around the no-host bar. On that warm March day the low afternoon sun spilled in through open doors, washed boxes of flowering daffodils. The primarily young crowd were in short-sleeved shirts and blouses, sweaters suspended from waists and giant sport shoes worthy of Mickey Mouse.

Uppermost in my mind was the need to put names to faces so that I could present Arethusa to those who would approach and politely expect to be introduced. That distraction made me less attentive to the stately companion who sailed at my side than I should have been.

The evidence of that was unsettlingly immediate. I was about to introduce Arethusa to an importunate decorator queen who rashly assumed that anyone at my arm was important and thus potentially useful.

"This is Orville," I began, only to find that Arethusa was not eyeing the slight figure in a tangerine shirt and tight black pants but two women at our rear. I turned too, to see a stocky woman in her fifties hungrily licking the earhole of her equally bulky, if slightly younger companion. Both women seemed quite oblivious of our presence until the ear-explorer smiled at my companion and generously invited, in the expansiveness of Sapphic sharing, my startled friend to have a nibble of her lover's nacreous lobe if she so wished.

Arethusa didn't glide up to me in her usual fashion but pranced like a startled elk in my direction.

Orville grinned broadly, revealing his second treasure, a set of niveous white teeth. (His number *one* treasure, prominently displayed via the tight pants, was half way between those teeth and his dainty little feet. He, like me, wasn't wearing Adidas or Roebucks.)

"I'm Orville Daubney. Have you noticed how Vancouver gets more *osé,* day by day? And to think we're here to see a movie about that old closet queen, Henry." He put a manicured hand up to his mouth. "Oh, *what* am I saying?"

Whether goaded by his flamboyance I'm unsure, but she certainly seemed to shed her reaction to the now *french-tongueing* women in a hurry.

"Did you say Daubney?" she asked, her voice several notches higher than usual. "Any relation to Kenneth Daubney?"

Orville curtsied. "My father," he admitted happily. "My first lover, as a matter of fact."

"I went to high school with him,"Arethusa told him hurriedly. "Prince of Wales?"

"The one and only," Orville affirmed. "I went there, too. Like it's all in the family—as I said earlier about darlin' Dad."

I steered her firmly away from him. Sapphic dalliance in public was one thing—incest quite another.

"Out of the frying pan into the fire" is just a rather shop-worn saying for some people. For me it sometimes seems a way of life. I veered away from Orville to confront Norman Winfield. Norman was a piss-poor poet and frustrated politician who vehemently believed I was just a reactionary blot on the gay radical landscape. He swiftly surveyed the glittering bulk of Arethusa before firing his first torpedo.

"I'm glad you brought a friend in drag, Davey. Where on earth did you find such magnificence? My, those sequins! And *what* a hairdo. Am I imagining things or do I see a white mouse peeking out from those peroxide strands?"

Desperately I tried a defense. "I don't know about mice, sweetie, but I'm looking at a rat. And if you don't mind my mixing metaphors, have you written any more *dog*gerel lately?"

Torpedo number two. "I *beg* both your pardons. Now I can see the resemblance. It's your mother, *n'est-ce pas*, Davey?"

My hand wasn't gently at her elbow but grabbing the fat of her arm as I elected retreat. I shoved her into the theatre where mercifully the screening was about to begin. But trouble was not yet done. As the film reached a moment of quiet solemnity, an actor reading from Henry's last novel, those two amorous ladies from the foyer who were sitting right in front of us, emboldened by the gloom, progressed much further with their mutual groping with one head even sinking down out of our sight.

Arethusa suddenly pinched my thigh hard before creaking to her feet and announcing in a hoarse voice I'd never heard before, "Let's get the fuck out of here!"

We did.

Jess Wells

Bird's Eye on Girls

I sat like a vulture, perched on the edge of the balcony, my hands gripping the railing as if they were talons. Below me, in Orchestra Sections A, B, and C, were three of my ex-lovers, each unaware of each other, and unaware of me looking at them from above as if they were the carrion of fifteen years of my life.

Roberta helped some young thing off with her coat; Claudia argued with her girlfriend over who should sit next to the man in their row; and Antonia stumbled down the aisle, laughing, gesturing the way she does when she's telling a joke that's at her own expense.

It couldn't have been worse timing. If the tickets hadn't been so expensive, and my involvement with my new date so on the edge, I might have gotten up and left.

My date and I were at *that* point. We had determined there were no Republican tendencies between us, that the sex was good, that each was reasonably prompt and relatively free of neurosis. She was crazy about me, she said. I genuinely liked her. Both our sets of friends had made encouraging gestures. Any minute now she was going to put her arm around the back of my chair and I was supposed to snuggle in.

Instead, I wanted to swoop off the railing and strafe the hairlines of my exes. I wanted blood.

Antonia was wearing that soft leather jacket I had bought her when it was our time to snuggle in. Claudia had no doubt driven here in the car we had bought together and that I had lost in the divorce. As for Roberta, I didn't want to think of all the pairs of sapphire earrings I had bought her that were now under beds all over town.

I didn't want to pick the meat off their bones for the things they had said, or the infidelities, or the anguish over property settlements and in-laws lost to loyalty. I just wanted to claw the optimism out of their chests.

Relationships are such pretense. We pretend that they're going to last forever. But we all break up. Inevitably. Invariably. Then we become best friends. So why do we even pretend that we're not going to divorce? Why all the soupy, sappy dialogue about forever? And since when is longevity the test of true love? Why should a recognition of the mutable nature of love be seen as inconsiderate? You have life insurance against the possibility that you might die early, and medical insurance against the 1:1,000 odds that you might get seriously ill, but you're not allowed to talk realistically about the 1:2 chance that you will break up. Tell her that you will love her absolutely and treat her like a queen for the finite time that your love lasts, and then that you will honour her and keep her as a member of your closest family thereafter for the rest of her days, and her friends will tear her away from you like you have a beak and a gizzard.

I sensed a wattle flapping under my scowling face. We pretend that it was actually sensible to buy things together, or that one of us isn't keeping track of who had paid for which book. We pretend that relationships don't mean you have to suddenly ask permission for everything—going out with your friends, coming home late from work, buying stereo gear, planning your weekend—or that you must suddenly make joint decisions about *everything*—television channels, restaurants, your car/my car, should we take coats, the windows opened or closed at night. We pretend that it is a better life to suddenly be at each other's side at all times for all things. Tell a woman that you'll live with her but will spend two nights a week in your room reading and one night a week alone with friends. See what happens. Give name to non-matrimony! I wanted to squawk down on the crowd.

But it was time to snuggle in with this new girlfriend of mine. We had recently gone from sleeping together three nights a week to just stopping by her place for clean clothes. It was *that* kind of moment. When you couldn't remember what your refrigerator looked like without her assortment of olive jars in it. When you start *assuming* that you'll spend the weekends together. Upon reaching this juncture in the past, I would have redecorated the bathroom in her favourite colours. The trip to Bed and Bath Superstore would have been some kind of foreplay. This time I wanted to sail away on my vulture wings, consider all the couples below me some form of rotting meat.

And yet for the honour of her love, I thought, turning to see her so dapper, so kind, draping my coat across the back of my seat, a relationship seemed the least I could do. It was a necessary evil, like taxes to pay for the roads. Shackles on your ankles to free your heart.

My dear one twinkled at me. "What would you like to do this weekend?" she whispered just as the lights went down.

I smiled sadly, nestling into the crook of her arm, while my fingernails gripped into my thighs. "I don't know, sweetie. What do *you* want to do?"

John Whiteside

A Tin of Cocoa

It's just a red cylinder, perhaps eight inches tall, with a gold legend reading, "Cacao Bensdorp," and below that, "Royal Dutch." A sticker on the side tells me that it came from Dean and Delucca in New York City. It's almost empty; there's at most a spoonful of cocoa at the bottom of the tin.

It's a grey, cold afternoon, one of those early spring days that makes you think the New England winter is never going to end, when the chill penetrates you to the bone in seconds and can't be shaken for hours. Living in an apartment that's half full and half empty has been bothering me; the spaces between pieces of furniture and the imprints on the rug where a chair was make it seem like the movers just took Alan's things out an hour ago. I decided to start with the kitchen cabinets, to spread what remains through the empty spaces.

The first time I saw this tin was five years ago, on a day much like today. Grey and cold, but it was December, when such days make sense. It was the day of our first date.

Alan's roommate arranged it. Somehow we decided that it would be easier if he accompanied us, and somehow it was decided that we should meet at three-thirty in the afternoon, although the plan was to have dinner. And so I found myself at a pub in Jamaica Plain in the middle of the afternoon, watching Alan walk in with his roommate and several other people.

"These are my friends from Atlanta," he explained. "I just picked them up at the airport."

We ate, and eventually we all ended up at Alan's house to trim his Christmas tree. The cocoa tin sat on a shelf over his old-fashioned sink.

The house was a classic Boston triple-decker, plain and comfortable, and it was easy to imagine a succession of Irish families living there, the children crammed into one of the small bedrooms, the parents walking up the block to South Street to catch the trolley to work. The house was untouched and unruined by modernization; no drop ceilings or wall-to-wall carpet, just the simple lines and wooden surfaces that had always been there.

Alan is very good at playing host, and so he made hot chocolate. The tin was almost full that day, and I remember a slightly awkward conversation in the kitchen as he heated the milk and his roommate pulled boxes of Christmas ornaments out of the hall closet.

For a while the tin sat on our kitchen counter in the South End. We moved in together in the fall, and that winter we seemed to have friends over for dinner every weekend. We'd walk to the supermarket in the Prudential Center, where most of the other gay men in the neighbourhood seemed to shop, and while I picked out the main ingredients for dinner Alan would choose the components of a salad—by colour, so it would look right. That evening, our small apartment would be filled with the sounds of our friends. The tin of cocoa gradually got lighter as the memories accumulated.

It's a nice tin, and I'm sure Alan would have taken it with him if he'd noticed it crammed behind a bag of sugar and a box of teabags on the top shelf of the cabinet. But I'm standing in my tiny kitchen, holding it and remembering another grey day, when it was full and it belonged to a man whose touch was filled with mystery and promise.

It looks very different today. Now it reminds me of comfort, of how warm this apartment used to feel on cold winter afternoons, of friends having dinner and Christmas trees and all the small things I'm going to miss. I feel embarrassed and a little bit maudlin, standing in my kitchen looking at a tin of cocoa, while tears well up in my eyes.

I set the tin on the counter, pull a tissue from the brightly-coloured box on the counter. Blowing my nose, I look back at the tin. It *is* a nice container. I pour the last spoonful of cocoa out of it, rinse it with cold water, and set it on the drying rack. Perhaps I'll keep teabags in it now.

Duane Williams

How to Find the Chair of Your Dreams

At fourteen, admit the truth to yourself. You are attracted to chairs. Vow to take your secret to the grave. Beneath your mattress, hide old Ikea catalogues. Worry that your acne is a sign of God's disapproval. In the presence of your mother, avoid chairs for fear she will notice your deviance.

Begin to despise your mother. Dream of her in a casket, wearing the lime green dress with seashells for buttons. This is a recurring dream. At a dinner party for her boss, throw the truth in her face. You have been with a chair. Your dead father's rocker. After extensive therapy, overcome your illness. Concentrate on school. Win the award for top student in calculus.

Move to Toronto. At furniture stores, become an uncontrollable slut. Realize, after more therapy, that you are really looking for love. Buy a recliner, a lawn chair, a bean bag, a stool. Eventually, find yourself on a pew, considering God.

Just when all hope is lost, spot the chair of your dreams at a party. At this fateful moment, your mouth is full of biscotti. Manage to smile from across the room. In a mirror, check your face for crumbs. The chair is mahogany with a strong back and carved legs. Walk over. Take a seat. Breathe. *This* is the one.

On the first date, determine your feelings for the chair. This is an important step to a healthy, long-lasting relationship. In your mind, hear the radio voice of Dr. Cindy, Shrink to the Lovelorn. Her voice instructs you to focus your buttocks. Shift your weight from one to the other. Push them into the chair. What do you feel? At midnight, open a bottle of Dom Perignon and feed smoked oysters to the chair. Hear yourself telling it that you are in love.

Forget to return your friends' calls. You are developing a relationship with your chair. Avoid the tendency to recreate the one which you have with your mother. Be passionate. Move slowly. This relationship will have lasting effects on the direction of your spine.

After moving in with your chair, bump into an estranged friend on your way to the therapist's. Say just enough to imply that you are miserable. Instead of leaving your chair, claim your entitlement to self. Secure your identity. There is a fine line between the self and your chair. Define this boundary. Read somewhere that denial of emotion, especially anger, can lead to hardening of the stools and, in severe cases, piles. Check this with your therapist.

Begin to stifle your chair. Ask that it be intimate with no ass but yours. Plant evil thoughts in its mind about cats and other animals with claws or shedding proclivities. Bar it from card tables, kitchen tables, any table that attracts single chairs. Your chair will be patient, understanding, faithful.

Become disenchanted with your chair. At the party for your first year anniversary, catch yourself eyeing an armchair with incredible curves. Do not, in any way, deal with your doubts. Let them drag on and on. Deny suggestions that your buttocks are not as loving as they once were. In spite of yourself, fall asleep in your chair, night after night. Have an affair with a public toilet.

Leave your chair, once and for all. In a drunken mess, call your estranged friends. They are screening your calls. Lament all that you've lost from being involved with your chair. At two o'clock in the morning, call your mother. Spill everything. Cry. When she starts in about how if you'd just listened to her and finished your MBA and pursued a lifestyle with a desk like everybody else, hang up. Vow to live the rest of your life motherless. Chairless. Sell your chair to an antique store, although it is not yet old. Take whatever they'll give you. With the money, go to a strip club. Stand at the bar. When a bar stool in black leather catches your eye, appear aloof. Look away. *This* is the one.

Barbara Wilson

The Woman Who Married Her Son's Wife

How did it come to this, the three of us with pancake make-up melting in the camera's glare, the talk show host, Allegra Mostly, demanding that we bare our heart's secrets to the raucous studio audience? The audience is waiting for our story, waiting with curled lips to lunge toward us, to demand, "How could you do such a disgusting thing? How could you betray your son? Your husband?" Will they call me a depraved mother and my daughter-in-law a perverse slut? Will my son be seen as pathetic and ill-used?

I see the audience waiting like lions outside the circle glare of our public trial; I hear them slathering, pretending to be normal, honest Americans who just wanted to attend Allegra Mostly's show because they admire her so much, because they think the issues she brings up are really important.

The only show of Allegra's I have ever watched was on Men Who Have Sex With Dogs. But that was in the old days, Elise assured me, when Allegra and the other talk hosts were competing so hard against each other. Nowdays they have cleaned up their acts, she read somewhere, pressured by Congress to deal with questions of more substance and decency.

"It will be tasteful," Elise said. "She's giving us a chance to explain our story. Our story could be helpful to other people in the same situation." And Allegra herself was kind enough to call to convince me. "Sometimes love knows no boundaries," she said, in that soft, firm, warm voice that is familiar to millions. "It's important that we talk about that."

It is a hard thing to acknowledge about my lover, now my new partner since her divorce and our ceremony, but Elise, so ordinary in some ways, wants very much to be famous. She has bought a new dress for the occasion. It is short and white, with rather silly capped sleeves. Her dark cap of hair is shiny and soft, and even before the make-up man got hold of her, she had put on foundation and lipstick and outlined her pretty green eyes with black—she, who always went around in jeans and a torn t-shirt. Beside her I feel ancient and wrinkled in my grey pantsuit and glasses. I am thirty-nine. I should know better. The other two are just babies, barely out their teens.

I remember when Darrell was born, and how I rocked him as a baby. I remember his first tooth, his first playground fight, his first girlfriend. He was not a smart boy, nor an athletic one; only good-natured and a little dull. I never understood what Elise saw in him, why she dated him in high school, why she wanted to get married. I told them they should wait; I'd gotten married young, right out of high school. Where had it gotten me? A divorce and the financial struggle to raise my son alone. "Wait," I told them. "Get jobs. Go to college." I was speaking more to Elise, "You're growing and changing so much now. In a few years things may look completely different."

Neither of them had jobs at the time of their marriage, two days after high school ended. They moved in with me, into Darrell's room. Elise wanted to get away from her parents. Darrell just wanted what Elise wanted.

It wasn't that I didn't like having them around. Elise and I had always gotten along. We joked and cooked together, watched television, read each other funny parts of the newspapers. She called me her real mother; I said she was the daughter I'd never had. When did it become something more?

Darrell took a job on a fishing boat that summer. He was gone three months, and returned in September. He had enough money to move out then, but Elise didn't want to. She said, "Your mom will be lonely." They quarreled and sulked until the following May, when Darrell went out with the fishing fleet again.

The first night he was gone Elise came into my room, just the way she had last summer, but this time it was different. This time she didn't just want to sleep. Sleeping wasn't what I wanted either. Last summer it had been all sweet flirtation and cuddling and delicious tension. All winter it had been awkward and sad. Now everything let loose; we could not pry ourselves away from each other.

"I'm not a lesbian," she said. And I told her I wasn't either. After all, we'd both married men. We pretended, at first, that we did what we did only because we didn't have men around now. But one day Elise whispered, pressed into the mattress, below my heavy breasts, all my fingers deep inside her, "This is better, this is better than with men."

It was all a secret. We didn't think about what we were really doing, whom we were betraying, until Darrell came home again and Elise said, "I can't sleep with you anymore, Darrell. Your mom and I are . . ."

I remember how he didn't look at me, only went inside his room and closed the door.

"It's not how it sounds," I want to tell the crowd of dressed-up women and men pretending to be decent, normal Americans. "I'm like you. I'm not crazy or perverted. I never knew these things about myself. If I hadn't met Elise, none of this would have ever happened."

She smiles across at me and again my heart stops. That dark cap of hair, those pretty green eyes, that lust for love and publicity.

"What if I had divorced my husband to marry his father? Would you think that so strange?" she is asking the crowd. "It's just the same. Practically just the same."

The audience roars, a hungry lion. My son looks helpless. I, his mother, never prepared him for this. I look at Elise. I feel her bones beneath me. When Allegra asks me why I did it, I can only say, "Sometimes love knows no boundaries."

Phoenix Wisebone

Revisions

Dear Margo,

You are the one I've waited for all my life. Without our love, I will perish.

Okay, I won't perish, I just won't get to stroke your ass like I've wanted to, or plunge my tongue into your wet, hot pussy.

Dear Margo,

My tongue longs for your clit . . .

Dear Margo,

My tongue is tied.

My clit is . . .

Dear Margo,

Would you please stop with the "I'm too shy to ask if I can fuck you" routine? We've been secretly ogling each other for twelve months now. I'm tired of pretending not to notice when you think I can't see you checking me out. Time and time again days have passed silently when we could've told each other how we felt, could've asked each other for what we wanted, could've had a rapt evening of wild, wet lust.

I'm tired of these polite chats about "the polyconfigurationalism of New Age thought." Save it for you doctorate! I've slept in twisted sheets for ages now. "Rise up my love, my fair one, and come away" is all I can say at this point.

Would we pass up this chance now, instead of seizing our day (and night) or prefer to wither for lack of each other's rivers?

Soon the year will be up. I'll be heading north for school—and where will you be? Locked up in your ivory tower of pre-doctoral propaganda passing for higher trains of thought.

What hasn't yet become can be, yet won't if we don't act fast. Will this be a fond farewell, or a melancholy "so long"? . . .

Dear Margo,

Thank you for sending me the photographs of your commitment ceremony. I hope the teaching post works out. I've given up on the honours degree and am settling for a B.A.

Decided to give up dating. I think I'll become a nun.

Nothing Kristofer Wolfe

Confessions of a Street Whore

I climb into your bed and over your cock. It fits into me like the wrong piece of a puzzle, scraping at my insides. I can hear your whispers, your secrets, your tales. Your breathing becomes rapid. Your tongue violent. I lay on the bed as you undress and the confessions begin.

Your t-shirt falls to the ground. Your body is large and hairy. I wonder how I could ever be able to have sex with you. I would never be able to make love to you. Of course, this is not love or sex. It is only a job.

I wonder what it would be like to kiss a boy, instead of kissing a man. Men are so rough with their lips. Their tongues. They think that I enjoy their clammy hands violating my skin. Do you lose coordination with age? Or is it just with sex? I wonder what it would be like to be a virgin again?

No, I do not have a home. I live in the alcove where you found me, curled up against my friend's skin. The people are nice to us. They never make demands, unless the cops hassle them about having kids sleeping on their steps.

I wonder why you ask me these questions. Do you really care? You must have picked up so many boys before. It is not like I am special or something. Soon, you will forget my name and I will just be another face in the crowd. You'll pass me by when I am stoned and I ask you for a quarter for a bite to eat and you will laugh in my face with your business suit and carefully parted hair. Don't you know how lucky you are to have a life?

Oh, I know how fun it is to run from cops at night when I don't have anywhere to go and buddy over there keeps asking if I want to buy some of his stash but everyone knows that you have some to unload yourself. Nobody's buying but everyone's carrying it. It is the wonder drug. It is sex. Sex. Sex. Sex. I know that you want it because you have brought me here today and—is that a package of smokes in your jacket pocket? Mind if I have one? It'll probably calm me down.

I'm sorry I'm being like this. I guess I just haven't done this in a while. My boyfriend left me with a bag of pot and that's almost gone. I was supposed to sell it for food but half of it got smoked—you know how it is. So here I am selling again to men like you. You wouldn't happen to have a light would you?

Would you mind if I called you Daddy? I hope that you don't—it's not an incestuous thing or anything like that. It's just that, well, you're warm like a teddy bear and I wouldn't mind having a Daddy like you. You know what I mean?

I wish that I was good enough to be your son but I'm sure that you wouldn't want me around. Who would want a son who has make-up smeared across his face and smells like stale booze and—did you know that they want me to be a girl? Well, my boyfriend does anyways. He says that I would make a beautiful girl and that I would make more money that way. I don't know. If I was going to be a girl, I think that I would be a dyke because I wouldn't want to waste my time with men like you.

You want to start already? God, I haven't even finished my smoke yet.

You toss it aside and your lips are on my body again. My pants are down around my ankles and you are sucking like you are addicted to my cock. I don't understand the enjoyment you receive having me in your mouth. My cum flooding your throat. Do I taste as sweet as sugar or am I bitter? I've never tasted someone who was sweet yet.

I close my eyes and pretend that you are not you. You are that beautiful boy who often passes me by. His hair is short and blond and he wears a blue flannel shirt. I guess it is really all he has to wear. I always thought he would taste sweet until the night he offered to rail with me and I lost all respect in him. I really don't like the hard drugs. They are too mind-stripping and sad.

My orgasm shoots through me like a bullet as it exits my cock shooting out jism semen blood stench and you lap at me like a wild dog then disappear into your corner. Ashamed to have even touched me. I guess you have a wife and kids to go home to. Do you use mouthwash to get rid of the taste of stale sperm? I guess you don't want your wife tasting it on you.

You quickly get dressed and I pull on my clothes. You call me some name that isn't mine and throw me some bills which will disappear in a matter of minutes. I fold them up carefully and tuck them into my back pocket. I follow you to the door and squint as the light hits my eyes once again.

You drive me back to the spot where my friends wait for me and sit in silence as I click open my seatbelt and climb out the door. We do not share goodbyes. We are strangers in this world where you are a criminal and I am a child.

Laura Wood

Into the Dark

A seaside town in winter. Breezes become gales and gales turn into reckless storms. Huge waves crash ferociously on this deserted shore where once little toddlers splashed and safely paddled. Everything is washed clean, rearranged, scrubbed down.

I look out to sea. The sky moves in giant strides toward me. Dark masses heavy with moisture loom above my head and the sky is criss-crossed with great shafts of light, like a vast articulation of cosmic emotion.

It is early in the morning. I walk slowly along the promenade and sit down on a bench. Innumerable men have had sex together in the toilets just below where I am sitting. I close my eyes and think about it. Two men are having a splash and staring at each other's dicks. . . . What happens next? I can't imagine it.

A woman walks past. She is wearing a black leather biker's jacket, loose-cut blue jeans and big black boots. Her hair is short on top and shaved at the sides. Her face is tough. Her eyes broken and deep. She casts me a bold half-smiling glance and walks rapidly toward a large unlit subway which runs beneath the promenade. She kisses me with that look. She walks in a muscular way, strides toward the dark tunnel and I follow her.

The grey sky turns black and bitter cold rain whips into my face. Water pours down the steep sloping gravel footpaths and soaks my feet as I splash toward the tunnel. She is waiting there, leaning against the wall with shoulders hunched, a cigarette in her hand. She smiles when she sees me come toward her. I lean up against the wall next to her.

"Smoke?" She flicks up the lid of a half-empty pack. I pull a cigarette out. She offers me a light. A gust of wind blows down the tunnel. She shelters the flame in her hands. I lean toward the flame. My cigarette glows. I draw in a deep breath and exhale clouds of smoke. I look into her face. She turns away. The leather of her jacket creaks as she takes the cigarette from her lips.

"Cold, isn't it," she says with a shiver.

"Freezing," I say in a huddled reply. She looks at me. I look down. Her look sends a thousand erotic sensations streaming through my body.

Suddenly we're embracing. I squeeze her hard. "I can't feel you beneath all this leather," I say. She laughs and rubs her hair in my face and kisses the base of my neck. We struggle in each other's arms. By now I am breathing heavily. Her face is damp and flushed.

So *fast*, I can't stop thinking, as I push my thigh between her legs. She presses down on me and uses my shoulders to pull us closer together. She unzips my fly and forces her hand under the curve of my groin.

"Let me," she whispers breathlessly.

"Yes . . . ," I relax in her grip.

She cups me and kneads me. Her hands are strong and I long for their power. I kiss her lips. She sucks my tongue. One finger at a time, she penetrates me until the whole of her big hand is inside me. I murmur in her ear, "Fuck me, fuck me. . . ."

"Yes . . . ," she says. She supports her hand with the weight of her thigh and pushes and pushes until the throbbing inside me bursts through my body like fireworks. She groans and calls out a name, then presses against me more gently. For a moment my head rests on her shoulder. I feel the softness of her face. I hold her in my arms.

She presses again, so gently. Kisses my hair. At last her fingers slip out and she pulls away. I fall backward against the wall. My legs are trembling. She looks upward into the dark. Her face is radiant. She puts her hands in her pockets, turns and walks out of the tunnel. My eyes follow. She doesn't look back.

Karen Woodman

Evidence

You were scared and sitting with her parents in that fancy restaurant because you wanted them to like you so much and wished they didn't have to. You fumbled with the cutlery and laughed when things weren't funny. Her mother gave you a long look when she thought you weren't noticing. You were telling them about the trip the two of you hoped to take. You wiped your chin with your sleeve, scratched your nose and swallowed a spoonful of soup that was too hot. The spices burned your throat and you made a small coughing sound. You wanted to cough louder and empty the water glass but you didn't. You held your breath, took a sip of water and swallowed and swallowed to stop the burning.

It reminded you of the afternoon you ran into your aunt on the street. She was sophisticated, had married a freemason and sometimes looked at you with a kind of bewilderment that made you uncomfortable. She asked what you were doing and you said you were just out for a walk, wandering around, doing nothing in particular. She said no, she meant what were you doing with your life and you said, oh, I didn't know that's what you meant and you tried to think of things that would sound significant, sensible, organized and ambitious. When she walked away you were relieved because it was already three-thirty and the welfare office closed at four. Passing the two security guards you were glad because the line-up was short. You got your cheque without any questions and sat in a hard plastic chair to fill out the stub. Do you still require assistance? Yes. Are you looking for work? Yes. A drop of blood fell to the floor. Your hand went to your nose and when you pulled it away, there was blood on your fingers. You held two fingers to the side of your nose pressing on the veins to stop the bleeding and looked around to see if anyone had noticed. No one was looking and you were glad, because you just wanted the bleeding to stop. Two drops of blood landed on your cheque and you silently cursed everything and nothing. You licked your fingers, dabbed your nostrils to wipe off the blood and brushed your nose with your coat sleeve. There were no mirrors or public washrooms in the welfare office, so you had no way of knowing if there was blood on your face. When you walked out to the street, passed the security guards, you hoped you wouldn't run in to anyone you knew, especially not her mother.

Raymond John Woolfrey

All Saints' Day

When Michael arrived for dinner Sunday evening, it was a perfect Halloween night—dark and gloomy. We settled into my kitchen at the back, leaving the front dark to ward off any candy-crazed monsters who might dare to ring the bell. Later, when Michael opened the front door to let himself out, we gasped. No, there were no monsters jumping and squealing at us; rather, five centimetres of wet, very cheerful snow covering the ground and sticking to tree limbs, car roofs and parking signs. So much for the Halloween look.

"Good thing we did our partying *last* night," said Michael.

"Imagine trying to get through *this* in high heels," I replied.

They had predicted snow, but I thought they meant a few dry flakes swirling out of an inky sky to melt a few seconds later at our feet. "It'll probably be gone before morning. It's too early for it to stay," I said, hopefully.

But the next day when I opened the blinds I was astonished to see the same, sodden "winter wonderland" raging away. The beech tree across the street, its leaves bright yellow for Halloween, now looked foolish coated in snow. The monsters of the night before—now masquerading as schoolchildren, with their multicoloured snowsuits that made them look like the bonbons they'd been gorging on—were beside themselves with glee. The snow was perfect for snowballs and, at recess, snowmen, no doubt. Weary mothers tagged behind them, their faces long with dread for the five or six months of snow and cold to come.

I couldn't help delighting in it all—there's always something thrilling about the first snowfall. Besides, surely it wouldn't stay, would it? But it *did* mean the end of cycling to work—for a while at least; and that meant using the old BMW: bus, métro and walking.

As the 129 bus to Outremont groaned its way through the Park Avenue slush and past Fletcher's Field, I looked up from my paper to peer through the windows' heavy condensation at the white, snow-capped trees. In the bus, a few male Université de Montréal students—about the only passengers—caught my eye. They reminded me that the first snowfall always makes me horny.

I went back to reading my paper, but soon looked up to study a young blond with a fuzzy helmet-strap beard who was frowning at his agenda. What potent lips, I thought. Then I felt foolish. It wasn't *horny* that the first snowfall made me, it was *romantic*. I needed someone to cuddle with.

That night, with no work the next day, and free schnapps with beer at La Queue Dorée, I wondered: Should I stay in on this cold night (the temperature had fallen to minus five), or should I venture out to celebrate the first snowfall with the other bad boys who like to stay up past their bedtimes? Will magic happen, and I'll meet friends and engage in mind-blowing conversations or even have a hot time with someone new? Or will it be boring and I'll stand by myself in a corner writing stories in my head?

The ice crunched beneath my combat boots as I headed for the bar. The cold, hard air stung my nostrils and bronchi like Vick's and formed small clouds before me as I breathed out, making me look like the bull I felt like. By February such nights will have become oppressive, but in the fall it's a welcome new sensation—a contrast to the stupefying August heat when its dirty, humid air feels the same within your lungs as without.

Once at La Queue, I settled in at a corner of the central bar to watch the crowd (it was thin) and allow the alcohol to slow down the thoughts that usually spin in my head.

About an hour later, a good-looking, dark-haired guy flashed me a smile from across the bar. I flashed one back. Soon, thanks in no small way to the couple of schnapps-and-beer I'd downed, I was on my way around the bar.

"Hi," we said. Pete was his name. He had a big warm smile and large brown eyes that shone and laughed. Thick curly hair fell down across his forehead. He put his arm around me, I put mine around him, and we caressed each other as we talked about unimportant yet interesting things.

He was standing on the footrest of the bar so that his head was higher than mine—I got a kick out of slipping my hand up into the back of a "taller" guy's shirt, and I thought this enactment of his little fantasy was kind of cute.

We left at closing time and went to my place. Pete's lovemaking was as fun as his conversation—it was six before we fell asleep.

The next morning was sunny and, with the snow still on the ground, whiter-than-white bright; but milder, so the snow melted off roofs and cars, and the white street slowly turned a glistening black as passing traffic flattened the slush into nothing.

After breakfast we brought coffee to my bedroom at the front where the sun was pouring in upon the bed. There we sprawled, our legs entwined, as Pete turned the pages of my atlas. He found the island in Greece from where his family had emigrated. "The endings of Greek family names are related to the area from which they came," he said.

The doorbell rang. I disentangled my legs and went to the front hall just off the bedroom to answer. It was Yves, my landlord—something about how Hydro was charging him at the same time I was paying. As I made him a copy of my bill with the fax machine, he poked his head into the bedroom and said jovially, "*As-tu vu les flocons hier soir? C'était pas de fantômes! Tu parles d'une joke!*" (How about those snowflakes last night! Not exactly ghosts, eh! Some trick!) Pete lowered his eyes and smiled bashfully. Then Yves asked for a shovel, and went back out to scoop the snow off the balcony.

"Do you think I should get off the bed before he comes back in?" Pete asked.

"Of course not. I don't care what he thinks—and besides, he's okay. He used to be a nurse."

"That's really nice of him to shovel your steps. My landlord would never do that."

As Yves made scraping sounds with the shovel, we resumed our study of the atlas. We curled up together, kissed a bit, and closed our eyes as the sun's warmth poured over us. Contented, I snoozed. The saints had given me a first-snowfall romance.

Jane F. Wrin

Monomum

Hello love, it's nice to see you, come in.

Yes, I'm all right, oh thanks. Did you get that nice bread from Greggs? I do like that, it's so soft. Would you like a cup of tea?

Oh, right then, how are you? Any boyfriends on the scene?

Sorry, I didn't mean to pry.

Mrs. Tatton came round yesterday, her dog has got rheumatism, sad really, I think they'll have to put it down and she's had him for so long now.

Yes, okay. Well . . . you sit down too. What's the matter, you're very agitated?

There must be something, you're like a cat on a hot tin roof.

I'm not nagging. I'll make a cup of tea.

All right, all right, love, I won't. What is it?

You're what, love, I didn't hear you?

Gay . . . that's nice, I mean, I don't know what's wrong with youngsters these days, they're all so gloomy. It's nice to be happy, jolly, gay . . . I'll make that cup of tea.

Okay, I'm sitting, I'm sitting. . . .

Yes, I know Helen, she's a good friend. Like me and Mrs. Tatton.

Don't get so irritated, I'm old, you know. You shouldn't be so ratty.

Yes . . . you and Helen.

I *will* make that tea.

Now listen young lady, I don't know what you're trying to say but I need a cup of tea.

I'm sitting, I'm sitting.

I *am* listening, but you're not saying anything.

Yes, you said you were gay.
Of course I know what that means. You're carefree, happy. . . .
Don't shout.
Yes, Helen and you. . . .

Michael Wynne

Spurning

In order to be there before the service starts, he leaves directly from the pharmacy which he runs with his boyfriend in Bangor. On the passenger seat beside him is a simple wreath for the dead boy and, lying underneath, the video of a skin flick, recently sent through the post and ignored since. As he drives over the backroads to Ballycastle he hums the contorted strains of a reel, his remembrance of his dislike for the dead boy, his irritation at his toothache-afflicted lover, and images from a rimming sequence that they played to accompany their peevish lovemaking the previous evening, at points all coinciding. At an oblique crossroads he interrupts his private air to say, "Here, like that young turd, people hung by their necks for all manner of deeds, buggery not being the least of them." He feels no guilt at referring to the dead boy like that. Instead he is suddenly horny at the thought of the butt-happy Latin men that helped sustain his desire and that of his lover last night, and strokes his throat, sore from sleeping in the draughty room above their apothecary.

When he reaches the grey terraced house he sees them, the young parents, unhappy and unmarried, standing outside and apart among a shoe-gazing group; and he gets out, conscious of his calmness, kisses the chilled cheeks of the mother—his half-sister—pats her strained-faced man on the shoulder-blade as gently, as manfully as he can.

He, the young father, whose face even in its desolateness bears traces of the confused delirium of adolescence, wipes his white dripping nose on the cuff of the navy suit left behind by his common-law father-in-law, who died the morning the dead child was born. On the lapel there is still the pioneer pin the former wearer sported all his life with pride, even in the face of discernibly suppressed ridicule; it remains because the young father, whose drinking has increased since his beloved was laid off, would not exactly be sure what it stood for, even if he had fully noticed it.

His neck-tie is navy also, and pencil-thin, but has a resilient look that would not enable an observer to rule out the possibility of its having the power to quiet a jumped-up little big mouth for good and all.

Later, while the larger-than-expected pine casket is being clumsily lowered between the level walls of clay, the pharmacist's eyes centre on this thin strip of navy; while people shuffle and sniffle about him, he concentrates on how the mishap, termed "freak" by the local newsrag, could come about. With the breeze, horse chestnuts in their spiked casings drop and ping on the polished coffin that, already, nestles in the earth. The bereaved mother splutters in awed grief, turning a fraction from the scene. Eyes unwavering, her half-brother lightly holds her elbow in comfort, and as she leans toward him, he dwells on the dead boy twirling and turning by the tie he had donned to play teacher, the weighted branch that had snared him, lowly, rhythmically creaking.

From beside the subdued bar of the squalid public house which they go on to afterwards, he phones his partner, can tell immediately from the note of petulant self-pity in his voice that he's still in pain.

"Have a couple of hot toddies," he tells him, "like I'm going to. Being around bereaved people always gets me in a reckless mood. And if the punch doesn't anesthetize you, there's a potentially hot little item resting on the seat of my car which should be able to work some sort of miracle this evening."

He turns and, on his way to the outside latrine, brushes past a religious relative of the chief mourners, a compulsively head-nodding nun with wrinkles whorling her jowls and crabbed hands.

Stepping over a trough-like drain that connects the toilet with the main building, he reaches for the scored door which opens at the brush of his fingertips to reveal the dead youngster's father, who shambles from the dark hut into the half light with his belt unclasped and open fly gaping. At the sight of the pharmacist he slopes into his ken, clamps his hands around his buttocks, begins to weep on his cheek. As the other edgily comforts him with "Keep it together, keep it together"—a line he picked up from a movie he caught in town the previous evening—the young father slides his face across his succour's, kisses him on the mouth with an emergent tongue which is butty, and layered with thick spittle. The pharmacist snatches back his head, holds his arm like a bar against the other's chest and, as he emits syllables of protest, sees in the downward stretch of the eyes before him not only the dimness he has for long despised but also, strangely, something in them of the snide knowing that provoked his hatred of the deceased young boy.

"Off," he spurts, and tensing his lower half from the tightening fingers, the pressing Y-fronted crotch, he draws free, sidesteps into the twilit water-closet, and shoots both bolts.

"Repulsive, repulsive," he hisses as the dark, steaming stream sploshes onto the stained bowl, "What taste has my sister: hitched with a mule, who's a closet-case to boot."

He doesn't partake of whiskey after this, but drives back to Bangor at once, pressing a lozenge against his palate and humming, on each long stretch of road, staves of a carol he crooned to the dead boy as a newborn.

Tonya Yaremko

My Club Too

So I walk into this womyn's club, a place I really couldn't call a regular haunt because the music is alternative, the atmosphere superficial, and I have always felt somewhat, no let's be truthful, incredibly uncomfortable there. Somehow tonight it's different. Totally different. What is it?

I try to figure it out as my date and I stand in the long line-up at the bar. The music is the same. The tables, the bar stools and the smoky atmosphere haven't changed. Womyn are just beginning to pour into the place and there are all sorts of bodies (mostly with crew cut hair, androgynous clothes and all manner of piercings) intertwining in strange and sometimes contorted positions on the dance floor. What's so different about tonight? I'm not sure. I sense, feel, analyze.

In the last two years since coming out I've been here frequently, but tonight, for the first time, for some strange reason, I feel welcome. Comfortable. My clothes are no different. My white blouse is unbuttoned and tied around my waste to show off my belly button and just enough, but not too much, of my favourite fashion item; a push-up, thirty-dollar, my-breasts-are-beautiful black bra. Same haircut, long and straight, flowing down my back. My jeans are neither too tight nor too loose. Lipstick and makeup noticeable; pleasant but not obvious. I'm looking good. I always do when I go dancing.

Tonight is the first time I've been to a bar with a date. My first serious girlfriend. Maybe that's it, I think, as we reach the bar and order our respective drinks. She has her regular beer and I order my I-refuse-to-play-their-image-games glass of white wine. I hate beer. Why should I drink it? I'm feeling comfortable. She's holding my hand and it feels right, but the amount of normalcy I'm feeling is unsettling. I've gotten used to having my guard up, my back tense, waiting for the stupid womon who's going to give me that What the Hell is She Doing Here look.

This is my club too. The mantra I've been saying to bolster an increasingly lower self-esteem raises itself in my mind. Maybe, I think, I've finally broken through. Two years of struggling to break into the lesbian community at dances, activism, pride parades. Maybe my face is recognizable now. Perhaps my guard no longer needs to be up. As my date and I dirty dance to the same old same old music, a womon with strong features and slicked back, short blonde hair smiles at me.

Wow! That's new. A friendly smile. Strange. I'm not used to this. I'm used to under-the-breath comments of "Straight" or "Breeder" as I walk by. But tonight there are no comments. Only smiles. I start to relax. Enjoy myself. Enjoy the face, the sweat and the laughter of the womon I'm with.

I had been frightened. Afraid of what she'd feel hearing those comments about the womon she's dating. Afraid that she, newly out, wouldn't want to face the cold stares, the rejection that has become part of the everyday fabric of my life. I remember another womon that I dated for a short time. Thirty-five years to my twenty-four, she told me she was frightened of what other lesbians would think of her for dating me. My girlfriend I know still needs, craves, acceptance in the eyes of other lesbians. I crave it too. I had just started to think I'd never get it. But tonight my fears seem ridiculous. Tonight the energy is unmistakably friendly. Perhaps it's been me all along. Insecurity. Fear. Internalized homophobia.

It's the first time my girlfriend has been to a womyn's club. She's so relaxed. Fits right in. I notice all the womyn, many whom I've seen here before, smiling at me. They never smiled before. I'm getting a sinking, sickening feeling in the pit of my stomach. I study my girlfriend. With her short cropped, wavy brown hair, her plain white t-shirt, baggy jeans and Doc Martens; she looks every bit the dyke. And I came in holding her hand. I'm with *her*.

A familiar, uncontrollable rage hits me. A fury so overwhelming I want to take a baseball bat and smash every one of those too-little-too-late smiles that now surround me. I'm with *her*. I'm a femme on the arm of a butch. So I'm welcome. I'm accepted. I guess I'm a Real Lesbian now. Sadly, at this moment, I identify too closely with those straight womyn who can only get into the Old Boy's Club on the arm of some well dressed man. At this moment, I feel like puking.

I want to leave. I want to run. I'm so tired of this. So fucking tired of the misogynistic bullshit I've faced my whole life from men and that now, it seems I have to face for the rest of my life from other lesbians. I want to hide. I want to retreat. I don't. My shirt comes off. My breasts proudly jut out. My guard goes up. Fuck you! screams through my brain. . . .

This, *is my club too!*

Gretchen Zimmerman

The Lesbian Nation

According to the latest census (assuming lesbians would ever be properly included in one), there are approximately eighty-seven lesbians in Canada. That there are so few dykes, or woman-identified women, in this geographically large nation, was proven to me this weekend.

I sat in a not-so-trendy east Vancouver café, having my usual, a double decaffeinated latte, with extra chocolate sprinkles and two sugars. The woman I shared a table with was my recent best friend's one-time non-monogamous lover. We sat in the front window of the café, watching the dykes go by, discussing the usual SM dyke stuff—leather, motorcycles, public sex, lovers, ex-lovers, motorcycles, ex-motorcycles, etc. She told me that she used to be in a motorcycle club in Toronto—dykes only, of course, when she said, "Yeah, this really cool woman Kathleen . . . blah blah blah. . . ."

I said, "You know Kathleen? Kathleen with big brown eyes and dark brown hair, kind of shoulder length, really butch, cute as the day is long, a big bottom?"

"Yeah, we were good buds," she said.

"She's my ex," I said.

"No kidding?"

"No kidding."

"I dated her friend Allison. She was my first woman lover ten years ago."

"Holy shit," I said.

And so it went, with various mention of other women and other motorbikes and leather and women and, well, you get the picture.

The census findings read: Of the eighty-seven lesbians presently residing in Canadian communities, it is reported that forty-seven of them live in and around the greater Vancouver area (the numbers of which have appeared to increase this year reflected in the decreasing numbers of lesbians residing in and around Toronto), nine lesbians reside in greater Montréal, four are reported in the eastern provinces, three in Chilliwack, two in Surrey (monogamously), and one in the Yukon (still looking for a partner).

None of the surveys sent to Alberta were returned answered, although the daughter of a rather well-known politician for the Reform party was seen dropping her census into a mail box in Edmonton. She has not been seen since.

As further proof of the census findings, allow me to illustrate. My current girlfriend's ex, who used to live in Vancouver but now lives in Toronto, one of the only lesbians to migrate east in the census, lives with my emotionally monogamous, but sexually non-monogamous primary partner's ex-girlfriend, who plays racquet ball with my ex, who is best friends with my present girlfriend's last lover. I also have an ex-lover who dated a woman who once slept with k.d. lang (a.k.a. one of the lesbians currently reportedly living in Vancouver), who is also, as rumour has it, supposed to have had a very "close" country-style relationship with a woman with the initials A.M., a woman not currently represented in the census as one of the three eastern province lesbians, as she will not yet come out, at least in public.

So, as some sort of formal logic might have it, I have slept with k.d. lang, six times removed, but, hey, when fame is involved, who's choosy? I just wish I had the memory to go along with that logic, however faulty it may be.

I have discussed the census findings with several of my closest lesbian friends (all of whom reside in Vancouver), and very few of them seem to believe them. One day last week while sitting in a café, my West End lesbian friend said, "The census can't be correct. There have to be more of us than that."

"The census is neither correct nor incorrect," I said. "It merely relays the information provided by those surveyed." Just as the last word of the sentence left my mouth, a woman entered the café where we were sitting, sipping on double decaffeinated lattés with extra chocolate sprinkles and two sugars.

"Ohmigod. It's my ex, Jen," she said.

"Jen's your ex?" I asked.

"Yeah, and she's dating the woman I'm currently seeing," said my friend.

"No way," I said. "Jen's my ex's ex."

"Who's your ex?" inquired my friend.

"Barb," I said.

"Barbara Johnson?" my friend asked again.

"Yeah."

"Barb's the woman I just started dating," she said.

The census is never wrong.

Author Biographies

Donna Allegra's work has appeared in anthologies including *SportsDykes, Lesbian Erotics, All the Ways Home: Short Stories about Children and the Lesbian and Gay Community, Queer View Mirror, Dyke Life: From Growing Up to Growing Old*, and *My Lover Is a Woman*.

Alan Alvare was a well-loved Vancouver writer and grief counsellor. His poems, stories and articles have appeared in sundry places, not always on walls. He passed away in December 1996. He is survived by his partner Tim Barker.

Lawrence Aronovitch grew up in Montréal. He now lives and writes in Victoria, B.C.

Tommi Avicolli Mecca is an Italian-American queer writer, activist and performer whose work has been published in various anthologies, including *Queer View Mirror*. He is currently an AIRspace artist in residence at the Jon Sims Centre for the Performing Arts in San Francisco. By day, he works at A Different Light bookstore.

Damien Barlow was born in 1963 and lives in Melbourne, Australia. His work has appeared in *Queer View Mirror, Campaign Australia* and *Australian Literary Studies*. He also regularly receives religious instruction from Michel Foucault and the women from *Prisoner (Cell Block H)*.

Russel Baskin is a writer and artist who grew up in London, England. She now lives in Vancouver and is currently writing a collection of short stories and poems. At the same time she continues to work as a teacher and visual artist.

Michael Bendzela has had stories in several North American periodicals and was the recipient of a Pushcart Prize for fiction in 1992. He works part-time teaching English, labouring for his partner's small construction company and taking care of a historic house and farm.

Persimmon Blackbridge is a learning-disabled-lesbian-cleaning-lady-sculptor-performer-video-artist-writer. "A True Story with Lies" is an excerpt from her novel *Sunnybrook*. As part of Kiss & Tell, she co-authored the Lambda-winning *Her Tongue on My Theory*. She lives in Vancouver.

Allen Borcherding is a radiation therapist, living a quiet life of ardent domesticity with his partner in Minneapolis, Minnesota.

Jacob Bowers lives in St. Claire Beach, Ontario. This is his first publication.

Maureen Brady is the author of *Give Me Your Good Ear, Folly* and *The Question*

She Put to Herself, as well as three works of non-fiction. She lives in New York and teaches at The Writer's Voice.

Alison Brewin lives in Vancouver. She has been a student, an activist, a lawyer, a political assistant and a businesswoman, but has come back to writing after each incarnation. She is presently working on a lesbian mystery novel.

David Lyndon Brown nearly wet his pants when his collection of stories, *Spilling the Beans*, was shortlisted in 1996 for the Reed Fiction Award. He is presently completing a novel. He is a natural blond.

T.J. Bryan is a spirited hellcat and Tart in Training (TIT) who believes in pushing her limits to expand consciousness. A co-founder of De Poonani Posse (a Black dyke cultural production house) and BANSHII, she is also on the *Fireweed* editorial collective. She lives in Toronto.

Giovanna (Janet) Capone is an Italian-American poet and fiction writer. Her work has appeared in various anthologies and journals, including *Unsettling America*, a multicultural poetry anthology. She is currently co-editing *Angie Loves Mary, Vinny Loves Sal: Writings by Lesbians & Gays of Italian/Sicilian Descent*.

Justin Chin is a writer and performance artist. He is the author of *Bite Hard* (Manic-D Press), a collection of poetry and spoken word texts. He lives in San Francisco. "The Cooking" is an excerpt from a larger work.

Kent Chuang was born in Hong Kong in 1960. He left Hong Kong in 1968 with his family, and is currently living in Sydney, Australia, where he is a landscape architect.

A.J. Crestwood is a writer living in Montréal with her partner of eleven years and her two children. She has had short fiction published in *Room of One's Own*.

Daniel Cunningham is an optician who can't see straight. Nor does he want to. He lives in Edmonton, Alberta where he is honing his writing skills and developing a taste for Raymond Chandler and single malt scotch.

Harlon Davey lives in Toronto. He occasionally writes for *Xtra!* and *Canadian Male*. He has completed a novel which is stuck on pause. All he really wants is to live by the beach somewhere warm all year round and relax.

Lisa E. Davis was born and raised in Georgia but has lived for a long time in Greenwich Village, New York. With a Ph.D. in Comparative Literature, she taught in the state and city university systems of New York. She is completing a novel, *Prisoners of Love*, about the Village in the roaring forties.

Nolan Dennett is currently the director of the dance programme at Western Washington University in Bellingham, Washington and the author of two novels, *Place of Shelter* and *Vincent's Tale* (both published by Sun & Moon Press).

Nisa Donnelly is the author of two novels, *The Bar Stories: A Novel After All* and *The Love Songs of Phoenix Bay*. Her short fiction and essays are included in several anthologies.

Annette DuBois is a Boston-area writer and editor with roots in San Francisco and dreams of returning to France. Her work has been published in *Sinister Wisdom, Backspace, Queer View Mirror* and as part of too many anonymous scientific papers.

Gary Dunne lives in Sydney, Australia. Since 1983 he has published three novels plus several anthologies of Australian gay and lesbian writing. *Fabulous Monsters*, a novel, is due out in 1997.

John Egan was born into a large Irish clan in New York, and has lived in Vancouver since 1989. An educator and consultant, he vacillates on whether to pursue a graduate degree in plain language or work in international community development. This is his first published piece.

Siobhan Fallon is a writer whose poetry and fiction have appeared in *Lesbian Short Fiction Anthology, Aphrodite Gone Berserk, The Alembic* and *Thirteen*. Siobhan is currently working as a volunteer editor for the *Abiko Quarterly* in Chiba, Japan.

Laurie Fitzpatrick was born in Panama, raised in east Tennessee, and now lives in Philadelphia, where she paints in oils, writes criticism for local publications and is the Senior Arts Editor of *Art and Understanding Magazine.* She is finishing a collection of short stories and is working on her first novel.

Reg Flowers is an actor and playwright. He is a native of Philadelphia, where he received his BFA at University of the Arts, and his play "The Men's Room Cocktail Bar and Lounge" was produced. His erotic fiction appeared in *Wanderlust* and *Southern Comfort* (both by Badboy Press). In 1995 he received the Ovation Award for his role in the touring production of the play *Angels in America.*

Rhomylly B. Forbes lives near Washington, D.C. with two gay housemates and various small animals. Publishing credits include stories in *Tomboys! Tales of Dyke Derring-Do* (Alyson) and *Close Calls: New Lesbian Fiction* (St. Martin's).

Michael Thomas Ford is the author of more than a dozen books, including novels, non-fiction and short-story collections. He writes the column "The Way I See It" for *Fab* magazine, and his humour column "My Queer Life" runs monthly in newspapers across North America. A collection of humourous essays, including "The Crown of Heaven," is forthcoming.

Debbie Fraker is a Southern queer writer living in Atlanta, Georgia. Her work has appeared in *Etcetera* magazine, *Southern Voice, Amethyst* and *The Chattahoochee Review.*

david michael gillis, Deyna to friends, is a Vancouver writer born and raised in the East End of the city. He now lives in Vancouver's West End.

Gabrielle Glancy's poems have appeared in such publications as *The New Yorker, The Paris Review, The American Poetry Review* and *New American Writing.* "The First Time I Saw Vera" is a chapter from her novel-in-progress, *Heart & Limb*, which chronicles the exploits of a girl-Cassanova in search of her Russian lover.

Robert Oliver Goldstein was born in Charleston, S.C. He began writing at age seven and now builds computers for a living. His work has appeared in such anthologies as *Sundays at Seven* and *Best Gay Erotica of 1997*, as well as in various magazines. His computers can currently be seen at San Francisco's A Different Light Bookstore.

Candis Graham lives in Ottawa. She is currently obsessed with her second novel, *Handmade Pleasures*, and a book of non-fiction, *The Places Women Take Each Other*. "A Second Time" appears in her book *Tea for Thirteen* (Impertinent Press).

Mikaya Heart is a Scottish lesbian now living in California. She is co-editor of *Lesbian Adventure Stories* and author of *The Straight Woman's Guide to Lesbianism*. "A Nice Scottish Story" is written in the same spirit: that of choosing to tell the truth.

Thea Hillman, once named "Most Likely to Bring Up Sex in a Conversation," is now reaping the benefits of her title. Her porn can be found in *Noirotica, Ragshock* and *First Person Sexual*, as well as in her chapbook *Nuts and Chews*. Magazine credits include *Black Sheets* and *Wood Technology*.

Welby Ings was born and grew up in rural New Zealand. He has written a collection of short stories, *Inside from the Rain*, children's books and several plays, which have won numerous literary awards. His gay writing focusses strongly on the lives of rural men, on their visions and experiences and the simple politics of being ordinary.

Alexandra Keir is a feminist lesbian who shares her life with Donna and Avril, Jasmine, Courtney, Brett, Alistair, Mantequilla, two horses and other creatures on a magnificent farm in "the land of my soul," Nova Scotia, Canada.

K. Linda Kivi is a mountain-dwelling, house-building dykely babe of Estonian-Canadian origin. Her publications include a novel, *If Home is a Place* (Polestar) and *Canadian Women Making Music*, as well as many slutty poems and stories.

Swan K. is a Bohemian Gypsy citizen of the United States. She was raised in a strict Catholic household and it did not help. She is still a femme lesbian witch.

Robert Labelle is a young writer and an aging punk rocker, being one of the founding members of the sixteen-year-old group American Devices. He lives, writes and rocks in Montréal.

Larissa Lai lives in Vancouver where she works as a writer, curator, critic and activist. In 1995 she was recipient of an Astraea Foundation Emerging Writers' Award. In 1996 her novel *When Fox Is a Thousand* (Press Gang) was nominated for the Chapters/*Books in Canada* First Novel Award.

Michael Lassell is the author of *Poems for Lost and Un-lost Boys*, the Lambda Award-winning *Decade Dance* and *The Hard Way*. He is the editor of two books of gay poetry, *The Name of Love* and *Eros in Boystown*, and co-editor, with Lawrence Schimel, of *Two Hearts Desire: Gay Couples Write About Their Love.*

Joe Lavelle is the adult child of an alcoholic. His writing has appeared in *Queer View Mirror, The Pink Paper, APN, The Poetry Now Book of Gay Verse* and *Refractions* (an Internet project). Joe is a member of Queer Scribes, Merseyside's queer writing group.

Karen Leduc is a twenty-five-year-old newly out and proud dyke. She lives in the Vancouver area with her fiancée and their family of animals.

Denise Nico Leto is a San Francisco area poet, writer and editor. Most recently, she co-edited the anthology *Angie Loves Mary, Vinny Loves Sal: Writings by Lesbians & Gays of Italian/Sicilian Descent*, due out by Guernica in 1997.

Shaun Levin is a South African writer who has lived in Israel since 1978. He has published short stories and reviews in Hebrew and English. His work has appeared in *The Evergreen Chronicles, Queer View Mirror, Stand Magazine* and *The Slow Mirror*, an anthology of new Jewish fiction.

R. Zamora Linmark's "Kalihi in Farrah" is taken from his first novel *Rolling the R's* (Kaya Productions). The author lives and works in Honolulu, where he is at work on his second novel.

L.D. Little has had work appear in a variety of publications. She lives on a small farm in northern Nova Scotia where she is working on a collection of short stories. She would like to thank the Canada Council for supporting this and other work.

Jannathan Falling Long teaches English part-time at Virginia Commonwealth University and is working on a book about a rural queer community he lived in for four years. He is part of the collective that produces *RFD, a rural journal for gay men everywhere.*

Michael MacLennan's play *Beat the Sunset* won Vancouver's Jessie Award for best emerging playwright, as well as the *Theatrum* National Playwrighting Competition. He is finishing a new play and a screen adaptation of *Beat the Film*.

Tom McDonald—a writer, artist, performer and educator—lives in his native Brooklyn. His first published story, "Louis & Willie," appeared in *Queer View Mirror*. He is currently marketing his first novel, *Egotists, Kept Boys, & Punks*, and doing stand-up comedy in the New York area.

Jim McDonough writes mostly what a friend once described as "friction fiction." His work has appeared under an assumed name in *Advocate Classifieds, Advocate Men, First Hand, Hot Shots, In Touch, Mandate* and *Nature in the Raw*. He is currently working on his first novel *Reckless Abandon*.

Rondo Mieczkowski's screenplay *Leather Jacket Love Story*, a gay romantic comedy, was filmed in 1996. He edited *Sundays at Seven: Choice Words from A*

Different Light's Gay Writers Series, and has received grants from PEN USA West and the City of Los Angeles.

Dalyn A. Miller is a native New Mexican who has recently migrated to Boston (go figure). He lives with his partner Jason and is currently at work on a collection of short fiction.

Tia Mitchell is forty-four years old and lives in Vancouver. She says telling stories is the healthiest way to express her feelings and tap the limitless capacity of her lesbian experience. She is currently working as a therapist in private practice.

Letizia Mondello was born in Italy and has lived in Melbourne, Australia for most of her life. She has had stories published in *Outrage* and in *The Outrage 1993 Australian Gay and Lesbian Short Story Anthology*. She also writes a column and book reviews for the *Melbourne Star Observer*, a gay and lesbian newspaper.

Merril Mushroom lives in rural Tennessee. Her writing has appeared in numerous anthologies and periodicals.

Lesléa Newman is an author and editor with twenty-two books to her credit, including *The Femme Mystique, Every Woman's Dream, Out of the Closet and Nothing to Wear* and *Heather Has Two Mommies*. She has recently completed a book of poems entitled *The Buddy Poems*, which details the friendship of a lesbian and a gay man with AIDS.

Laura Panter is a twenty-five-year-old graduate of Queen's University. She currently lives and writes in Toronto, a city she once despised but now begrudgingly adores. Her work has appeared in *The Queen's Feminist Review* and *Queer View Mirror*. She was recently awarded a Toronto Arts Council grant to produce her first play.

Gerry Gomez Pearlberg's poems and prose have appeared in numerous publications, including *Hers II, Women on Women 3* and *Chelsea*. She is the editor of *Queer Dog: Homo/Pup/Poems*, an anthology of dog poems by lesbian and gay poets (Cleis).

Jane Perkins is a writer living in Brooklyn, N.Y. She has just completed her first novel and is working on her second.

Edward Power is a freelance writer living near Waterford City in southern Ireland. He is at present completing *The Sepia Zone*, a novella with a gay Anglo-Irish setting. He describes himself as a latter-day *von Aschenbach* seeking his *Tadjio*.

Cynthia J. Price, who is referred to by her two children as "Mother Queerest," lives in a coastal town in Kwa Zulu Natal, South Africa with her wife. After a mixed career of medical technician, mother, part-time student and crocodile handler, she is now a boring bank clerk who writes to remain sane.

Gary Probe is a writer and performer who lives with his partner Larry and his cat Claude in the Commercial Drive area of Vancouver.

Mansoor Punjani lives in Mumbai (Bombay), India. When not attending to the personal needs of his seventeen slaves, he researches and writes about SM. He is presently completing work on a book called *Algolangnia* (*Pain Lovers*).

Wendy Putman is a forty-year-old Jewish lesbian grandmother who just found herself a single parent, again. She is a corporate publisher by day, a literary publisher by night, and a writer in whatever time is left. She lives in Vancouver.

Carol Queen's work has appeared in *Switch Hitters* (which she co-edited), *Best American Erotica 1993* and *1994*, *Best Gay Erotica 1996*, *Best Lesbian Erotica 1997* and more. Her most recent book is *Real Live Nude Girl: Chronicles of Sex-Positive Culture*.

Keith Rainger was born in London in 1940. He taught French and English before retiring early to write short stories and chair a monthly forum for gay and lesbian teachers.

Lev Raphael is the author of a story collection, *Dancing on Tisha B'Av*, which won a 1990 Lambda Literary Award, and two novels, *Winter Eyes* and *Let's Get Criminal*, as well as the non-fiction books *Edith Wharton's Prisoners of Shame* and *Journeys & Arrivals*. He has also published four books with his partner Gersh Kaufman, including the bestseller *Coming Out of Shame*.

Jeff Richardson is a Toronto writer and creative writing instructor. He gave up smoking on October 15, 1986, for which he, his beloved partner of fifteen years, and their three cats are very grateful.

Susan Fox Rogers is the editor of six anthologies, including *SportsDykes: Stories from On and Off the Field, Close Calls: New Lesbian Fiction* and *Solo: On Her Own Adventure*. She also co-edited *Portraits of Love* with Linda Smukler.

Patrick Roscoe is the author of five books of fiction; his latest, *The Lost Oasis*, appeared in 1995. His short fiction has been widely published in North America and Britain, has won two CBC literary competitions, and is frequently selected for the annual *Best Canadian Stories* anthologies.

Meredith Rose lives in Berkeley, California. She has taught writing and reading at City College in San Francisco, San Quentin State Prison and at adult literacy projects. Her chapbook of short short stories, *Lesbian Neurotica*, was recently published by Square Tree Press.

Lawrence Schimel is the editor of *Food for Life and Other Dish, Switch Hitters, Two Hearts Desire: Gay Couples on Their Love* and *Tarot Fantastic*, among others. His own writing has appeared in over 100 anthologies, including *Queer View Mirror, Nice Jewish Girls* and *Weird Tales from Shakespeare*.

D. Travers Scott is the author of *Execution, Texas: 1987*, to be published by St. Martin's in 1997. His work has sullied such publications as *Best Gay Erotica 1996* and *1997*, *Sons of Darkness, Switch Hitters, Reclaiming the Heartland* and

Forbidden: New Defiant Lesbian Fiction. He is currently editing *Strategic Sex*, an anthology on calculated fornication.

Ken Smith is a former Royal Navy officer and many of his stories have naval themes. His work has been published in *Mister, Vulcan* and *Zipper*. He is currently at work on *The Intruder*, a series for StarBooks USA.

Linda Smukler is the author of *Normal Sex* (Firebrand) and *Home in Three Days. Don't Wash.*, with accompanying CD-ROM (Hard Press). She has been a Lambda Literary Award finalist, and has received poetry fellowships from the New York Foundation for the Arts and the Astraea Foundation.

Sam Sommer lives in New York with his lover of thirteen years. He has recently completed his second novel, *Jacob's Diary: Sleeping with the Past*.

horehound stillpoint is the hotwired alter ego of greg taylor, a queer forty-four-year-old waiter (single) living in San Francisco, who studies Vedanta and slams poetry.

Matt Bernstein Sycamore is a shitpoker and much more. His writing appears in *Queer View Mirror* and *Flesh and the Word IV*. He currently lives in Seattle, but moves frequently.

Robert Thomson is the author of *SECRET THiNGS*. His fiction and journalism have appeared in various publications. He lives in Toronto and is managing editor of *FAB* magazine, as well as operating Immediate Press. His second book, *Signs of Life*, will be published in 1997.

Sarah Van Arsdale is the author of *Towards Amnesia*, a novel published by Riverhead Books/Putnam. Her poems have been published in many literary magazines. She divides her time between New England and San Francisco.

Mary Grace Vazquez was born in Bayamon, Puerto Rico. Her writing has been published in *Bless Me Father: Stories of Catholic Childhood* and her photographs have been published in *The Femme Mystique*. She was a Grey Nun of Montréal from 1962 to 1967, at which time she came out of the convent and out of the closet.

Chea Villanueva is a tough little "old school butch" of Filipino/Irish ancestry. She is the author of three books, *The Chinagirls*, *Jessie's Song* and *Bulletproof Butches*. Her fiction and poems have also been published in numerous anthologies. She is single and lives in San Francisco looking for the femme of her dreams.

David Watmough's work has been anthologized in *Cornish Short Stories*, *On the Line*, *Certain Voices*, *Indivisible*, *His, Volumes 1 and 2*, *Queeries* and *Queer View Mirror*. His latest short-story collection is *Hunting with Diana* (Arsenal). He lives in Vancouver.

Jess Wells' seven books include *AfterShocks*, *Two Willow Chairs* and an anthology, *Lesbians Raising Sons*, due in 1997 from Alyson. Her work has appeared in more than twenty anthologies, including *Women on Women, The Femme Mystique,*

Lavender Mansions, Lesbian Culture and *When I Am an Old Woman*. She is a two-time winner of the Lebhar-Friedman Award for Journalism.

John Whiteside is a marketing manager and writer in Washington, D.C. His non-fiction has appeared in *Bay Windows* and *The Encyclopedia of* AIDS. This is his first published fiction.

Duane Williams lives in Hamilton, Ontario. His short stories have appeared in *Queeries, Queer View Mirror* and *queering absinthe*. His poems have appeared in *The Church-Wellesley Review, Kairos, Afterthoughts, The Harpweaver, People's Poetry* and a recently released chapbook, *Taste the Silence*.

Barbara Wilson is most recently the author of the novel *If You Had a Family* (Seal) and the memoir *Blue Windows* (Picador). "The Woman Who Married Her Son's Wife" is a retelling of an Inuit (Kulusuk) myth from east Greenland, first collected in *A Kayak Full of Ghosts*, "gathered and retold" by Lawrence Millman (California).

Phoenix Wisebone's pursuits include cartooning, folk singing/songwriting and living below the poverty line. Her poetry and articles have appeared in queer, feminist and literary publications in Canada.

Nothing Kristofer Wolfe is a twenty-year-old writer whose influences include Poppy Z. Brite, William S. Burroughs and Lynette D'anna. His short stories and poetry have appeared in *Slice Magazine*. He is currently attending Langara College in Vancouver.

Laura Wood is an anchorite and painter who makes a living doing odd jobs. She lives with her life-time partner in Brighton, England.

Karen Woodman is an artist and writer who makes her home in Vancouver.

Raymond John Woolfrey grew up in Montréal, where he presently works as an editor and translator. He has published short stories in Canada and abroad, including *Queer View Mirror*. "All Saints' Day" is part of his collection of Montréal stories (in progress) entitled *East of the Big Q*.

Jane F. Wrin lives in Merseyside, England with her computer and too many books. She is a member of the Liverpool Writing Group Queer Scribes, and is currently engaged in dividing time between research and writing.

Michael Wynne was born in the West of Ireland in 1971. In 1990 he published a story collection entitled *Speak of Angels* and his work has been published in several anthologies, including *Quare Fellas*, the first book in Ireland celebrating new gay fiction. Since 1994 he has written for *Gay Community News*, Ireland's only gay/lesbian newspaper.

Tonya Yaremko is a ferocious Vancouver femme who has worked as a fibreglasser, trained as a plumber and holds a degree in communications. In 1996, she was diagnosed with learning disabilities; as a result, she is now gaining the tools she needs to fulfill her childhood dream of becoming a published writer.

Gretchen Zimmerman is a thirty-year-old boy dyke. Since meeting her wife, lover, boyfriend, bottom, husband, boy, sister, friend, she has discovered that colours are much brighter.

James C. Johstone and **Karen X. Tulchinsky**'s first collaboration appeared in the Lambda Award-winning anthology *Sister & Brother: Lesbians & Gay Men Write About Their Lives Together*. This inspired them to co-edit the original *Queer View Mirror*.

James works as a Japanese language interpreter and tour escort. His writing has appeared in *Q Magazine, Prairie Fire, Icon, The Buzz, Flashpoints: Gay Male Sexual Writing* and *Food for Life and Other Dish*. He is currently editing *Quickies: Short Short Fiction of Gay Male Desire.* His greatest pleasure is being Jayka's daddy.

Karen is the author of *In Her Nature*, a collection of short stories which won the 1996 VanCity Book Prize. She co-edited *Tangled Sheets: Stories and Poems of Lesbian Lust*. Her work has appeared in numerous anthologies and she has written for several magazines including *Curve, Girlfriends* and *The Lambda Book Report*. She is currently editing *Hot & Bothered: Short Short Fiction of Lesbian Desire* and writing her first novel.

James and Karen live in Vancouver.

Also available:

QUEER VIEW MIRROR

Lesbian & Gay Short Short Fiction

Edited by James C. Johnstone & Karen X. Tulchinsky

"A rich feast. . . . For the courage to demand 'that place at the table,' we must continue to feed our souls. *Queer View Mirror* gives the kind of sustenance we need." —*The Lesbian Review of Books*

"The editors have created a mosaic of mirrors of gay life that are both common in the global queer nation and as highly various as the individuals involved." —*The James White Review*

"Masterly condensations written with style, humour, honesty, and imagination."—*Fab Magazine*

Featuring work by Lucy Jane Bledsoe, Maureen Brady, Beth Brant, Michael Bronski, Dennis Denisoff, Nisa Donnelly, J.A. Hamilton, Michael Lowenthal, Lesléa Newman, Felice Picano, Michael Rowe, Lawrence Schimel, Wickie Stamps, Kitty Tsui, David Watmough, Jess Wells, Paul Yee, and many, many more!

ISBN 1-55152-026-5

$19.95 Canada / $17.95 U.S.

Available through your local bookstore, or send a cheque or money order to:

Arsenal Pulp Press
103-1014 Homer Street
Vancouver, B.C. Canada
V6B 2W9

Please add shipping/handling charges of $3.00 for first book, $1.50 per book thereafter (plus 7% GST in Canada only).